Re...

SLICE

PAN
HORROR

PAN BOOKS
London, Sydney and Auckland

First published in the USA and simultaneously in Canada 1990 by
Onyx, an imprint of Penguin Books USA Inc.
First published in Great Britain 1991 by Pan Books Ltd
Cavaye Place, London SW10 9PG
9 8 7 6 5 4 3 2 1
© Rex Miller 1990
ISBN 0 330 30440 2

Printed in England by Clays Ltd, St Ives plc

**For
Carol**

"... under the law almost everything is purged with blood, and without the shedding of blood there is no forgiveness of sins."

Hebrews 9:22

CHICAGO

"**M**organ the dragon in flames made of aspic," the junkie said poetically, fumbling around inside the packing crate. At least it sounded like that. It could have been.

"Margo, you're a drag and I'll find me an ice pick . . ." Or any number of other junk-fuzzied weirdnesses, but to the junkie doing the mumbling only one thing counted, and that was copping. With dope there was hope.

His years of scholarly pursuits into the nature, soul, limitations, and validity of human knowledge had been cooked down to a bubbly blood-thick essence. The epistemology of "dopology." Get it and do it. Do it to it. Do it to me till I scream. Do it to me till I cream. Do it to it till I dream.

Finally he finds his filthy fit and gets his bad self tied and fried. Ohhhhhhhhh, yeah. That's right. The spike bites and he jacks it again and it rushes through him, and how can anything that feels so good be bad? No way, Oh Jay. He jacks it again, fascinated as he watches dopy blood bloody dope, and he nods off into blessed relief from those nagging aches, the agony of defeat, the heartbreak of psoriasis, the cold hawk, all gone and forgotten.

Morgan the dragon and Margo the drag queen are all forgotten in the mystical, foggy land of the Wizard of Smack, but reality doth intrude, and he awakens, hallucinating, on the nod inside a packing crate in the shadows of an alley off West Erie. Glad to be in a nice, cozy shelter from the coming storm. But sorry to be halluci-

9

nating. So sorry to be hallucinating a human monster thing.

He is no stranger to hallucinogenic experiences. It was only yesterday or last month or sometime he saw a building levitate. High as jet contrails and tight as a bird's asshole he watched the side of a building begin to rise to the sky and he almost shouted in amazement and then the building held fast as the billboard some company had painted on their electric garage door slid out of view and he realized he'd been bamboozled by the oldest gag in the book, the garage-door billboard trick.

But this hallucination is so real it will take some doing to shrug off. This thing, this huge and awful gigantus of humanity, it STINKS. It looks so real you could reach out and touch it—or worse, it could reach out and touch you. It is a man thing. An immense, stinking giant.

The hype would curse his luck for having chosen *that* particular packing crate in that particular alley, because as the blurry-eyed addict came off the nod, a gigantic thing emerged from the depths of the street in a poisonous swirl of the most fetid, disgusting, noisome, and putrescent stink it had ever been his dubious pleasure to experience. And it was then that he realized this was no hallucination that would evaporate like a dope mirage.

Survival instincts being what they are in the human being, even in his advanced state of chemical euphoria and physiological ruin, the junkie had the good instincts to stay chilly as the apparition moved past his hiding place. He remained inside the upended packing crate, transfixed by fear, and he would later recall that a loud thunderclap exploded just as the thing came up out of the sewers, causing him to momentarily lose control of his bladder.

What he witnessed then was a sight few men had ever seen. The scary, scar-faced, monstrous mountain of a fat man stood quietly there in the alley, sensors ticking, frozen as if he was listening for something. Tick . . . Tick . . . Tick. . . . Time seems to stall, the sweep of the second hand sluggish, moving as if through glue.

The hype has never seen anything human look quite

like this. Not just the size, but there is an animal awareness to the movements, a strange machinelike precision,
almost a daintiness in each studied and careful motion
and then—it freezes.

As the thing freezes and becomes inert the junkie also
freezes, literally as well as figuratively. Freezing motionless and chilled to the bone in the breath of the dark
hawk that has blown this cold Chicago rain down upon
his world, freezing in terror at the specter that confronts
him. Will it smell him as he has smelled it? His own
dripping and dope-ravaged body fights off a shudder of
cold fear.

A small quadruped makes a noise nearby and scurries
away, but the huge man's killing hand remains clenched
involuntarily and he continues to stand motionless. The
big man wonders if he has imagined this rain, and inside
the crate the hype wonders if he has imagined the huge
thing, but he is afraid to move even a junk-addled muscle
in spite of having a chill spasm stab through his bones, in
spite of his discomfort, in spite of being doped to the
gills, and in spite of being half an alley's length away
from where the huge man now stands menacingly.

The rain opened up then but the man continued to
stand there without moving. Waiting with infinite and
frightening patience. Again he imagined he was hallucinating this night rain, just as his presentience had mistak-
enly caused him to think some human was nearby. He
drank in the fuel-choked city air like a drowning man and
then, satisfied he was alone, he tore his clothes off and
stood there in the shadows, nude, trembling, and soaping
his massive, filthy, blood-encrusted bulk in the hard rain-
water. A tower of blubber and muscle. Stone-naked,
only a few blocks from Chicago's Loop, washing blood
and grime off in the night rain. A hype's surrealist
nightmare.

The monstrosity's face was tilted up into the rain and
he felt his other eye finally open and then he could see
the stark patterns of old time transformers visible against
the night sky, their lines crisscrossing the alley that re-
sembled something out of a time warp, a bit of architechture
unchanged from the 1950s. He stood there carefully wash-

ing himself as the traffic rumbled by him only meters away, tires singing through the wet streets, and as he slowly soaped himself again and again, he slowed, stilled, slowed, stilled his vital signs, breathing in the city's pollution—to him a tasty piquancy—soaking in the rain, absorbing the power that was surely to be his alone, listening to the heartbeat of the darkened city.

And he made a sudden, loud barking noise that badly startled the dazed addict. It was the closest sound the beast could make to that of a human laugh.

At last he was able to remove at least the outer layer of filth from his body. He continued to stand nude, waiting there in the blackest part of the shadows. In his killing hand he held a heavy, taped tractor-strength chain nearly a yard long. And his grotesquely stitched face beamed in a dimpled grin, like a caricature of an insane killer cupid.

He had survived. He was alive! And his hunger had returned. And he knew now that he was safe. And his smile was the smile of complete peace of mind, knowing as he did that finally he was invulnerable.

The disgusting hulk watched the cars carefully now, watching the slower ones, waiting for the moment when his inner clock would tell him that the timing was right. And he grinned with pleasure at the thought of the next one he would take. Death. Waiting naked there in the dark, chill Chicago rain.

The hype hunkered down now with his eyes shut, afraid his heart was going to give out on him while he was in the packing crate, afraid he'd cough or sneeze or puke or do some terrible thing that would alert the monster to his presence. Afraid to look. Afraid not to look. Afraid he was starting to get real sick. He prayed he could be very still and he curled into the fetal position, shutting his eyes as tightly as he could, so that all he would witness would be the sounds of movement, slamming of a car door, things like that.

The enormous human almost made a move on a car but he let it pass and then about two minutes later he felt real good about the next one and decided to take it. He waited until the slow-moving car was almost even with the alley and he shot out of the darkness with explosive strength.

When the slow car came almost abreast with the alley, the driver saw a huge and terrible THING suddenly appear in front of him, waving its arms wildly as the motorist tromped down on the brake, not quite in time, the left fender actually giving the huge man a hard clip as he barely threw himself past the vehicle and the driver was screaming something at this apparition that had materialized in front of him. But he saw the worried face of the big man, the face like a crudely stitched wound, and this was obviously someone who needed help so he cautiously lowered his window and in that first shattering moment of awareness he knew he had made a serious mistake, a grave error, but it was too late then and a powerful force was upon him and all over him and the behemoth was in the car with him and doing something to him and then he was dead and on the dirty floorboard in an ignominiously arranged posture, the penultimate humiliation he would suffer.

And with dimpled smile hideously affixed, the murderous beast was alive and well and wedged behind the wheel of a year-old Tempo GL with half a tank of gas, money in a wallet, and a fresh kill at arm's length. And something pinged in his mental computer and he drove back two blocks and came down the alley from the other side, cruising very slowly with the headlights off, but he saw nothing. No surprises waiting for him near his duffle bag.

That lucky, *lucky* hype who had only minutes earlier cursed his luck had fallen asleep in his crate, and it would be much later that he'd recall seeing something about a fat killer who lived beneath the streets, and he'd know he had lucked onto a fucking score. Lord knows it was his turn for a break. So far, without bad luck, he'd had no luck at all. And now—shit fire and put out the matches—he'd seen a GHOST!

This was no ghost. This was Daniel Edward Flowers Bunkowski, six foot seven, 460 pounds of serial killer. A battered and molested child who had managed to survive, then grown into a two-fisted payback machine "bigger than a fucking truck," institutionalized nearly half his life, pulled off death row and sent overseas so he could kill for Uncle Sam, surviving—always surviving—escaping deactivation by friendly fire, returning to the world to do murder and mutilation, tracked down and shot by a cop, only to survive again. He was Chicago's Lonely Hearts killer, the one who liked to rip his enemy's heart out and *eat* it. The one they called Chaingang.

Chaingang was alive. He had one shot, as he saw it, sitting in a freshly stolen car. He needed $10-to-$12,000 cash and he needed to get it now. Then he needed to completely vanish into fat air. Lay chilly and bite the bullet. He would have to dramatically alter his appearance in some way.

Having run through all the plastic-surgery and disguise scenarios and not liking any of them, he was left with only a couple of possibilities that held any promise: massive weight loss and then the acquisition of a partner. Either male or female would do, but upon consideration he decided a woman would be preferable. He was facing certain biological needs. He would proceed. He'd get money and then a woman. Then he'd lose weight. When the time was right he would make Jack Eichord pay.

First—money. He ruled out banks because of the surveillance cameras. It was vital that nobody know he'd survived the shooting. He considered grocery stores. Too busy. He stole fresh plates, changed clothes, and began casing successful small merchants with big cash flow and moderate in-store traffic.

Sam's Meats was perfect. He watched the store for an hour and saw thirty-seven customers. Not bad. He knew what meat cost. He drove up the alleyway and parked near the back entrance. He tried the door. It was locked. He knocked with a fist like a huge rock. Movement inside. The door opened.

"Yeah?" A young man's face showed in the doorway.

"Sam want those ribs rena cranus in back here or what?" That's what it sounded like to the employee of the meat market.

"Huh?"

"I said do you know if Sam wants me to bring those . . ." But by then Chaingang was inside and upside the head of one Tommy Crockett, now bleeding on the concrete floor, and the massive, bloodied chain is beside his leg and he looks inside. Nothing. A large, dark, and empty room with office to the left, swinging doors in front that obviously lead to the market. He steps forward cautiously, locking the door his wide girth had just squeezed through, and peers into the market. Two butchers working. A woman buying something. Ring of cash register. Voices. And he pushes the door open where the other butcher can see him but where he's still hidden from the woman and the other man and he says softly, "Hey, bud?" The big dimpled smile in place, showing the uninjured, right side of his face, cleanly shaven, grinning, trustworthy, he says, "Can you come help us a second? Need somebody to hold that door open." A vaguely nodded head. The butcher coming in to see who the hell this guy is and suddenly a world of pain and he is unconscious and Chaingang opens the door and says, "Yo. Give us a hand here a second."

And the owner of Sam's Meats, holding a sharp cleaver at the moment, looks at the stranger and starts heading back into his storeroom. But a meat cleaver isn't enough and he is on his face in some blood that is not his, a chain wrapped around his throat and a great weight on his back.

"Where is the money?"

"Cash register. Hey, shit, yo're breakin' my damn back, man."

"THE REAL MONEY, not that chickenfeed."

"I don't know what you—"

"Watch. Here. Over to the right." And the butcher looks to the right and feels the weight shift and a thunk, a wet splat a horrid soggy sound of crunching blade into bone, and there is a hand. It is Tom's hand severed from his arm.

"Yours next," the basso profundo rumbles calmly, "if I don't like the answer. Where is the REAL money." Said without a question mark.

"My office. Lower left-hand drawer. Black metal box."

"How much is in there? Don't lie."

"I dunno. Day's money—ready to go to the bank. Over ten thousand, I know that."

"Where's the key?"

"Key to the drawer's the small gold key on my ring. Right pants pocket." The lights go out.

Very quickly, faster than most human beings have ever seen him move, he hurries into the office. Second key works. Fits. The drawer opens. He takes the black box. Back into the doorway to the market. He sees two women and a child waiting, looking around the store for the butchers. Quickly he slices each of the three throats with his huge cleaver, stepping carefully around the blood, wiping the prints off both doorways and the bloody cleaver, keys in the sack with the black box, all of this in a cardboard box, out the back door again with handkerchief over the handle, pulling it shut and hurling his bulk into the front seat of the stolen Dodge Charger just as the woman opens the door to the back room and sees the bodies and screams. Soon he pulls over to the side and counts the money in the box. He has $15,825 in cash. Another $3,800 in checks, which he shreds and lets blow out the open window as he starts up and wheels the Charger back into the traffic flow: $15,825 for less than ten minutes' work. He never knew there was so much profit in fresh meat.

To you in your safe nest of a world his murderous actions are the bestial acts of a madman. Throats being slit with a knife is an image you won't ever have to deal with. Not up close and for real. Only the catsup splatter of Hollywood gore. The real feel of the cut, the way you slice first, then pull it roughly through, ripping on down quickly to sever the artery of a human, this is something you'll fortunately never see or feel. But to Chaingang it is a movement as natural as slitting an envelope flap with a letter-opener.

And if you insist on teasing, taunting, tormenting your babies, abusing and using and confusing and sexually misusing your children, battering and splattering your youngsters for perverted kicks, you risk creating one of these boys. Or girls. One of these two-legged monsters who will seek organic payback in the form of the torture, degradation, and slaughter of as many of your kind as the fates will allow them. And the ones who become highly proficient at the death arts, they will seek your brothers and sisters and sons and daughters out in their quest to destroy your likeness again and again and a hundred times over.

CICERO

He spent a couple of hours resting in the Charger, with the car parked on a quiet industrial side street. Then he had a nudge and started the car and drove out to the nearby town of Cicero. He found a fairly secluded home. Lawn overgrown but no for-sale sign. He parked a block away and checked out the house. Nothing. He drove in and parked out of sight in the garage area in back, slipped the lock easily, and penetrated the dusty stillness of the dark home.

Furniture. Clothes in closets. Food in the refrigerator. He gorged. Went in and showered. Ate again. Relieved himself. Put the television on without sound, a flickering ghost in the next room. Prowled through the house on those huge, splayed feet. Touched things and wondered. Decided to take another shower. Found a bottle of cooking sherry and tried to drink some of it but spit it out onto the living-room carpet. Finally found a small decanter of something that proved to be brandy and poured himself a large goblet full, not finding a proper snifter.

He sat in the darkness in front of someone's TV, his naked body drying in the still, warm house in front of an electric snow screen. He shook his head at the miraculousness of life. Trying to assimilate all this new data. Only hours before he had been dead. Beneath the streets with the old sewer woman who had found him and nursed him back to health like her three-legged dog, the pet that hobbled gamely wherever she went. Now here he was. In some monkey's living room watching the tele-snow. He sighed and got up with a grunt of effort.

Chaingang changed his dressing and went back in to finish the brandy in front of the TV, but he felt the hairs on his arms prickle and something was out of tune. He quickly gathered up his clothing and out of habit wiped surfaces of prints, hid the obvious signs of his penetration (only much later would the family discover that Goldilocks and the Three Bears had raided their refrigerator), and drove away from this darkened house that no longer "felt safe" to him.

Within ten minutes he was parked in a field between a building that appeared to be abandoned and a thick hedgerow, and he sat there calmly in the darkness trying to remember what had gone wrong, what had brought him to this state of wounded confusion. The last thing he could remember vividly was being in the sewer and the cop Eichord coming down after him, shooting at him, and he remembered him putting that gun to him and the way he jerked his head quickly as the gun fired, and then the lights went out and there was nothing. And when he awoke he was dead.

Had it all been a dream? Had he imagined the old woman who lived in the sewer? Was she like the old woman who lived in the shoe and had so many children she didn't know what to do? Or was she a real person who had found him floating up on the filth-covered concrete shores of her mad world, this phantom hulk of bloody being who at first appeared dead to her? She found many such things in her underground world, but they were almost always dead.

At first he too believed that he was dead and that the song he heard was the song of angels from some half-forgotten story wrenched from the guts of his tortured childhood. But it was not the sound of angels, and it was then he felt an alien sensation of fear. It was fear of the unknown, as he understood that he was being held submerged below the surface of the sea, deep in the black cold, far removed from the noisy, burbling, human wave above, far above him somewhere in the living world.

He smiled when he recognized the source of the noise, amused and pleased that he would have a chance to study

the sad, strange, haunting, melancholy, squeaking, unde-
cipherable, gentle song of the whales. He was listening to
the courting song of the killer whales.

Daniel E.F. Bunkowski who had torn the hearts from
countless victims and left their poor, terrorized, mutilated cadavers strewn across Southeast Asia and much of
North America, was at peace. In harmony with his surroundings. Because if Daniel loved and hated, his love of
nature and mammal and animal life was at least the equal
of his fierce and abiding hatred for humans. So his frightening and massive death mask of a face crinkled in pleasure at the sound of the singing whales.

And a chill slowly crept over his enormous bulk like a
dark shadow, and the mysterious song of the whales
intensified into an electrical sound, not unlike a human
scream, and then he slept.

Do we really know what it is to experience fear, horror, terror and awful, mind-paralyzing shock all at once?
Few of us ever have such an experience. We might survive a car wreck, adrenals pumping, heart pounding, and
we pull over by the side of the road, and tears streaming
down our faces, we begin shaking uncontrollably in the
preamble to emotional collapse. This is only aftershock.
This is nothing. But to know the terrible and numbing
fear that Eichord felt that time in the sewers of Chicago
as he confronted the wounded killer, is to come face to
face with your limits and thresholds—physical, mental,
and emotional.

The monstrous killer had emerged from his manhole to
destroy Jack Eichord, the serial-murder expert, but Eichord
had shot him, and the huge madman known as Chaingang
had fallen back down into the depths. Eichord missed
with the next two shots, then climbed down into the
stench, and seeing a woman and a child he cared for,
both miraculously alive, there was that cruel moment of
relief. And when he let up for just that half-second, the
monster came alive again, coming up out of the puddle of
slime and charging him like a wounded rhino.

To know and taste and feel the emotions and fears and
sensations that ravaged Eichord in those moments, as he
shot him again, firing point-blank at the wounded killer,
is to understand the fragile balance of the human gyro.

From the proximity and the blood and noise and impact, Jack thought the beast was dead, but he was not thinking clearly. He'd just been shaken to his core by the bellowing, seemingly unstoppable onslaught of the man whom he'd just thought he'd killed. And when he bent over the inert form of the huge heart-ripper, up close and with a shaking service revolver, imagine his total terror, the woman and child huddled nearby, as he places the barrel in what's left of Bunkowski's mouth and fires again. Two more rounds. The shots echoing like cannons in the dank, foul enclosure. Eichord shaking so badly he nearly drops his weapon as he jams it back in his holster and tries to get the survivors out.

But it was pitch-black down below the Chicago streets, and Eichord, frightened half out of his mind, had failed to mortally wound the beast called Chaingang. Lady Luck still hovered over the killer. What Jack had done was give him a severe head wound, graze his skull, and turn his cheek into a sieve. Because when he bent over the killer's form he had placed his weapon into the shattered mouth and fired more rounds through the side of his face. And a cheek is quick to heal. And Daniel Edward Flowers Bunkowski was no normal human being.

He had recuperative powers, tolerances, immunities, appetites, defense mechanisms, involuntary reactions, reflexes, tactile skills, sensory gifts, and cognitive powers that were partially biochemical and physical compensations for a lifetime of deprivations and subjugations and inhuman treatment. Where others might have perished, he built scar tissue, and developed weird immunities or strange receptors that could counter the most painful injury or violent attack. He was not an easy man to destroy.

We all know of cases in which individuals have survived the most bizarre wounds and the most extreme and apparently fatal traumas. A man recently survived for weeks without food or water. A child recovered from a long immersion in freezing water and nobody could explain it. A woman fell from forty stories, suffered two broken ankles, but lived. Every day the headlines carry a tale of someone who would not die. And these are ordinary persons, not CHAINGANG BUNKOWSKI.

Bunkowski floated off in the rising tide of water that flooded into the submain. The water made his huge bulk buoyant and carried it off into the black recesses of the subworld. And that was it. Hours became days. There was brief, flickering consciousness, then only more cold, gathering darkness. But Daniel's body was like no other. A massive storehouse of inexplicable tolerances and virtually inhuman powers. A uniquely self-sustaining death machine. And slowly the great bulk began to heal.

His first memory was of trying to see. He opened up his one eye as much as he could and saw only Vaseline. It was like the time he was a kid and had been in the reform school and caught "pink eye." He remembered his eyelids seemed stuck together. One eye was like that now. It refused to admit light. The other one saw only a smear, as if someone had taped one eye tightly shut and smeared a couple of pounds of petroleum jelly over the other. And it was such an effort to try to see up into the jellied covering that he let the deep sleep take him again.

The next memory included sound. He had come awake shivering. Stone icy cold to the bone. Frozen to the marrow. Freezing to death, he thought, and he struggled to move and could not. And struggled to open his eyes again and saw only the jelly. And, freezing, he shivered and made a kind of whimpering noise. And he heard his mother say, "Now, now. You just lay right there like a good boy."

"Nnnnnnnn," he tried to tell her, and reassured by the sounds of his beloved mommy, he fell back into the arms of Morpheus.

Finally, he came to for longer than a couple of seconds. He was awake for perhaps two minutes this time. Once he had tried to instinctively open his eyes and went through the Vaseline routine again, but he stopped struggling and just trembled. Not from fear so much as from the cold.

"There, there, Baby Boy."

"Nnnnnn," he said to his mommy.

"Good boy."

"Mmmmmmmm." Beloved Mommy.

"Big Boy. Good boy."

"Nnn."

"Rockabye, Big Boy, in the treetop," the woman sang tunelessly.

"Ooooooh." The huge man made a shuddering sound as he trembled from the cold chill that had penetrated to his core.

"Lah dee dah dah, the cradle will rock."

"Nnnnnn."

"Now, now. Good boy."

"Mommy.

"Big Boy, Momma's big boy."

"*OOOOHHH.*" Another massive shudder racked his body.

"Oh! You scared me. Such a big boy," she crooned to him. She was holding his wounded head in her lap.

"Ooooh." So cold. He would never get warm again.

"You go back to sleep now, my big boy." She loved to care for things. Doctor things back to health: small animals, cats hurt in fights, dogs run over by cars, derelicts, junkies. She'd never cared for anything as big as this one, though.

"Mmmmmm." He made another moaning noise and snuggled against her and passed out. She wondered if it would live. Well, it won't get done with me sitting here, she thought as she got up, letting Daniel Bunkowski's bloodied head splash down unceremoniously in the filth.

And he was close to death for a time. The dark angel who he knew so well from hundreds of previous encounters, the ominous angel of death hovered over his body, freezing him as it blew the icy breath of mortal coil's cessation across him. And Daniel slept. And in the sleep of death he dreamed of his own murder. Of a policeman who threatened him with the symbols of his tortured childhood and then came and hunted him down in the sewers and shot bullets into him, blasting him apart in a screaming hot blinding deafening explosion of fiery pain. Then he opened his eyes and saw the black angel settling on him and he died in his nightmare—this beast who had caused so many nightmares he renewed his acquaintance with the ultimate bad dream.

He is cold. Inert. Unmoving. He does not seem to breathe. Although his great bulk is covered in a mound of rags and newspaper placed there by the old lady to allow the dying one to retain its body heat, he feels like he has been entombed and packed in ice. His tactile senses have finally ceased to exist. Hearing, deafened by the up-close blasts of Eichord's service revolver, shuts off, leaving a ten-decibel electric hum like the buzzing of a faraway bee. Sight, blinded by the gunshots into his face at point-blank range, winks out. He sees nothing. Even in his imagination he cannot conjure up the image of the blues and brilliant reds and yellows that one sees when you "see stars." His sense of smell long since vanished from the assault of his environs beneath the Chicago streets. His taste is dead. In fact, he wonders idly if his jaw has been shot away. And in this altered state the huge man realizes that, by definition, he no longer exists. So this is what it is like, he thinks, to be dead.

And that is when he sleeps the longest sleep of all, the one that takes him to the brink and beyond, and then he escapes the sharp talons and the chill and the black, and one of his eyes tries to open but it cannot but at least he knows he is not dead, and he is drenched in his own foulness and bathed in poisonous sweat and the flood of perspiration beneath the mound of impromptu covers unglues his eye and he sees his mother there—MY GOD HE SEES HIS MOMMY—and he tries to speak her name and the old woman hears the dead thing go "Nnnnn." And she whirls around, nearly jumping out of her skin in fear.

"Big Boy is alive," she says to him. Mommy says to her baby boy. "Whaaaaa. You gave me such a start. I thought you was dead." She comes down near him and he sees the outline of Mommy's face and imagines the warm smells of her as she takes him and coos and comforts him and holds him and rocks back and forth talking gibberish to herself and she tells him her name.

"*My* name is Pippy. What's your name, my big boy?"

Chaingang just lies there and lets his mommy hold him.

"I'll bet you've never heard that name before. Isn't that a pretty name? Old Pipper is taking care of you now. Making you big and strong again. Pippy found you all dirty and bleeding. You was in baaaaad shape. But you're a fine sight now, oh sonny boy yes indeedy you're a fine sight now," the old woman tells him as he shakes with pain and sickness, his body racked by infection and fever.

"You best get your rest now. Go back to sleep. Get your forty winks. And then pretty Pippa will make you a nice hot bowl of soup. But right now, Big Boy, just have to go night-night and live off the fat of the land." She pokes him gently in the center of the huge mound to emphasize her point and cackles like a cartoon witch. And, grateful for his mother's comforting nearness, his head in the folds of her skirts, Chaingang Bunkowski lets himself drift off again, racked with pain, sweating like a pig, on the lap of his long-dead mommy.

He is starving to death when he wakens the next time and he feels a tide of relief wash across him as he pops his eye open and sees the woman looking down on him.

"Wake up now, Big Boy. Pippin must get some soup into your jib. Ready for your nice soup?"

Feed me, he thinks.

"Okay," she says as if she was reading his mind, "here we go." And she splashes something liquid across his face.

"Now, now, boy. Now, now. Big Boy is a bad boy. Big Boy mustn't bleed for Pepper. We'll have to fix that, won't we?" And she goes and gets something and then Mommy does an unspeakable thing to her trusting baby boy as Chaingang's eye opens wide in horror at the sight of his mother coming to him and plunging something sharp some awful stabbing sharp silver thing into his face. Oh don't, Mommy, I'll be good I swear I promise I won't ohhhhhhhhh noooooooooooooo, and the woman hears the thing grunt "NNNNNNNNNNNNNNNNNNN" as she takes the huge needle and begins sewing the side of the man's wounded face together with sailcloth thread she retrieved from a garbage dump.

He begins to wonder if he has hallucinated the injury to himself as he once dreamed that he might have hallucinated the rape and murder of an exquisitely beautiful woman. He was not given to many hallucinations. But trauma, pain, illness, some powerful disease, had shaken his iron resolve. Was he alive? Yes. Was he dead? No. Was he a dying man? Perhaps. He ran it through his

malfunctioning computer. He smelled—no, that isn't the
right word—tasted a foulness that permeated every waking breath he took. At first his computer told him it must
be coming up from diseased lungs. He thought he had
lung cancer. He wondered how long he would live and
what he should do next.

"Waaaaaaahhhhhhhh." He coughed and spit the foul
taste out in a hawking effort that racked him with a
convulsive pain spasm and a woman's voice said, "Bad
Big Boy." Which made no sense to him whatsoever. He
knew he was alone. He tried to open his eye wider but
the light was so bright and he shuddered with chill and
yet he was soaked in sweat, and the side of his face felt
pinched shut.

"Bad, bad doggie," the old witch cackled, but Chaingang
Bunkowski did not hear the voice and he was taken down
again into trauma and unconsciousness. He did not hear
her say "Bad, naughty puppy dog. Bad boy spit and
make him face bleed for pretty Pip. BAD boy." The
crazy old bag lady watching him as he passed out again.

Much later he awoke and it was all black and he
thought the cancer had killed him and he assumed he was
dead, but the thought was but a fleeting awareness as he
was sucked back down into sleep and then the bright
light and the noise, and he made an effort to open his
eyes but one seemed swollen shut and something was
wrong with his face and it was the old woman saying
something: "You was never gonna get up, boy. Are we
hungry?"

He tried to nod his huge head and the massive effort
almost took him down. He tasted feces, coal oil, death,
stale fish, an awful stench beyond the worst halitosis
from acute gingivitis becoming the worst peritonitis and
then the ultimate case of death breath on record. He
tried to spit and could not, and then tried to swallow and
the voice said, "Here, open wide for Mommy."

"Mmm." It was his mommy? He tried to assimilate the
information.

"Eat."

"Nnnnnn." He agreed to eat. He was ravenously hungry.

"There." It tasted like hot water but he was able to

swallow the liquid and for the second it took to swallow it the awful taste in his mouth was gone.

"MORE," he rumbled, and the old woman dropped her spoon, then laughed.

"Baby boy can TALK. Boy's first word to Mommy: MORE. All righty, we've got plenty of good, nourishing soup here. Yes indeed, pretty puppy, Pipkin has plenty of good soup." And she fed him another spoonful of hot water.

"More," he said.

"Yes. You'll get more now. You can talk. What is Big Boy's name?" He said nothing and she got another spoonful down him. "My name is Pippa. Do you think Mommy is pretty?"

"More."

She obliged him. "Feeling our old selves now, are we?" He blinked. "Is Peppy's big doggie going to be up and wagging his tail soon, eh?" She cackled madly.

"Mmmm." He tried to make her give him more again but it was just too much work to get the word out. Fortunately she understood and nodded and dipped the soup spoon back in to the can.

"MMM-ummm, good," she sang tunelessly, and he managed another swallow. And the small nourishment was sufficient to pull him back off the edge. He turned his head and felt the pull at his face. What had happened? He remembered the blinding gunshot. He wondered if he was blind in that one eye—perhaps from the point-blank explosion? No. He knew on some mysterious level that he was all right. He was going to be all right.

"More," he rumbled.

"At's a fine, Big Boy. We'll have you up an' at 'em in no time now." And he saw her dip the spoon, which was Silver and marked Palmer House, into the can that said Campbell's Minestrone Soup, and his brain told his arm and his hand to move and he reached out and took the can and tilted it up and swallowed the soup.

"HA!" She was pleased. Another stray being nursed back to health. "Big Boy ate allll his soup."

He smelled it now and knew that he was wrapped in foul rags, and he realized for the first time that he was lying in his own filth. Why hadn't he been cleaned? What sort of a nurse was she? This wasn't his mommy. This was . . . what? He saw where he was then. He was down in the sewers. And this creature who had given him soup had done something to him. He remembered her plunging something sharp into his face and hurting him, and Chaingang looked at the old lady and thought how easily he could snuff her out like a dirty candle but the thought washed over him like a dark and heavy cloud and he could only swallow, a major effort, and he let his upper torso and head fall back down into his nest of rags and he slept again, feeling himself pulled down into the black sleep whirlpool as the woman's voice sounded far away, "Rockabye, Big Boy, in the treetop" and something about something breaking, and he was gone again.

"That's my good big boy. Sleep good now for Mommy. And when we wake up we'll have a FEAST. We'll slay the fatted calf," she said with a delighted screech at her rapier wit.

But Chaingang was far away, dreaming of the face of the cop and the things he would do to that face, the ways he would change that arrogant appearance, and the thought of it stretched part of his own face in the rictus of a bloody smile, and then the big man dreamt of the song of the killer whales and slept.

SOUTH
BUCKHEAD

"**L**isten to *this*," he said, reading in a loud voice anyway so he could be heard in the next room but screaming the words he wanted to emphasize. "Designer Bob Mackie attaches a *muff* to this classic evening fur. All right. Check it *out*." He was getting louder by the second. "I'll go muff-diving in *that*! HEY, you listening?" There was no comment from the dining room, where the long-suffering woman sat at the table with a pile of bills. The wife of Eichord's old pal Chink.

"C'mere, you gotta see this, hon," said Detective Sgt. James Lee. "Listen to the way these people down there live. West Palm Palace highlighted by a spectacular two-story cathedral-ceiling living room this magnificent home is enhanced by a beautifully landscaped half-acre lot that includes a marble pool. Gourmet kitchen," his voice squeezed into his version of the late Mr. Gleason's how-sweet-it-is voice, "four guest accommodations. Now reduced to sell at only two million four hundred thousand." He stopped and laughed and turned a page. Perusing in silence for a few moments, then beginning to read aloud again, the awe apparent in his voice as he read, "Unique in all the world. Exquisite Palm Beach oceanfront estate. Walled castle, twenty-seven rooms, beautifully furnished. For the uncompromising. Property includes three-bedroom stone caretaker's cottage on grounds. Eight million, two hundred thousand dollars. *EIGHT MILLION DOLLARS*, are you listening?"

The woman in the dining room spoke for the first time, "What did you charge to Visa that was $37.92?"

"Don't bum me out with that. Prestigious ocean view in panoramic setting. Five bedrooms, four baths. *FOUR BATHS*! Oceanfront deco breakfast nook. Entrance foyer with glass walled elevator facing the Intercoastal. This gorgeous showplace is perfect for entertaining. Covered loggia overlooking the Olympic-size pool. What the hell is a loggia?" he asked, mispronouncing the word.

"One million eight hundred and forty-five thousand dollars! Who the FUCK are these people?"

"Hey," The woman screamed at him. "Watch your language in there, that's ENOUGH!" She scared him and he flinched at her voice, which was louder than his. "You're not with Dana in some bar now. This is your home."

"Sorry, I just read these things and . . ." He trailed off.

She put the stack of bills aside and came in the living room. "What are you reading? You shouldn't read this . . . your blood pressure. Where did you get this? What is this? Who sent you this?" She had the habit of asking the same question about eleven different ways as she spoke, and she leaned over and read, " 'Oscar de la Renta's opulent version makes this one of Palm Beach's favorite . . . Oh, what a lovely stole. Where did you get this? Who sent you a paper from Palm Beach? Who do we know in Palm Beach, FLORIDA?" For a second she couldn't remember what state Palm Beach was in, California or Florida? She'd never been to either place.

"Beats me. I got it in the mail. Look," he said, turning the page, "Mediterranean elegance. This beautiful home is designed around an inner courtyard complete with fountain. Formal dining room, sixty-foot living area, spectacular paneled library of seven thousand leatherbound books in sets, five bedrooms including two master suites, servants' wing, four car garage, wine cellar, silver vault—*SILVER VAULT!*"

"Don't read any more," she said, taking the paper from his shaking hands. "Who sent this anyway? Who do we know in Palm Beach? Do we know somebody down there? Jeff, maybe? Would he have sent it?" She didn't care about the real estate in Palm Beach; her only interest was in who might have sent her husband the foreign newspaper.

"Mmmmmm," he said, mm-ing "Idunno," giving the words a three-syllable count of grunted sound in the familiar articulated shrug.

"I wonder who sent this." The paper was an alien artifact to her and she looked at it in awe. Something that had dropped off a passing spaceship. The *Martian Daily News*.

"Guys buying their wives Bob Mackie muffs you be lucky you get a CLOTH coat every five years." He shook his head.

"You hear me complaining?" She stood in back of him looking down at her husband of nearly twenty years.

"People living like goddamn kings on the ocean, we got to figure out how to pay the credit-card charges. You shoulda married some rich joker and not some schlamazzle cop don't got fifty cents in his pocket."

"You hear me complaining?" she asked him again. "Come on, get up, I gotta vacuum. Outta my feet." She had a unique speech pattern and frequently left English words out of a sentence. "Outta my feet" translated as "Get out from under my feet." He got up.

"We got a card from Jeff. Dawn loved those little stick-on earrings you sent her. She wore 'em to her tenth birthday party."

"Guys be giving little ten-year-olds diamond earrings. I give stick-ons," he muttered as he went out into the yard.

He went outside and tried to decide where to sit. He looked at their shabby lawn furniture with the cracked pink-and-gray arms and went over and sat on the wooden bench he'd made. The sparrows roosted in the tree above it and they had left droppings all over the bench, but he decided it wouldn't bum him out as badly as sitting on that cracked plastic.

The white bird droppings didn't bother him but here and there, where a sparrow had ingested some berries, a disgusting streak of red- or purple-colored excreta decorated the bench.

He sat gingerly and put his arm across the back of the bench, propping the part of the paper his wife had failed to confiscate across his arm and read "Tradewinds luxury: sumptuous estate on .75 acres with tennis court, pool, maid's quarters, 5 bdr, 6 bth, guest house, private security fence with electric eye gate, sunken loggia, $2,900,000." He let the paper slip from his hand and flutter to the ground.

It was then he realized for the first time that he had his arm resting in some birdshit.

CHICAGO

It was very cold down there on the bottom of Lake Michigan with the rest of the singing killer whales. But he fought the strong urge to wake up from whatever it was he was in—this state of grace that allowed him to enjoy the rare and treasured privilege of studying their mysterious, melancholy mode of communication in this way. It was so restful, reassuring, restoring, to wait here in this dark, cold, untroubled place.

He would like to wait here until all humanity passed by, wait until their systems had relaxed, wait as he listened to the interplay of the great whales, experimenting, as always, reaching out with his unusual mind, hoping to find the level that would allow him to eavesdrop and manipulate their subaqueous thoughts as he enjoyed their sad songs, and then he would float back up to the surface, coming up under the carefree people he hated so passionately—how easily he could kill them then—and he smiled as he let himself match his strong pulse to the distinctive, throbbing theme music of the movie shark. And this was a unique thought for the killer, as he thought, Ta-dum, ta-dum, in his mind, thinking the notes in tempo with the heartbeat music of the white shark, because it was one of the only times he had ever told himself a joke. And the smile on his bandaged and blood-encrusted face was as wide as the wrapping of taped rags would allow, and he came to fully for the first time and pulled himself up saying, "Get food," and the old woman nearby almost had a heart attack at the sound of the deep voice in back of her.

"*OH!* Shit, boy. Oh, my stars. Land sakes alive, Big Boy

33

gave Pippy a start then. Oh, Big Boy mustn't startle
Mommy." She looked at him with her head cocked to
one side.

He thought how easily he could pinch that ugly face in
his strong paw and snap that withered neck. He could kill
her, even in his current state, as most people could swat
a fly. *"GET FOOD."*

"Yes, sir," she said, and began fumbling with a can
opener and something he could not see. He was having
trouble getting his eyes to focus. He felt intermittent waves
of dizziness, but he sensed they would soon pass. He must
have nourishment. While the old lady opened a can of something he dragged the huge duffel bag over and rummaged
around in it until he found several things he wanted. He took
out some money from a secret hiding place and unfolded
a ten-dollar bill, then a twenty, then larger bills, which he
hid again. Then he took the small metal mirror and looked
at himself for the first time. He was a thing that could not
be shocked, but he was almost shocked at what he saw. He
began peeling the mound of bloody rag from his head.

"Don't do that, Big—"

"SHUT UP," he roared at her, and she looked away.
He removed the filthy rags. The thread or whatever she'd
used had made the wounds in the side of his face look
like something out of a horror movie. "Give me clean
water," he commanded, and the old woman handed him
a small pop bottle with cloudy water in it. He began to
clean off his wounds and then studied her handiwork. It
would suffice to hold the skin closed for now. He put a
battle dressing on and gave her some money. She drew
back her hand, but when she saw he wasn't going to hurt
her, she reached out and took the money.

"I'll tell you what I need. You go get it and bring it
here. Then I'll give you this." He showed her a fifty-
dollar bill.

"Okay," she said brightly, and he immediately sensed
she was quite deranged and that the lure of money would
not be what would pull her back. He told her what to get
him but he could see she would not be able to carry it out.

"How long have"—he chose his words with care—"you
and I been here." She smiled at him. "How many days?" He
thought he might kill her then if she refused to answer him.

"Pippy will count up," she said, and turned away from him. He felt nausea and dizzy waves that shook his body. He picked up the cold can of tuna fish and began eating out of the can, devouring great hunks of the food and then washing it down with the rest of the cloudy water that was in the bottle. "Sixteen days," she said proudly. "Oh, look! Big Boy ate all his dinner like a good boy. Pretty Pipper will give him a nice dessert now."

She reached for something and held it in her hands where she alone could see it, and made a show of peering into her hands. Then she laughed and offered it to Chaingang, holding out her hand as she said, "Big Boy's nice dessert treat." She was holding a tiny dead mouse in her hand. He stared at her in disbelief as she dropped it and cackled away into the darkness. Insane and lucky.

He tried to get to his feet but the effort was too much and he sat back down with a splash, realizing then that he was still immersed in his own dried filth.

It was then that intense hatred probably saved his life. A surge of scarlet hate poured through him and the raging tide propelled him to his feet, forcing him up at the thought of the cop who had done this to him, and the momentum carried him forward as he plunged ahead into the wet black stench looking for a way up.

Soon he had forced himself to return through the malodorous sewer tunnel to the place where the old woman was waiting, and he tapped the last of his strength to glean what information she might be capable of dispensing. He learned how she had happened upon him, his body half out of the water, washed into a nearby submain where she sometimes went to seek shelter. He learned how she had found his huge "bag of pretty treasures." And from what he could gather, nobody besides the crazy sewer lady knew that he was alive.

He sent her scurrying off on his supply errand, the dog limping along beside her, and as soon as they were gone, he gave in to the soporific pull of his total exhaustion and fell into a deep sleep.

BUCKHEAD SPRINGS

It was a good, solid marriage, this crazy, hot thing of theirs. It broke some rules but, hell, a lot of great things break rules—that was what rules are for. She broke some of Eichord's rules about women, and with every misconception shattering, with each new stereotypical cop thought breaking like so much cheap glass, his smile would get a little wider. She was good for him, and the reverse was also true.

She'd saved his butt one time and she was a good-enough lady that she never looked back and said, Way they go, or patted herself on her gorgeous back for it. She was a caring person. She genuinely liked people. There'd been a time when all that had hung precariously in the balance and Eichord had been a part of that case. He'd asked her out and she wasn't having any of him, or men in general, having been at her lowest all-time ebb, and the two of them had pulled each other up.

There were only two things she didn't like about the marriage: she had to leave Dallas, which was so much a part of her she couldn't shake loose from the Big D sunshine, but there was sunshine here too. The people were a little different: closer in, tighter, kept more to themselves, not open like she was used to knowing. But she was a monogamous family-oriented lady and she'd build their own world around her lover.

Their new friends were a problem. She'd left a couple of girlfriends of years' duration and in trade had inherited a couple of stuck-up, nosy neighbors, and a bunch of "hard-on cops." The closest thing Eichord could deliver by way of what ordinary folks call friends or close acquaintances.

It had taken the passage of some time and then the constancy of the hot sex had tapered off to something approximating normalcy, whatever that was. All that meant is that they didn't do it every waking hour. They just couldn't get enough of each other. It wasn't like they were snowbound and had nothing else to do, or like they were trying to prove they were still kids. Eichord especially was reaching the point where he couldn't ball four, five times a night nonstop like he could when he was a kid.

Nobody cared. It was the nearness and warmth and love and touching and sweet companionship and trusting and, most of all, the laughs. They just knocked each other out. There was a lot of laughing. And any marriage where there's a lot of laughing and a lot of touching—you don't have much to worry about. Nobody's counting how many times you get it up. You're both too busy laughing. There'd been plenty of sex and a lot of ha-has and as much genuine caring as both of them had hoped for.

After the honeymoon year they'd reached the point where they could get out of bed long enough to have a few of Jack's acquaintances and buddies over and have a party. It was a borderline disaster. To say that Donna hated his friends would be unfair. It would be true, but it would be unfair. Now they'd learned to laugh about that too.

"We about ready for another cop barbecue?" She smiled at him.

"I don't know. I think you and I can handle it but I'm not sure Tuny's up for it yet." They both laughed. Dana had cornered Donna in the kitchen. It had been ridiculous, offensive, and she couldn't believe it. She had taken Jack aside and whispered, "Who's that big, heavyset dude? What's his name—Tuna?"

"Dana. Dana's drunk. Why "

"He hit on me in the kitchen," she had whispered to Eichord, who could not hear above the noise of the party crowd and music. There was barbecue in the back yard. A big wet bar going inside. Party time. Very domestic.

Donna was in a sexy black hostess gown. Dana Tuny was plastered and had come onto her in the kitchen.

"He WHAT?" Eichord had thought she'd said Dana had hit her in the kitchen. He couldn't believe it. He was flying pretty high too.

"He propositioned me. Is he supposed to be a friend of yours? Some friend."

She looked so serious Jack had broken up. And they went in the bedroom amidst jeers and naughty remarks and he told her abut Dana. Yeah, believe it or not. He's a kind of friend, he'd said, hell, not kind of, he IS a friend. He had told her, "He's a pain in the ass, even when he's not bagged. Tomorrow he'll get up, and if he remembers it, he'll be so contrite he'll fall all over himself apologizing. He gets a little booze in him he's a lost soul. But he's covered my ass more than once. Come in behind me when the captain was laying for me and made it right, back when I was on the sauce so bad. Went in to cover me against a dope gang one time, him and me with handguns against a couple of wise guys with submachine guns. He was right there. Something like that you don't ever forget. It cuts a lot of slack for somebody."

So she had gone back to the party and later Dana had cornered her outside and she had smiled in his fat face as he breathed a hundred-proof fumes in her ear and whispered, "Hello, beautiful. Wanna sit on my face?"

She never missed a beat; she had backed off and said loudly, "I'll pass personally, but if you want some oral sex I think I've got you a partner."

"I'm your man," he had replied as the people around them chuckled.

"She's right next door. She'd go for you."

"Huh?" She had gestured toward the fence.

He had said, "Your neighbor lady, you mean?"

"No! Lord, no! The neighbor lady's chow is in heat."

The cops still ragged Tuny about that one. They'd tell him it was Donna Eichord on Line One, calling to ask Dana if he wanted to go and get some chow. Things like that. She had really put them all away with that one.

"Yeah," Jack said as they laughed about it, "you zinged him once and for all with that one."

But the ha-has still took a back seat to the romance.

"You're something, you know that," he said to her, cupping her long lovely neck and feeling the smoothness of her bare shoulders as they got ready for bed.

"Something is the word. But is it something good? That's the question."

"Something awfully good." He stroked the long fine hair that she would comb out, letting it fall nearly to her waist. "Like corn silk."

"What does a city guy know about corn silk? Bet you never shucked an ear of field corn in your life."

"Wrong," he said, making a buzzer sound. "Sorry, ma'am, this means another article of your clothing has to come off for an incorrect answer. Pay up." He slipped the straps of the nightgown over her beautiful shoulders. She had large, firm breasts. He was always asking her when the silly putty was gonna shift. They were too good to be true. She was built like a Texas hourglass. With plenty of sand in the top.

CHICAGO

The huge man wakes in darkness and fumbles for his flashlight. He switches it on and sees the form of the sleeping woman nearby.

"Wake up," he rumbles, and she sits up blinking like a bat, the blinding light in her eyes.

"Eh? What? Who's there?"

"Get up. Light the lantern," he tells her, and she slowly sits up, rubbing herself. "LIGHT THE LANTERN." She comes awake fully and begins obeying his command. Eventually a coal-oil-kerosene-like odor permeates the stench of their immediate surroundings and he says, "Did you bring me what I told you?"

"Okay. Pippy brings the good boy his fine things." Amazingly she had brought him a sack containing some of the items he'd asked for. So she wasn't altogether useless. He snatched a can of Spam and quickly keyed it open, slapping the rectangle of meat and congealed grease out into his huge hand. Without even wiping the packing gelatin off, he took a ferocious bite, swallowing two-thirds of the meat in a single bite. In less than five minutes the old woman watched him consume the entire contents of a bag of groceries. "Good Big Boy eats all his fine dinner." She waited for his next utterance.

He looked at her with some degree of irritation. He had tortured and killed people who had irritated him less than she did. Yet he felt no particular rage against her. She was somewhere along the evolutionary ladder between mankind and animal. He might let her live awhile longer if she didn't annoy him further.

"Look, see Pepper's puppy. He can walk just like the doggies with four foots. You look real close and only see three foots on puppy. See?"

He lurched to his feet, taking the heavy bag in one hand and the lantern in the other.

"Listen to what I tell you, sonny boy," she commanded in a stern voice that caused him to glance at her, and the hard eyes looked for just a fraction of a heartbeat but she wasn't worth bothering with, and he was too tired to even shrug. Daniel turned away from her, the light sending ghostly movement of oily shadows over them, and he could hear her voice from the blackness behind him saying something about "pretty Pip would eat her dessert" as he lumbered out of the subworld for the last time.

He had known where he was going to come up and he scrutinized the street carefully before he felt comfortable with the idea of coming out of the manhole. There was an alley immediately behind him, and as he slid the heavy cover out of the way and squeezed through the opening, a Billy Batsonizing boom of thunder cracked down out of the sky and Chaingang's mighty lungs filled with the almost overpowering pungency of "fresh" Chicago air.

WINDER (EAST BUCKHEAD)

The two rednecks were in a cheap motel on the outskirts of town. Wire-skinny and hard-rock tough, the mean mammer-jammer calling himself Bo Johnson crumpled up the empty Bud and flung it viciously across the room in the direction of the wastebasket. He glowered at the white trash peckerwood he'd gotten saddled with.

"I mean, sweet *JESUS* you gin' ta hafta start LISTENIN' TO ME ya goin' to end us both up back inna fuckin' slammer, ya know." He was pacing the small room and his nervous energy was as scary to the other man as a loose high-voltage line crackling in the air beside him. It had been different inside.

Them and the other white boys against the smokes and Messicans. But shit, he wouldn' let up onna man.

"Well, hell," he began.

"Well hell iz right, John. Sweet JESUS youuns can fuck somp'n up. DAMN. I couldn' fuckin' BELIEVE it, I mean we go up air'n shit 'n ya go 'n write MY fuckin' name inna damn book. What in the seventeen sweet names of the damn DEVIL couldya be thinkin' about, huh?"

"Shit, it ain't mah fault, Wendell, an' I didn't write YOUR name any more'n you wrote MY name,"

"I wrote YOUR name? WHAT THE HOLY HAPPY FUCK YA TALKIN' ABOUT, BOY?" The stupid one, whose name was John Monroe, flinched at the screaming, wondering if the people next door would hear the hollerin'. He made the calm-down gesture with palms out

42

in front of him, as if warding off evil, saying, "Ya done wrote PARTA my name," talking in a whisper, trying to placate the other man with his tone, "JOHN-son. Get it? Ya done writ Bo JOHN-son onna damn card 'n, shit, ya know, then I got sorta confused an'—"

"Ya got sorta confused awright." At least he was talking in a halfway normal voice you couldn't hear a block away if you was deaf. "Well, hell, man, I jes' writ the first fuckin' thing come in my head, so I put down there I was Bob Wendell, now that ain't using—Well it is your name but I mean it ain't either 'cause hell anybody lookin' for somebody named Wendell De Witt, they ain't gonna' put two and two together there ya know like Bob Wendell don't even sound like Wendell De Witt or nothin' and even—"

"See what I mean, John, you don't fucking LISTEN to what I'm tellin' ya. You got to start payin' attenshun to me, goddammit." He smacked a hard fist into his other hand and it sounded like the loudest possible tooth-rattling slam of a door. "JESUS IN HEAVEN, ya goin' ta git us tripped up iffn' ya don't pay a-fuckin'-TENshun." Monroe imagined what it would be like to get hit in the face with that hand.

"I'm sorry."

"You're sorry," he mimicked, "you're confused. See that don't help. Ya understan' what I'm tryin' to tell ya?" Monroe nodded but he had to say it,

"Yeah, but if we 'uns had stayed in the same damn room we wouldna hadda write on two cards we coulda writ like we was brothers or somethin'."

"I done already said in the car." He was shaking his head in total exasperation." I don't WANNA stay in the same room like a coupla fuckin' faggots."

"Hell, I ain't no faggot."

"I never said ya was a faggot. You're as dumb as fuckin' stone but I never done accused ya of being no dick-suckin', ball-lickin', cunt-asshole turd-packin' faggot. What I said was—and listen to what I'm sayin' 'CAUSE I AIN'T GOIN' TA SAY IT AGAIN, I never said ya was no faggot. I said I don't-want-to-stay inna-same-fuckin'-room-like-we-*was*-two-faggots. Get it? AW-RIGHT."

"But—"

"I had my fill of that shit when I was in goddamn jail and that is plain enough of that shit for me. I ain't stayin' inna same room with somethin' I ain't fuckin'. 'Less you want me to start dickin' YOU inna ass ya better git that shit straight goddammit."

"Shit I can be with that awright. I never could abide no faggots myself. I let one suck me off one time when I was out in California—"

"Yeah, well I don't think we got time to go in to all that shit right now, man. We gonna do somethin' here or not? Because if we ain't, then I'm gonna make somethin' happen on my OWN, ya unnerstand?"

"Hey." Monroe tilted his head. "I hear ya'. I want to go for some of that shit."

"That's the way I like ta hear ya talk. Now let's plan how we're goin' ta git them pipes."

"Dale's got him a nice little Beretta, man." He pantomimed holding a handgun and played like he shot the lamp. "PPPPSSSSSSSSSHHHHHHHHHH HHKKKKKK KKKKKKKEEEEEEEEEEWWWWWWWWWWW!"

"We ain't goin' ta use no traceable pipes, butt-wipe. Ack like you got some fuckin' sense."

The other man as if in agreement hawked up a gooey oyster and spit it in the general direction of the motel wastebasket.

"What we goin' do is go down to Helferd's."

"Uh-huh."

"Go down there about eleven-thirty onna Friday night when the cops is all out lookin' for pussy or eatin' goddamn donuts, and we goin' ta throw a couple bricks through the fuckin' window and take the first three or four guns we can grab outta there."

"Don't they got no burger alarm?" he asked, unconscious of his malaprop.

"Jesus sweet Christ. Of COURSE they gotta fuckin' BURGLAR alarm ass-wipe, we ain't gonna STAY there fer shit's sake, we goin' ta SMASH the fuckin' glass, GRAB the fuckin' guns, an' BOOK. How long ya' think that'll take?"

"Oh, I guess—"

"It'll take nineteen SECONDS is how long it'll fuckin'

take." He was proud of his command of the situation. "I got a piece a' windshield glass, and that shit is strong, and timed what'd take to sledgehammer through it 'n reach in and take a couple a' pipes and book. Nineteen seconds. A cop cain't wipe his fuckin' heinie in nineteen seconds. We're outta there."

"How about bullets? Where we gonna—"

"We BUY some bullets. Okay?"

"Yeah, but we need pistols or some shit. They ain't got nothing but big-ass rifles inna window of Helferd's last time we was by there. I want me a nice Beretta like double-o-seven, 'n go—" He pointed at the door and went "PPPPPPKKKKKKKKKKKKKKKKEEEEEEEEEE WWWWWWWWWWWW! PSSSSSSSHHHHHHHHHKK EEEEEEEEEEWWWW!" Sweet Jesus, the man named Wendell De Witt thought. I've got me a fuckin' imbecile here.

"We take what's inna window. We ain't goin' in an' fuck around all night with no goddamn showcases. We grab rifles if there's rifles inna window, we grab shotguns iffn' nair's shotguns. Okay?"

"Yeah, sure, that's cool. But how we gonna go walkin' inna fuckin' bank with fuckin' big ole hunting rifles with goddamn telescopes 'n shit all over 'em?"

"Mmmmmm." He sighed as if he hurt, pulling the tab on another Budweiser and flinging it away from him. "I swear ta Christ. We're gonna saw them off." He said this with patience in his tone, that sweet sound he got right when he turned real mean. John Monroe had heard him talk like that once right before he proceeded to kick the living *shit* out of these two slick dudes in the goddamn gas station. Just *whomped* on the sides of their heads till the gray shit come out. He didn't say nothing, only nodded yes.

"Okay." Wendell smiled. "So now we got our pipes all nice and sawed off." He pointed his finger at Monroe and went, "PPPPKKKKKKKKKKKKEEEEEEEEWWW" the way a person will try to do when you can tell they ain't never played guns when they was a kid because they can't make the noise. "And then we go ask some a' these fuckers to part with their money. How does THAT sound to ya?"

"Let's do it. Shit. I know a perfect place. That new little American Finance office out there where Long John Silver is, ya know? Onna highway?"

"Fuck that. I had a guy I knew in jail hit a little place like that 'n he only come out with three thousand dollars in his sack. Shit. I ain't goin' to do the crime if I cain't have a time. We'll hit a fuckin' bank."

"Yeah. Shit, we can hit a bank," John Monroe said without an ounce of conviction in his voice.

"Yeah."

"Like ta make sure they ain't a whole buncha assholes standin' around. Shit, they can throw an' alarm and shit an' you know, a couple a' people cain't cover no whole fuckin' bank."

"We ain't goin' that route. We're gonna waltz innair with the fuckin' president of the damn bank."

"No shit?"

"I wouldn't shit mah favorite turd, would I?" he said with a big mean smile.

BUCKHEAD

He was getting as flaky as the nutbaskets he worked with, Eichord thought. That morning leaving for work he'd showed Donna what he'd bought for Dana.

"What'd you buy him?" she said with a smile.

"Little sign for his desk." He'd found a bumper sticker with the word on it and found some desk signs in a drawer upstairs at headquarters. He'd slid one of the signs out and the bright Day-Glo sticker word fit perfectly across the plastic insert. When he slid the sign insert back into its stand, it looked like it had been custom-made for it. Wordlessly he sat the sign on the kitchen table and she screamed with laughter.

"Perfect."

"I'm getting as fruitcake as he is."

"I love it." Her smile wrinkles deepened and she said, "When you invite them over, be sure you tell Dana that your wife sent him a special invitation—from next door." They both laughed.

He put the sign back into the sack. This domestic stuff was all right. He could get used to this real quick. They sat finishing breakfast leisurely and he thought to himself how much he'd missed sharing things with someone. Even a stupid joke. Just to have someone you genuinely cared for meant so much. He looked over at this lovable lady and couldn't feel anything but a boundless joy.

"Now whatcha grinnin' at?" she asked him through a bite of toast.

"My luck, baby," he said, and went over and had a

47

taste. Crumbs, grape jelly, Donna Eichord—the whole works.

When he finally got to work he was carrying Dana's new sign in a little brown sack that looked like his lunch, and he could hear Chink's voice all the way up on the first landing.

"How come you wanna play *Hill Street Blues* again, dammit?" he could hear them arguing. "It's been off for a hunnert years."

"I liked it."

"Keerist. You liked the *Flying Nun*. You been sick since they took *Kojak* off."

"Go jack off? Go jack off yourself, you little kamikaze reject, if you can find that miniature gherkin you slopes laughingly refer to as a cock." They went on like this all day. He always wondered how they could have kept it up all those years. After a while it made you tired to hear them. But he loved them, he supposed. And you overlook someone's faults when you love 'em. He knew they had covered for him a thousand times over the years. Covered for him back when he stayed blitzed to the gills on the job. Of course, they never let up about it either. That was their style. Anything was fair game for these flaky friends of his.

"Good morning," he'd say, and Lee would look up and shake his head, "Swacked again," he would sigh, "Four hours late to work. Pathetic. All we ask is whatever you do don't breathe on the captain's shield. He just got it shined yesterday."

"Yeah," Fat Dana would chime in, "and that heavy a concentration of alcohol will tarnish gold fastern' saltwater'll eat out the bottom of a '64 Olds Cutlass."

"Speaking of heavy concentrations of things that eat," he'd say, and the thing that sometimes passed for witty repartee in Buckhead Station would begin.

Eichord's walk coming down the flight of steps was unmistakable to them and they made him halfway down, and he "overheard" them begin to discuss him at the top of their lungs.

"And another thing about that mother grabbing, headline-grabbing Jack Eichord, man, his EGO is so

damn big he no longer thinks he has to shower or bathe.
Have you noticed? *PHEW!*"

"Oh, shucks, yes," Lee's partner could be heard to
say. "Eichord stinks like a wet Saint Bernard's crotch.
It's getting so bad—"

"The real question is how you assholes know what a
Saint Bernard's crotch smells like," Eichard said as he
reached the door of the Squad Room.

"Hey," Lee acknowledged his friend's presence. "Don't
you love it when he talks dirty."

"And now, ladies and gentlemen," Tuny boomed in
his announcer voice, "the Major Crimes Task Farce
proudly prevents . . ." He cued his Oriental partner for a
fanfare.

"Taaaah-daaaaaaaaaahhhhhhh!"

"That Sherlock Holmes of winos, the old skid-row
supersleuth himself, let's hear it for the boss of the Bourbon Street beat."

"Taa-daaaaaaaaahhhhhhhh!"

"Lovable, intoxicating, Blackjack Eichord, human
distillery!"

They broke up as Eichord, who had moved behind
Dana Tuny, reached over with both hands and gently
squeezed the man's prominent chest, which bulged his
shirt out to a noticeable degree,

"Up to about a fifty-two-C now, are we? These are
getting ripe."

"A fifty-four-D-cup actually, Officer," Dana told him,
"and I wish you wouldn't stop. I'm getting kinda hot
from that."

"A teacup?" Lee said incredulously. "Did you say a
TEACUP? Hey, that's bullshit. You couldn't fit those
baby blimpers into a teacup. You be lucky to squeeze
one into a casserole dish."

"I'll squeeze you into a casserole dish, you little dink
handjob. I'll fuck you over so many times you'll think
you're the center on a Greek football team. I'll—"

"Hey, Big D."

"Eh?"

"Donna sent you something."

"No shit?"

"Yeah. Really, it's starting to bug me a little. I just don't like the way my wife's always thinking about you."

"Uh. Well, what can I say? She knows a real man when she sees one." Lee screamed with laughter at that one. "Shaddup ya fuckin' pickleprong. Whatta YOU know about it?"

"Yeah," Eichord continued, "she just can't get you out of her mind. Wanted me to give you a little something. What do you think we got for you? Huh?" He held up the sack the way you might do with a kid.

"I'm a genius now I know what's inna sack, for shit's sake. What do I look like Bobbie Fisher?"

"You look like CARRIE Fisher through the tits there, but what's in the sack? Give up? Maybe something you can put on your desk so we'll all know what you are—eh?" He slipped the sign out and put it on Dana's desk. Lee started screaming hysterically as soon as he read the sign. He fell from his chair to the floor and began pounding it with his fists.

"Jesus, cheer up," Dana told him. "It ain't THAT fuckin' funny."

"Oh . . ." He could barely catch his breath he was laughing so hard. "Chunk, my man," he roared, "oh, yeah, that's perfect—you are a fucking *CHOWHOUND*!" He went into another fit of screaming laughter.

"Fuckin' flakes."

"*Chow*hound," he said as he fought for air. "Oh, I'm gonna' fucking *DIE*."

WEST ERIE SUBSTATION

■ ■ ■   " so anyway, the bitch's layin' there on the slab 'n, you know, he's been boffin' the good-lookin' ones all along, right? So, shit, he pulls back the sheet and goes, Hey, check THIS out. 'Cause you know, she's a stone bitchin' fox, right? And he feels her up a little and, shit, she ain't even that cold yet. All fuckin' RIGHT, so he's horny enough to fuck mud anyway, and he's got his skivvies down—"

"Uh, 'scuze me, is Detective Shy here?"

"Hold it, Bud. So anyway, he's got 'em down and he's climbin' up in the saddle, right? And he puts it in and he's pumpin' away at this dead bitch 'n all of sudden she comes to"—the detectives laugh—"an' he goes, Whoa, SHIT. And he pulls his razor outta his pants, he's gonna cut the bitch's throat and FINISH, right? And he gets so excited tryin' to get the razor outta his jeans he slices the end of his own fuckin' THUMB OFF!" Screaming in the squad room. "An' that's when ole Elmer comes boppin' around the corner of the hallway and here's this naked broad runnin' out of the morgue with blood all over her and he thinks he's got the goddamn dee-tees." Laughter.

"I want to report a—"

"And he goes, Hey, you ain't supposed to take 'em in there before they're completely DEAD!" Screaming.

"I was told come in here to report this. Is Detective Shy here?"

"Yeah," he said, laughing, "that's Scheige over there. The one with the magazine." He pointed out a skinny

51

detective looking at a centerfold, and the cop called out his name.

"Hey, Scheige?"

"Hey. Check out the bongos on this," Scheige said, holding up the magazine.

"This guy wants to see ya." The cop tilts his head in the direction of the hype.

"Yeah?"

"Detective Shy?"

"Whatcha need?"

"I was told to come in here and report this to you. I seen that guy in the papers. You know the big, fat murderer? They said if I give you the information you could—uh, you know, pay me money for being, uh, er, uh, giving you d' information?"

"This oughta be good," one of the detectives muttered under his breath.

"What big, fat murderer you talkin' about?"

"In da paper dere. The one d' cop killed."

"Oh. You saw the one the cop killed. Uh huh."

A couple of giggles.

"He was naked and taking a bath in the alley off West Erie."

Every cop in the room screamed with laughter as the hype stood there reddening.

"That's wonderful," the one called Scheige said. The moon was full. The day before a guy had come in to "swear out a warrant" against someone called Voltan X, swearing he had information the extraterrestrial was the head of an interplanetary kidnapping ring that was taking lawn elves and pink flamingos in the mistaken belief they were our children.

"I seen him ALIVE. Takin' a shower in d' rain, buck-naked right dere in d' alley."

"Wonderful," Scheige said, dissolving in hysterics.

"Hey, man, this is for real. I ain't shittin'. I seen him—" His voice was drowned out.

"Bernie, jew ever hear about the time me and Mac busted Sweet William Trace?"

"Huh uh," a cop replied.

"Sweet William was sniffin a whole shit pot o' glue back then, and he was in the back of his limo all glued up, ya know, 'n he was naked, beatin' his meat and wearing a German army helmet. You know those old time Kaiser helmets with the big spikes? So anyway, Mac and me made the limo and we was just gonna stop it, I forget—some bullshit probably—and we have 'em pull over, and fuckin' Sweet William comes outta the back, stone-naked, glued to the max, wearin' a German army helmet—he weighed about three-fifty, you know, 'n Mac'd never seen him and he said he liked to pop a cap on him when he come outta that back seat!" The cops laughed.

"Did you ever hear about that sheep-fucker we nailed over in the twelfth?"

The hype turned around disgustedly and left the squad room and the flaky, laughing cops who didn't want to lay a taste on him for the good information. "Fuck it," he said, sniffing and rubbing his arms.

NORTH BUCKHEAD

"**H**ow ya like this jam, boy?" he said to John Monroe, meaning the car he'd borrowed.

"Fucker's tight. Cherry ride absolutely." It was six-ten and there was already traffic inbound, but they were boogeying out Cypress Road.

"Boy, I can pick 'em. Big ole Crown Vic. Shit. Be lookin' for thirty-four hunnert." He looked over at the dipshit next to him.

"This is, shit, 1900 'n somethin', Wend—uh, I mean Bo, they ain't got any numbers on the fuckin' houses or nothin'."

"Whatjew call me?"

"Huh?"

"Jus' now. Whatjew call me then?"

"Bo."

"Uh huh." He gripped the wheel like he was strangling it. The voice starting out in almost a whisper, very softly, exaggerated sweet tone of voice, like to a baby, "Lissen up now, John, because iffn' ya go an' call me that when weuns inna house, or iffn' ya go shoutin' at me across the bank," the voice changing to a column of steel sticking John in the ear like an ice pick, 'HEY WENDALL I MEAN BO COMMERE 'N KICK A COUPLE MORE HOLES IN MY DUMB SHITTER F'R ME,' why, ya jes' won't leave me no choice. Ya do understand that, doncha, John?"

"Sorry, man I won't—"

"I mean, there we'll be inna bank an' shit I'll just draw
down on ya and drop your goddamn fucking dumb ass
right there in the fucker. DO YA GIT IT? Ya got to
screw down your damn head, John, and Concenfuckingtrate,
all right?" Sorry cracker trash.

"Uh. That's the two thousand block so youuns goin' in
the right direction, Bo. I'm sorry, I won't forgit again."

"I'm sorry, I won't forgit again," he mimicked him.
"Man, ya can try a person's fucking soul with that shit.
Ya *GOT* to git y'r shit together now."

"Okay."

"An' don' say NOTHING inna house or the bank. I'll
do it. Ya just do what I tell ya."

"Right." John Monroe nodded.

"Ya go in back and cut everything ya find like I tole
ya. Jes' like I showed ya yesterday with them bolt-cutters.
Right?"

"Right."

"Cut ever' fuckin' thing. Phone lines, air-conditioner,
the goddamn antenna thing, the fuckin' copper water
line. I don' give a rat fuck what it is, *CUT* that sucker.
Right?"

"Right."

"Then youuns come on back around real fast 'n come
right on inna door behind me. Got it?"

"Gotcha."

What a fuckin lamebrain. He looked over at the imbecile that bad luck had saddled him with in the joint. What
a fuckin' mistake.

"Twenty-one hundred block, Bo."

Shit, now the dumb fuck was a gonna call out the
numbers of every goddamn block to him like it was the
countdown f'r a fucking rocket. Well. Fine.

"Real good, pud. Jes' keep callin' out them numbers
an' thataway we might git lucky and not drive by the
thirty-four hundred block, eh?"

Donald Fields had just looked at the clock. It was
six-fifteen A.M.. He missed Clara and little Bud. Usually
he and Clara had coffee and chatted together in the
breakfast nook while they woke up. He never saw the

boy before he went to work because he got up so early, but with them at Earline's, he missed the kid's presence in the house and was glad they'd be home by the following night.

After Clara got her heart started, she'd make him another cup and fix them cereal and freshly squeezed orange juice all icy cold, and he'd read the paper until six-forty or so. He liked getting there about five-to-seven. Seven at the latest. Come in a full half-hour before anybody came to work. There'd be the maintenance man and the night guard there and he'd unlock and go on in and arrange his day.

He loved that time and always looked forward to that first half-hour when he'd be in his nice office and it'd be so quiet out front, and he'd sit there arranging the day, getting it all just so. Smooth and prepared. He was going to have to sit down with the boy this morning. "The boy" was what he called his top man. A young hotshot named Joe Gillespie. He was problems. Short-fused. Thought he was the only kid who knew anything about the banking business. He'd had an offer from that asshole at American Fed and he was pressuring Donald for a vice presidency and all the usual. Fields was chewing over in his mind how he'd handle it. He wanted to keep the boy. He was a killer in trust work.

Fields was putting his pocket items in his trousers when he heard the noise downstairs. It didn't startle him that much because he was always hearing noises in the damn house ever since they bought it two years before. There was something wrong with the dining-room lighting fixtures, big white globes that fit into metal retainers on the ceiling. About once a week, BANG, one of the globes would drop down out of the retainer, never dropping all the way out, but good Christ it always scared them to death, because when the globe would catch on the outer metal lip it sounded like glass breaking. He wondered when the damn thing would fall on them during dinner one evening. He'd looked at it a dozen times but the globes looked identical to the ones in the kitchen. He was no handyman. He could barely change the bulbs in them, and he just told Clara to call somebody and see if she could get them fixed so they wouldn't drop out, and this is the prosaic and mundane and trivial thought he could recall going through his mind as he started downstairs to make sure the glass hadn't fallen out and a tall thin vicious-looking stranger was there on the stairs with a gun pointed out at him, saying, "Youuns jes' be sweet now an' turn aroun'." As though in a dream he held his hands up just the way they do on TV and turned and felt one of his hands being pulled back and something going tight around him. Then the other hand went back and—OUCH—it was tight. He heard the door slam. Someone else was coming in. He thought, OH GOD, a whole gang of them, coming in to rob and assault and kill him, and thank God Clara was gone. The other one telling him not to move or try anything and was racing around him and up the stairs. Footsteps were coming up behind him, and a stench, and he heard another voice snarl as it pulled him back down the stairs,

"Yessireesir. Git y'r faggot ass down them stairs, ya' lily-white pussy boy. Ya' don' wanna make me *HURT* ya," and on the word "HURT" he felt all the wind shoot out of him and he was down on the carpet with an intense and awful pain in his kidneys and he could feel tears of anger about to well up in his eyes and fear as he wondered what these madmen wanted. If he could just get to the alarm in the front hall, he thought, but he was on his face with his hands behind him, and doors were slamming and he heard the tall, thin man saying to another one, "Pull the car up to the door. Go on." And he was being rolled and something heavy and bad-smelling was around him and he realized he was being rolled up in a throw rug. Why were they doing this? And then doors slammed and he was lifted up from the floor, and he said, "Please just tell me what you want," and one of them snarled a response, but he couldn't hear it through the rug. Then he was afraid he was going to suffocate, he was being crammed into something tight and he couldn't breathe and he thought he was being kidnapped and these insane men were going to make Clara pay to get him alive and he never connected it with the bank until several minutes later when the car stopped and they took him out in an open field and explained to him what it was they wanted.

"Now youuns lissen up real good, heah?"

Fields nodded. His hands were bound but he was otherwise unhurt. He wondered how far he'd get if he tried to kick the one in the groin and run. Just take off running into the nearby trees.

"We gonna untie ya, and weuns gonna all go downta the bank. An' ya'll gonna go in and get me a lotta money, unnerstan'? 'N iffn' ya fuck us over we'll drop you right there like a DEAD ROACH, ya git it?"

"Yes." He nodded that he comprehended.

"We gonna go now."

"Uh, sir?"

"Eh?"

"The time lock doesn't disengage until seven A.M. I can't get you any money until seven."

"What the—" the one named Monroe started to say. "Hold it, shaddup, what the fuck ya' talkin' about time lock?"

Donald Fields explained to them about the overnight procedures, how all monies were locked up in a vault with the time lock as a safety precaution.

"And we can't open the vault before seven." It wasn't true, but he thought it might buy him time.

"Shit, that ain't no problem. It's almos' seven now anyway, shithead. We gon' innair, and jus' waltz on inna that vault with ya, and *you* gon' git us alla money ya can carry in sixty seconds. 'At's alla time ya got. At sixty one seconds I start pullin' the trigger." He fired a round into the dirt beside Fields' feet. It sounded like an eight-inch naval gun going off. Donald Fields wondered if he'd make it through the day alive and in one piece.

"How many people's innair at seven?"

"Just the night security man and the maintenance man most of the time. Then people start showing up a little after seven. It varies."

"Fuck it. Les' go." They got in the front seat. The tall, thin one in the driver's seat, the other one on the passenger side, with Fields between them, his hands still bound. He thought about how to signal to a cop if he saw one;

how to pantomime the word HELP with his mouth. It might be worth a try.

They pulled up on the east side of the bank at one minute before seven and the driver untied him. Fields tried to rub the circulation back into his hands and arms. His confidence was returning. He thought about what he could do. Weighed his options. The driver had been asking about his wife, wondering why he had been alone in the house. He was expert at sizing a man up and these were stupid men. He could outthink them if they gave him half a chance.

Then they were all getting out of the car. He'd been instructed on what to say and do inside. The vicious one was going to go with him into the vault. The stupid one would watch the guard and janitor. Nothing about alarms, cameras. They weren't professional bank robbers. He doubted if they were professional anythings, these hill-billy jerks.

He unlocked the east door of the bank as he'd done four or five thousand times before, but he was shaking so badly he could hardly fit the key into the lock. They came in behind him and he threw the main lights on, the way he always did, and as he hit the switch he felt a pistol jammed against his spine,

"I'm just turning the lights on." They walked on into the main part of the bank, coming in the east door, and Fred was mopping and said, "G'morning," like always and the stupid one motioned at him with the gun and a finger over his mouth in the shut-up sign, and the janitor dropped his mop and raised his hands just the way Fields had, only he said, "Oh, please, don't—"

"SHUT CHUR *FACE*" the vicious one snarled at him in a stage whisper, poking Donald Fields in the spine again for emphasis, and they all walked across the main lobby in the direction of the big vault. "MOVE GOD-DAMMIT," he snarled, and they moved quicker, Fred and Donald first, the other two behind them with their guns out, looking for the security man, who for some reason was nowhere in sight.

The store burglarized the week before had decided to display a couple of handguns with the rifles in their window. It was something they almost never did but the .380 auto had been returned by a customer who nitpicked about rust on the case-hardening, and the big Colt Python had been gathering dust in the showcase for so long they thought that maybe if they moved a few pieces around a little they'd shake something loose. They shook something loose all right. Two nights later thieves broke the window and took both handguns out.

"Hurry," the mean one whispered in Fields' ear, bathing him in a foul mouth odor, "ya' got fifty-nine seconds to *MOVE!*" And it seemed to take forever to unlock the gate and swing the big, heavy door back, and they walked in over the wire grate that of course Fields hadn't disengaged, and the silent alarm was thrown for the second time. Fields gathered up the seven zippered teller pouches with the bait money, taking as much time about it as he could. The vicious one ripped the pouches from his hand and took off running screaming across the lobby at the stupid one, who was standing there with his gun on Fred the maintenance man, "LE'S *GO!*" Which is when the night security guy, Floyd Coleman, stepped out from behind one of the pillars with his .357 Magnum revolver just like Clint Eastwood in the movies only instead of saying, Make my day, he started to say, Drop those guns or drop your pants or drop something, but only the dr came out because John Monroe had pulled the trigger of the .380 auto, shooting him smack dead bang in the ticker and knocking him back like he'd been punched in the stomach by a heavyweight and he sat back and the four of them watched him die with his gun in his hand, dead as he sat there with his eyes still open, going slowly back, toppling over backward almost as an afterthought, the gun firmly in his hand but pointed over to the side, and Monroe and De Witt shagging ass with the teller pouches full of money and almost out the north doorway. But somebody opening the door, a girl named Kelly Pierce who'd only been with the bank for two years, who Donald Fields suspected the boy was secretly poking, Kelly with the famous low-cut dresses and the nice cleavage, Kelly was coming in as they were running out. Bam-BOOM, everybody knocking one another ass over teakettle, money flying every whichaway, the pouches unzippered, bait money in the air like autumn leaves, Kelly knocked on her pretty tush, the vicious one and the stupid one scrambling for money like contestants in a mad quiz show, one of them firing the big Colt back into the bank putting Fields and the man Fred flat on the floor as the thieves snatched and grabbed and jumped into the car that Fields would describe to police as a "dark-blue or midnight-blue Crown Victoria—maybe a year or two old, not sure of the model year." And two uniformed cops coming on the scene and doors being locked and people being herded into offices and interrogated, and cops everywhere.

And at 07:04:10 the dispatcher gave a coded "robbery" at an address that everybody obviously made as Buckhead Mercantile Bank and Trust, and at 07:06:00 Bureau cops picked up a "robbery-in-progress" changed to "robbery with shooting" and they gave it in the clear to homicide, who of course only take over if there is a dead body on the scene, and the five detectives working the midnight-to-eight graveyard tour were all in-house and rolled on it en masse: Bill Brown, Marv Peletier, fat Dana Tuny, Jimmie Lee, and Harry Ecklemeyer.

At 07:21:00, there were fifteen cops by the crime scene. Two uniformed officers, Ramírez and Jones. Four agents of the Federal Bureau of Investigation led by SAC Howard Krug. Five Buckhead detectives, with Detective Sgt. Lee in charge of securing and seizing and protecting and preserving intact the evidence of the crime scene. Lee was in charge, as there had been a homicide committed in the course of the robbery, but he was working "with" the Federal Bureau of Investigation—plus the captain himself no less, in person, and two two-man teams of backup uniforms, all with the light bars and the sirens and the hoo-hah and the evidence van and the ambulance and employees showing up and milling around everywhere as general chaos prevailed.

But it had already happened by the time the feebs arrived with their high tech and higher self-esteem, imbued as they were with a mandate from the Lord on High Himself. It had happened long before the captain had arrived in a cloud of Gordon's and toothpaste. (Christ, the fat son of a buck must use the stuff for a mouthwash.) It had happened when what is usually called "opportunity" presented itself, when the detective sergeant in charge had put his people to work measuring body position, taking the money measurements, searching for spent bullets, processing the crime scene, protecting the evidence, seizing . . . especially the seizing part.

Lee'd gone through the doors where the bills were scattered everywhere—these deliciously crisp green rectangles of spendable, dependable, expendable lettuce leaves with TEN and TWENTY printed on them. These collectible, delectable, beautifully minted, verdantly tinted photographs of dead presidents that he was WALKING through, STEPPING on, this shlamazzle cop who didn't get ten cents walking through this newly mown field of crisp twenties, and intoxicated by promise he opens the door and there's some more of the tellers' pouches and that's when James Lee saw the opportunity and that's when he crossed over the line.

You draw a line somewhere. Right? Right. Draw one. Draw it wherever it makes you comfortable. It looks like any other line—right? It's just a line.

Wrong. It's your line. If you cross it, you put yourself on the other side of the line and at first, because it's only a line, it looks the same from the wrong side as it did before you crossed over. Right? Right.

Every night at Buckhead Mercantile, after the federal people make their pickup, whatever was there from the afternoon's business generally went into the seven zippered tellers' pouches. At close of business there'd been $28,000 and change on the premises. That put a nice, round $4,000 in each of the teller's drawers, not counting the $500 in bait money that each of them always set aside in the special "grab" tray inside their drawer. It was what went in the sack first when a man stuck that Saturday-night special in the girl's face with a note that read, "Put all the money in the sack, this is a robbery," while the hidden surveillance cameras took some charming shots of him for posterity. The bait numbers were on file with law-enforcement agencies for such a contingency.

Just one of the hassles of a robbery/shooting like this was that they'd have to sit there working late putting all those bills back in order, figuring out which were the bait bills and which were the regular bills, making all those neat rectangular stacks, thumbing through those crisp lettuce leaves fast and sure, the way only a bank teller can do, stacking up all those green dreams.

And what Lee saw when he let the door close behind him was three teller pouches and small bills scattered all over. There was one big stack by itself, like somebody had a fistful of cabbage crammed together and it had been knocked loose, but when it hit the floor the tens and twenties and fifties had somehow stayed together. Lee just swooped the stack up, not thinking, bent over with nobody looking and took it. He was a little hot along the ears the way he got sometimes when he was uptight, but he was ready to explain it, like somebody caught shoplifting a candy bar. He just dropped that great big handful of bucks into a deep, inside jacket pocket, out of range of prying eyes, hidden surveillance cameras, the FBI, and his fat partner. Only James Lee and his maker saw him take the step. And just that easily, he stepped over the line. And by definition he was now one of the bad guys.

And he about exploded with joy. He was so happy. He knew it was wrong, but good GOD, it felt good that little bulge of bills, that happy weight of paper in his pocket. Untraceable, embraceable, irreplaceable pounds and sawbucks and cee notes. Smiling faces. It was all he could do not to hurry as they wrapped up the initial processing and seizure work and made their way back to the station.

Lee had an envelope always ready in the trunk for whatever might come up—not like he'd anticipated this—but hell, sometimes it helped if one could flog a little coke sample off a dealer for an emergency holdback. A man never knew when it would come in handy—just tuck it down behind the seat of a car for a probable-cause swindle. Something to lay on a snitch as a thank-you for the Big One. A little taste just in case.

He just put the money in the big, thick manila envelope and dropped it into the first corner mail depository he came to. He mailed it to himself care of that post-office box that was always such a cheap insurance policy. And sure enough, that's where the money went. He couldn't even count it. He tried and hit a big stack of solid twenties. A hundred double-saws in a tight stack. Two thousand dollars just in that half-inch or so of money, so he knew he had some serious bucks in there. All those fifties he'd seen had made his ears flaming red, he was sure, but when he glanced up into the rearview mirror they were still the color of yellow jaundice. He was too nervous to count it now. All he could think about was those asshole feebs and IAD and what they'd do to him if they caught him dirty, but as much as it scared him he wasn't about to go give it back. He was glad he'd picked up the lovely green stack of dirty money. The line looked the same from either side.

BUCKHEAD SPRINGS

Donna walked through the room in which Jack was sitting reading some reports, with his back to her. She wore very short white shorts and matching sandals, and not even the voluminous, cantaloupe-colored sweatshirt could disguise her fabulous breasts, which were quite large and unusually high and firm.

She felt a glow of warmth just at the sight of those broad shoulders and the unruly black hair that was now flecking with more than a bit of gray.

"Old man," she teased gently, her fingers in his hair from behind, "you are getting white up here."

"Umm," he said.

"Did I ever tell you that white-haired men turn me on?"

"Hmmmmm."

"Really. The sexiest thing in the world is a guy with a great head of pure white hair. If you get gray let's dye your hair, okay? Bleach it out real white." Her hands slid down on the big shoulders. "You need a haircut, by the way."

"Nag, nag," he said.

"That's me." She came around and sat beside him, scrunching up very close. "Nag, nag, nag," she was whispering right in his ear, and he let the report fall to the floor. "Hope I'm not disturbing you," she kidded him gently. "Were you reading something?" she asked him with mock innocence.

"Reading? Who, ME?"

"I'm sorry if I bothered you," she lied as she took the lobe of his left ear in her teeth, then leaned around into his face and kissed him ceremoniously, carefully, as if she were passing a mouthful of sacramental wine to him. Or like people playing a game in which they had to pass something with their mouths and couldn't touch each other with their hands.

He received the kiss in kind with his lips and tongue only, neither of them touching otherwise, finding a new way to say it by mouth-to-mouth exploration, kissing the way they so often did.

"Kiss me forever," Donna said.

"Yes." Jack knew what she meant. He wanted to kiss her each time like it was going to be the last time. He would kiss her sometimes while getting ready to leave in the morning and he'd be late to work by ten minutes because they couldn't stop and it would inflame them. They learned to plan around it and he started leaving earlier. They would never let this marriage reach the peck-on-the-cheek stage. Huh uh. Not this one.

"You taste good. Did you just brush your teeth?"

"Hmmm," she told him. They kissed with the unashamed abandon and sense of fun that marked all of their lovemaking. "You taste good, mmmmmf," she said, and he shut her up.

Then she began kissing him more gently. Little kisses. Hot, quick, wet smooches around his lips and in the hollow above his chin, and he kissed her softly on the cheeks. Her cheeks always felt so surprisingly smooth to him, so satiny and feminine. He could never get used to the surprise of her wonderfully smooth skin. And he kissed her eyes closed, barely touching the silky lashes, and a hand touched her. The hard point of a breast shot an electrified current through the palm of his hand and his kisses slid off of her face and onto the pulse at the side of her throat and soon clothing was on the floor and he was seeking the source of that strong pulse with his lips and tongue.

He kissed her heartbeat where it throbbed beneath her beautiful chest and worked eastward over to the side of one of her large and ripe breasts, where he mashed his face into a lovely expanse of white skin and told her everything she need know about them in an eloquent statement of adoring, hot kisses. He spent a lot of time right there on the side of the mountain and then he climbed to the top, moving around to the nipple, then back to the other, moving back across the heartland, then climbing the other, just because it was there. He let it excite him the way it invariably did, sucking both breasts then, tongueing nibbling chewing hungrily devouring then going south down through tummyland, south of the border, traveling down with those inflamed kisses and a tongue that was starting to set her on fire. But he didn't make the trip this time because his hardening desire was pulling him back up, and then both of them were back on the sofa, and she was opening up for him and they were coming together like two halves of a puzzle built in separate rooms, assembled independently; then the pieces joined together in a mating that never failed to delight each of them with the perfection of the fit.

"I want you," she said in a hot whisper.

"Yes, honey," he agreed, "I want you too. So much."

But the reality was that he was somewhere else in that part of him where the deepest desire was kindled. He suddenly realized that he had crawled inside himself and was watching his own performance. GRADING himself or something. And the ludicrous discovery softened his ardor just as she heard him say, So much, and she wondered what she had done. She had been accused once of coming on too strong by a previous lover and it had stayed with her, as the fiercest critiques so often will.

He said nothing. He only kept kissing her, but now in a different way, and after a bit he rolled over, wondering what it was that had passed through his subconscious, like a cold, dark shadow. Donna wondered what she'd done this time to attack the fragile male ego bastion. Both of them thinking these things but said nothing. Donna wanted to say, "It's okay, my sweet. No big deal." But she thought it inappropriate and dangerous and silly anyway. Saying it was no big deal was saying that it might have been a big deal, having all this go on inside her head. Jack wanted to put his face in that pillow of luxuriantly dark hair and just breathe her in till the badjazz blew away. But neither of them did anything.

CHICAGO

He spotted her on Randolph, walking slowly, looking straight ahead, and his eyes targeted first on the thin fabric of the white dress that reminded him for some reason of an actress in the movies. His computer showed him a mental image and he pulled the car over to the curb, lowering the window as he forced a huge, crinkly smile onto his face. She was thin, ordinary-looking, anywhere from nineteen to twenty-three years old, alone, and she met all the requisite minimums.

One may have trouble understanding how this 460-pound killer with the bandaged face could work his magic. The fact that this was not an unattractive young woman makes it all the more incomprehensible to some, but age, sex, personality, they have very little to do with the phenomenon that a man like Daniel Bunkowski exploits.

His eyes saw a female form alone and zeroed in on the legs, which were silhouetted through the thin material of the dress by the sunlight. The fact that she wore a dress—that alone triggered a whole battery of responses in him. Then there was her vulnerability. Who can say why some individuals project this quality and others do not? Vulnerability runs the full range of a wide and complicated spectrum of auras—from projected vulnerability, a far different thing, to true vulnerability, the brand of the profile one so often sees among life's casualties. This young woman had that thing. It was a quality the starmaker machinery looks for in females. When you find it in concert with overt sexuality, the package is dynamite.

But in this one it simply said to Daniel, I am vulnerable
to the taking.

Even as he pulled to the curb, hitting the electric
window controls and reminding himself not to turn his
face too far to the right while he was speaking to her, he
was sizing up his pitch by her appearance, the clothing,
the shoes, the degree of cleanliness, the gait of her walk,
the purposefulness or lack of purpose in her physical
movements, the tilt of her head now and the way it
changed when his voice drew her eyes, the eyes themselves—which so often will give it all away even in the
most practiced liar—the hair, the hands and what she was
carrying, everything about her told him a quick story. It
said, VICTIM.

"Hi." There was no response as she turned. "Excuse
me," and a mumble of words followed, calculated to pull
her over by the side of the newly stolen wheels.

"What?" She moved a little, warily.

"Do you have any idea why I can't get across the
[something] to the other side of [something else]?" The
inflection was that of a sincere question, his eyes cast
downward as if in a map, his Pillsbury-Doughboy-meets-
FrankenKong face a pleasant, beaming, lost, wrinkled,
jowly, and deceptively cherubic mask of fat and friendly
exasperation.

"Huh?" She had moved closer and looking into the
front seat of the car she saw a huge man of indeterminate
age staring and shaking his head at a street map.

"Can you help me?" he asked, pointing at the map.
She moved closer, right by the window and he had her
then. He knew if he could get them within touching
distance he had them. Always. That was the reality of the
track record.

If they were reluctant to get within arm's length, it
usually meant that they were too wary to con into the
vehicle. But if they got that close to him, he always had
them. They'd get in a car with Daniel Bunkowski no
matter if he was bleeding, drenched in sweat, covered in
sewer filth, or immaculate and in a rented summer tux.
The ease with which a victim went with Daniel seemed to
be in almost inverse proportion to the social acceptibility
of his appearance. It was as if anybody who looked like

THAT couldn't possibly be a bad guy too. It was too much of a cliché, perhaps.

The trust factor. He began working on it now with the girl. His eyes never looked at anything but the map, and at her eyes. He let himself blink a lot, squint, shake his head, and put more movement into his normally static and inert facial features, smiling, grimacing, scowling, licking his lips, shaking his head, all the while the torrent of words flooded out of his mouth, a river of busy verbiage lapping against her resistance.

"When I tried to cut through there it was a one way street, see?"

"Yeah. They got the town all screwed up now with the one-ways."

"Yeah. They got the town all fucked up now." He said the word to her naturally, really bummed out by the crazy street system. "You can't find your way around for shit." The big head moved, the words testing her probing getting the lay of the land and the temperature of the water.

"Yeah," she agreed, laughing, the phrase "fucked up" as common to her as blue sky.

"I haven't been here in a few years," he said. "Are you from here or what?" Big friendly smile.

"God, no. I came here with Mom a couple years ago. We're from California."

"No shit," he said, his face lighting up like a Christmas tree. "Where 'bouts in California?

"Bakersfield," she told him.

"Oh, God. That's wild. I'm from L.A."

They both laughed.

"No kiddin?" she said, having to stop herself from saying "no shit." And he was telling her the first thirty-five things he could remember from doing time with cons from the Los Angeles area, saying things about how great it was out on the Coast, how much it sucked back here, and in the wave of California dreaming and nostalgia for the palm trees and the ocean and all, she was soon sitting in the front seat of the car and the car was moving then as he talked and, yeah, she agreed,

"I can't wait to get outta this shitty city." And he laughed like that was the funniest remark he'd ever heard in his life. And she smiled at his recognition of her wit and acumen and personality.

"God, what happened to you?" she said, natural as you please. He told her about the accident on his Harley, and they talked bikes for a while. God. How cool, she told him, "I love bikes." And before he could stop her she was off and running on the long and intensely boring tale of how somebody named whatever asshole name—Kevin or whatever—used to take her riding in the "hills," and that went on to the point where it was starting to give Daniel a headache to concentrate even fractionally on the pitch so he finally had to interrupt her and say, "Hey, excuse me and all, but shit, I just gotta ask. Have you ever done any modeling?"

"Modeling?" She looked over at him like she'd never heard the word before in her life.

"Yeah. You know. Posing for pictures in magazines. Being photographed. High fashion work. Swimsuits. That sort of thing."

"Naaaaw." She laughed a little and looked to see if he were putting her on.

"Boy," he said, his face deadly serious, "what a waste. You know, that's what I do."

"Photograph models?"

"Well, no, *I* don't photograph 'em. Oh, sure, the story-boards and all I do, but I'm a concept producer, and I work with beautiful models all the time. God. You put 'em all to shame. You're a knockout if you don't mind me saying so." His eyes remained straight on the road, so sincere you'd think he were sitting next to Brooke Shields now. He began some double-talk gobbledygook about concept production for the "big slicks." And she was beaming from the compliments.

"You know," she said, "you might laugh at me but I've been thinking about trying some high fashion modeling."

He couldn't believe the nitwit said it—TRYING SOME HIGH FASHION MODELING. What an idiot. He smiled and shook his head in amazement. "I just can't believe nobody's ever asked you. Wow! Listen, I don't know if you'd have any interest, but I'm on my way back out to the Coast to do a big spread for a major advertiser and I need a girl who looks just like you. But she has to be un-spoiled-looking, pure, beautiful—like YOU. I need some-body new. A new face." He was really getting into it now. Riffing. The rumbling basso profundo lapping at the listener's brain, never letting up, the stream of vocalese scatting away at reason, the rising tide drowning them in compliments, favors, begging, imploring, dangling lost opportunities and rich promises in front of them, giving their own language back to them slightly altered, the sea of words taking the victim under. "I need . . . I can't use those skuzzes out there. I have to find a new girl."

"Hmmm," she hummed in agreement, hanging on his words.

"Would you have any interest at all in going with me? I would pay all your expenses, and when we got to California you'd be getting a big cash fee for just a few hours' work. How does that sound?"

"God! Yeah. I mean it sounds real good. What would I have to do?" Her face was wary.

"That's the beautiful part." He beamed his biggest smile yet. "Absolutely nothing!" And her smile crinkled the corners of her eyes and he read her for an easy yes.

"When would I have to go?"

"Well, see, that's the thing." He was very earnest now, hurried, intense with the excitement and challenge and just that soupçon of threat mixed into it, like you know—"if we don't go right away you'll miss out on the job, and it's so perfect for you, and you're so beautiful and I can't believe my luck." And on and on until she fancies herself a free spirit and she goes, "Well. Shit. Why not? I'll go home and tell Mom," and what a crazy, spur-of-the-moment chick I am, and let's do it. Devil-may-care me, I'm always ready to try anything once, ha ha.

But then Chaingang tells her, "I've got even a better idea than that," and he begins spinning this bullshit about how they can surprise her, and the best way to handle things of this nature based on his past experiences, and how he is going to personally buy her AN ALL-NEW WARDROBE so that she doesn't even have to stop to pack, not even pack a toothbrush, and here's a dime to call Mom and stuff soon as we stop for clothing, and he hands her a ten and peels it off a role of bills the size of a grenade that he can barely jam back in his pocket, or so it appears.

And even as she starts to protest, his foot has gently dropped just a little on the pedal and they are moving toward the city limits even as he speaks, that overflow of wordplay still inundating her with the dream of sunny Cal and the beach and the tan—my God how great she'd look with a deep tan.

"Yeah. I been wanting a tanning bed, but—"

"Why would you want a tanning bed when you can lay out in your new string bikini on the golden sandy beach—" But he misread her and she says,"Oh, I hate the hot beach," and before the word "hot" has had time to resonate in his computer he has rephrased the whole thing and they are talking about how he will buy her the finest tanning bed on the market, and which kind of tanning bed is the safest, and he pours out the pitcher full of liquid charm and she settles back in the seat of the big stolen car, thrilled to her core that this is happening and beginning to consider the possibilities of this ego-stroking act of kind fate, and he intrudes upon her daydreaming fantasy as he says, "Hey. Listen. I don't even think we introduced ourselves. I'm Daniel. What's your name."

"Oh, yeah. Hi. Sissy Selkirk."

"Sissy?"

"Yeah," she said apologetically, "I way—" but he quickly stopped her before she could begin some interminable tale about her goony name.

"Sissy is real different. Pretty. I like it. Like Sissy Spacek."

"Yeah, I spell it same as her."

"You LOOK a little like her too," he lied. She was very ordinary-looking. Far from pretty but not homely. Her face was attractive in profile, but when she turned, the jawline was exaggerated like Sub-Mariner's in the old comic books, and she was so thin as to be almost without a figure.

"Sometime when I get two thousand dollars I'm goin' to get my boobs done," she said.

"Pardon me?" He had no idea what she'd said.

"You know." She touched her chest." I think it would

give me more confidence to model and that. Kevin said I should get boobs exactly like Morgan Fairchild's." She showed with her hands approximately where Morgan Fairchild's breasts would be if they were on her chest. For the first time Chaingang had just a little tremor of nagging regret. She was almost too stupid. He wondered how long he'd be able to tolerate her as a cover before he let the tide of rage wash over him and he lashed out and killed her.

"Morgan Fairchild's," he mused aloud, having no idea who that was. "Well, we'll have that two thousand for you soon enough. What are you going to charge for modeling—do you know yet?" Anything to keep talking.

She didn't know what to say. He could sense he'd erred again, asking her a question that required some degree of intellect to respond to. He quickly said, "You'll have to set a fee. A bare minimum. Get it?" He laughed inanely. "A BARE minimum—for when you do bikini modeling."

"Yeah!" She laughed with him. He seemed like an okay dude. She thought for a moment and asked carefully, "How much do you pay?"

"*Thousands*," he said expansively, nodding to show her he was serious, "so the bare minimum is even good." They laughed again. Rarely heard, his natural laugh was a weird kind of barking noise. He knew it frightened the hell out of people, so he had learned to fake a passable human laugh, a cross between laughter and the sound of an outboard motor starting.

And there they were, Daniel Bunkowski and Sissy Selkirk, two strangers in the warm afternoon, getting to know all about each other in the front seat of a stolen car rolling along toward the sunset across the distant horizon.

Fifteen minutes before, Sissy had been on her way to pick up something she'd put on layaway downtown, just walking down Randolph minding her own business. And now she was sitting next to a perfect stranger, a 460-pound lunatic killer, on her way to God knows where in California to model for thousands of dollars an hour. Life can sure play some big surprises on you, she thought, her heart beating rapidly with the unbelievable rush of this exciting offer.

Soon Daniel would begin his tale of how they'd need
to keep their expenses as low as possible to get her a
wardrobe or whatever, and would she mind terribly if
they'd SHARE a motel room? And that would be just
the beginning.

But the suggestion, while not even a hair off-key in
tone, jars some vestige of caution in the girl and she
begins a big number about how she just can't leave
without calling home.

"I gotta tell Mom. God, she'd shit if I, you know,
would just leave 'n that—not say *anything*. GOD! 'n you
know, I gotta get some things, 'n I gotta—" And he
smiles, nodding with her as he decides how he'll handle it
when Mom draws the line. He has a fluid game plan. He
will go with the flow as always. Ride with the tide.
Boogie with the oogie. What a MORON. I gotta feed my
goldfish, wipe my ass . . . He has tuned her out as he
searches for a pay phone at sidewalk level. One where he
can closely monitor the girl's side of the conversation.

He is parked. She is depositing money. He catches
fragments of a no and he begins to formulate his next
move until he hears, "HEY WELL YOU KNOW JUST
FUCK IT THEN IF THAT'S THE WAY YOU FEEL
FUCK IT!" The girl slamming down the receiver, Daniel
fighting to look sincerely worried as she hurls herself
back in the car. "You know, like you said, I just won't
bother with any luggage 'n that. I mean, we can PICK
UP whatever I need. Right?"

He can't believe it himself. "Right, sure. Absolutely."
He starts back into traffic as she begins recounting the
lifelong battle of wits between mother and daughter.
Bunkowski scores again. Too facile, perhaps? Yes, for the
average person, maybe. But he does not have Daniel's
inner compass which points toward the vulnerable heartbeat. Somewhere you have your Sissy Selkirk. The thing
is, you and Sissy may never meet. If you DO find her,
will you be able to spot her in a crowd? Chaingang can
always find them. It is part of his nature.

He looked over at the girl as if he'd homed in on that
excited throbbing in the childlike bosom smiling his most
disarming and trustworthy smile, the gruesome, bandaged face turned as far away as possible, the right side

crinkled in warmth and good humor as he eyed her flat chest, smiling, beaming at her wonderfulness, and when she paused for a gasp of air, saying, "Morgan Fairchild," nodding slowly, knowingly as he looked at her. "Yes. I think so. Definitely." And that was just the incentive to set her back on course, and she started off on a long, aimless, circling butterfly flight of airheaded jabber as he let himself tune out with a contented smile.

WINDER

"**O**h, man, shit, Bo, I done drew DOWN on 'im."
They had ditched the Crown Vic. "God DAMN
that's a good fuckin' feelin'— SHIIIIT." John Monroe
was toked and stoked. He started counting again, one
hunnert, two hunnert, three hunnert, damn . . . He lost
track ag'in. "Oh, man. I mean I was cocked 'n rocked,
weren't I?"

"Uh huh."

"Bo, that sucker come out from behin' that post 'n shit
'n just pop outta there like a rabbit tree'd outta a damn
cornfield, POW—pops up and goes, Awright, Louie, drop
the gat, er, some ole-timey shit an' I just go cooler'n a
damn snake I go PPPKKKKKSSSSSSSSSSSHHHHHHHH
HHHHEEEEEEEWWWWWWWWWWWWWWWW! 'N
blast that fucker onta his shitty ass." He laughed like it
was the funniest thing he'd ever seen. A man dying. "Up
jumps the devil and PPPPKKKSSSSSSSSHHHHHHEEEW
WW! One rentacop"—he made the finger scoreboard
gesture— "ten points! Hot dawgies."

He started to count again, this time out loud, "Twenty,
forty, forty-five, ninety-five, and, uh, ninety-five and twenty
well call 'er a hunnert and twenty, hunnert and forty,
hunnert forty-five, two hunnert and forty-five, two hunnert
and sixty-five—"

"John." Patient. Calm. His sweet, syrupy put-on voice.

"Ya sure kin shoot, John. I mean f'r some dum-fuck
bum-fuck ya' kin drill, boy."

"Ain't that the fuckin' truth, Bo. Two hunnert and
eighty-five. Three hunnert and eighty-five, uh, four hunnert
and forty-five— "

"Real fine on the draw there. Ya done real good with that there pipe."

"Yeah." He didn't like Wendell's tone. He kept counting in silence, six hunnert . . . seven . . . eight. Another thousand stack. That was . . . what? He'd already lost count. Fifteen? Seventeen. Most he'd ever seen.

"Hey, Bo. Weuns got us about eighteen, nineteen thousand dollars here. Motherfucker! 'Atsa most gawdamned money ah'v ever seen in mah fuckin' LIFE. Maybe nineteen, twenty thousand dollars." It was getting more each time he said it.

"Uh huh. Thing is, f'r somebody with a fast pipe like youuns got that there was some serious BAD fuckin' reflexes at the door. Ya know that, doncha, boy? Ya know ya fucked up back air—now say it, eh?"

"Huh?" He didn't like the tone at all.

"Yeah. Ya fucked up real purty, John."

"I don't know whatcha mean, Bo. I didn't do nothin' wro—"

"'N another thang take 'n spit out that there fuckin' foam rubber in y'r cheeks ah cain't understan'a fuckin' word—okay?"

"Yeah." He spat out the window. One of the sides he had to dislodge with a finger. " 'N we can shave these mustaches off too like ya said. They gonna be lookin' f'r two theefs with them caps 'n pussy ticklers and big ole chipmunk cheeks."

"Ya fucked us out of about twenty thousand back air."

"Huh?"

"Ass right."

"No way, man." He didn't have to take that shit. He'd gone and saved their shitty butts back there.

"Twenty thousand. My half is ten. So you owe me ten outta youuns share." He was deadly serious.

"Shit. You was JOKIN' with me." He got it now. He thought Wendell had been serious. "You got some sense of humor, man. Shit chew had me a-goin'. Hell's bells."

"Uh huh."

ONE MILE FROM I-57

He drove through the congested traffic with a tenth of his mind, not even that, a fraction of his brain channeled on what he was seeing with his eyes and the rest of him out on some faraway level.

The noise in the car was sufficiently disconcerting that it might have disturbed some lesser being. The radio was blasting a big-beat tune straight from the heart of old time rock-'n-roll—thumping, toe-tapping, undeniable kind of music—and it was the sort of non-formula rock that came from the most real point on the musical compass forcing the listener to either love it or leave it. You had to get with it or get away from it. You couldn't be indifferent. Chaingang was the exception. It didn't exist for him.

The girl on the seat beside him was running her mouth as she always did, and with perhaps the bottom hundredth of his awareness he was able to follow some vague semblance of her meandering tale of woe about a jealous suitor who had followed her everywhere, and he would hear snatches of her voice pop in and out of his consciousness.

". . . him if he kept following me around I'd have to get the law on him and he said okay, but then when I went to . . ." And getting enough of a sense of it that he knew it was of no danger to him, nothing he had to correct or stifle or steer back on track, and though for many it would have been disconcerting or annoying to the point of distraction, to him it was less than the buzzing of a fly. He found her voice somewhat pleasant.

She spoke in a kind of babyish, controlled, soft-spoken way that made a person want to lean forward and listen until he realized she wasn't saying anything of importance.

". . . and she said he'd been over at her house parked outside waiting for me for about two hours and so I said to her that if he ever—" It was sort of like chewing gum with words, a reflexive thing some people have in the proximity of others; a need to constantly fill anything resembling quiet with noise. The sportscaster syndrome: the need to keep talking.

Daniel found the girl's voice bearable. He liked the fact that it was soft and always respectful and low in volume so that his powers of concentration could easily tune it out. In a way he supposed that it was better she had plenty to say to him, because they would be together a lot and he had absolutely nothing to say to her. Nothing. They had a grand total of zero in common. He might have come down from Mars for all he was able to relate to her world of mundane troubles and nothingness.

". . . when they came and they just warned him and a' course he told them he hadn't been following me, which was nothing but a lot of lies, and so the next time he called me up I just said . . ." A lulling kind of not unpleasant, soft, background noise to let him know she was still alive and functioning beside him.

He could not look at the traffic without being amazed by it. It fascinated him, so alien the sight of masses of human beings was to his nature. What were they all thinking? Where were they all headed? A dirty, long-unwashed, grimy gray used car of some kind swerved into the lane immediately in front of him. Daddy and Mommy, with a kid between them. Three more in the back seat and hanging out the windows waving and laughing and screaming maniacally like a family of chimps. God, how he detested the sight of them. A family "having fun." It pleased him greatly to think in that instant how close they all were to death. They were a whim away from the Reaper.

How easy it would be for him to take them out. He was so experienced at it, he knew all the tricks of the trade, the techniques to put people at his mercy to lead them by the nose into the dark places where they could cry for help at the top of their lungs to no avail, where no prying eyes could see the horrors they would be subjected to in their closing minutes—or hours, if he was lucky.

His experience at this was unparalleled. He knew just in that second, all the dangers, all the possible permutations, the accidentals, serendipitous happenstances, fortuitous lucky breaks that might save them. He knew by instinct and lust and long, long experience how to make that quick, instant assessment of their level of threat to him.

And in that fleeting second, as he looked at the screaming monkees and the weary Ma and Pa with their brood in the old car, even a lawn-mower handle or something protruding from the filthy trunk lid which was tied down and flopping back and forth as the old car bounced along, in a big hurry to what? Go mow their lawn? They fascinated him. What could they be thinking, these monkees.

How easy it would be for him to tap their bumper, and the twine would break and the lawn mower would do whatever it would do and the trunk lid would pop up and the man would panic and brake and pull over and Chain would be on top of them in a heartbeat. And instinctively his mind planned a scheme whereby he could insert himself into their peaceful, nothing, alien lives. Saw their monkee reveries apart with a nasty, serrated steel edge. Hammer into their plans and boring lives of predictability with a fury that would leave them bloodied and screaming from pain and terror. Rip apart their lawn-mower lives of weed-eating, water-sliding, tractor-pulling ignorance and blissful stupor. Make them beg for merciful death to take them under. And the heat of the fantasy kindled an old familiar hunger.

BUCKHEAD SPRINGS

Party animals uncaged.

"There are eight million naked stories in the city and—"

"Eight million STORIES, ya fuck," Lee corrected his partner.

"That's what I said, eight million stories in the whore. There are"—he took a deep, boozy breath—"eight million naked bimbos in the city and I'll poke every one of 'em."

"You guys flyin' pretty good already?" Eichord said, sipping his nonalcoholic cooler.

"What ya drinkin?" Dana Tuny peered at the glass.

"He's drinking Seven-Up same as I am," Donna said loudly from the next room.

"Canada Dry," Jack said.

"He's drinkin' Canada Dry," Lee said.

"Shit, Eichord already done drunk Canada Dry a long fucking time ago," Tuny mumbled.

"Tuny, if brains was worth a dollar and it cost a quarter to go around the world you couldn't get outta sight, ya' fuckin' imbecile," Lee whispered.

"If dick was worth a dollar and it cost a quarter to get laid, you couldn't fuck a cheerio, ya' slant-eyed little squid-eater."

"My dick is bigger than that little hernia you carry around."

"Come on, girls, let's not fight," Eichord admonished as they walked out into the yard.

"Listen, picklepecker, remember we done SOLVED

this question long ago when we measured them whores—
mine was six inches longer than yours an' I only pulled
enough outta my pants to beat ya."

"The only thing ya ever pulled is your pud, and you
hadda do THAT with a fuckin' tweezer, numb-nuts."

"Poor Peggy." Fat Dana shook his head in mock sor-
row at the thought of her suffering. Unaware of the
singer, Lee's wife had changed her named to Peggy when
he'd brought her over. "Just imagine—she's never known
nothin' but a li'l ole two-incher." He held his fingers out
in measurement. "Li'l fucking firecracker of a hard-on
about the size of a dink cherry bomb."

"At least Peg GETS a hard dick once inna while," his
partner said. "Not like poor ole Bev. God, I feel so
sorry for Bev. Married to d' blimp here." Lee discussed
the weighty aspects of the problem with Eichord.

Jack knew that when they joked like this, these old-
time partners of a hundred and fifty years or whatever it
had been, they were TALKING about dicks but they
were talking ABOUT something altogether different.

They'd been together so long they could probably communicate by sign language, and Jack often wished they
would, when the banter wore thin. But there were odd
moments of oblique and surprising subtlety when they'd
be exchanging their goofy rap back and forth and Jack
would suddenly realize they were having some kind of a
discussion during the nonsense. They managed a between-
the-lines dialogue of sorts, something about work, or
whatever, hidden, subliminal, sandwiched in between all
the crap. In this way their chauvinistic, vulgar, silly de-
meanor served as a kind of vocal camouflage. A code or
word smoke screen. He wondered what it was all about
tonight.

"That ain't no bullshit about the hard-ons," Dana ruminated, his tone sobering slightly as he thought about it.
"Shit, I love that woman and we don't even hardly kiss
anymore. 'Course we don't kiss any LESS either."

"Peggy says if she ever got hurt in a traffic accident I
wouldn't be able to identify the body," Lee said.

"Umm." Dana smiled. They were still walking, out of
Eichord's yard and down the darkened street, three old
coppers who loved one another. "I can't enjoy it any-

more. I don't mean Bev. Shit, I love Bev. I can't hardly get it up. Christ, I don't even play with it." His voice was serious.

"Bullshit," Eichord said.

"I ain't had a blue veiner in weeks. It's pitiful, man. I don't even wake up with a piss-hard anymore."

"Who does? That's kids get piss-hards."

"I gotta piss hard now."

"Ya fuckin' pissant."

They laughed.

"It's terrible never to even get a soft-on."

"Remember that time we busted that old guy in the whorehouse over on Canal and Mary?"

"Yeah." Dana chuckled.

"That's when I knew you couldn't get it up."

"Huh?"

"Yeah. You remember that big blond one?" Eichord asked him.

"Yeah."

"One day I hadda go back there when I was doing the follow-up on the dude that got dusted." They'd been together while Lee was out for some reason, working on a murder in a low-rent brothel. "One day I hadda go back there when I was doing the follow-up on the dude that got iced, and she said 'Where's that no-dick partner of yours?' She was trying to give me some shit about what a fizzle you'd been in the sack."

"What's all this shit?" Lee had never heard this one.

"God's truth," Eichord said to James Lee, "Dana and me were taking the stories and what-not and he says, You cover me—I gotta go back and boff Blondie. And he goes back in the back with this one," Eichord was whispering.

"It's true," Dana told his partner, smirking in the darkness.

"She says, Where's that no-dick? The fat one? That worthless no-dick partner of yours couldn't even get it up."

"That's true."

They laughed.

"Pathetic," Lee said to his partner.

"Well, shit. She had hair."

"What the fuck?"

"Shit, she had more hair on her fuckin' legs than you do." They all laughed. "That's no shit."

"Lying fucks."

"Hey. Really, man. I still remember that bitch. Big ole' watermelons like this onner." Dana gestured in the shadows. "Looked pretty good. Long blond hair. Shit, I didn't know how long. I took her back there and Christ almighty, she's whippin' those clothes off and here's all this fuckin' hair under her arms, looked like little black forests growin' under there. And she had this garter-belt deal, and I can still remember those legs. Nice legs, man, but there's all these old black hairs mashed down under them hose. I go—" He makes a little descending whistle noise that they both recognized and know he is also holding his little finger in front of his fly and letting it droop with the sound effect—Dana's drooping dick schtick.

"Well," Lee said, "hair or not, I'dda fucked her."

"BullSHIT!" Dana laughed. "Be like tryin' to fuck Lyle Alzado." They laughed. "Really, man. Fuckin' big shoulders and legs onner. Big old hairy thing. Be like tryin' to put the pork to Dutch Hornung."

"Who the fuck is Dutch Hornung?" Lee asked seriously.

"JESUS, you simple midget, don't you fuckin' know anything, Paul Hornung, f'r Chrissakes. Don't you—"

"Lower your voices." Eichord was laughing. "Come on—shit, these people around here don't know I associate with riffraff like you guys. Come on, let's go back."

"Who the fuck is Paul Horney?"

"That guy used to be on the radio." Dana gave his voice a distinctive inflection, "and that's the way it is, the whole fucking story—"

"That was Walter Cronkite, goddammit, not that other guy—whatjasay—Dutch Hardon or whoever."

"Don't you know any fuckin' thing about sports?"

"Just submarine racing."

"Muff diving."

"The fifty-meter broadchase and leaping humperjump."

"The three-minute free-hand jerkoff."

"I took some money." Lee said, in a cold whisper.

"Huh."

They stopped.

"Yeah."

"Whatya talkin' about?" Dana laughed.

"I took some money. A lot of it."

"Bullshit." Not meaning bullshit at all, Dana recognizing the chilly tone.

Lee was suddenly very sober and serious. "I don't want to talk about it."

"Uh huh." Eichord said nothing. They stood there, the three old friends, with their empty glasses in their hands and their withered old-cop dicks in their pants, standing in the darkness of Buckhead Springs.

"Fuck it."

"Whatya fuckin mean ya took some money a lot of it."

"You know what I mean. You know exactly what I fuckin' mean. I took money."

"Don't tell me this shit," Eichord said, and turned and started back toward the house.

"It wasn't on the arm—"

"I don't care. I don't want to hear that crap."

"I had to, man. It was a LOT of money."

"How come ya didn't gimme any?" Tuny said to him, half-joking but seriousness in his voice.

"Want some? I'll give ya some. Then when those butt-sniffers bust me and they make me tell what I did with it, I can bring YOU down too, izzat whatcha want, ya dumb zeppelin?" Butt-sniffers was his name for Internal Affairs cops.

"You serious." It wasn't a question.

"Yeah. Believe it."

"Who the fuck be dopey enough to give YOU a lotta money."

"Nobody GIVE it to me, jackoff. I took it."

"Where? When?" He sounded like Peggy. Where? When? Who? Hah?

"At Buckhead Mercantile."

"'I'm not hearing this shit," Eichord said, and he walked back toward the house.

BAYLORVILLE

Even without his frightening and lethal abilities, a physical precognate—that rarest of the presentient humans—who planned and prepared with the degree of dedicated concentration that marked Chaingang's best efforts, was all but unstoppable as an adversary. As a manipulator he had few peers. The afternoon before, still in the stolen wheels, he'd begun to lay the groundwork for the next move.

"I definitely think so," he told the girl.

"God. You really think I could be an ACTRESS?"

"Absolutely," he told her, shaking his head no, but sending the vibes of a totally convincing yes. The bandaged face was held carefully to minimize his frightening countenance: the dimpled, radiant, ear-to-ear grinning and beaming smile was in place and doing its thing, hampered only slightly by the wounded cheek. "I see it as you talk. The way you hold your head. The way you move." The way you sip your tea. He couldn't believe how easy she was.

"I mean, I've never thought about acting. Well, I thought about it but I mean, every girl thinks about it. Aunt Pearl said I oughta be an actress or a model. And I thought about goin' down to the TV station and trying out and that. And then, you know, Toby, this one boy, he said I oughta try to get on TV, you know, like national, and Aunt Pearl said I should write a letter and, you know, send my picture to Johnny Carson, and then this other guy he said, No, Johnny Carson probably gets a lot of mail and the picture might get lost. And then I decided that . . ."

He tuned out and sighed as he nodded along. This was going to take a lot of his patience.

Finally he could stand it no more. He wanted to get his point in and interrupted her, as he usually had to do, saying, "Yes—I can see. I understand. I do think you might work toward becoming an actress in addition to your high fashion and bikini work. Maybe posters, too. But I think we should start tomorrow with lessons."

"Lessons," she said with a catch in her voice. It was a word or phrase like screen test or starring role. A word out of a tabloid in the supermarket. A word out of an article about Morgan Spacek/Sissy Fairchild having taken ACTING LESSONS SINGING LESSONS MODELING LESSONS LESSON LESSONS, a buzzword from the beckoning, impossible world of a thousand million Sissy-girls since the beginning of show biz.

"This is the Stanislavsky Dihedral Method," he said, enjoying himself as he toyed with this nitwit, "and it comes from the reliance on believing your character. I want you to pretend that you are my niece."

"Niece?" It was such an odd word. It meant nothing to her. He sensed that. She was used to having some guy want her to pretend she was his slave and get on her knees and do whatever he said. No, he'd approach more directly.

"We're going to play like you are going away to college—no, to Hollywood to be a model. And your uncle, who is rich—me," he beamed, "is buying you a car. You go into the dealer and you say this—" And he began to coach her on what he would have her enact the following day. She tried it and it was easy. This acting thing was a breeze. She had no idea that the next day he would hand her thousands of dollars in actual real money and she would have to go in and buy a car. They spent the night in a motel. Uneventfully.

The following morning they drove to a place he had spotted and he gave her some "notes" to rehearse, care-fully printed in large, block letters neatly made with a black marker by a hand that mushed the pen point down with each firm and precise stroke. She studied the words

like they were her opening lines in a new hit on Broadway.
Showtime. To this moment she'd not been told it was for
real.

He'd spotted a gleaming black Caprice parked between
a Celebrity and a used Nissan something-or-other. He
saw the words on the windshield in white "$5,245 . . .
50,000 miles! Loaded!"

"Wait here and be rehearsing," he told her, extricating
his near-quarter-ton load from the car. He waddled toward
a pay phone. The model year wasn't readable on the
windshield but he knew it couldn't be over four years
old. It looked about right to him. Chaingang checked the
directory, dropped some change, and heard a busy woman's voice.

"Mannschrecker's."

"Sales manager, please," he said. A long pause.

"Hello."

"Sales manager?"

"Parts."

"I was waiting for the sales manager. Can you recon-
nect me, please?"

"Sure." The line clicked. Then obviously disconnected.
He dropped more money and dialed again with his usual
total concentration and unswerving perserverance.

"Mannschrecker's." The same busy voice.

"I was holding for the sales manager and was cut off,"
putting a bit of fake edge in his tone.

"Sorry you had trouble, sir, just a moment." Click. A
tune by the Beatles performed by some butt-kissing, nothing band played in the bowels of a far and unnecessary
hell, then— "Here you are, sir," again unnecessarily.

"Tim Brinkman, can I help you?"

"Tim, I was in last week looking at that black Caprice?"

"Yeah." Friendly tone. Meant it had been on the lot
for at least a week. Good.

"I just drove by and see you still got it. I just was
wondering here, uh, tell ya what, Tim, I just don't wanna
go five thousand for it like I talked to somebody there.
But, uh, let me say this: you let me have it forty-five
hundred and I'll come in right this minute and write you
a check."

"Who's zis?"

"Oh, Tim, you don't know me. I'm wantin' a car for me but I'm gonna let my niece take it when she goes away to college," he started the story he'd concocted for Sissy. Using the name the way he'd want it on the registration.

"Bud, ah can't do it. I mean, that Caprice's a honey. Hell, it's LOADED. I might knock a couple hundred down if you came in right NOW with the check, but, no, I just can't—"

Chaingang cut him off, "I understand that. But that's for comin' in there right now an' writing a CHECK. I got us a better idea."

"How's that?" Suspicious tone.

"Suppose a feller like you wanted some immediate cash flow. And a feller like me wanted a nice little ole' Caprice for forty-five hundred dollars. Looks like there's some way we could strike a deal?" A pause and Bunkowski knew instantly he had him and he closed it. "So I say I send the girl on over with the cash money, an' you write it all up real nice any old way you like. You understand what I'm telling you. We're not talking financing. We're not talking checks. We're talking those nice dollars. CASH money, Tim. Forty-five hundred and we'll drive it off the lot now."

"When you think you could get here?"

"Oh, I'd say about five minutes." He was looking at the lot.

"You got five minutes," the sales manager said in his best sucker-con voice and hung up. Chaingang walked back to the stolen wheels and over to the girl's side.

"Memorize your part?" he asked, smiling in the window with the right profile toward her.

"Yeah. You want to hear it?" She was ready for the applause. If this was all there was to acting . . .

"Okay. Let's really try it out. I got an idea," he said with sudden animation, and in a burst of energy he chugged around and got in behind the wheel, perhaps for the last time. "Here. I want you to try your luck. Go across the street there and—" He pulled out the big roll and started counting big bills off to her. She almost fainted. Welcome to the big time, she thought, not really believing it but not NOT believing either.

"This is five thousand," she said to him somewhere in between the inflection of an interrogatory and an exclamation. Five grand could do a lot to make disbelief go up in a puff of lime-colored smoke. Five thousand in real money. She'd never dreamed something like this could happen. She'd hit the bull's-eye that people talked about. This was it.

"You really want me to BUY a car?" She couldn't quite let it register.

"Yep. I want to see if you can do. Uh, that is, I want to let you have this *acting* experience. Think of it as a lesson you can draw on later." That magic word again.

"And really GET a car. BUY a CAR?"

"That black Caprice, right there. He pointed, letting his hand graze her leg and she sat there calmly.

"You gonna be there."

"No. Talk just like we rehearsed. If I'm there you won't be alone ON STAGE. This way you're the lead actor. You get experience in a starring role. Get it?"

She nodded, the money feeling good in that big stack that dried her throat just at the exciting thought of it all. "Yeah."

"Can you pull it off?"

"SURE."

"Okay."

"But don't we trade THIS car in?"

"No." He had forgotten she had a functioning human brain. It was by far her most intelligent question or statement, and he had to take a beat to frame an answer.

"See, the deal is, most people TRADE and they lose so much in blue book. What your best deal is—you SELL your own car to a private individual, then amortize your collateral or if you have a mortgage or submortgage your equity, you see—then take the difference and put it into your refinancing."

"Oh," she said, satisfied at the double-talk. "Okay. Do I have to do anything else?"

"No. Just the way we rehearsed it. Then get the temporary tags, and after you pay tax and title and all, you be sure you have the motor vehicle registration, the pink slip we talked about. That's it. You drive 'er back over here."

"Okay," she said with a luminous smile. She looked pretty to him and he patted her leg and the smile didn't change. And Chaingang realized how horny he must be.

"Okay," he rumbled. "Outstanding."

"Now?"

"You're ON," he told her, his huge, dimpled grin straining at the battle dressing. "Break a leg."

He watched her get out of the car, pushing her dopy sunglasses that were held by a cord around her neck back up on her nose and starting across the street with the money in stolen bills clutched in her small, bony hand.

"SISSY," he called to her, his bark startling her, and she spun around, hurried back, and stuck her head in the car window.

"Probably be better," he said, smile fixed in place, "if you didn't have the money in your hand like that. Ya know? Why don't you put it in your purse now? Then you can hand it to the man when you get the thing all signed, eh?"

"Yeah, okay." She opened her purse and stuffed the money in. "Good idea," she told him.

He thought how he'd like to pull her right in this second. Grab that hair and just yank her in, slapping her hard enough to break her puny neck and then masturbate into her open mouth while she died. How easy it would be to waste her. He watched her walk across the street, her thin legs outlined through the cheap dress.

BUCKHEAD

Agent Pfeltmann was reading the chronological sequence report in a loud, slightly adenoidal, singsong voice,

". . . constitutes the relevant and known sequence of events in the investigation of the bank robbery and shooting death of Mr. Floyd Raymond Coleman, of 2802 Brook Valley, Buckhead, which occurred on the morning of 3 July as per attached 52-11.

"Time: 0610. Occurrence: Two armed male Caucasian subjects gained entrance to the Fields residence at 34822 Cypress Road, North Buckhead, by means of prying the front door loose. All power lines to the home had been cut but the alarm system line, which was buried under the home, was not severed and—"

"Too bad they didn't cut that too, we wouldn't have to screw with this." The alarm system in the Fields home was triggered so that a cut in the line for longer than three minutes signaled the local police. They had complained of many recent inconveniences caused by interruptions in the power by the local utility company.

"Yeah. Anyway, it goes on about the wife and child being out of the house. Mrs. Fields substantiating and corroborating the husband's story. Blah, blah. Two armed subjects ordered Fields to accompany them to the premises of Buckhead Mercantile Bank and Trust, 1705 East Broadway, where he is employed as a manager. Goes on about the surveillance video." He read ahead silently. "And the fingerprints from the home and the crime scene, and goes on about the vault. Let's see, he described the vehicle as a late-model dark colored Crown Victoria, either dark blue or midnight blue. What the hellsa difference between dark blue and midnight blue. Okay, goes on about the guard. Coleman blah blah, fifty-two years old, blah blah, coroner's report, ballistics, the forensic analysis, spent projectile report, again referencing the surveillance video," his voice going up and down in a bored little song, "okay, now we get to the nitty.

"Silent alarm 07:01:30. Dispatched uniformed officers Eleven-Yankee-One. Backup car Eleven-Yankee-Six. Robbery in progress. Okay, here BOI gets the robbery-with-shooting call. Man down. Buckhead homicide rolls on it. We roll on it. SAC, you, me, Delgado. Two uniforms inside when we arrive on the crime scene: Ramírez, Jones. Five clothes: Brown, Lee, Tuny, Peletier, Ecklemeyer. You got the janitor, Jefferson. You got Fields. You got the broad. What's her name? Kelly Pierce.

"Fifteen people besides the two perpetrators who had fled. Now our good friend Mr. Monroe is telling us *they* got sixteen thousand dollars and change. That Mr. De Witt did, rather. We got Mr. Phillips telling us they got twenty-eight thousand and change. What is it? $28,145 I think it says on the 52-11. Okay. So what are our options? What are we lookin' at?" He took a piece of white chalk and started making marks. He printed on the blackboard the same way he talked, in screeching little singsong, bored strokes.

"ERROR you got. Somebody didn't count right. Whatever. THEFT BY BANK. Cover embezzlement. That kinda thing. Phillips, or a teller, or the one with the tits. Sees it as an opportunity to cover a mistake. Phillips looks good if you're gonna hypothecate. He could pick up twelve kay and who'd know? He might bet we're not gonna get the perps. So we look at his life a little closer. But from a cursory glance he don't NEED twelve thousand. The janitor picks up some money. When? You got the surveillance tape against that. One of us. We didn't get there soon enough.

"PERPETRATOR you got. John Monroe decides he'll burn his partner and walk away from a Murder One. Shit. Homicide committed during an armed robbery of a bank? He'll burn for it. So he squirrels away twelve

grand and calls us with his story. He looks sorta good for
that until you spend five minutes with him." There was
laughter in the room.

"So this leaves THEFT BY INVESTIGATING PO-
LICE." He wrote DIRTY COP on the blackboard, and
the chalk scream as if tortured.

ROSEMONT

They stayed the night in a motel in Rosemont. Chaingang began weaving a tale that was calculated to cover their next move—a move that would surprise her.

"You have all the tools," he told her in his concept-producer voice, "all the gifts." A big, dimpled, lop-sided smile. "And you're beautiful. But remember where we're going ALL the girls have all the tools and all the gifts and they're all beautiful. I want you to learn the whole thing. I want to give you EVERYTHING so that when we get to California we'll blow the town apart, right?"

"Right."

"But, Sissy, this won't be easy."

"Yeah. Well, that's okay."

"So you are willing to work?"

"Sure."

"You really want this?"

"Yeah."

"Well"—the huge head tilted—"what this means is lots of hours of practice, coaching, meditation, thinking, soul-searching, and GUIDANCE. More LESSONS. Understand?" She nodded yes. She had no idea, but whatever. She was game for it. "Here's what I think we need to do. I think we should PREPARE for a few weeks; you'd be on full pay of course the entire time, but spend a few weeks in preparation before we light up the town with your big entrance."

"What do you mean. I mean, what do you want me to do?"

"This is just a spur-of-the-moment idea, but I know this man who owns some property out in the country not far from here. I was thinking an arrangement might be made where we could stay there and polish your new career until we were ready, and then . . ." And the words poured out, clouding her mind in a billowing smoke-dream of heady possibilities, and she nods yes. And he is pleased and makes sure she is fed, watered, settled cozily in front of the television set, tucked in, and his game locked down tight. Then he excused himself to "take care of some business."

His horniness was not the issue. When he was moving from the black Caprice, his first legal wheels, to the motel room, a pair of punks had pulled out of the parking lot beside them in a red pickup and Chaingang had seen the driver's face laughing at him and then looking over at the passenger beside him as they both roared in derision. But this is not what had distressed Daniel Edward Flowers Bunkowski. Something else, the crooked smile, the set of the upper body behind the wheel, something stabbed at him.

Daniel was a man to whom taunts and ridicule had no effect. He was oblivious to the scorn of the monkees. To a man whose life had been a saga of abuse, torment, torture, anguish, unbearable pain, distress was a catalyst—a hair trigger in a gun loaded with suffering, confusion, misery, bewilderment, and the paralysis of dread and fear. It had kept a child immobile, willing his heart not to beat, willing his tiny penis not to leak or drip, not to pee, willing his bladder not to burst, slowing his respiratory system to death's threshold, taking his mind all the way to its limits and beyond into the darkness of consciousness's edge, willing himself not to scream in his childhood's hellish, unending nightmare rending the mind and heart and soul and rendering the victim a frozen, cowering thing riveted with terror and abject fright.

To this man, whose horror is more jolting than any electric shock, whose fear and hatred is more hallucinogenic than any combination from acid to lithium to peyote to paregoric, those hideous, violent, psychodynamic origins and psychogenetic developments cause Daniel Bunkowski to see hear smell feel taste touch and perceive —to say the least—a distorted reality.

And so the set of the punk's shoulders or the bared teeth of the punk's smile is enough to trigger it. And it comes in a hot, brutal tidal wave washing his senses in the mad desire to kill and in just that moment of derisive laughter from a passing pair of punks, in just that hot heartbeat of memory-jarring reality, Daniel's kill lust was kindled. So he said his piece to Sissy Selkirk and was in the black Caprice and the flickering telephone poles whipping by were a hypnotic thing ticking at the edge of his vision as he drove into the darkening night, driving over newly painted yellow line, aimlessly yet with singular purpose, driving toward the heartbeat of an unknown victim.

He would not remember what triggered it, later, or how he knew to sit for so long in the parked car. The infinite patience and mysterious self-confidence always his trademarks. Nor would he remember why he zeroed in on Harmon Schmitz when he saw him. It was a thing of balance. The inner clock. The gyro. The thing that was his automatic pilot and regulator.

Harmon Schmitz was a faggot. A simpering, mincing, limp-wristed, queenish, full-blown, cruising-for-a-lip-bruising sperm-sucking fag. He was as gay as a fucking fruitcake. He had good points. He was smart. He was a good worker. He loved his mother. But he had this problem. The idea of putting a stiff male erectile member into his bodily orifices got him crazy. He was smart enough to know if he wanted to keep his gig out at Cat's Paw he would have to act butch during the day. And he liked the bucks and so during the day Harmon Schmitz was a regular guy. No sly looks. No hand on the hip. All he needed was a palomino named Fury and he was Straight Arrow.

But with the coming of nighttime Harmon Schmitz underwent a wild and gay metamorphosis and Lon Chaney, Jr., became the wolfman under the lunar luminosity, but instead of getting hairy he got horny and instead of wanting to sink his fangs into somebody's neck he wanted to sink his lips onto somebody's beaver-cleaver. A total, God-help-me-Mary-I'm-coming, Hi-there-sailor, screaming, swishing, knees-to-the-men's-room-floor queer.

And he was in mortal fear day and night, not of being found out, he wasn't worried about coming out, he was worried about shagging a nice, virulent, unstoppable case of killer AIDS. Scared out of his wits. Frightened half to death. Not to the point where he'd stop cruising, you understand, but very seriously afraid. He already had three friends who were in some stage of the devilish disease. And it was all he thought about when he wasn't horny.

I mean, when you think about it, what's so wonderful, what's so exciting, what's so thrilling about the rubbery, cock-sweaty, tasteless taste of a penis? What was the big attraction about gobbling a few cee-cees of nasty, warm cum? Why couldn't he give it up? He didn't know. Harmon Schmitz just plain loved to suck the boys' things and that was all there was to it.

He liked the humiliation, he supposed, of subjugating himself to another man. The way they'd look at him when he let his eyes travel down to a guy's bulging crotch and back up to look him in the eye and let him know. The way one of them was always dominant and one was always the more passive. He loved the passive role but he'd play it either way to get laid.

He liked it in the mouth in the butt in the hand, he would take it in his armpit if that's what got some stud off but the important thing was the cruise. He liked finding it. The tingling and decadent erection that would threaten to rip through the front of his pants the moment he saw a guy. He liked all the numbers out there and it was then that his thoughts would be far from AIDS and the other dangers of the mean streets.

Harmon loved "dating," which is the name he gave it in his mind. And when the number wasn't too rough sometimes they would date and it would be an even greater ecstasy in anticipation of the climax of the evening. But he liked the toughest trade too. Liked, hell he craved it. Craved the suicidal impulses and self-destructive urges that led a fellow down that path.

He loved the language of the game. The illicit kick
of the stalk and the final moves. He loved the positioning of
the belt buckle and the hip pocket handkerchief and all the
lore and the secret mating signs and the self-advertising
clothing and mannerisms of the gay brotherhood. He
adored the rites of homosexuality. He got off on the
ritual, like an inveterate pipe smoker reaming away at
the dottle and dreaming about the sweetness of what he
was going to be sucking. He could write a book about
sucking.

In fact, that is exactly what Harmon Schmitz was thinking about when this hulking behemoth stepped out of the
shadows and rumbled something at him and he turned
and it was like a rowboat looking up at the looming
Queen Mary but sometimes you take what you can get
and with his caution switch on overdrive he turned and
said something clever and the voice rumbled again, some
nonsense about how to get somewhere and he was both
relieved and mildly disappointed that this big thing wasn't
a number just someone asking bothersome directions and
he replied he didn't know and started off and the voice
rumbled again, "Hey!" And he turned back, frightened,
but then it spoke to him again and it wasn't menacing the
guy just wanted to get directions and so he made himself
stop and think for a minute and the man said, "Isn't that
Scranson Something going east?" He didn't catch the
name but when the huge Goliath pointed and said,
"There!" so insistently, he turned his head to look to
make sure, Oh that, he thought, that's only Kings Highway but he never got the thought enunciated because as
he was turning back to speak a building fell on him and
he died.

Nothing fell on him really, but when Chaingang turned
back to his left, moving his right arm that powerful
killing arm to his left to point in front of the victim,
pointing out toward the street, his arm going right in
front of the man's face where he'd have to turn and look
and as the man's scrawny, pencil neck turns Chaingang
smashes that battering ram of an elbow back into the
side of the man's temple, and as he fell to the ground
he killed him then and went over to the waiting vehicle

and packed him away and Harmon Schmitz died as he lived.

He died a heartless death. He died as a piece of meat is butchered. And one cannot overlook the perverseness of the irony that had Harmon Schmitz known that he would be killed so that a madman could eat one of his organs, he'd never in a million years been able to guess which one it would end up being.

Life is funny.

BUCKHEAD SPRINGS

She'd first told him about it that night coming back from Peggy and Jimmie's when they'd gone over for dinner and cards afterward. Lee not seeming as downbeat as he'd been and the evening a pleasant one, with no talk of the Job or any other subjects that might bum anybody out, and they were both in a cuddly mood when they drove home that night.

He loved the look of metropolitan Buckhead after dark. It always seemed to him to look like the best of both worlds, the familiarity and predictability of a small hometown environment coupled with the pizzazz and dazzle of a big city at night. Invariably Jack would recharge a bit at the look of the lights of the city skyline and the surprisingly big-town feel of a vast cosmopolis when he drove through South Buckhead and down Main toward Buckhead Springs, and saw that string of bright lights and all the glittering nightlife in the distance.

She rode close to him and her perfume was intoxicating. She seldom failed to arouse him up close like this, and as always, when he glanced over at this lady he could never quite fully believe she was his, she stirred that kind of desire and admiration in him. Donna's scent mingled with the car interior making the vehicle smell newer, more luxurious than it was, and her nearness made the lights a little brighter. They had Laurindo playing on the tape deck.

"That's nice."

"Just your basic unamplified, six-string, open-face guitar sandwich. He do play."

"He play good, Laurindo do."

"I play good too. Wanna play later?"

"Umm. And I wanna play Saturday too but not what you think exactly." She snuggled against him. "I want you all to myself all day Saturday."

"I'll have to look at my calendar. I have a very busy schedule. My dance card is very full at this time of the season. I'll check."

"You do that little thing. Make room in your busy schedule for Donna. All day Saturday. Really."

"Okay. Whatcha got planned?"

"Just something," she told him mysteriously.

"I don't like surprises. Tell me."

"I won't tell. You can do anything you want and I won't talk."

"Are you saying your lips are sealed?"

"I won't go THAT far." She giggled a womanly giggle. "I mean let's not get crazy here. I won't say that my lips are sealed but I won't spoil my surprise. Just be mine alone all day Saturday."

"I'll see if I can clear the decks. Tell Racquel and Heather I just don't have time for them Saturday."

"You're too kind to me. Whatta guy."

"I know."

When Saturday came she woke him up with kisses and fresh juice and coffee and they had breakfast in bed.

"I made you a card." And she handed him a card with the legend HAPPY BIRTHDAY written across the front and then he remembered it was his birthday. "I hope you like homemade greeting cards because I couldn't find one I liked." He told her he did and opened it and inside a drawing of a big heart she'd written his birthday message. He read it out loud.

"I love you, my husband. You have made my life a dream that I thought would never come true. When you are away from me I feel the way you hold me and when I make up our bed it makes me tingle just to see your imprint in the sheets. I love you a lot and I will be yours forever. You are the best man I've ever known. All my love." And he turned and they kissed over the Xs drawn across the bottom of the card.

"That's enough. That's for later," she said, drawing away from him. He looked at her with such love and in that second he couldn't imagine that he'd ever had a life without her.

"You drive a hard bargain," he told her.

"So. Get dressed and come into the Official Birthday Room." The Official Birthday Room was the living room. There was a box, a large, beautifully wrapped box, and he opened it. There was a beat-up baseball and two well-used gloves, together with a note.

THIS IS THE OLD-TIME SATURDAY YOU TOLD ME ABOUT. REMEMBER THE WAY IT WAS WHEN YOU WERE A KID? PLAYING CATCH WITH YOUR DAD? GOING TO SHEPHERD'S DRUGSTORE WITH YOUR PALS? THEN READING A COMIC BOOK OUT UNDER THE TREES? GOING TO THE DOUBLE FEATURE AT THE ORPHEUM? HAVE FUN! LOVE—XXX, DONNA.

"I'll be your dad. I get the catcher's mitt, so—let's go, son," she said. She had a little trouble keeping the cap on all that hair. Finally she hairpinned it in place somehow, a Met's cap that had been a gift to Eichord from a guy he'd worked with once, and he followed her out into the yard.

"Burn it in there," she said. She had on one of his old shirts and a pair of shorts you couldn't see somewhere under the shirt tail. "Burn one in to your old dad."

"Hate to say this but you don't look anything like old dad." She pushed out even the voluminous shirt front.

"Cut the talk, son, 'n burn one in."

"Okay." He pitched one to her.

"Come on, boy," she told him, "you can throw harder than that. I'm not no sissy girl."

"Right, Dad." He threw another.

She hopped around blowing on her hand. "Okay," she said, "that wraps up the catch game. Besides I gotta get these rented gloves back." He laughed. "You made Dad's hand sting. Later you can kiss it and make it well."

"I aims to please."

"I hear that. Okay. It's time to read our comic book under the tree." She went and returned with a sack in her hand, motioning for him to come with her. They sat under a red maple.

"Look what came in the mail."

"What on earth?" It looked like one of the old-time comic books that he used to subscribe to. Sure enough, there was an old mailing sticker on the familiar brown paper with his name and his address where he'd grown up. "Where in hell—"

"I'll never tell." She had found an old copy of Children's Activities Magazine and soaked his mailing label off the cover and glued it to the wrapper she'd made for the comic. He removed it gently from the container and opened it.

"MY GOD! Walt Disney's Comics & Stories! I haven't seen one of those in thirty years. Where on earth?"

"Some guy up in Missouri sells old comic books. I remembered you telling me about the covers."

"Huey and Duey and Louie with Uncle Donald," he said, smiling one of the biggest smiles she'd ever seen on his face. The nephews were watching Donald about to go skiing. But two rows of tiny animals, birds, and assorted hangers-on had lined up on the back of each of Donald's skis. "That's the way I remember them. I got this one, and Tarzan and Red Ryder. Three comics a month from the same company—I'll never forget it."

"I know—I know. I wrote it all down. I thought about getting you a Tarzan, too, but I didn't know how you'd feel about my selling the car, so I held off on that one." They laughed.

"Okay," Donna told Jack when he'd finished perusing the adventures of the ducks. "Let's go to the drugstore." They went off to the side of the house and there was something about the size of a Volkswagen parked in the space between the Eichord's house and the next-door neighbor's.

Eichord said, "I think I can guess. By the size of it you've purchased a time machine and we're going to get in and go back to 1947?"

"That's right," she said, going "Tadaaaaaaaa" as she pulled the sheets off the surprise.

"Oh, NO!" He laughed. "Where on earth did you get THESE?"

"That's a long story. When we were in Dallas I remembered you talking about the drugstore, and drooling about the old days at the drugstore, and those sundaes and the ice water after the ball game, and your description of the big fan overhead, and the little wire chairs with the heart shapes, and the marble table. Anyway, I saw an ad for the table and chairs at a garage sale, so I got 'em for us."

"Perfect."

"Well, the table is wood and not marble but you can pretend."

"Yeah." He sat down on the tiny chair with great care.

"Wait there," she told him. She returned from the kitchen with a sundae, complete with fudge topping, nuts, whipped cream, and a cherry.

"AHA," he yelled in recognition as she also placed a glass of water in front of him.

"Yes, sir. Only the best for my darlin'. A genuine Coca-Cola glass full of old-time ice water."

"I love it," he said with heartfelt feeling, taking a delicious, incredible bite of the ice-cream concoction and a sip of the cold water. "Just as I remember. Wonderful."

"Okay."

"Fabulous. Pure essence of Shepherd's Drugstore." He finished in a wave of nostalgic contentment. Some wife.

"So far so good. Let's see—the game of catch. The comic book. I got 'em out of order but anyway—then the drugstore. Okay. Time to go to the show." She pulled him back into the house and led him to his easy chair in front of the television in the living room and picked his feet up, sliding an ottoman up under his legs, then slipping his bedroom shoes off. He was still dressed in slacks, T-shirt, and his old Leo Gorcey pinback hat that he'd worn to play catch in. Nobody's perfect, he thought wryly.

She sat a small box in his lap.

"You're KIDDING! A CRIME CLUB movie! A serial! MY GOD IS THIS REALLY THE GREEN HORNET! FROM 1939?" He read the tape labels out loud. "How in hell did you find these?"

"Same guy I got the comic book from." She took one

of the tapes from him and went over to their video machine. "I've been practicing. Watch." She had learned how to insert the tape. She pushed play. "Have fun. I'm going shopping," she said, leaving Jack Eichord mesmerized in front of a buzzing hornet's image as his childhood began to flash before his eyes.

He watched four chapters of the old Green Hornet movie, wishing there was someone he could talk to who would understand the delight of the experience. Somebody he could tell about Al Hodge, whose voice had been synched to the lead character's speech. Al Hodge, out of the time warp on Eichord's happy birthday. He was halfway through the Crime Club movie when he heard the car pull up.

Donna blew in with her arms loaded down.

"Need a hand?" he said, revealing no intention to move from his seated position.

"I think I'll be able to manage. You having a good time?"

He smiled and nodded.

About fifteen minutes passed and he heard a radio playing or some music coming faintly from the bedroom. Another ten minutes or so and the movie ended, so he shut the equipment off and got up, then went into the bedroom to tell her how much he was enjoying his day.

"Mmmmmm," he said. Donna was in a wispy thing that covered her shoulders and most of her large, high breasts. Matching wisp of a bikini. "Nice." God, she looked good.

"Fire-engine red."

"Yeah," he said, his heart in his throat.

"Come on over."

"Okay," he said, wasting no time.

"Do I know what you like or what?"

"You know what I like."

"Do I know the way you like it?"

"Nnnn." He tried to answer but his mouth was busy.

She took him through the sex just as she had the rest of his birthday surprises. Making it all for him, leading him, orchestrating it so their lovemaking would be just the way HE wanted it, just the way any man would like it. Biology and Mother Nature took over and when she was through he was spent, spread-eagled across the bed in blissful, or so it appeared, immobility.

But inside his copper core that thing that was with him all the time now remained cold and untouched. It was loathsome, whatever it was, because it had diminished the joy of the day and made fabulous sex routine, and the thing was all the more annoying because he couldn't put a handle on it.

He labeled it as apprehension, and Jack suspected that Jimmie was bringing this down on him, but when Jack felt apprehensive about something he could normally isolate the reasons why and do something about the emotion. This was something else and it was dogging him all the time now. A dark, unidentifiable silhouette of something too far away to see with clarity.

Neither the Hornet nor Kato nor Donna Eichord's tastiest ice-cream treats could manage to dispel the sense of foreboding he carried. A shadowy thing that he knew would be taking form soon. A paranoiac, ominous suspicion and dread that made Eichord unfit for the company of lovable ducks.

STOBAUGH COUNTY

By midafternoon they had reached Stobaugh, and they crossed over the county line. Chaingang was totally tuned out as the girl hummed and sang contentedly with the radio. He was physically as well as mentally in another time and place. He was back in Southeast Asia with Michael Hora.

What would Sissy have thought had she known the truth or even vestiges of it? Could she have begun to comprehend that this thing beside her with the deep voice and the huge girth and the strange mannerisms and the bandaged face—that this man was a true genius of sorts? A genius of assassination? He had been discovered on death row in Marion, most fearsome of our federal prisons. A security arm of the intelligence community, as it is laughingly called, had found him and in the sensitive early years of the war created a small, secret unit around this unlikely figure.

He had been tested, and a gamble was taken. He was sent to Vietnam along with other similar individuals, programmed—or so they hoped—to work in covert, counterinsurgency assassination teams. And he had performed his function better than they had ever dreamed. Bunkowski was a unique entity. Godzilla and the shark from *Jaws* or its human counterpart and the Pillsbury Doughboy all in one remarkable, bestial, freak mutation. A human being who truly lived for only one reason: to kill. A killing machine.

In Southeast Asia he killed the little people with a mad

fury, both "good guys" and VC alike. In truth he saw no
distinction. And there come a time when the security
masters tried to terminate the members of the anomalous
band that was fast becoming a dangerous potential liabil-
ity. Chaingang and Michael Hora were two of the only
survivors of this execution attempt, and they escaped.

They had not been close or even casual buddies. In
fact, both of them were friendless, dangerous, self-
contained killers who lived only for number one. Chaingang
did not particularly respect Hora's abilities as a fighter,
and Hora of course viewed Bunkowski as a monster or a
total maniac, but they shared the common enemy and
that had been enough for at least a begrudging relationship. During this time Daniel had learned of Hora's
"place" south of Chicago. For a price, he was sometimes
willing to shelter those on the run from the law. It was a
piece of minutia to be filed away for possible future
retrieval.

Now, these many years later, Chaingang Bunkowski
looked at some old notes in the back of his "bible," a
ledger of escape plans he had worked on while in prison,
and he saw the map of how to find Hora, assuming the
man were still alive and the property still his. The thing
that kept Bunkowski one step ahead of his adversaries
made him feel confident Michael Hora would be there.

"Well, it won't be long now," he told the girl, and
presented her with an item from the trunk. She bright-
ened when she saw the sack of magazines. "I think it's
important for you to study for an hour or so. Read up on
all these stars so you can learn their ways." He handed
her some of the schlock grocery-store tabloids and movie
magazines.

"Sure. Great." She was delighted and he knew she'd
stay riveted to her important homework while he checked
out the lay of the land.

"I should be back in an hour or less. But just wait
here. You can sit over there"—he pointed—"or stay in
the car. But stay nearby. Okay?"

She nodded.

He moved with the curious grace of the very heavy.
That peculiar flat-footed, splayed, deceptively easy gliding movement that is somewhere between lumbering and

waddling. From the distance his vast upper torso appeared to be propelled by the great tree-trunk legs, arms swinging slightly as he moved. Only when he was tired and his bad ankle could not fully support the bulk could you discern the slight limp.

The field ended with a tree line and he eased over some long-forgotten, rusting barbed-wire fence that had broken and been slowly crushed down by the unstoppable tide of vetch and poison ivy and creeper vine and pigweed and honeysuckle and multifloral rose and God only knows what kind of grass and weed and abomination of Mother Nature. And he was through the trees and weeds and in an overgrown parcel of pastureland that backed up to the property.

He moved steadily and on a perfectly straight line, thinking of nothing in particular but with the mixture of awareness that he carried right beneath his mental surface feeding his on-line terminals. Telling him the field was full of snakes. A few would be poisonous. There were cattle milling off somewhere in the wooded acreage to his right, and water nearby. And he knew there would be dogs. People. The taped tractor chain swung against his leg, the heavy weight a comforting presence.

The junk began before he had cleared the far edge of the pasture. He'd seldom seen anything like it. A panorama of blight. Huge, rust-encrusted mounds of everything imaginable. Filth-covered bedsprings and the guts from a hundred junked television sets. Ancient pumps and what was left from an old hay saw. Broken I-beams and cracked engine blocks and parts of tools and discarded appliances. Pieces of transient lives and memories and throwaways and investments gone bad and farms gone sour and marriages gone awry and a thousand broken, burst, busted, bummed-out vestiges of the American Dream left to mold and mildew and oxidize and collect weeds in the hot sun and cold winters of the great midwestern pastureland. All the white, gray, gunmetal, blue, silver, chrome, oilslick shades and hues and paint jobs had been worn and ground down to the same color—an ugly, ferruginous brownish shit red.

But this is not what he saw as he walked through the snaky weeds. He did not see broken dreams and bedsprings. He did not care about tanks, transmissions, trucks, clodbusters, cultivators, combines, planters, Plymouths, plows, rippers, rollers, refrigerators gutted to make pump houses and left to turn to rust. He saw hiding places, coffins, burial grounds, camouflage, ambush sites, killing zones, field expedient resupply, death and torture and escape and evasion.

He was Chaingang then, not Daniel, walking through the tall fescue and the creeper vine, the heavy chain swinging against a tree-trunk leg, and if you crossed him out here, in all this overgrown world of desolate junk, you dropped. You disappeared. You bought it. Because this was a world he could relate to. The kind of things he gravitated toward. Junkyard dogs and snakes and lonely, frightening places with no one around to hear a cry for help. Nobody near to blunder onto a freshly dug grave. This was snuffie country.

He was aware of Michael Hora's presence then. Not that he thought Hora was watching him through a scope or anything. It was just a subliminal feeling that there was a dangerous man somewhere nearby. He was close now. And as he walked, guided by that inexplicable compass inside him, never hesitating for even that fraction of a fleeting second, one saw what Chaingang saw as he moved toward his destination, homing in on human heartbeat.

He saw the shape of Stobaugh County the way it fit between the four adjacent, touching land masses, and the surrounding and interlocking blue features, and the way the fishhook looked. This was his name for the part of the state he was now in, and he had looked at it for a long time, then redrawn a portion of it to scale on a page of the ledger, making clean, ultra-precise lines with a draftsman's hand, and the eye of an artist. Very close to true scale he had drawn what he called the fishhook shape of this land mass, bisecting it with the Sandy Road and Lingo Road, and Talbot's Mill Run, and Johnson's and Hunter's Ferry Road and the old Althea School road, crisscrossing the fishhook and neatly printing the names that were still only names to him.

But he had memorized the placement of Hora's to the Big Pasture, and the surrounding Rowe's Field, and South

Spur, and Dutch Barrow, and Fast's, and Kerr's Store, and Bayou Landing, and he would know in an emergency situation how to get to Indian Nose and Hurricane Lamp, or where Thurman's property line was, or Texas Corners or the McDermott Cemetery. He'd been there for half an hour but he retained in his memory the place-names and roads and routes and geographic locations of the area better than some old-timers who'd been there for fifteen years.

Because his life might depend on his being able to make it through Lightfoot Swamp to Breen's Hole. He might have to find the burial mound south of Clearmont Church in a hurry, and he wouldn't have the luxury of calling Triple A or stopping a friendly stranger and asking directions. He might have to negotiate the twists and turns and surprises of County 530 in the pitch-black night, escaping with his life up through Dogleg and Hibbler to Whitetail Island, or Number 22, and when the time came it was all filed away inside his computer, the lay of the land and the escape routes. He believed that if you planned hard you won.

He smelled humans now and it was the scent of people nearby. He walked around vehicles, and a barking dog on a chain penetrated his faraway thoughts as he came around part of a rusting pickup and saw a heavy young woman sitting on the porch of a decrepit, tar-paper-covered house.

"Howdy," he called out from a distance, beaming a smile in the woman's direction.

"Where'd jew come from?" she asked without interest, her mouth not unlike his, a small slit that opened in a shapeless mass of dough.

"This way." He gestured vaguely, stepping around toward the front of the house but not going up on the porch. "Michael around?"

"Michael?"

"Yeah."

"Michael *who*?" she asked with a smart tone.

He thought how easily he could snuff her out. Go up on the porch, chain-snap her once, and butcher the fresh hog.

"Tell Michael Hora it's somebody used to work with

him," he said in a voice loud enough to carry to the
surrounding buildings. He felt eyes on him for just a
second or two before he heard the flat voice to his left
and to the rear, "Bunkowski? *Chaingang?* Jesus!" he
said as Chaingang turned and saw the man standing there.
He had not heard him come out of the building. "Whatchew
doin' here?" He didn't seem that happy at the prospect
of a reunion.

"I gotta proposition for ya."

"I ain't in that line no more."

"No. Not that."

"Okay. What?"

"Need to go someplace we can talk in private."

"She don't hear nothin'."

"Uh huh."

"Go on. Speak your piece."

"I need a place to stay."

"So?"

"Someplace where people don't get too curious."

"You're hot then, are ya?"

"Oddly enough—no. But I need time to myself."

"Umm."

"I remembered you had a big place down here. I
thought we might work out some kind of a deal."

"Howzzat?"

"I need to have something to do to occupy my time. I
plan to go on a, uh, training regimen that will include a
diet and lots of hard work."

"Diet. Work." He repeated the words like they were
foreign phrases he'd never heard before.

"Right. And you have work that can be done, right?"

"I cain't afford to pay for no work right now."

"No. You don't understand. I'll pay you. Also I'll do
some of the work. Whatever fits into my schedule." They
talked some more and Chaingang pulled out a thousand
dollars in cash. "For a month in advance?" Hora walked
over and reached for the money. "Oh, and I have a
woman with me."

"Where?" Hora looked around as if she might be
standing in back of him.

"Back in my vehicle."

"You two ain't runnin'?"

"She knows nothing."

"Umm."

"A thousand a month up front. Anybody asks, I'm help you've hired to do the heavy work."

"Heavy work." More new vocabulary. "We can try it for a month, I reckon." He eyed the money. "Jus' don't bring down no heat on me."

"No way," Chaingang said.

"Reckon you can use the ole sharecropper shack. It's over yonder"—he gestured—" 'tween here 'n the ditch."

"What work is there now?"

"Say what?"

"What kinda work needs doin'?"

"Shit." He laughed. "I dunno. Gotta unload these ties." He gestured at a huge pile of railroad ties. " 'N these here timbers." A flatbed truck was piled with landscape timbers. "Always somethin'. Weeds need a cuttin'. Shit like that." He shrugged. "Do whatever feels good." He laughed again.

"Okay." Chaingang turned to waddle off in the direction of the pastureland.

"I didn't hear the bell go off." It was a word they used for a certain kind of alarm device they had used to safeguard their nighttime defensive perimeters. Nothing to do with a bell at all.

"I didn't ring it," Chaingang said without turning. He added as he lumbered off, "Stepped over the trip wire."

Hora looked at the huge fat man's back and said nothing.

BUCKHEAD METRO

"**D**on't say it. Whatever it is. I can tell by the look on your face. Whatever it is I just don't want to hear about it. Keep it to yourself." Eichord was half-serious.

"How can you tell anything about anything by the look on my face. Don't you know I'm an inscrutable fucking slope?"

"Not today. You're very scrutable today and I don't like what I see in your scru."

"Scru you, too, G.I." He twisted in the seat. Paranoid.

"Promises, promises." Eichord looked in the direction of his old friend's glance. "Chrissakes stop that shit you faked me right out of my shoes, man." They laughed. Jack had teased Lee for years about his inscrutability and his head fakes.

"Fucking NFL lost a great wide receiver when you joined the cops," Lee said, shaking his head and laughing. "Jesus, I hate it when you do that to me. I'll be saying something and you look so SERIOUS all of a sudden and those eyes go *BOIIINNNG* like you just saw a naked lady in a tree and every damn time I look where you're looking. Remind me never to play touch football with you."

"I'm antsy down here. Fucking IAD could tail us ten different ways. Put a beeper under the car like in the movies. Shit. Tap the cigarette lighter."

"I really don't want to hear that shit, man. How many times I got to say it. Keep all that shit to yourself."

116

"I can't."

"Say what?"

"I can't, Jack. I know you don't want to hear it but I got nobody else I can talk to. I can't put this shit on Dana, you know that."

"Oh, right. You can't put it on precious Dana but old Jack—that's different. You can put it on me all right. No sweat."

"You know that's not what I mean, asshole. Dana, shit, he's like my brother. I love that fat schmuck. But he's . . . weak. You know what I mean. He'd fucking go to pieces under this. You're all I got, pops. I gotta talk to somebody. I—I can't put this on Peggy. And Dana. Shit. All he wants to know is should HE take some."

"Uh huh. The question is, why talk at all. I ain't the confessional."

"Shit, I can't help it, man, I'm scared," and with that this hard-nosed, two-fisted, tough-talking wiseguy-type Detective Sergeant James Lee, the same James Lee who had saved Eichord's butt in the Orient, James Jimmie the Chink Lee, was bawling like a little baby and Eichord was looking at him not believing it and knowing that it was the beginning of something bad. Then again, Lee cried easily.

"What the fuck," he said in his quietest voice when Lee had gotten the giggles and stopped sobbing. "Just where I want to be tonight. I'm married to the most beautiful woman in the world. She's made me a nice, cozy home. Where am I? Am I home kissin' my lady? Roasting my toes in front of a roaring bowl of popcorn? Nooooooooooo. I'm in the basement of Metro Parking watching *you* have a fucking nervous breakdown. What did I do to deserve this?"

"It's too hot to roast your toes in front of a roaring bowl of popcorn. Roast your balls on one of these." Lee popped the tab on a beer can and passed it to Eichord as he snuffled. Lee then realized what he'd done and snatched it away spilling foam on Jack's hand.

"Sorry, man—"

"Oh, thanks a ton." Jack wiped it off.

"Shit. I forgot," he said meekly.

"Nu?"

"I took twelve thousand dollars." Just like that. No preamble. Nothing. Just—care for a beer? Or by the way, I know you don't want to hear this but would you mind becoming an accessory to robbery?

"Ohhhhhh," Eichord breathed out and tried not to inhale again. Ever. It didn't work.

"I'm sorry."

"You're telling me."

"Okay. So why am I in trouble, you ask. I mean, I'm a big boy. I take twelve kay and I got my reasons. I must know I can deal with it. Am I having guilt pangs? Second thoughts? A troubled conscience? No. I'm scared shitless I'm gonna get caught." Lee poured out the whole story, Eichord saying, "You goddamn MORON," or some variation thereof, every few minutes. At the end of the summation Lee said, "So meanwhile, they got the dudes. One of 'em rolled over for immunity. And you know the fucking feds, man. So this thing gets tallied up, it's a $28,145.00 bank robbery, and they've backtracked $16,145 up to the doors of Buckhead Mercantile. So somewhere in between the shooting of the guard inside the bank and the front door, twelve grand got lost."

"Ummmmm." A groan of pain. He just wasn't fucking believing any of it. Not a word. "You ARE going to tell me this is some awful put-on you and the dirigible devised for my torture, aren't you? Say yes even if it's no."

"Yes."

"Wonderful. Just as I thought."

"No."

"Yes."

" 'Fraid not, Papa-san."

"Well?"

"What do I do now?"

"You know the answer as well as I do."

"Unnn?"

"No choice."

"What?"

"Don't gimme that WHAT shit."

"*What?*"

"You know what you got to do."

"No. That's it, man. I don't."

"You don't have a choice, Chink. You've got to tell 'em."

"Bullshit," he whispered.

"Tell 'em you fucked up and give 'em the money back."

"You know I ain't gonna do that."

"You gotta."

"I can't." A long silence in the car.

"Sometimes I think I've been in more deep shit than a plumber's friend."

"Yeah? I've seen more shit than the inside of a dinosaur's asshole."

"Well," Eichord said as he started the engine, "you don't need me for THIS shit. You already GOT both halves of a comedy team." He pulled out of the shadowy parking stall and started up the ramp toward the street.

Jack said, without looking over at him, saying it one more time just to hear himself say the words, "Think about it, babe. You *gotta* give it back."

But his friend was snapping his fingers, in Tahoe by now, on stage silently doing Tony Bennett's act: tux, Guccis, Ralph at the piano, rug in place, Basie's guys behind him, a big roll of hundreds in his pocket, singin' and swingin'. The best thing Eichord could hope for now was that he wouldn't start singing out loud.

STOBAUGH COUNTY

"**S**umbitch ain't gonna make it, workin' that fast."
"I give him three hours," the wife, who was "slow," said.

He worked from nine-thirty to four-thirty without a break. Seven straight hours unloading treated timbers as fast as he could. For the first four hours he was lightning-fast, pulling them from the big truck bed as fast as he could touch them. Then he'd grab a timber in each huge paw and waddled over to the slowly escalating stack he was making alongside the building. At the end of four hours he had a large, neat stack of timbers. He'd off-loaded more landscape timbers in four hours single-handedly than a two-man crew could handle in a full eight-hour day. He'd lost an enormous amount of water and was replacing it too quickly, drinking too much water from a nearby garden hose.

"Fucker ain't gonna' last much longer," the man said. The slow woman only shook her head in disdain. They had been sitting there on the porch watching him for four hours straight, as if he were a television game show. Fascinated. Neither of them had ever seen anything like it. The man got up and stretched. "Ah'm gonna sack out awhile. Fuck it," he said, and went in, the screen door slamming. The slow wife said nothing but continued to sit on the rump-sprung chair watching the big man from the porch.

The water intake hit him hard. He felt a terrible rush come across him. Vaguely like the red tide that would wash over him and make him do the bad things, but he figured this one was maybe heatstroke or blood pressure. Either way, he thought, I work. He wet a bandanna and tied it around his neck, put on his floppy boonie-rat hat, and slowly went back to work.

He could feel the heat had sapped him. He could no longer pick up a landscape timber in one hand. His fingers would let it go. When he dropped one on his foot he quit trying. But he stayed with it, working slowly, methodically, using both hands to pick up each timber, walking slower now, feeling a little twinge in his back as he set the heavy timbers down on the stack, which was taller and wider than a pair of double beds.

About three-thirty the man came out, yawning. He looked over and said, "Shit. Still at it." He walked down the rickety steps and across the junk-strewn yard. "Hey," he called out aimlessly. Chaingang may have tilted his head slightly but he said nothing. "Y' better ease up 'air, hoss." His tone was jovial.

Chaingang grunted and kept working. The man disappeared back into the house, taking the woman with him this time. After another hour or so Chaingang finished.

He was hurting in his back a little, but not too bad. He'd worn a large hole in one of the work gloves. His ankle was sore as always. He had a headache. He was having a little trouble breathing. Just tired more than anything. He went into the sharecropper's shack and drank a little more water from the jug. Flopped down on the mound of blankets and was snoring immediately, fully dressed, filthy dirty, and sweat-soaked. Dead to the world at a quarter-to five in the evening.

Sissy had been out in their "back yard" looking at all the sights. There were ducks, two kinds. Turkeys. Pea fowls. Peacocks strutting around. Dogs. Cats. It was something. All the junk fascinated her as much as the animals. She came in and was surprised to find Daniel sound asleep on the blankets. She didn't know what to do next so she went back outside and watched the ducks and turkeys and peacocks and junk until dark. And then she came in and lay down by the snoring mound that was her new mentor.

The next day Chaingang did no work. He couldn't. He

could not get off the blankets on the floor, much as he tried. His back felt like it was broken. He had dreamed about this, that two of the blacks in D had taken baseball bats to him and he wondered if his kidneys were bad. He could not get up to piss, so he rolled over and urinated out the door.

Then he saw his ankles. Both ankles were swollen. His right ankle, the bad one, was the size of a large grapefruit. He knew there would be no point in continuing this sort of work as long as his weight was so great. The building process might cripple his weak ankles. He'd forgotten what it would be like to carry all that weight on top of his own. He had to be able to walk. This wouldn't get it.

He was finally able to roll into a sitting position, and he pulled himself up by the strength of his upper torso. Using a broken wooden chair for a kind of walker, he hobbled outside with his big fighting bowie, moving toward the ditch that ran through the middle of the property. On the way he cut himself a huge crutch from an oak tree, and he limped through the field of weeds in the direction of the running water.

He removed his clothes and immersed himself in the ditch, which was ice-cold and muddy brown. It felt so good to let his weight push his sore feet and ankles down into the cool mud. He stood motionless for a long time. Then he washed his clothes in the cold water and, pulling himself out with the aid of a nearby, overhanging tree, managed to get back on the bank. He soaped himself thoroughly and went back into the water, washing himself as best he could. His enormous pants and shirt dried like blankets in the nearby willow limbs. The sun was hot and he came back out and sat naked on the bank, thinking of nothing, trying not to feel the pain and soreness and the aches in muscles he'd forgotten he had. He stayed there on the bank through the noon hour when he went back to fetch Sissy.

"Come on," he told her. It was only the second thing he'd said to her in two days and it was enough to make her smile and start a flood of pent-up commentary about everything she'd done or seen or thought during the last forty-eight hours. He heard not a word of it as they walked toward the hidden vehicle, back through the over-grown fields bordering the junkyard.

". . . and he says they're called coots, those little black ones, you know, or mud coots, somethin' like that, and they'd come up . . ." And then they were in the car and moving toward town. Sissy was happy again, and her soft stream of chatter was like playing a radio low in the background.

The first stop was at a medium-sized grocery store in a small would-be shopping center that had a laundromat, a Radio Shack, a video store that was apparently out of business, and a Western Auto. Chaingang went in to get them their lunch. He came out with a can of V-8 juice that he'd paid for, and pockets full of apples, a package of cold meat, and a tomato, which he plucked out of a sealed package. Nobody could shoplift like Daniel. While the clerk was ringing up the V-8 he dropped some mints into a voluminous pocket. He had plenty of money, but he always stole on principle.

He got in the car and handed Sissy her apple. "Here's your lunch."

"Thanks," she said. "Is this all we're gonna eat?" She wasn't complaining. Just asking.

"Yeah. You need to lose weight for your modeling. Tonight you'll fix the meat, some greens, and tomato." He had their menu all planned out.

"You know," she said, telling him for the tenth time, "you're the only guy I've ever known who didn't think I was too thin."

"Ummm," he grunted as he drove across the expanse of parking lot toward the Western Auto store.

"I went to this one doctor, ya know, and I was getting a physical and he was you know going on about how I was too skinny and all and . . ." She was so pleased that this man who had actually had professional experience producing model layouts would be truthful with her. She had always suspected she was too heavy for high fashion work, and even though she hardly ate anything she just couldn't lose weight. Chaingang, the ultimate mind-manipulator, had instinctively played to her most secret fear. That she was FAT! A borderline anorexia victim, Sissy could sometimes stand in front of a mirror and look right at those protruding, skeletonlike pelvic bones and see only disgusting bulk. He heard her singsong little-girl voice say with great earnestness, "And I sure do like for ya to be honest like that with me," and she touched him.

He was turning off the ignition when he felt the little bony hand reach over and rest on his leg, and she almost bought it right then and there. Some miracle stopped that steel shotput from crashing out and stilling her simple brain. He loathed being touched by anyone when he wasn't expecting it and he almost took her down as an involuntary reflex, but somehow he caught his reaction in time. All she saw was a little tremor like a flinch as he slid out of the vehicle, the springs creaking in relief as he removed his bulk from the car. She thought to herself, Interesting, and knew then that they would have something between them.

He went inside and a jovial, redneck clerk boomed out, "Hot enough for ya?" which Chaingang ignored as he searched the row of merchandise.

"Whatcha looking for there, Tiny? Can I help you?" The man had no earthly idea how close he was right at that second to shuffling off his mortal coil. For some reason Bunkowski's huge bulk evoked that sort of a response in a certain-type person. People who worked in hardware stores, gas stations, tire retailers—they weren't used to seeing a 6-foot-7-inch 460-pound man waddling though their aisles. It upset them, put them off their feed a little, these certain jolly types, and they "kidded" him sometimes to help smooth over their surprise. Some he didn't even hear. Others he ignored. Once in a while he would go over and hurt them in some way. Something would fall on the person. An accident. A can of paint would drop on their foot. Or he would shoplift an unusually large amount right in front of them in silent revenge.

"Where's the whipsickles?"

"Where's the Popsicles? Haven't you et lunch yet?"

"Whipsickles? Weed slingers?" Chaingang beamed. It was his most dangerous smile.

"Right over here," the man said, sensing something and backing off a notch. But it was too late. As Bunkowski walked past him, filling the aisle with his massive body he "brushed up against the man and lost his balance," as he said later, and 460 pounds came down viciously on the clerk's arch and the man let out a bloodcurdling scream, "AAAAAARRRRRRRRRRRRRRRRRRRRRRRR."

"OHHHHH" Daniel echoed as if he too were hurt and out of control, pushing against the man as he threw his poundage into the witty clerk, who slammed backward into a cascade of about four hundred cans of aerosol paint spray, and then Daniel let himself fall, just so, slapping the hard floor just as he timed the fall, and screaming, *Oh, my back,* surreptitiously pocketing something, then getting up limping.

There were apologies all around. Daniel wished he could help the clerk pick up all the paint cans. If he only had more time. Outside, Sissy had heard the screaming and racket and was peering intently trying to see what was going on inside the store. Chaingang said he wanted to leave a tip for the accident, and he left a ten-dollar bill on the counter. The weed slinger was $8.49. SPECIAL! He couldn't wait for the man to ring it up.

He tossed the tool into the back seat and drove out of the shopping center. He drove a couple of blocks and pulled over to a garbage can behind a café, where he took the money from the clerk's wallet. It was only twenty-six dollars but it pleased Chaingang greatly. He found nothing else of interest and threw the wallet and cards away. It would be hours before the clerk realized he'd lost his billfold, and he would never connect the two events.

"Ask that man where a welder is," he told Sissy, interrupting her accounting of how she'd thought he'd "got into a big fight with that guy inside the store."

"Where's a welder?" she shouted out the window in a high, birdlike voice.

"Heh?" a moron said, walking over and looking in the window to hear better.

"Where can we find a welder?"

"A welder?" he repeated, looking at Bunkowski. Daniel had noticed that everyone around these parts had the habit of treating ordinary English words as if they were astonishing surprises. He was pleased by his choice of locations for a "fat farm," as surely this part of the country could lay claim to some of the most obtuse, moronic, and vapid imbeciles he'd ever encountered. And the stupider the human, the less the possible threat to him.

"Somebody who can weld? A welder? Do you know of a welder around here? Somebody who does welding?" To weld. Transitive verb. To allow metallic parts to flow together; to unite by heating, or by hammering, or by compression without heating, or compression with heating; to anneal, strengthen, toughen; TO WELD, yes. Do you speak English? Even as a third language?

"Oh, yeah. You want a BLACKSMITH. Oh, well— yeah." The moron ruminated, his face lighting up like a neon sign as he chewed over this dramatic, earth-shaking turn of events. "Uh. Hemphill's done retired. He was the blacksmith hereabouts."

"Do you know of anyone else around here who can w—can do blacksmith work?" Chaingang smiled his most dangerous killer-gargantuan grin.

"Um. Herb Cannell might can. He's over acrost from the bank catty-corner."

"Thanks."

"Go ta the second stop sign an' hang ya a left and go—"

"Thanks," he muttered in a foul-tempered rumble. He didn't hear the last of the directions, as he was halfway there by the time the man finished.

He pulled up in front of Cannell's Repair and went in. A man was talking to someone on the phone and he hung up in what appeared to be a rage and snarled at Chaingang, "Yeah?"

"People say you're the best welder in four states. They say you charge the fairest prices and that you're the most expert welder in this part of the country." He looked at the man with his most trustworthy and genuine smile.

"Um. Well, I reckon that there is true. Leastways about the fair prices. 'Course NOT EVERY GOD- DAMMNED BODY THINKS SO."

"Well, personally, I'd be PROUD to have ya do a piece of welding for me—if ya was of a mind to." Chain beamed.

"Yeah. Well." He took his glasses out of his pocket, calming visibly, and walked over to the huge man. "Whatcha need welded?"

"I want this reinforced." He held the cheap whipsickle up in front of the man's face. "Here," he said, touching it, "and all along in here. Could that be done?"

"I suppose it could, but why in the hell would ya WANT to?" The very idea offended him.

"Good point. Because they don't make things worth a damn anymore. Sloppy workmanship. Lack of care. Inattention to detail. A craftsman—somebody like YOU—is a genuine rarity today." He pronounced it gin-u-wine, which he thought gave it a nice touch.

"That's for goddamn sure."

"I'm TIRED of goin' out in the fields and workin' and the least li'l bit of heavy-duty usage and the daggone whipsickle blade busts, or the shaft snaps . . . I'm tired of it."

"You can't BUY a damn tool anymore."

"It's the damnedest thing," Chaingang agreed, speaking the words in the man's exact speech cadence as he shook his head. The two of them stood there, shaking their heads at the sorry state of affairs.

"Feller could run a brass strip along here. Not just an ordinary piece of shim." He took the whipsickle out of Daniel's hands and walked away, talking to himself. "I gotta brass strap here someplace that might work . . ." Ten minutes later Chaingang was standing outside the shop watching the white-hot blade cooling blue and then red as the new brass-reinforced weed slinger cooled in the water.

"How much?"

"Two dollars be about right?"

"Right as rain." He smiled, handing over some sweaty ones.

The man pulled it out of the cooling trough and gingerly touched the blade to see if it could be handled. He gave it to Chaingang.

"NOW bust 'er."

BUCKHEAD SPRINGS

"I like that. I do." He wasn't doing anything. Just holding her very close with his face pressed into the hollow of her throat. "I like it a lot. Don't stop for a thousand years."

"Ain't doin' nothin'," he said into her neck.

"Don't care. I like it," she told him. "I know what I like and I like it."

"Mmmmrfk it too."

"Yeah?"

"Mmmrf mmm."

"I know just what you mean. I feel the same way. Roof-moof."

"What I said was we fit good."

"I know that. I heard you loud and clear." They kissed. Again. Again.

"You know something?"

"Eh?"

"I love you so much."

"I'm glad," he said. "You know something? Aw, never mind."

"Tell me."

"I will—but not now." And his tongue touched hers. They made love and he tried for the longest time to be as gentle as he could. That was the idea. To show her how much she meant to him. That she was porcelain dolls fine china breakable heirloom vases treasured satsuma capo di monte royal doulton steuben all the stuff that goes crunch the fine stemmed goblets and the fluted this and

the delicate that and the nouveau lamps with shades like
wafer-thin eisenglass and the thing is though she wouldn't
break and she'd told him a couple dozen times she wasn't
fragile and as gentle as he started out to be the heat of
her warmed him inflamed him made the old volcano
rumble and molten stuff in there start to flow and then it
got a little wild and then he made up for it by kissing all
the places where he'd made her body hot, kissing those
sweet spots maybe ten thousand times just to show her
. . . just to let her know. Gentle kisses from head to toe,
covering her in as much love as he could bestow, but she
didn't wan't him down there smooching on the sides of
her knees and she told him so, to which he replied, "But
don't you see, woman, I adore your knees."

"And they adore you, sweetheart, but I want you up
here where I can look at you. "She sort of pulled him up,
body weight notwithstanding, kissing the parts of him she
could reach, first a hand and then the top of his head and
then his face. "I wish I could have your child," she said
out of nowhere.

"I'm glad you feel that way." It was enough for both of
them and more and they went to sleep like that. Holding
each other, not in the fitted curves of tummy and hand
and stomach against back and groin to butt, which is the
way they so often fell asleep, but in each other's arms,
with their faces almost touching, pillows pressed together,
as close as they could get.

He'd known since Dallas that Donna couldn't have
kids. It meant next to nothing to him when they'd first
married. It was only after she'd told him a few times that
she wished she could bear his child that he even allowed
himself to think about it. He had never fathered a child
nor had he felt the usual, normal fatherly urge to propa-
gate. In fact, with the abrogation of his first marriage
he'd assumed that his age and profession and life-style
would preclude children. It was only later, growing close
to a child—Lee Anne Lynch—and letting his heart fill
with the joy a child could bring a man, that he allowed
himself even the luxury of an occasional thought, wondering, as a man will, what it might be like—fatherhood.

It was clearly something Donna wanted but neither of

them had talked about the possibility of adoption. To Eichord it was as remote as a faraway planet.

But when she said it this time, told him how she wished she could have his child, told him with such intensity of feeling and longing and regret, it stayed with him. And he supposed it was kicking around up in the old brain wrinkles when the thing happened at work, and maybe it was one of those surrogate things. Whatever. In any event, a couple of nights later he was in the garage talking to himself.

"I'll never leave you again," he was saying. "No. I promise. Never. You'll never be alone again." Nobody else was with him. He was talking into a box.

He went in and found her, and he took her hand and led Donna back into the bedroom the way she'd taken his hand and led him through his birthday treats, and she looked at him with a quizzical smile as he positioned her on the bed.

"What?" she said, sensing something.

"Well," he said as he handed her his homemade card, "just a little something." She stretched out on the bed in her slightly décolleté top, French jeans, and heels, looking good enough to jump right there, he thought, and she read the card aloud as he had hers, "Dearest wife," penned in a carefully drawn heart, "when I look at you I never fully believe my luck. I love you so much it makes me laugh out loud when I think I'll be able to come home and find you here waiting for me. You give more than you could ever take. You're the best woman I've ever known." She looked up at him with eyes that looked moist and beautiful and he had her close them.

"Keep them closed for sixty seconds. Just lie there please," he whispered. She didn't hear him leave the carpeted bedroom until she heard the steps going down the hall, but she stayed where he'd put her and kept her eyes closed wondering what was cooking. She heard him open the door to the garage and then close it and he heard her voice down the hall. "I'm getting awfully curious back here all alone in this big bedroom." And she could hear him say almost like he was talking to a baby.

"Well, we won't be alone in that ole bedroom anymore, eh? No. Not anymore. Nosiree. No way." And saying to her from the hallway, "Are those eyes firmly closed?"

"Yes, Officer."

"Just keep 'em that way, lady, I'll instruct you when to open them." And she heard something, a kind of skittering noise against cardboard or paper, and felt something moving, touching her.

"OH!" she opened her eyes and saw what was standing on her. A little gray kitten. Very young. A baby one. Standing, or doing its best to stand there, head cocked at her. It weighed nothing. A ball of gray fluff.

"His name is Tuffy," Eichord told her.

"Tuffy," she whispered softly, and the cat liked it so well he spun in a circle and fell off her stomach in a tumbling kind of somersault and then did a few acrobatics on the bed. "Guess what?" she said to the kitten. "I LOVE YOU!" It was a whispered rush of adoration, to which she added, "BOTH of you," and Eichord smiled.

"We feel the same way, my sweet."

"Oh, thank you," she said in her softest tones, smiling at this fluffball attacking her leg. "Oh!" She laughed. "I don't know what to say. I just adore you, Tuffy. I think you're great."

To which the little gray cat responded by opening his mouth wider than she'd have thought possible and yawning a great yawn, and showing a mouth that was shocking pink like the inside of a seashell, and Donna laughed with glee.

"What a guy," she said.

And Eichord smiled like he'd knocked one out of the park.

VARNEY

Daniel would never have expected the girl to accept this weird turn of events in her life so easily. She was perfect. He sensed that he couldn't have done better if he'd had a hundred shots at picking up somebody who would suit his needs to the nth degree. Sissy was one of those people who, once dedicated to a person or a cause or a goal, hoped only to please. She required some direction or she would be aimless and rootless. She was not a self-starter. She needed positioning, guidance, but once she had that she could function with surprising smoothness.

Sissy was of a gentle and placid nature. A girl who had never known a father, or even a particularly strong maternal influence, she took to Daniel as would a duck to the wet stuff. He would tell her precisely what would be expected of her within the framework of each given day or event. Never really bossing her or being domineering, she felt, just telling her the way it was to be. He expected NOTHING from her in return. No sexual favors. Nothing. It was so new to her, this sort of a benevolent, guiding hand, and she took each word from the huge man as if it were handed to her engraved on stone.

She was used to BOYS not men. A boy who would want her only for sex or for companionship on a date, and who would say, "Hey, wanna go to the Steakhouse tonight?" and she'd say, "Sure, sounds great." And then she'd think for a minute, thinking for both of them and say, "But, uh, Toby," or Kevin, or whoever, "*do you have any MONEY?*"

"Um—uh, no," he'd say. "Uh, can you let me borrow fifteen dollars?" And now here was a guy, a man, who would hand her thousands of dollars and trust her to do the right thing.

She fully expected he'd been conning her when he pulled her off Randolph Street but, God, wasn't it worth a shot to find out? He was so interesting and so convincing and obviously experienced.

Life had not been especially rewarding to Sissy Selkirk. People had told her she was pretty, she was this, she was that. But nothing had ever come of it. Only more of the same boredom and let downs and hand-me-downs. She had failed at school. A boy had taken her virginity. She had gone out into the workplace pregnant and been taken advantage of by an employer who saw in her only the easy sex and vulnerability, paid her minimum wage, abused her, and when she was big with child, abandoned her as her teenaged lover had. She had not picked her men well. She had given birth to a little boy, Guy, named after her unknown father, and she had failed at mothering. Her ways were "unconventional," and they had taken Guy away from her, and called her unfit to be a mother and put Guy into a foster home somewhere.

This was the first time in years that it looked like something good could happen to her. So when Daniel came in from a hard day of work out in the fields, she was quite content to feed him and watch him leave again "on business" as he often did, with no more dialogue than "You can watch TV or read, okay?" To which she would nod and smile and say, "Sure." She knew enough not to ask when he was coming back. And then late that night she would hear the rumbling engine of the black Caprice, which he now parked beside the old sharecropper's house.

This night he was heading on a northeast course, driving to Varney, tired from the day's work and his stomach a shrinking, aching tub that growled at him as he drove, putting him in an even darker, more violent mood.

Jesse Keys had been tossin' down a couple in there makin' eyes at ole Caroline and tryin' to wind down after a hellacious week working for the Brewster outfit up at

Hubbard City. He had swallered just about enough happy juice and looked at that little ole gal long enough he was ready to put the pork to a dead Mexican, an' then he decided he better just cat on home and pork the ole lady instead, and he goes outside and gets a big whiffa that nasty fresh air and his sore, tired feet hit that concrete and he was right back where he started. In a bad-ass ornery mood.

The job at Brewster's was a bitch. He was breakin' a new kid in who wouldn' listen to shit, doin' ever'thing his own way, and he figgured, Hell, about another day of that an' I'm gonna cut him loose. He'd druther work by himself. Fuck up his own job. If that's all there was to it.

He'd be up at five A.M. and seven he'd be on the job, and they'd be pourin' if the weather held. Christ on a crutch, he hated concrete. He wished the devil'd never thought of it. It hurt your feet, he thought, even in new metal-toed, cleated ostrich kicks from Hubbard Western Wear, damn stuff wasn't fit to walk on.

All those years at McCullough's on that fuckin' hard shit, that's what had really done him in. Hell, he blamed concrete for nearly every bad thing that ever happened to him. It got him so steamed, he made himself quit thinkin' about it and started thinkin' about the way that ole gal was comin' on to him. Ooooooooooweeeeeeeeeeee.

Damn! That little ole' gal Caroline could start lookin' good toward the end of the night when you was gettin' about three sheets to the wind on that there bourbon and branch water. Why was it just as soon as he'd get about half-drunk them little ole' fillies would all start up lookin' like Dolly Parton to him? Shit he'd be damned if he wouldn't fuck a bush if he thought there was a snake in it. He was so horny right now he'd learn to play golf just so he could fuck the holes.

It was the story of his whole damn life and if THAT wasn't a soap opera—well, hot damn, nobody ever writ one. His tallywhacker had got him in a shitpot of trouble and he couldn't do nothing about it either. That was sad. Plum pitiful. If you cain't learn by your mistakes, you jes' ain't worth whippin'.

He'd been with little Jane and then he'd met Darla Palmer and that stuff was all he could think about. Crap.

Ole Darla could just squeeze a man to death with them big, hard-muscled legs of hers. First time he ever climbed up onner he started goin' limp like a damn fairy. It was like you was puttin' it to another man. HARD legs. She'd been a dancer, and ole' Darla had them long, hard legs. Hot damn! She could wrap them around a man, and she knew other tricks too, that little bitch. Darla could fuck your brains out. And so he ended up puttin' everything on a single toss of them ivories and crappin' halfway out and him and Jane got into this big-ass courtroom battle and he swore, he said, "God, now I don't pray to you, as you know. But I'm jes' asking this ONE favor, Lordy, oh yes, sir, I beg ya, jus' give me Darla and them two boys and I'll never take a drink nor fornicate outside my marriage bed again." But the Lord punished him and only gave him one of them boys and that was better'n nothing, and he got Darla, but shit, it waddn't two months before he was out drunk 'n tom-cattin' but hell that was jes' men, he reckoned. He couldn't help it none that he had certain desires. And they'd give him a big, stiff cock between his legs like tonight with little Caroline in there showin' him everything she had, and what was a man to do?

He'd go home now and bomb the old lady. Make Jane so sorry she hadn't held on to him she'd faint, make Darla claw the damn walls. Put it to the woman till she flat out begged for mercy. Plum get some for serious and do the cowboy two-step till you drop, ladybug. He did a little shuffle in his Saturday-night boots.

Damn! He jes' hated concrete with a passion. Jesse Keys thought how much he hated the son of a buck as he walked across the darkened expanse of parking lot, metal-cleated boots ringing on the hard surface. He wished right then that he had his nice soft work shoes on. Them earth shoes or whatever you call 'em that Jane always bought him. Big, thick, soft-rubber soles between you and the hard world. Every step galled him in the boots. He wished he could turn the clock back sometimes. Shit.

He'd spent sixteen years standing on them damn feet eight hours a day and overtime on the main line at McCullough's, sixteen damn years less vacation and sick leave, standing in front of that big drill press and if he wasn't so bumfuzzled right now he could do that math in his head; sixteen times fifty, let's say, was shit how many weeks. Let's call her eight hundred. Okay, then take and multiply by forty hours plus. That's 3,200 or 32,000 hours he'd stood there, he couldn't make up his mind where the fuckin' zero was. He suspected it was 32,000 anyway. Call her 40,000 hours in front of those big fucks.

Oh, that concrete would get hard after six or seven hours. Stood there 40,000 hours with his young life sappin' down through the soles of his feet. For what?—for some piddly-ass $474.15 when he left. Shit the damn punch-drunk shift foreman who done good to even read or write his name, he was draggin' forty large a year plus on the side. Once in a while his boys'd steal somethin' off the loading docks or outta the warehouse and kick it back partly to him. Only way Jesse never moved up the sumbitch threatened to kill him if he put in for promotion and the little bastard meant it. His shift boss had been a pug. Fought welterweight. He'd look at you real hard and you would go on and quit whatever you was doin' and move along. Jesse'd seen him hit this one old boy, lifted him plum off'n his feet and he kicked the dude right in the fist with his foot as he went down and that's no lie. He'd never seen anybody get hit that hard.

But it wasn't a bad job. Man could work there blind or forever. Go in floatin' on pills and wine at eight A.M., drink a couple beers, hit that morning break and him and Eddie Lawson and Slater and ole Joe Bob would go kill a pint between them and come back and coast. You could hold a job at McCullough's if you could crawl. Stand there on the big line—concrete as far as you could see—noisy ole machines a-goin'. Not that computerized shit. Hands on. You did it all, two-fisted. Had a Hammond when he quit. Couldn't remember what them other two had been. Sixteen fucking years. Him and Eddie had quit the same day; Eddie got himself a job driving for United Parcel, and Jesse started pouring the shit. Fucking concrete. His entire life had been fucked over by concrete and he hated the stuff.

He should have stayed at McCullough's. You never worried 'bout shit. Never took nothin' home with you at the end of the day. You could stand there and smoke even. Mellow out while you ran your press. If the bosses came you'd see 'em a mile away and nobody could smell shit in there so everybody knew it was cool and they smoked pot and partied and hell's bells it wasn't like it was a damn death sentence or anything except that it killed your feet standing there like that.

He thought maybe he'd come back tomorrow night about an hour before they closed 'er down and see if Caroline would like to go out and turkey-trot a little with this ole cowboy and he was moving across the hated concrete when the thing wrapped around him and sort of pulled his head like you'd wrap a string around a yo-yo or a top and as the string or in the case of this particular moment in the life and death of Jesse Keys the chain is pulled, the top is spun, and Jesse went a-spinning out in a violent centrifugation his head seeing a blur of lights in this spinning, blinding whirlwind that cracked out and spun him into a parked truck. It was the last thing he saw, the flashing lights of the spinning horizon, right before the intense pain and the sudden death.

You know how it is when you get hit real hard with a chain? Well, what happens is—nothing. See you don't feel anything right away but the impact of the blow just numbs you out. It's later, that second or two or ten seconds later when the feeling starts coming back that you start screaming and holding yourself and shitting all over your new $375 cowboy boots from the intensity and blinding shock of the unendurable agony because as you well know there is nothing quite like being hit by 2½ feet of taped tractor chain. It will flat out put your raggedy country-and-western ass in the big hurt locker. It was a good thing he died real soon thereafter as it spared him a lot of terrible pain.

Shows you there's a good side to almost everything.

It just ain't reasonable to expect you can two-step through life without kickin' a little cow flop from time to time. It ain't nothin' personal it's just the way of the world. Once in a while you're gonna get them size 11 Justin Full Quill Ostrich jobs (regularly $495, special at Hubbard Western Wear only $375!), in the doo-doo. Life is not blue skies all the time. You got to be a philosopher about the thing. Into every life a little chain must fall.

BUCKHEAD

"**A**. C. Wiegrath, please," the voice tells the woman over the telephone.

"May I tell him who's calling, please?"

"SAC Krug at the Bureau."

"Oh—yes, sir—just a moment, please." The line goes click and there is a momentary pause and he hears the familiar voice answer.

" 'Morning, Howard."

"Arthur."

"You get a chance to go to school on my memo?"

"Yeah, I did. I pretty much think we need to push on with this. I see what you're saying but we're getting boxed in with the investigation if we don't move."

"Well"—the man's raised eyebrows and shrug could be heard over the telephone in his tone and the sigh—"you know the sit-chee-ashun as well as I do. You're on egg-shells. Something like this. I think you have to do what you think best. Buck stops with you."

"Yeah. Well, we got only three possibilities. First Mr. Fields hisself, which doesn't make much sense—guy can buy anything he wants now—Christ, djew look at his financial statement?"

"No, I didn't. He's got a few?"

"Yeah, you could say that." They chuckled. "For a rainy day. You can say the boy Monroe put it in a cigar box and buried it. I guess we can't dismiss it."

"What'd the poly do?"

"Shit," he said contemptuously.

"I figured."

"We took about forty man-hours combined with that damn videotape. He looks awful good for it. He's in there in a shot one minute, he's outta the shot the next minute."

"Christ almighty, I think . . ." He trailed off.

"Arthur, if there was ANYbody else looked ripe for it I wouldn't press it. I mean the girl. Shit there's no way. Just no opportunity. The video narrows it down by eliminating everybody else including the two uniform guys. I think we're lookin' at Fields, John Monroe, and the investigating officer in charge. That's it."

"Detective Sergeant James Lee out of Buckhead Station."

"Yeah." Long pause.

"I think we got to get a court order and the whole shootin' match."

"Lee's telephone. Fields' telephone. What else?"

"All the usual. For now. Then we'll just wait and see what drops out of the trees, I guess."

"Jesus. You know, for a measly damn twelve, insured at that, you know what *I'd* like to do with this one."

"Hey, really. Amen to that. It just don't work that way."

"I know, I know. Okay. I'll put it in the works."

"Thanks, Arthur."

"No problem. Get back to you after a while."

"Right," Special Agent-in-Charge Krug said, hanging up the phone.

The man sitting on the other side of the desk from him anticipated what Krug was about to say and said, "I can appreciate how he feels. We don't like it much either."

"Right."

"But we both know we got a dirty cop here."

"Looks that way, I'll admit."

"Yep."

STOBAUGH COUNTY

He had always counted on his surprising quickness and it had never failed him. He was amazingly surefooted until he grew tired, and his unexpected speed and agility had surprised more than one adversary to death. Daniel had always been careful about revealing his secret quickness of movement, even in combat, and he regarded it as a special, delicious treasure quite rightfully.

But while he could sprint fifty, sixty, seventy-five feet with dazzling speed for his obvious corpulence he was then dead in the water. Running more than a few city blocks, even at a slow jog, was impossible and to him unthinkable. What would be the point? Stamina has its limits.

He knew himself the way you know a reliable machine, every tolerance, every interrelated movement within the system, and his capacities and limitations were known, calculated, and trusted. First his wind would give out, then if he kept going—his ankle would pain him—and soon he'd be moving like a wounded hippo, favoring the bad ankle and moving in a kind of half-lurching half-waddling plunge forward, almost out of control, and uncharacteristically vulnerable as he gulped in mighty lungfuls of air. It was worse than if he'd remained in place and fought, or hid, or whatever. So of course he never ran.

Now he had to run. He had to do it all—the whole aching, killing, hurt-filled, boring, lonely, frustrating, play-through-the-pain program designed to tire him to the point where he wouldn't eat. To make him sleep on a huge, screamingly hungry gut that demanded attention as it shrunk. What was his speed? Could he run the forty in 4.4? The hundred in 14.4? He hadn't a remote clue. He decided not to buy a stopwatch, as he could count up to sixty minutes by the second and not be more than four seconds off either way. Hell, he WAS a clock.

So he bit the bullet and did it. He'd pull off his huge shirt and, Ace bandage carefully wrapped around the right ankle, take off at a quick double-time toward the nearest ditch. At first he could only run one way—but slowly, day by day, he'd run a little farther before he gave out, exhausted, collapsing in a wheezing, beached-whale heap wherever he fell, gasping for air, his ankle throbbing with pain to which he would steel himself. His heart would be threatening to burst through the enormous, meaty-titted chest, and he'd be angrier, at that moment, then he could ever remember being when the hot and red waves of kill fury were not present.

Finally he'd manage to get back to his feet, and—still fighting for air—he would gamely walk back to the shack, the soaked towel in his huge hands. It was then, on each of the trips back from the edge of Hora's property line, he would take the soaked bathtowel and wring it. JESUS CHRIST WRING IT DRY AND THEN THE HANDS WOULD GRIP IT LIKE IT WAS A HUMAN THROAT AND THEY WOULD WIND THE TOWEL TIGHTER AND TIGHTER, TESTING THE STRENGTH OF THOSE MIGHTY, POWERFUL SHOULDERS, BACK MUSCLES, NECK, UPPER ARMS, FOREARMS, WRISTS, AND KILLER HANDS AS HE PULLED AT THE TOWEL RIPPING THE JAWBONE OF A MAN LOOSE OR TEARING THE HEAD FROM A WOMAN OR SPEAR-THRUSTING INTO THE SOLAR PLEXUS AND COMING UP UNDER THE RIB CAGE AND FORCING THE FINGERS UNDER THE LOWER RIBS AND PULLING WITH ALL HIS MIGHT DO YOU KNOW WHAT POWER IT TAKES TO PULL A HUMAN RIB CAGE APART YOU SPINELESS, PENCIL-NECKS IN YOUR SAFE, HAPPY WORLDS OF CALM AND POISE AND FREEDOM? DO YOU KNOW THE WILL THE CONCENTRATION REQUIRED TO FORCE THE THUMBS IN BEHIND THE EYES AND POP THEM OUT LIKE SO DO YOU KNOW THE FORCE IT TAKES TO RIP A HEART OUT WITH YOUR HANDS?

Oh, he hated them all so. Hated their smiling faces and their foolish, sheep ways and their lives that seemed to mock him just by their mere existence.

Sissy knew instinctively that she must communicate something to this quiet and excitingly dangerous new man in her life. She wanted him to understand that his violent nature was quite acceptable to her. She was no stranger to violent men. She didn't mind a big, strong sugar daddy looking out for her. It was reassuring. So this became the hazy focus of her running commentary.

Chaingang hears fragments from a long, disjointed story about a guy she was with named Toby Something, and a rambling, pointless anecdote about a gun and his mind tunes in momentarily as she tells him, ". . . picked it up and pulled the trigger, and I didn't know, you know, it was loaded, and the gun went off. I was real close to him, you know, like from here to there"—gesturing—"and it went off right in his face and he got burns from the, uh, gun going off and . . ." She laughed at the memory of it. "And you should have seen the look on Toby's face when I pointed that gun at him and pulled the trigger. He looked so surprised when it went off, and for a second I thought I'd—" And back into the long, drawn-out, ridiculous story as he tuned out.

And now he looks at her as she drifts back into the boring nothingness of her past, fascinated by herself, and he lets himself enjoy the lulling effect of her soft, childish voice, the voice of a little girl, and the not unpleasant singsong delivery of the unending, muted flow of verbiage. And to illustrate her point she aims a thin finger at Chaingang and cocks her hand like a gun. SHE IS POINTING AN IMAGINARY GUN AT HIS FACE. He has to beam a horrible smile at the irony of it and he is suddenly awash in the red tide that so frequently engulfs his mind and emotions and makes him do the bad things.

His smile widens at the ease with which he could reach out and break that bony thing she points in his face, snap that finger like a pencil, holding it in the massive vise of his grip that can squeeze flashlight batteries and with no exertion simply press down and forward breaking the finger, giving him the joy of seeing her delicious agony as she suddenly screams and falls, him still holding the finger to control her movements, and then bend it back farther and snap and tear and wring it effortlessly ripping it loose. How much pleasure it would give him to hurt her right this second and thought nearly becomes deed as the feelings flood over him.

He diverts the flow, this time, and lets the scarlet roar and pressure of the blood heat rush through his loins like an infusion of liquid flame and it stiffens him and he goes over to her as she talks and spreads her legs, ripping the flimsy little bikini panties off her, wetting the head of his engorged sex and ramming in, squeezing her soft white thighs, and she is letting herself be manipulated and still valiantly trying to finish the story as her upper body goes back on the bed and he hears, ". . . as bad as Toby, and I'd wake up and he'd be doin' it to me in my sleep, ya know, or I woke up, like this one time, 'n I was so sore that—" Three, four minutes he bangs away, holding her to him in those vise grips. He ejaculates, pulls up his pants, buckles his huge belt that required the entire length of a dead cow to supply a sufficiently long piece of continuous leather. ". . . 'n of course I suspected what he'd been doing to me"—and he pats his pockets for keys—"and like this one guy who took me home one night from this place that me and Mary Beth went to, the Triple Nickle? So we got"—and he picks up the heavy jacket—"so drunk and we were partyin' outside after" —pats the special canvas pocket—"and this guy who I knew starts"—feels the reassuring weight—"partying with us"—she laughs at the humor of the night, all as real to her as the moment—"and man, we really got"—the weight of the heavy chain excites him anew—"fucking WASTED, you know"—and he heads for the hand pump—"and, God, I didn't even know where"—she hears him in the small, adjoining room, pumping water—"I was or what I was doing."

Daniel Bunkowski's sperm inside her, Sissy sees her man leaving, and she tells him, "The next morning I knew he'd taken advantage of me, you know, 'cause I was so sore."

The door of the shack opens and she tells his huge back, "Uh, hey, you know maybe next time you ought" —but he is out the door now—"to take [SLAM]—some precautions . . . ?" she asks, her voice trailing off into nothingness. A small tree falling in the forest.

BUCKHEAD STATION

It was unusually quiet in the squad room, but Eichord only noticed the stillness when it was shattered by a phone on Brown's desk, and the ensuing one-way conversation that Jack tuned out. Eichord, Lee, Tuny, and Brown were all doing paperwork. The clack of Tuny's typewriter and the deep sonority of Brown's resonant tones had a lulling effect on Jack, who was sleepy and bored and clock-watching at three in the afternoon.

He was doodling. Drawing a picture of the little kitten, a terrible likeness. Filling in the clearly delineated M in the middle of the cat's forehead that seemed to mark so many gray cats, a species of animal about which he knew next to nothing.

But he thought about Boy, their dog the day it was killed. He still remembered Boy, whom he'd adopted, or who had adopted Jack, while he was working on a murder case in Dallas. He remembered that last day he was holding the dog in his lap and he told the animal, "It's hard to imagine you used to be a starved, puny mutt. Now look what we've got." He patted the dog. "I guess I've made you what you are today," he said as he affectionately patted the obese canine's low-slung belly. "Fat," to which Donna had said cheerfully from the next room, "I certainly hope you're not talking to me," and they'd laughed. That same day Boy had run out in the street in front of the wrong truck. *Adiós,* Boy. He was glad he'd

145

brought the kitten home. He was sitting there thinking about Tuffy when Lee said, "Jack!"

"Yo."

"Quit that daydreamin'."

"Right."

"You had a weird expression on your face. What were you thinking about?"

"Pussy," he answered truthfully, "gray pussy."

"I ain't never had any that old yet. Peg's starting to look a little gray but it may be only a urinary infection. That's what we suspect anyway."

"I'm beginning to suspect YOU'RE a urinary infection. I know you sure can piss a person off."

"Hey, that's not bad. Well, that's all right. Shit. I was starting to wonder if you'd lost it. Long as you can still zing one now and then I don't have to worry. In case *tub*"—he gestured at the rotund cop typing at the desk next to his—"ever gets hold of a bad burrito and pulls the pin on me I at least know where I can get a partner with a sense of humor."

"Listen to this shit," fat Dana said. "There's a Peter Drier in Records down at Metro. Dig it, girls, we ain't even got a washcloth in the men's room and those assholes have their own *Peter* Drier!" He screamed, stamping his feet the way he'd seen Sammy Davis Jr. do once on TV. "Oh, damn, I'm funny."

"Uh huh," Eichord said, yawning loudly.

"Yeah," his partner said as he turned, "Chunk, you really are a fucking ton of fun."

Jack got up and stretched. Then he shoved his chair up to the desk and left for home. Shank of the afternoon. He'd had it. Fuck it. He was tired of listening to the phone ring and wondering when it would be IAD wanting to talk to Jimmie Lee.

And every week that went by without another problem Lee would say to him when they were alone—nudge, nudge,

"See. I tole ya. Nobody's gonna know nothin'," and Eichord would let his shoulders droop and he'd close his eyes and just stand there, his entire body screaming, No . . . WRONG . . . But Lee would get all the more ada-

mant about it. How it had been "just one of those things."
And it was all over. But they both knew it wasn't like
that. Eichord had done a lot of stupid things in his time
but he'd always been wise about money. And he knew
and he knew that Chink knew: stolen money never spent
well.

STOBAUGH

With the injection of sex into their bizarre relationship something else changed between Daniel and Sissy. He began to notice her for the first time. This, in itself, was not good. He was beginning to notice that she was THERE, a human presence where for so many years there had been nothing. He had never tolerated proximity of any kind, even slammed down tight behind bars he was the classic example of a con doing his own time. Daniel was a loner.

Now he would come "home" after his days of exhausting work and be vaguely irritated that someone was there waiting for him. And one day he noticed something that would completely alter his life. He almost never spoke to Sissy anymore, and of course from the moment they'd begun having sex the whole Hollywood and model fantasy had been dropped. Neither of them ever spoke of it again, almost as if by mutual consent.

Neither of them spoke about much of anything. She had tried to initiate conversations but even Sissy ultimately caught onto the fact that her man was neither listening nor responding to anything she said, so she settled for what he gave her, which proved to be a warm place to stay, a roof, a sufficient amount of caloric intake to stay alive, a TV set, animals to play with, the odd moment of brief sexual usage, and no further demands on her physically or intellectually.

He had lost an enormous amount of weight already. The first week alone he knew he had dropped over

twenty-five pounds just in water. Although he was too
heavy to be weighed on ordinary scales he could easily
estimate his own body weight and calculated he'd lost
between sixty and sixty-five pounds and it was still melting from his hugely corpulent frame. The thing is, he had
noticed something that had all but turned him around.
His stomach was getting smaller, but hers appeared to be
growing larger. At first, without consciously thinking about
it, he'd assumed her weight gain was due to a totally
sedentary life. Then, as he made more new holes in his
belt, cutting more excess leather off the other end and
cinching up the baggy pants he was wearing, it dawned
on him that he'd impregnated her.

"Why didn't you tell me you were pregnant?" he said
suddenly, confronting her outside the shack. He towered
over her like a grizzly.

"Umm. Well. I wasn't sure at first."

"But you're sure now?" She looked up at him and
smiled. She nodded and blinked her eyes, waiting for his
reaction. There was none. He walked over to the Caprice
and got behind the wheel, noticing that the steering wheel
didn't wedge against his gut quite as much as it had, and
motioned for her. "Come on—get in." He drove into
town to the local one-doc clinic and had her examined.
She seemed to be healthy, and about ninety days along.

The doctor had regaled them with stories about all the
women who went three and four months without a period,
and made sure that Daniel understood, ahem, that his
weight on top of her after a certain point, cough, might
cause discomfort. Checked out her plumbing. Gave her
two aspirin and a pat on the head and told her not to
smoke or drink too much caffeine.

"How do you feel?" Chaingang asked later, paternally.

"I have to pee bad," she said, completing one of their
typically crisp exchanges of dialogue.

And he went back out into the fields with his special,
blacksmithed weed slinger and worked until he could no
longer see, smashing out at the stubborn and infinite
vetch again and again, the sharpened blade slashing into
the obstinate weeds, the smoothly welded brass straps
helping the fiercely slung tool cut a path through the
overgrown meadow. Ten with the right hand, ten with

the left hand, ten with the right hand, over and over and over, the rhythm never slackening, never changing, the man showing no signs of tiring, of ever stopping. He kept swinging his blade of vengeance, chopping at the vetch like the Grim Reaper, relentlessly hacking his way through this vast acreage of Mother Nature unattended, slashing through Mother Nature rampant, defying her with every brutal blow. Weeds, grass, vetch, all the thick stuff flying into the air, sometimes over his shoulders, showering his head, coming down on his back, the strong man oblivious to everything as he concentrated, swinging the cutting tool, slashing hearts, ten with the left, ten with the right, ten more, ten more, each vicious swing in heartbeat tempo, *fuck* Mother Nature, *fuck* Mother Nature . . .

BUCKHEAD SPRINGS

Eichord was out under the big red maple thinking about the birthday Donna had given him. The treasured Disney comic book and the tapes of rare hero chapters were safe inside. He loved the idea of what she'd tried to do for him. He could no longer lose himself in nostalgia the way he had once been able to do. Either cop burn out . . . too much shit . . . or this thing with Chink. God, it bugged him. It bugged him that Jimmie would TAKE, number one. Number two, he wished he'd never been told about it. What would he do when IAD pulled him in and said, "Did you know?" Fuck it.

What it boiled down to is he would lie. No question. To protect a real friend like Lee. Who's kidding who? He'd stonewall it just the way all the other assholes did these days. He'd smile and cross his legs and protect his balls to the walls. What more could you do? Or what LESS could you do, in his case? He owed the kid that one.

Jack remembered their trip together. Years and years before, back at the beginning of the whole thing. Before McTuff had ever heard of a cat named Eichord. He'd been sitting there, a fish out of water, partnerless, no track record, a strong candidate for the drunk tank, and listening to fat Dana, not so fat back then, and Lee talking nostalgia.

". . . those fuckin' Buicks with the outrageous portholes on the side. God they were sharp. Every time I drew a picture of a big ole limo in school I'd draw three or four portholes onnit."

"That was the damn Chrome Decade: 1949 to 1959. Began with the Riviera and ended with the Seville. Remember the '59 El Dee? Oh, my, mercy sakes. Big ole righteous fins on that sucker. God! Wouldn't ya like to have been rich enough you coulda got a '53 El Dee when you were born or somethin'—you know, like your first words to mommy when you're three: 'Get me a '53 hog!' "

"Put it in a garage somewhere and pay the rent."

"Yeah, keep it cherry. Pay rent on a garage from 1953 to now—shit! If you'd put that in gold you'd be Nelson fellering Rockefucker by now."

"I'll tell ya a classic vehicle. Wanna hear a classic?"

"Yeah."

"Here ya' go: the 1948 Chevy Fleetmaster stationwagon."

"Oh, fuck. Wait a minute. You want a classic—get serious. Here's a classic. Ya ready?"

"Unnn."

"The '56 'Vette."

"Wait—the ultimate. The '51 Buick LeSabre rag top."

"Here ya go. The 1957 Ford Fairlane." There was a long pause. "THE '57 FORD FAIRLANE? You're crazy!" And on and on. Little Deuce Coupes and '51 Starlites (what the hell was a Starlite?) And being smuggled into the drive-in in a '37 Chevy coo-pay. That whole mythology of chrome and full mills and speed-shifting and dual H-wood glasspaks, and how the shift levers impeded the flow of romance way back then, and before long Eichord couldn't stand it. He had to go to the files and look through the old crime reports where the pictures of the cars were.

So in a way Lee had given him his career. It was there on the page with the grainy Kodak shot of the old car. It was a story about a homicide.

The picture of the car hadn't turned him on much but the homicide report caught his eye, and he took it over to the desk and sat there immersing himself in the old crime reports the way a curious detective will.

It was a homicide of "ancient history" even back then. Today it would be over thirty years old. It was 1957 and the main witness looked awfully shaky. The more Eichord read, the deeper he got into it and pretty soon he was on the phone and getting records pulled out of dusty boxes. He started talking to people, dredging up ancient facts and suspicions, and—he thought he had something.

It began with the suspicious crib death of an infant and ended with the death of a husband. But as Jack examined the reports more than a few contradictions loomed. The more he checked, the more the facts began to tear at the old contexture of interwoven lies. Then he found the woman's first marriage, which she'd been so careful to hide from the prying eyes of history and police, and he found the other mysterious infant crib death. The same MO. Suffocation. He saw a portrait of a killer emerge. It was a Buckhead homicide that would take him to the Orient.

He devoted weeks to it. Backtracking. Hiking over long-gone trails. Stirring the dirt where the forgotten ashes had long since been blown away. He found opportunity, and then motive, and then . . . the key. One of the accomplices had spent too freely. He saw what it had been all along. A careful, smartly planned insurance fraud.

She was sixty and living in Hong Kong, the last anyone could determine. He took it by the numbers. The reports. The requests. The channels. The warrants. The long series of confabulations with the Hong Kong cop shop. Extradition conferencing. The considerations of the circuit attorney and the assholes in the State Department. But Eichord wanted her badly, so he hung in there and persevered and pissed and moaned and caused a stink and generally irritated everybody to the point where they'd give him his way just to shut him up. He was going after her.

He would have to take along an interpreter, and a Chinese-American detective by the name of James Lee was right there in-house, and why the hell not? So off they went. In the end he'd solved a case that had been on the books "forever," and the positive ink it pulled for the department had changed his way of life completely, catapulting him into the hot seat when the Dr. Demented shit hit the headlines.

All because of Lee. He'd probably never have nailed

her had it not been for Lee and the man from Kowloon. The incredibly fierce warrior who allowed them to penetrate the bamboo veil of one of the ultra-secret societies called triads—the ninja who would slice off his tongue to prove a point—the fearless, frightening, awesome, and awful man who Eichord always thought of as "the man from Kowloon," but who was Jimmie Lee's older brother.

HUBBARD CITY INTERCHANGE

When his face had finally healed it was nowhere near so disfigured as one might imagine. Bullet wounds can heal to be little more than small puckers as the damage recedes with time. Knife, gunshot, and other wounds will sometimes completely disappear with the years, or leave great, sunken cavities in the flesh. It just depends.

Bunkowski's face was badly marked if one looked at it in profile. Two of the punctures looked like what they were, bullet holes, with the third wound having more of a superficial furrow effect.

But straight on or from other angles the marks were not so unusual or noticeable. Unless one inspected the three wounds they appeared to be almost a series of pockmarks the way they were joined so closely in the plump contours and distended bags of his face—what was once referred to as baby fat. They were like insect bites on an otherwise featureless face.

Additionally his face in repose was quite a different face than the one in animation. At will he could manipulate his rubbery mask to reflect any emotion from beatific, disarming innocence to fearsome menace. If you squinted a bit the bullet wounds became little more than dimples.

By working with a mirror he was soon able to learn how to hold himself so the people he came in contact with would see the face at its least alarming. By holding his mouth in an exaggerated way and causing the fat of the cheek to dimple and pucker he could conceal, to some extent, the ravaged appearance of his cheek.

The motorist pulled over and the grateful hitchhiker ran to catch up with the car.

"Hi," the young man said as he opened the door tentatively.

"Hi," the huge man said in a deep rumble. "Where ya headed?"

The youngster, just a kid really, tilted his head in the direction they were pointing. "North."

"Where you bound for?" the man asked, jovially, as the car pulled back out into the traffic.

"Lincoln." He was shirtless. He tossed a small duffel bag into the back seat. "Nebraska."

"Well, I haven't been up there for years."

"You been to Lincoln?"

"Yeah. I was in sales up there years ago. Good town."

"I guess so," the boy said without conviction, obviously of a different opinion.

"How old are you?"

"Fifteen." The boy smiled. He had a pug nose and a very deep tan. Rather long hair worn in the current fashion.

"Fifteen," the driver said in amazement. "I figured you for seventeen or eighteen easy."

"I'm almost sixteen," the youngster said, as if that explained it.

"Where you hitchin' from?"

"Huh?"

"Where did you start out from?"

"You mean this morning?"

"No"—what an idiot—"you know, when you started out on your trip? Where did you start from?"

"Lincoln," the kid said, as if he'd had this boring conversation three hundred times with motorists who'd picked him up. "I hitched down to Jackson," it sounded like he'd said.

"Jackson, Mississippi?"

"Florida."

"I've never been there. Where's Jackson, Florida?"

"Jacks. You know, Jacksonville."

"Oh, Jacksonville. Sure. That's a fun town, I hear."

"Absolutely," the kid said, shaking his head. "Bitchin' party town." He smiled as if he couldn't take any more party.

"So you sound like you had a good time."

"Had a real good time. I hate to go back."

"I bet. Your folks'll be relieved to see you, though, huh?"

"Don't have any. I live with my sister 'n her, uh, boyfriend. But I gotta go back."

"You in school?"

"Naw. I quit. Couldn't handle it."

"If you don't have to go back to go to school how come you gotta go back?" The big man had unconsciously already picked up the tone and language of the youngster, subtly easing into his speech rhythms.

"I run outta money." They both laughed.

"I hear that all right."

"Yeah. I ain't ate since yesterday."

"Oh, hey," he said jovially, "we can't have that. I'll tell you what—are you in a big hurry?"

"Naw." The boy shrugged his bare shoulders. "Not really," he said, looking at the big man behind the wheel.

"Well, I was just thinking. I gotta look at this piece of real estate for sale over by the river. If you have time you wanna go with me?" The man looked up through the windshield. "Looks like it could open up rain anytime."

"Yeah, it sure does."

"And, you know, if you think you can spare the time, you could ride with me and look at the ground with me and when we get done I'll take you to McDonald's or someplace an' get you some chow, and then I can drop you back on the Interstate."

The kid laughed. "Yeah, okay." It sounded as good as any other way to kill the morning. "I ain't got anything else I got to do I guess."

"Be a good way to stay out of the rain."

"Yeah," the kid agreed.

They rode in silence for a while.

"I'll bet you have some wild times on the road hitch-hiking, am I right?"

"You better believe it. Man, I mean . . ." He trailed off.

"I guess it gets pretty crazy, huh?" The kid looked at him and nodded agreement. "What's the weirdest thing you've had happen so far?" Just making conversation.

"Guys wantin' to blow me."

"Huh?"

"Yeah. Lot of guys wanted to give me, you know, blowjobs."

"No shit." The big man appeared incredulous at the possibility of such a thing.

"Yep."

"How many fags have you run into?"

"Oh, I dunno, I guess about half or maybe three-fourths of the guys that pick you up want to give you a blowjob."

"Jeez, really? I can't believe there are so many fag-gots, eh?"

"Yeah." The kid laughed.

"What do they say to you? I mean, how do they, uh, ask you 'n that?"

"I dunno. They just say . . . oh, different stuff. Some-times they just come out and ask me if they can suck my cock. You know." Like he was talking about the weather.

"How do you handle that?"

"Huh?"

"Well. You know. A young man like you, fifteen—almost sixteen like you say—and a grown-up guy 'n all, but still, by yourself. What do you say to these faggots when they want to suck you or whatever?"

"I"—he shrugged with his face and arms and shoulders all at once—"uh, just let 'em blow me, I guess." A little pause. "I mean it's THEIR MOUTH, ya' know?"

"Yeah. Right." Their mouth. What a punk.

"But that's it."

"Mmmm?" Eyes on the Interstate, waiting for the exit road.

"Nothing else. I mean I'll let 'em give me a blowjob but that's it. Nothin' else, ya know."

"Right." And then Daniel blinked and looked over at the boy and asked "What else do they try to do?"

"Some of 'em'll try to fuck me in the butt if I'll let 'em but I don't go for that shit. No fuckin' way." He shook his head. The driver said nothing. "For one thing I don't go that way, 'n another thing, you know, you got to be careful now."

"Izzat right?"

"Oh, yeah, that AIDS 'n shit, man."

"Oh, yes." His mind had drifted elsewhere as he was watching for that road.

"This one kid I know in Lincoln, he's eighteen. He was getting guys to take him to the fuck movies, ya know, 'n he'd let 'em suck him off and butt-fuck him 'n that, an' like—onna weekend he'd make like three or four hundred bucks easy."

"Really?"

"Yeah, an' this one guy they found out, this guy was stickin' him in the asshole alla time, he's got AIDS, man!" The kid laughed. It was funny to him to think about it.

"What's the wildest thing you've let a guy do to you?"

"The WILDEST thing?"

"Yeah," he said with a dimpled smile. "Just curious, ya know?"

"This one guy"—the kid started to laugh but he changed his mind and said seriously—"he jus' wanted to stick his tongue in my ass."

"Jeezus."

"Yeah. Crazy son of a bitch. You know, I go, Well, it's your tongue, man."

"You let 'm?"

"Yeah." Shrugging again. "I let him eat my asshole out, what the fuck do I care, man? If he wants to stick his tongue up my ass that's cool."

"What did it feel like?"

"Nothin'. You can't hardly feel nothin'. Just a tongue in your ass. That's about it."

"Wow. That's pretty freaky."

"Back home I'll make a couple hundred in two days just letting these three guys suck me off all weekend."

"Two hundred bucks?" As if he were interested.

"Really. These same three dudes jus' wanta suck my cock over and over. An' they'll be beatin' off or whatever, and I just let 'em suck me and then another one'll start. And I don't have to do nothin'. I'll just mellow out, you know, an' smoke or whatever, and just kick back.

And these three guys'll blow me over and over all weekend long. And they . . ."

Chaingang tuned out on the boring story of the kid's sex life as he planned what he would do next. He was pulling over onto a service road that ran parallel to the busy traffic.

"You a real-estate salesman?" the boy asked, snapping him out of his reverie.

"Right. Yeah. I'm a developer."

"We gonna go look at a development?" the kid asked, not even knowing what he was talking about. He was hungry.

"Yeah. Well, no, not exactly. A land site. I'm considering developing the property." There was a gravel road and he eased the car off the service route. A pickup zoomed by him, the driver in a hat with an ad on the front, and Chaingang saw the man lift a finger from the wheel in the universal rural motorist's greeting. Chaingang automatically smiled and lifted one of the fingers of his left hand from the wheel. There would not be much traffic along a road like this.

He drove about three miles along the gravel, the kid talking about blowjobs or whatever as Chaingang took the winding curves slowly. Cottonwoods and towering hackberries and maple, choked with weeds of every description, hung out over the road ditches that flanked the twisting gravel road, and you couldn't see opposing traffic until it rounded the curves and was right on top of you.

After three miles or so he came to a county blacktop and he drove slowly across it and up a mud road set into the face of a steep levee. It felt like he was standing the car straight up for a minute and the kid said, "We're out in the boonies."

No shit, the man thought. Brilliant, punk. But he grunted noncommittally.

"Yep," Chaingang finally said after they had eased down through the dark barrow pit, pronounced "barr pitt" by the people who lived there. "But this is potentially good property. You can still buy it right." He mumbled some nonsense about land.

They drove slowly through a field that appeared to be

maybe eighty acres or so planted in beans. And Chaingang stopped in a small access path that ran adjacent to a tractor turn row. He got out and the springs of the car groaned in relief. For the first time the boy got some idea of the bigness of the driver of the car.

"Let's go over and look over there. That's the part that I'm considering buying." He intuitively knew that the kid had just felt a quick stab of uncertainty when Chaingang had gotten out of the car, and smoothing those feelings over now as he talked reassuringly of land and profits and business deals, popping the trunk and taking a blanket and some other things with him, and they began walking.

"All right," the kid said as they walked through a crowded stand of willows and they saw the river for the first time.

"Man, it's hot," Chaingang said to the kid as he pulled his huge shirt off.

"Right," said the kid as he shook his head in agreement. Chaingang threw the old army blanket down on the bank under the willows. "We gonna stay here awhile?" the kid asked somewhat rhetorically as the huge man lowered his bulk onto the blanket and patted it for the kid to sit.

"Might as well be comfortable, right?"

The kid was relaxed now that he knew what the score was. He'd been down this road before. Big dude was all right. He'd get a ride and a blowjob and a big meal out of it, just like always. He sat very close to the big man.

"Man it's hot, ain't it?" the huge man said as he laid a gentle paw on the kid's Levi'd leg beside him. The boy seemed to move imperceptibly closer as he whispered, "Yeah. Really hot," very softly.

"Slide outta those jeans. Let's see what all those fags have been sucking on," Chaingang said to him, and the boy shrugged slightly and obediently began unbuttoning the fly of the bleached and faded Levi's. He wore cotton shorts and the big man said, "Take those off too." As the boy was complying he felt something encircle one wrist and then another and his hands were suddenly behind him and there was a click as the steel bit into his wrists and it all happened as fast as he realized it had occurred,

all in a quick, smooth, metallic SNNNIIIKKKKK that
pinned his hands together behind him first one and then
the other and he went, "Hey!" Still not scared just surprised, and the big man leaned over right by the boy's
ear and whispered, "Now no big deal. Don't worry. I just
get off this way, dig? I like to have a guy—you know,
vulnerable." Big smile. "For MY protection. I mean I
could be doing something and you hit me in the head and
take my car. I don't know you from Adam." And then
he was putting his weight on the boy and doing something to one of the legs and more steel no this time a kind
of nylon rope was being snugged up around his knee,
then again at his right ankle and the big man getting up
with a great effort and waddling over PULLING THE
BOY BY THE ROPE as he walked, pulling him effortlessly, the boy protesting but even as he did so feeling his
leg pinned up against the trunk of a willow. The kid
feeling the first fear now for real. Leg right by the tree,
and the man pulling out a huge knife.

"Hey, now, mister, please—"

"Oh, no sweat, babe. Really. I'm just cutting rope
here." And Chaingang bent over with a smile still plastered to his scarred face and sliced the rope near where
he'd made it fast and brought the cut end over and
started to tie it around the other ankle and the boy was
going to kick the hand away but Chaingang had the ankle
before he could make a move and then he ran the other
end over to another tree, not tying it as tightly.

"There," Chaingang said, repositioning the blanket and
dropping beside the kid's body with a groan. "That's
better, eh?" The kid was now nude, on his face in the hot
sandy dirt, hands handcuffed behind him, legs spread.
Nobody within howitzer distance. A passing barge maybe.

"OH," the kid cried out.

Chaingang had eased the handle of the knife into the
boy's rectum. Just playing.

"Sorry, I didn't mean to frighten you." Very tender.
And with that Chaingang took his own pants off and
entered the boy from the rear. In that position the kid
looked just like a girl from the back, he thought, and he
began doing it to the boy, who only grunted under the
enormous pressure.

"You like it, don't you?" he said to the boy.

"Yeah," the kid said unconvincingly just as Chaingang quickly orgasmed. The kid saw a blur of movement and Chaingang was off him and up and moving away from him. The kid wondered if the crazy man were going to leave him trussed up like this. Damn. He had to get loose somehow.

"Yes," Chaingang said with an immense, dimpled grin spreading across his doughlike face. He pulled a well-worn .22 Colt Woodsman, blued metal with checkered wooden grips, from the kid's belongings. He would bury everything else. "Yes," he repeated, "I think we'll just hang on to this." He looked at the kid on the ground. "As a souvenir." And he racked a long rifle round into the chamber and tried it for balance.

It felt good and he aimed to the left of the kid's head about an inch but he missed, shooting the boy in the back of the left ear. There was screaming and lots of blood, and he barked out a laughing cough and muttered, "Calm down. I'll get the hang of this with a little practice." And he shot the boy again, this time on purpose. "See? No problem." He squeezed the trigger again. The trigger pull was crisp but it was okay. He could live with it.

HONG KONG (1977)

"They know where she is," Eichord said to the smaller man beside him at the rail of the ferry.

"Yeah." Jimmie Lee nodded. "I 'magine so. You have to understand the way these people think. This ain't Chinatown, Jack. This is a"—he searched for the right word—"whole world with a set of laws and rules and traditions you can't begin to realize."

"Try me."

"You're not just an outsider here, coming in to investigate a murder in Chinatown. With all the aura that goes with any policeman in the States. All the force and backing and cultural influences. But here"—he shook his head at the hopelessness of it—"they see you as nothing. Or me. Any cop from the Occidental world. Our ways have no meaning to these people, so our laws don't either."

"Yeah, well, there's law and then there's right and wrong. This woman is a killer—and she's murdered again and again."

"Thing is, Jack, it's a society that takes care of its own. And she is"—again Eichord felt him trying for a way to put the disparate values into currency a Westerner could spend—"connected to something that is bigger than anything you've ever come up against. No puny Mafia or organized religion or even philosophy can touch this thing the Chan woman was. She is"—and he said a Chinese name—"which means Shadow Clan. But that is not what it means at all."

164

"Yeah?"

"You don't give a shit, right?"

"Right. I don't shiv a git. I ain't goin' back without her."

"Right."

"Not after coming this far. Not after having my chain yanked by those asshole lawyers. Not after fightin' 'em even to ARREST much less fucking go after a twenty-year-old prosecution. And then get all THAT rammed through and then track her this far and then lose her murderous old butt because she's, uh—"

"Shadow Clan," he supplied in a quiet voice.

"Frankly, Scarlett, I don't care if the bitch is Knights of Columbus. We're going to take her down."

Jimmie Lee stood looking down at the water beneath them. "You just don't understand. To you everything is cut and dried. Right and wrong."

"Yep. In this case that's what it is."

"Law and order. Rules and regs. Bad guys and good guys. Black hats and white hats."

"I know if a woman is killing little kids and a husband she deserves to fall no matter how connected she is."

"By rights . . ." He paused. "By rights I shouldn't have pursued this once I found out she was in the thing." He looked at Eichord. "That's what makes it all so impossible for an outsider. Even ME, as Western as I am, as far removed from this culture as you can get, James Lee, the all-American chink, *I'm* connected to her. If you want to look at this thing theoretically."

"How so?"

"Literally, in that my father was her brother. My brother too."

"Huh?" Eichord was shaking his head.

"All the clans are interconnected. By the secret societies—the triads they call 'em now. The brotherhood."

"The triads are CRIME societies. Your family isn't part of that." Lee said nothing. "Right?"

"The triads back home are one thing. The triads here go back thousands of years. Before they were the triads the brotherhood was a sort of caste system of warriors. My father was a descendant of that. My older brother chose to emulate that life-style. I was never a part of that. I wasn't raised here, as you know. I never even knew my father, and my family now regard me an outsider—a stranger. I'm not part of their world." He tried to explain about what his father had been, about the codes and systems that had been a part of the old ways.

"Are you telling me your father was a warrior like a ninja—if I'm saying the word right?"

"No. But you're on the right track. The ninja were like our early mercenaries," he began, "but there is a vast difference between the Japanese and Chinese cultures." He told Eichord about the codes and castes of feudal Japan, and their concept of Shugendo. How men of honor formed an elite, professional warrior class. Fearless, militaristic, practicing old martial arts and sciences of violence, purity, and austerity. Building lives on a dying caste system. He told him about the code of Bushido. The way of the warrior. The ninjitsu. The ancient ways. He compared the Shadow Clan to the feudal Kunoichi, with their secret death vows. He linked that world to the children of the samurai who still practice the ways of the warrior class in Japan. And to the Japanese Yakuza.

"We have the brotherhood in China. What you've learned about the triads, the crime societies in America, and here"—he pointed—"is only the cutting edge of an ancient system." He tried to explain to Jack how all the things he had told him about were Johnny-come-lately descendants of what had evolved from China centuries before. "What you know about the Bamboo Gang, or the Dragons or whatever—the Hui Dao Meng—these are only one element within a brotherhood that embraces every imaginable religious belief, cultural aspect and code. Some are bad. Some are good. But they are interlocked by history and"—he searched for some way to say it—"attitude, you know?"

"And your brother is part of this?"

"Yes."

"Can your brother find her for us?"

"Of course." Lee said. "If he will."

"Then let's give it a shot."

"That's what we're doing. He'll talk to me. But he is very orthodox in his beliefs. I think I know what he will say." Lee stared ahead as they approached the Kowloon peninsula.

When the ferry reached the other side, Lee's brother met them. There was a cold exchange of greetings. They did not embrace. The entire conversation was in Chinese and it became very heated. The whole time he was in his presence Lee's brother never acknowledged that Eichord was there except when Jimmie had first introduced them and Jack heard his name; the brother glanced at him and perhaps gave a slight nod of his head. To Eichord, who would never forget this man, he would never be Lee's brother. He would think of him only as The Man in Kowloon.

Lee and Eichord left, eventually, with the woman's whereabouts. Lee had, he said, blackmailed his brother. "I told him about the crib deaths. That by sheltering her they were protecting the worst kind of human filth—a child killer. That's what did it. He says anything there was between us is gone. We are no longer brothers. I've forced him to compromise his honor. And so forth."

"I'm sorry, man." But he wasn't at all. Not yet. That would come later.

"Well"—he said, tilting his head—"if that's the way he wants it, that's all right. He never really thought of me as a brother anyway. I was the American cop to him." Lee looked at Eichord. He wants us to come before the brotherhood as payment for obtaining the information. I'll have to go. You don't."

"What do you mean, come before the brotherhood?"

"He wants us to see what giving this information has cost him. He's going to . . ." And Lee started to choke up.

Eichord didn't understand what the hell was going on but tried to console his friend. "I don't understand. What do you mean, Jimmie? What HAS it cost him? Why does the brotherhood have to find out?"

"They know." He wiped at his eyes in anger as much as sadness. "They already know. He told them what I wanted. He said," he tried to say something but started crying again. He stopped himself, "He wanted me to learn the cost of my actions by coming to him for this information. He wanted me to know what price he would pay."

"What do you mean?"

"He is going to vow his silence tonight."

"Yeah?"

"The crazy son of a bitch," Jimmie said, his eyes filling with tears, "he's going to cut off his own tongue." Some kind of a joke.

"Come on, man." Eichord wanted to laugh in his face.

"No. He could not live with himself if he didn't. It is his way of preserving his honor. He'll do it."

Eichord could say nothing. He simply stared at Lee in disbelief while the man told him about the implacable, ritualistic, unswerving code by which his brother lived. His self-discipline, dedication, loyalty to the clan.

"He has no choice. It's either that or suicide."

"But shit, man, that's nuts."

"Not to him. Self-mutilation is part of the Shadow Clan culture. It is quite common in secret societies like you'll find throughout Asia and Europe. Even in America you have the penitents."

"Nobody cuts their tongue off, pard."

"You've just led a sheltered life, buddy. In the old country," he said, gesturing vaguely, "they used to cut their fucking BALLS off."

"Eh?"

"Didn't you ever hear of the castrati? The castrators? The Skoptsi of old Russia? Shit, Jack, they believed if you wanted to worship you had to bear the Seal of God. The lesser seal was when you took a knife or razor and sliced your testicles open and ate your goddamn nuts."

"JESUS."

"The greater seal was when you reached down there and took the ole pole itself." He wiped at his face. "Now *that* took some balls," he said, without humor.

"None of this is happening."

"It's happening, all right. Welcome to fucking China, baby."

Eichord and Lee found the woman and made the arrest easily. She was just an old woman. She didn't look like a murderer. So often they don't. The thing he'd always remember about her was when she was interrogated. She admitted the husband had been greased for the insurance money: $75,000 was a fortune back in 1957. But why the baby girl and then, in the later marriage, her own baby boy? She told Eichord, through Lee in part, that she'd grown tired of trying to find baby-sitters. It made as much sense as anything else about the case.

That night, with Mrs. Chan safely under lock and key, Jack Eichord went with James Lee. It was one of the rare occasions when outsiders would be permitted to witness such a ritual. It was admission by invitation only. It was a scene that Eichord would dream about a hundred bloody times, no matter how hard he tried not to. His dream of the Man in Kowloon.

CENTERBURG

Jenny Weiss had come out of one disaster of a marriage and wasn't about to leap into another just to bed down with Marc Thompson, cute though he was. She had little Jerry for one thing, a wild and precious two-year-old from the train wreck of a liaison that had swelled her belly with child and left her penniless and bruised and alone in Dayton, Ohio. When the grand and glorious and spectacular Mooney Kyle Shows came through for a week, compliments of the Dayton Jaycees, and Jenny had wandered down with Jerry to take in the sights, she'd seen Marc and Marc had seen her and the idea of a kid was no problem to this fast-stepper and first thing you know she was Cincy-bound in the passenger seat of the aging Thompson pickup, a decrepit house trailer locked to the tow hitch.

She'd taken to the carny life at first. The family-under-siege mentality had appealed to her and for the first year Marc hadn't let her come up for air to see the one-nighters and fortnighters of shows and carnivals that were their on-the-road life-style. Marc was a ride supervisor, and he'd gotten Jenny work with a variety of flat joints, including an alibi joint that she'd taken to pretty good and she'd worked alibis from then on. But she was starting to get the itch to settle down. Enough is enough. She was going to have to give Jerry more than this constant moving.

Jenny was twenty-three, with good legs, a great butt, a nice face wreathed in long, auburn hair, a sexy smile spoiled only by a cheapo cap job that dated back to her years in foster homes, and nice, high breasts, still firm after little Jerry. Nice little hooters that made the town creeps and marks drool and come back to drop more coins at the alibi. She didn't know what a bra was, and with her hair combed, some makeup, and a tight yellow sweater she could still make some heads turn and put a rise in some Levi's.

She saw the man in the car saying something to her but she ignored it. Townies were always yelling some shit—she didn't even listen. She was going to feed their dog and then . . . Well, for Christ's sake.

"Huh?" She couldn't understand what the guy was yelling.

". . . dering if you were with the show." Something or other, the word "show" triggering a familiar note. She wandered over to hear what he's saying.

"What?" A big fat guy was sitting in the car, sun-burned, smiling a friendly smile.

"Sorry. I was wanting to know if you were with the Mooney Kyle Shows."

"Yeah," she admitted. Not thinking that it would be obvious to anybody passing the rides to see all the cheap trailers parked beside one another in back of the rides. Those would be the spouses of the show employees back there.

"Your last name is what?"

"Thompson," she lied, warily.

"Doesn't your husband work over there?" He gestured toward the midway area. He must know Marc.

"Yeah."

"His name is—what?"

"Marc."

"Sure!" His face lit up, "Marc Thompson. I know him. Helluva dude."

"Really?"

"Me 'n him use to work together."

"You're kidding. When?"

"Here's a photograph of Marc—I got it here some-where when we were, uh—" She leans forward to see what he's got and sees him pointing the pistol and her heart almost jumps up in her throat, "HEY!"

"Listen to me. I won't hurt you if you do exactly what I say, but that sucker you're married to owes me money and if you don't do what I tell you right now, I'll put a hole in your head and you'll be dead in this fucking street."

"Hey, comon now—"

"Shut up," he rumbles, keeping the barrel pointed at her and reaching under with his other arm and opening the door. "Get in here a minute—I want to ask you some questions."

"Huh uh, I ain't—" She's shaking her head and he raises the barrel up on the back of the seat where anybody can see the pistol.

"I SAID GET IN THIS CAR OR I'LL *SHOOT* YOU I SWEAR TO YOU."

"Okay, okay, be fuckin' careful with that thing," she says, and slides in and there's people all over the place why aren't they helping me? She's right on the edge of screaming for help, so he lets her have one above the left ear. Not anything serious. Just a good firm slap with the long barrel of the pistol and she goes, "Owwwwwww!" Her head seems to drop to her knees and he rather gently pushes her to the floorboard as he gives the gas pedal a tap and they pull away from the spectacular Mooney Kyle Shows employee parking area. Soon they are where nobody could hear her. Her hand was just about broken as he pulled it back, cuffing it ferociously, all but dislocating her arm as he jerked her to a nearby tree.

"You shit-ass son of a bitch," she cries.

"Get over her and suck this," he demands halfheartedly unzipping his fly. But he was thinking about where he'd bury her.

"Fuck you, you fat slob."

"Suck it or die. Which will it be? You have three seconds and please no help from the audience." He is just going through the motions and she is too angry to be afraid.

"Suck it yourself, fatso," she tells him, straining at the cuff.

"Right," he says calmly, pulling out the big fighting bowie and smiling his biggest smile. "You're going to be nice and tasty, I can tell that right now." And he slashes her open across the front as she screams.

There is a second before he goes into the chest for her heart while she is still aware and in that beat she has time to think of her little Jerry and that she never got to settle down and she'd just learned to run the alibi and wasn't it a shame to die so young, and unfair and, shit, all of that in the one heartbeat or so, proving that sometimes your life does in fact flash before your eyes at the moment of death.

BUCKHEAD SPRINGS

Jack Eichord dreams. He dreams of the icy depths of Sugar Lake. He is clad in rubber, a tight suit of black neoprene, and he spits into a visor, puts the mask on, and dives. There is nothing to see as he swims along through his own bubbles, circling the muddy bottom of the lake, swimming through the frigid underwater shadows. Diving down in the cold lake where the childhood bullies of his nightmares, Whortley Williams and Cabrey Brown, once held him under until he almost drowned. He forces himself to go down in the lake and relive it again.

But all he can see is a picture of his friend James Lee, telling him about how he took the money at Buckhead Mercantile, making Jack an accessory. And Eichord knows that Jimmie has forgotten something very important. He has forgotten the code of the street: you don't do the crime if you can't do the time.

He swims into the Kowloon dream. Swimming into clarity he first sees the crown colony of Hong Kong at the mouth of the Pearl River. He sees it as a teeming squall of life fighting for survival, then for economic superiority in the industrial renaissance—a tide of monkey humanity slowly melting in the cultural caldron. The edges of the races blurring with each new generation, the culture changing, amplifying as it resonates into the fuzzy space expander of high tech.

But he sees it as a colony of chittering monkeys, yuppies, new-wave pirates, all in a mad race up the steep, sloping

174

sides of a giant rice bowl. The Man in Kowloon does not belong to his world. He is an anachronism. He does not belong to this chittering, squalling, teeming time and place. He belongs in another century, alone and aloof in some mountain retreat, far from the crowd and the market-place. He does not belong to a world where a woman will roll over onto a crying child to crush it and suffocate it because she has grown tired of finding baby-sitters to watch her babies while she goes out to take a lover. They are not of the same species.

The night is fire that always burns Eichord's eyes. The color is that of brilliant gemstones or broken glass. The smell is mass, fish, fear, electricity, mob smell. The sound is screaming, chanting, car-horn tympany. Cymbal crash. Oriental singsong lute mandarin samisen songbird fugue for panflute.

Then he is in the chamber with the drunken, chanting men. Lee's brother scowls fiercely into the face of his ancestors and picks up a short, gleaming sword. The flames from the torches flicker on the walls like dancing demons, ritual remnants of the antecedents who gave the clan its name. Light sparkles from the blade like sunlight on a golden Buddha. He takes his fingers and shapes them into a claw and oh God no don't let me dream this again don't let me see him pull his tongue out like that oh Jesus Christ oh please oh God don't let me see him start that sawing make that first sawing cut across that tongue that will prove so impossibly impossible to cut to sever to oh God don't make me see that first ridge of blood as he slices across his own AHHHHHHHHHHHHHHHHHHHHH!

DARNELL'S FIELD

Each month, like clockwork, Daniel would wait until Michael Hora was outside and alone and he would walk up to him and hold out the money. A thousand dollars. This would usually constitute their conversation for the month. There was no contact whatsoever. The few times that Hora spoke to Bunkowski he discouraged any conversation. Chaingang became more and more paranoid as he stayed in one spot for such a long time. The thought had occurred to him that Hora, while probably on the run himself—if only from the U.S. military—might consider a few probes to see if there were any serious money on his head. On the other hand, Hora had established a counterculture reputation of sorts for his "farm." It had become known as a place where runaways, wanted men, mercs, and similar rogue elephants might seek temporary shelter from the eyes of the law and government.

But time had a way of eating at security. The greatest hideout in the world was vulnerable to bad luck. And there was Chaingang's natural disinclination to have someone know his whereabouts. Another factor was the regularity of the payments. At what point would Hora decide a thousand a month wasn't up to the spiraling cost of living, and his old pal would have to sweeten the pot? Because he had the precognate's mind he anticipated such events, and they filled him with unrest, while stirring his natural desire to waste Hora. It was just a matter of time.

Sissy was well along in her pregnancy, and rather than become enraged by it and stomp both her and the fetus out with a monstrous bootprint, he was pleased by it. When he was ready he would go for the cop Eichord and inflict a payback on him beyond anything he'd be able to conceive in his most torturous nightmare, and what better cover than a pregnant wife or—better yet—a wife and a baby. It dimpled Daniel's pockmarked, doughy face in an immense grin—just the thought of his blade of vengeance slashing out at Jack. He would come with something quite delicious. Perhaps render the cop into a living stump, keeping him alive, one of those freaks you see in New York scurrying around on a skateboard. Or one of those pathetic creatures you find begging for handouts in places like Thailand and India. He'd love that. He'd turn Eichord into a freak and give him a tin cup and some pencils.

It was payday for his landlord again, and Hora saw the man lumbering over in his direction. The protuberance of his belly was nowhere near so obtrusive as it had been only a few weeks ago. Hora was amazed by the amount of work Chaingang, whom Hora secretly called Gangbang, had turned out. How he had leveled that eighty-acre piece of overgrown pastureland with a weed slinger was beyond anything imaginable to him.

"Hey," he called out.

"Yeah." Chaingang grunted and handed him ten filthy one-hundred dollar bills. Hora, none too fastidious himself, always had the urge to wash his hands whenever he'd had to touch something Chaingang had touched.

"Listen. Uh, you know that ole barn over 'tween my ground and the Darnells' field?" Chaingang said nothing. "It's up to you. But if you're lookin' for somethin' to do you can wreck it. Just as soon see it down, but I want the cypress logs and them shaker shingles. Okay?" The big man nodded. He took a double-bit ax and started off toward the field.

"You ain't gon' to be able to chop her down. Need to get some crowbars and a sledgehammer 'n a—" but Chaingang just kept waddling off so Michael Hora shrugged and muttered, "Fuck it then," and went about his business.

The Bunkowski wrecking company had its own way of tearing down a barn. He went into the woods and felled a thirty-five-foot ash with the ax, chopping as fast as he could, moving around the base of the tree with little precise shuffle steps as he swung the sharp ax, watching the blade *thwock* down into the hard wood. After a few minutes he'd broken through to the center and he smacked it once more and stepped out from under the big falling tree.

He then chopped all the lower limbs off flush with the trunk and started working on chopping through the tree at about twenty-two or twenty-three feet from the base. Finally he had himself a 22 ½-foot pole of stout ash, and he was in the wrecking business.

Hora and the slow wife and Sissy, each on a different part of the farm, could all hear Chaingang working. He was popping boards and shingles and ceiling timbers off the old barn. They'd hear a loud hammering noise and then a kind of fast-fire effect as the smashing sounds echoed from the Darnell place across the flat pasture. *WHAP!* as a timber broke loose. *POW! POW! POW! POW! POW! POW! POW! POW! POW!* Shingles flying from the roof of the barn and into the nearby field. Chaingang standing dead center in the middle of the filthy barn, a bandanna over his face and safety glasses over his eyes, standing in a rain of ancient sawdust, nails, dead bugs, rat shit, God knows what, as he pounded timbers and shingles out into space with a 22 ½-foot ash battering ram, gripping it in a death grip with those extra-large leather work gloves and thinking about how pleasant it would be to tie the cop to a tree somewhere and work on him with the big pole. Breaking kneecaps and crushing the rib cage and the groin and pelvis and thinking these thoughts as nearly four hundred pounds of hell on the hoof smashed its weight up against the roof and timbers blasted loose and shaker shingles flew crazily into the cloudless sky *WHAP! POW!POW!POW!POW! POW!POW!POW!POW!POW!* Smashing the pole into the man who had sought him out the way you'll seek out a human target in a firefight and dog the man and try to kill him. *WHAP!* Smashing those knees and pulverizing that arrogant face into scarlet pulp *POW! POW! POW!*

hands that could squeeze a flashlight battery or rip a rib cage loose were ramming that big tree trunk up at the thought of this cop he'd come to hate.

Because of the unusual sound-carrying acoustical properties of the land they all heard it easily three hundred yards away. It sounded like somebody was blasting apart the barn with a machine gun. And by sundown there was no barn at all. Just piles of rotting debris.

BUCKHEAD SPRINGS

Donna and Jack Eichord and Tuffy were playing on the living-room floor of their house. That is, Donna and Jack were laughing; Tuffy was doing the playing. He had a little crumpled ball of paper that was his favorite toy of the moment.

"A month ago," Eichord said when he got control again, "somebody says, You're gonna be buying cat toys, I woulda found it a little hard to swallow." He'd just gone into a store and purchased a fake mouse.

"I know. But the little guy is so much fun to watch. What a mess," as if Tuffy had heard her he attacked the paper with renewed ferocity, and as it skittered away across the rug, he went with it, end over end in a mad scramble. "Look at him!"

"Tuffy, you're gonna kill yourself."

"If you live that long."

"That's why I named him that. When I saw him playing in that cardboard box Shari brought down to work, he was running at the walls like a kamikaze pilot. He looked like a daredevil cat to me."

"I hate that word."

"Cat?"

"I hate words like 'daredevil.' I don't even like the guy's name—Mr. Kuh-neeval. The first name. I don't like that word."

"Yeah?"

"I don't like spooky words. Tuffy doesn't like 'em either. However, we DO like the word 'spooky.' "

180

"Good name for a little black cat." Eichord looked the way he did when he was only there with the surface of his mind. "I know what you mean, though, about words. I have some words I don't like to hear either." His face grew serious. "A few proper nouns I'd just as soon never hear again." He had that look in his eyes she'd learned to recognize in Dallas, and she smiled and quickly changed the subject.

"Hey."

"Yeah?"

"Sex aside," she said, snuggling close as Tuffy watched them, his tiny pink tongue hanging out after all the rambunctious activity, "I want to know which of your official birthday goodies you liked the best. Tell me."

"Sex aside, you say?" he said, snuggling next to her. "Well, that's number one shot down. I guess my favorite was the quick game of catch. I thought you were dynamite in that shirt and cap. Cute stuff."

"You liked ole Dad, did you?"

"Posilutely."

"You liked burnin' 'em in to old Dad?"

"A regular Bob Feller."

"Who's Bob Feller?"

"Who is BOB FELLER? You jest, surely." She shook her head no. "Even a youngster like you shoulda heard of Bob Feller. Hmmm. Well. Bob Feller. He was a pitcher. They used to say Feller only had three pitches, a fast ball, a burner, and a high hard one."

"That's all any man needs."

"Yeah?"

"Sure. You guys can do just fine as long as you got a couple of balls and a hard one." She said it very seriously.

"Uh huh."

"Be right back," she said, getting up off the floor. "Don't you two go away."

"We won't," he promised.

"I'll be right back," she repeated as she bounced off down the hall. A few moments later she reappeared. The sweatshirt and jeans were gone. She had on his shirt again, and the Mets cap.

"Hello there," he said, checking her out. "That was a quick costume change."

"Like you always say, I aims to please."

"Uh."

She was bare legged and wore no shoes. And the shirt was open in front and he could see the beautiful swells of those proud twin globes. She pulled the shirt apart a little farther and said, "You wanna come inside and play?"

"Right," he said hoarsely. He got up and followed her down the hall toward the bedroom to inspect her fast-breaking curves.

Tuffy was busily batting his crumpled ball of paper all over the living room, his little fur ball of a body flying at top speed until he chased left when he should have chased right and ran right smack dab into a wall. The little kitten got back up, dazed, shook it off, and looked around.

Where the heck did everybody go?

When Jack snuggled against her something was changed. She could tell immediately, even as he was touching her, that her husband was just going through the motions, and to Donna Eichord it was a confusing irritation. This time she couldn't hold her tongue and said, "I can tell I'm driving you insane with desire," in a tone that made him draw back from her and he smiled a little and kept touching her but he didn't try to fake a response.

"It isn't you, love."

"That's good news," she said.

"Come on," he said very softly, feeling her draw away from his touch. "You know better."

"I thought I did, but . . ." She knew how she must sound. She let it trail off into space.

"Really," Jack said, sighing, "it's work. You know. Sometimes it just doesn't shake off at the front door."

"That's okay. But you know, before, we've always talked about it if something is bothering one of us."

"I know."

"I'm starting to wonder if I'm doing something wrong."

"Hey. Don't be silly."

"I don't think it's being silly. Obviously something is out of kilter all of a sudden," she said.

"Nothing about us. I just have a lot on my mind."

"It hasn't been a problem before." (Let UP for crissakes—what is *your* problem?)

"I love ya a lot, you know that." He touched her

lightly on the tip of her nose. "I'm just having an off week."

"Okay." She smiled. "If you feel like talking about it . . ." Jeez, kid, she thought to herself, why can't you shut your trap? But she couldn't. It was too important not to let anything ever wedge itself between them. "You know I'm here to listen. Whatever it is."

"Some things are just better left unsaid." He sat up against the headboard. "If you really want to hear about it I don't mind telling you about it. It's no mysterious thing. You really want me to tell you the details?" He could no more stop himself now than she could.

"It might make YOU, you know"—long pause—"feel better to have, uh, to be able to talk about it. I don't mind." Her voice very quiet.

"A multiple homicide and robbery in a Chicago butcher shop. It was something got called to my attention. Just one of those awful killings where the sickness of the perpetrators keeps screaming at you. So we make bad jokes. We do this and that. Usually we can let it all drop at the front door. This one's just been harder to shake. Somebody butchered the butchers, you might say. Cut their throats in a very cold-blooded way the same way you might slaughter something for food." She seemed to shrivel as he told her about it. And the more Donna recoiled from it, the more it irritated him that she'd goaded him into telling her about it. And the more he told her of the gory details, the more he felt like he did when he was trying to gross out some woman reporter in the squad room, or some TV schmuck at a crime scene. And when he'd finished she was still irritated, and he was irritated, and nobody was feeling very loved, and something awful and sick and horrible had inserted itself into the intimacy of their warm marriage bed.

"It has NOTHING to do with us," he said, knowing even then that what he'd just said couldn't be further from the truth.

STOBAUGH

Daniel had a trot line in back of the Darnell's Field, and adjacent to a place known locally as Gum, which led to the New Cairo Ditch. But he'd never walked that far, nor had he ever wanted to go through all the tall weeds, swamp, quickmud, poison ivy, and thickly overgrown areas between Michael Hora's ground and the New Cairo. There was also a shallow ditch that ran down through Gum parallel to the Sandy Road, running past Darnell's, Hora's, Thurman's, and the Lingo Field to the extreme eastern edge of the land on this side of the river, the point of the fishhook. The top left of the hook as one saw it on a map would be the New Cairo, a deep and swift-moving ditch that curved back around the farmland feeding into the river. There was good fishing in the New Cairo, and Daniel had driven all the way to Texas Corners and put a line in there, which he ran when he thought about it.

He had decided he was going to try to walk the whole distance, a long, boring, tough, solitary march to wear himself down. Just one more variation on his daily theme—to tire himself to the point where he could ignore his hungry, screaming belly, which was shrinking just as his companion's seemed to grow more prominent by the day.

So it was a new experience as he cut down through the swampy Dutch Barrow, plowing through the high, wet grass, moving up a little weed-covered hill full of cottonwoods and willows, down over the ditch bank, and in that eyeball click he was back in Vietnam.

The McDermotts had 160 acres of rice and this is what he saw as he came through the overgrown ditch bank foliage, stepping out into a rice field that lay across his field of vision all the way to the far tree line. Chaingang had gone over the bank and between a pair of cottonwoods and a willow and some horseweed, but he came out in high elephant grass between two palms in the Rung Sat Special Zone, in another time, another lifetime.

To the mind of this insane killer and precognitive genius and childlike retard and atavistic two-legged mastodon—a strong emotion or a quick psychic jolt will not be the same as it will be for you or me. This bestial man draws on a lifetime of cruelties; tortures and deprivations beyond the line of normal human tolerance.

To us a surprise or shock or consternation will register in a different way. We forget our coffee, which has been sitting there for a quarter-hour and we lift the cup to our lips, preoccupied, busy with something else, and the unexpected coldness is a minor, unpleasant moment. Nothing more. An insignificant annoyance. But to this man, a sound—the metal-cleated footfalls on certain surfaces—or the smell—a feces-clogged tenement toilet—or the sight—a tattooed arm reaching out in a certain way: these are the nuances that can trigger fast, steel-muscled, relentless, deadly responses that strike out to silence the nearest human heartbeat.

And Daniel Bunkowski steps between the rustling cottonwoods and the high weeds and Chaingang emerges into the heat and fearsome dangers of the Rung Sat, and it is the 1960s and the big man is there for only one reason—to KILL—and it is open season on humanity. And he sees no one but he SENSES . . . SMELLS THEM . . . the little people, and he moves cautiously, moving backward, stepping exactly where he has just stepped before, moving back between the palms disappearing back into the high elephant grass and saw grass, into the myriad, mysterious, many shades of Vietnam green and melting back into the shadows to wait and plan his ambush.

This is Charlie's. Everything is his. Jungle. Delta. Mountain range of straw-carpeted, deep caves. Tiny spider holes that dot the land like cancer. Massive, intricate tunnel complexes. And a mined, bobby-trapped, pungi-

sticked paddy running between here and the blue feature. And Chaingang lies chilly in the tall grass. Frozen.
Waiting for the cover of night when he will be ready to
run the game back on Victor Charles. When he will take
it to him.

The Stobaugh County Army Corps of Engineers had
just run a piece in the Hubbard City paper about the
paddy situation, but Chaingang didn't read the paper. He
didn't know he was looking at a rice field that would
soon have its dikes leveled so they could simply let the
levee water in and help the farmers who had until now
been forced to implement the costlier and more time-
consuming methods of irrigation. He looked out and saw
only the paddies and dikes of the Rung Sat Special Zone.
He waits, frozen, hiding in the wet shadows of the Dutch
Barrow Pit, but in his mind he is at 331/STAR RACER,
at the edge of an area of marshes on the Long Tau River,
and he is surrounded by Charlie.

To visualize the area, picture the exaggerated hourglass of a woman's figure. Facing her, the large left
breast is the Long Tau, curving around marshland, curving back into the woman's waist, the tree line of palms
and cottonwoods, the exaggerated woman's hip curving
back out around the field of flooded paddies and an
overgrown path leading to the blue feature.

The huge man is not in his geographic location but is,
instead, somewhere south of the pagoda woods, to the
east of the woman's right breast, north of the rice fields,
and west of the comic's edge, like the early stories of
Christopher Columbus, who would surely fall off the
edge of the world. He is out of body, back in time,
transported back to the hot, stinking hell of the RSSZ,
Republic of South Vietnam. It is monsoon season, and
he is caught in a tidal stench, alone, surrounded by things
that could hurt him to death, not the least of which was a
company of Ho's fiercest who were using the woods for a
base camp and reppo depot.

He preps for the night ambush, sitting there in the
scorching down-state sun, in the Vietnamese blast furnace of the foul-smelling Rung Sat, and he begins methodically taping every loose piece of gear, every clanking
metallic thing that moved, taping with his precious black

friction tape, or slick black electrical tape, pulling out the huge tractor chain and painstakingly taping each individual link so that nothing clicked, snikked, ticked, rattled, clattered, bang, shook, chinged, pinged, or thumped a unnatural noise of warning in the night. No shiny metal will take the reflected jungle moonbeam and light up his night in sudden and fiery pain.

And the shiniest metal imaginable, a slashing, razor-sharp bowie that weighs as much as a small sword, a flashing silver blade that could sever a one-inch manila hemp line the way you could shave a hair from your arm, a monstrous killer knife is drawn from its oiled sheath and he begins running the blade back and forth across a spittle-wet, oiled whetstone. Ffffsssssssss. Ffffffffffssssssssssssssssssss. Long, measured strokes with the blade carefully angled to produce maximum results without feathering the razor edge. Long, patient, unhurried sharpening pulls across the rough stone. Ffffffffsssssssss. In tempo with his heartbeat. Then, when he is satisfied with the keenness of the cutting edge, he slices into his wiping cloth and wipes off the filth, laying a light, almost invisible coat of oil on the bright, perfectly hardened and tempered steel that had killed so many times.

He smelled them. They would be coming as the tide moved back in. When the rains came and the monsoon torrents swelled the river over the banks and the rice fields became awash and the whole of the RSSZ became one putrid, dangerous swamp, he would have to find the high ground, and they would be there, a company of the enemy's toughest elite, waiting to kill him.

But they would not kill him. He had heard of the rewards offered among their little soldiers and the ones in the villages who were their spies. They would give much to have the huge man alive. To take him and make his dying a slow and precisely choreographed pain play, a tapestry of agony. They'd enslave him first as they liked to do—keeping him in a hell they would devise to match his worst fears, prolonging his suffering as few races could do better than the hard-hearted North Vietnamese.

He wondered how it would come. His presentience would warn him if capture were inevitable. He would kill many, many of them. But when the M-60 was out of ammunition, the claymores gone, the frags expended, the pistol clips empty, the belts shot up, the explosive used, the chain lost—he would kill as many as he could with the bowie and then turn it on himself. He knew he could summon the resolve to stab himself in the heart and stop his own life force. Or he could save a grenade for the last. Or save one bullet. One special round tucked away for the end.

He absentmindedly finds himself with the oiled bowie in hand, holding it in a death grip, and without thinking, for no reason other than emphasis, makes a deep, quick downward slash over his strong heart.

It is funny. He smiles widely at the sudden bloodstream. It is a deeper cut than he meant to make but of less than no significance. A prank. Nothing more than a jailhouse tattoo, a heart stabbed into the arm from boredom, filled with a poison of inks to darken and dye the skin. LOVE and HATE inscribed upon the knuckles. A pachuco cruciform at the webbing of the thumb. A slash over the heart for luck.

He is hunkered down beside his huge ruck in a small woods at the edge of an area of marshes on the Long Tau, where the spike team was to effect an ambush of Viet cong guerrillas who had terrorized a small, nearby hamlet, torturing and brutally killing a province chief and his family. Intelligence believed that the VC were using the ruins of a pagoda in the woods in back of him for a supply cache near the hamlet, but Chaingang knew it was a setup and he had gone on a different course, alone, waiting and watching. The team had been wiped out by mortars and sniper fire. Set up by hoi chanh dinks who had been double agents or quadruple agents or . . . who knows? And the boat was gone. There was no radio. And Chaingang was alone.

He knows he will wait until dark and then make his way to the New Cairo Ditch, which is the Long Tau River in the IV Corps Tactical Zone, 331/STAR RACER, Spike Team M-1350, Republic of South Vietnam.

THE RUNG SAT
SPECIAL ZONE(1965)

The LZ, which is named with some ridiculous woman's name, is perhaps fifteen clicks out and the birds change pitch and it signals his on-line terminal that this is the time he hates about to materialize and manifest itself in the sudden drop to the decks, and suddenly your lunch is in your throat and before you can drop your socks and grab your rocks the 101st Airbone Division (Airmobile) has set them down through the small opening in the green, and a commo "adviser," a marine sergeant is yelling at them to double-time it to the blue feature.

They are soon jammed onto a PACV from some riverine unit and roaring up the snaky waterway into the Long Tao's fanged mouth. The Hovercraft is called a patrol air-cushion vehicle and Chaingang thinks of the blue feature as a water snake, winding the way a serpent will, flowing and twisting into the Rung Sat.

These are spooky Charlie-held streams that weave a web of blue and brown lines through the jungle delta and sprawling Vietnamese marshlands. There will be no medevac back in here. No arty. Nor resupply. This is a lonely game to be played by the chosen few. What did they say on the commercials? The few—the proud. If you get your ass kicked back in here you are permanently fucked up.

Chaingang sees the tributaries as a thousand water snakes, their names sounding like notes played on a busted musical instrument by a deaf man without hands, music that reverberates and twangs and echos shrilly with

189

Asian monkey vibes of bad luck and slow death and omens of evil.

Water snakes feeding into the arms of Satan. Warping the drug-ripped minds of these children. Injecting them with massive shots of instant paranoia and fear tremors that rumble deep in the gut like the New Madrid Fault Line, and the boys hope they can get their fatigues off before the fear erupts, because as everyone knows Ho Chi Minh's revenge takes no prisoners.

The PACV comes coasting into the Long Tao at dusk in a ratfuck of off-loading mania and hand signals and everyone sweating bullets, wishing they were aboard her when the chief petty officer makes her a memory. And the team is moving out to dig in the night positions before the blackness of Victor Charlie country comes to blind and befuddle.

They are moving into the darker green of the jungle. Wet. Soggy. Putrid. Foul vegetation and rotting plant life and dead fish clog the humid air, making it impossible to breathe from the stink and the asphyxiating humidity. And this is the GOOD time. When that tide goes out the Rung Sat becomes a barf city mudhole of the most evil and poisonous stench the devil ever shit on earth. Stinking slime pops like the sound of enemy coming, and you can only hope that the worst thing in your nightmares will be the red ants and leeches and venomous snakes and big, growling man-eaters and alligators as big as Chryslers and vampire bats that come to suck human blood.

Charlie lives here. It is his base camp. Ammo dump. His triage. His resupply. Charles' R & R. Charlie owns this bitch. Welcome to the Rung Sat Special Zone. Four hundred square miles of the most frighteningly danger-ous, stinking, deadly mangrove swamps and river delta in the Nam. The name translates as the Assassin's Forest. A slimy, smelly, murderous mass of vampire feces that lies along the Long Tao, connecting Saigon to the South China Sea.

331/STAR RACER is an operation being run up the VC's nostrils by the U.S. Naval Advisory Group, the Crotch, and assorted spooks, grunts, and snake-eaters from various units. Because the mission is aimed through,

if not around, certain elements of the ARVN, it becomes
the property of one covert spike team, carried on the
books as M-1350, written in invisible ink and guaranteed
to NOT go down in history.

The Hoi Chanh dinks have butt-fucked intelligence
once again, and the unit is wasted. Its ass is well and
truly waxed, and Chaingang, who is a self-contained
hunter-killer unit moving slower than the pack, never
following the path of least resistance, working solo, is
now operating alone. No radio. No spike team. No chopper. No boat. Surrounded by VC and worse—he is in the
heart of an NVA base camp—and the monsoon rains will
come soon.

Somewhere, GHOST TOWN, the exfiltration team,
awaits the radio signal. A coded crackle of words sounding like routine grid coordinates: India—Whiskey—Novem-
ber—Yankee—Zulu—Foxtrot—Golf—Papa—Lima—
Golf—Papa—India. Twelve simple words. IWN. YZF.
GPL. GPI. What could be simpler to remember? But
there is no mike to key. Not static-filled radio to speak
the exfiltration sign into. No way to tell them. So he will
WALK out of the Rung Sat. He will KILL his way out.

He makes his way again to the edge of the shadowy
tree line and comes out at the edge of a rice field, moving
quickly across the muddy paddy dike. Sweating profusely
in the scorching heat and energy-sapping humidity of the
dreaded RSSZ. Fifteen quintuple-E bootprints mashing
down in the muddy earth, leaving a trail that is danger-
ously clear. He wishes he had extra grenades or even a
pie or two, which is what he calls the claymores, that he
could use to leave a little surprise in his pathway. To
"close the back door" behind him.

But he is out of 'nades, mines, even ammo. Worse—
although he prefers the personal killing modes—he has
lost his long-range destroyer. It is his tool for dispatching
the little people as the current situation and terrain dic-
tated and he missed the comfort of the weight on his left
shoulder.

It had been R & D'd by the Bridge Tool and Die
Manufacturing Company, of Philadelphia, Pa., and made
by Inland Steel—the Inland Manufacturing Division of
General Motors—and it was Chaingang's pig, the M-60

LMG. Twenty-four pounds of slope killer. A gas-operated, 550-round-per-minute, 43½-inch death machine fed by a disintegrating link belt system, which the government had phased in to replace the venerable .30 Browning.

Under ordinary field conditions the M-60 would easily lift a hundred-round bandolier vertically, and the auto-fire recoil was sufficient to actually hold the weapon in place when fired from the hip, making it the most reliable heavy-duty piece that was sufficiently mobile for a single man to carry into combat.

He liked the weight of it on the special shoulder pad. He enjoyed the way it felt cradled in his arms as he thought about how easily he could cut a man in half with the projectiles from this tool. How easy it would be to stitch a line of bullets through the middle of a human, blasting him apart with the mere touch of a trigger.

But his M-60 and ammo were gone. No pies. No 'nades. Not even his Hi-Standard with the suppressor. Only a pitiful Colt Woodsman and half a dozen .22 rounds, his chain, and his blade.

He stepped over a deep set of ruts. Tracks had been along through here and there was water in the deepest ruts. He spotted the shotgun shells, but to him it was the spent brass that you see everywhere after a mad minute. The litter of a firefight, perhaps.

Everywhere he looked he saw the trash that was the calling card of both the multimilitary and civilian incursion/occupancy/habitation. The whole country was a garbage heap. He looked for bootprints, broken limbs, disturbed nature, as he tromped down away from the beaten path, his sensors purring as he moved toward the blue line.

Nature's noises were building in intensity the way they do the deeper you go into the boonies, and Chaingang thought he might be nearer the big ditch than he'd calculated. It looked just like a steep ditch bank and he was surprised not to see water as he came up over the rise, moving cautiously, keeping his boonie-rat cover down even with the surrounding tree and bush line, taken aback to see the huge, dry creek bed and the remnants of a blown bridge. He eased down into the fly-infested hollow. Eyes scoping across the cracked mud floor for sign. He found more shells. Spent brass from another firefight. The whole thing could be a bomb crater. He crossed the expanse of mud and pulled himself up the other side and felt something. He stopped.

There was somebody, something nearby, a living thing. He neither saw nor heard anything—just that stab of awareness. He felt it like a chill on his skin and it froze him to the spot. Absolutely motionless.

Stilling slowing stilling the vital signs. Breathing twice as deeply but half as often, slow, heavy, measured intakes of air, filling the immense lungs and slowing stilling slowing the heartbeat as he tuned in on the presence. He stayed frozen so long the birds began singing loudly as they will if you remain unmoving for several minutes. He heard loud animal noises, faraway engines, a chopper high in the sky and far away, and something moving close by. The killing hand held the taped tractor-strength chain, his "flexible club," in a steel death grip and whatever it was was right beside him now and he tensed and it moved slightly and the camouflage was so good it had been very close all this time, and he had to stifle the cough of laughter as he spotted the tiny brown furry creature in the deep weeds.

Very carefully and gently his left hand reached down and scooped under the baby rabbit and he lifted it up to his level and looked at it like he'd never seen one before. He poked around in the weeds but could not find the mother or any other babies, so he tenderly sat it back down in the deepest thickest weeds he could see and backed away. His hands had become so toughened he had not felt the soft fur or the barely discernible thumping of its tiny heart. It was the first rabbit he'd seen in-country in a long while. The baby rabbit hunkered down in the weeds, having a small heart attack as the giant human moved off.

He thought about how they mistreated the animals here. Especially our soldiers. He enjoyed thinking about the one boy who had teased the duck. He watched him later, and when he went into a latrine to shit he rapidly fragged the door and when the punk came out . . . He had to pull his twisted thoughts off the fragging of the punk, something was demanding all the powers of his concentration.

Chaingang was all but impossible to booby-trap. He could be shot, bombed, fragged, destroyed in any number of ways. But to expect him to step on a poisoned bamboo stake or to trip a bouncing betty or a whip or any of the hundred other traps they could deliver to the unwary, was simply to underestimate his abilities. So at one with his environs was this killer that the slightest off-key factor—the smallest detail out of harmony with its surroundings—and he would see it as if it wore a bright flag. The other thing man has never duplicated is nature, be it camouflage or neorealist art, and however impressive, man's artifice could do no better than a shiny wax apple.

It was not the fear of mines or hidden chi-coms that nagged at him. He had yet to put a label to it, but he knew that to ignore such vibes was to do so at his own peril. It could be this piece of ground. For just as there are persons in whom the trace of evil is prominent and assertive there are geographic locales in which that trace is strong. And as the men and women and children touched by evil reflect no obvious commonality, the traces can be found anywhere. At the bottom of the sea, in a complex of cities long buried by the winds of time and evolution, in a certain desert, or on a variety of hills, valleys, ravines, mountains, temples, desolate landscapes, shores, wastelands, swamps, urban sky-rises, remote countrysides, and boondock ditch banks alike. This was one such locale.

He tasted it, smelled it, it prickled his skin as the synergy of the place and person combined to form a deadly bond. He also was beginning to sense that unnamed thing again, and he realized what it was when he came over the next steep bank and saw that he was at the ditch. There was a Cong fishing boat, or what was left of one, tied to the overhanging willows by a piece of rope that had all but rotted through.

He pulled the boat up onto the bank easily and tipped it over on its edge, a 275-pound wooden jon boat, tipping it like it weighed fifty pounds, letting it plop back down in the muddy water. It had been badly caulked and the caulking was only partially holding in the cracks, but it appeared to still be halfway sound. Bunkowski checked to see how the bottom looked and, satisfied, he gingerly stepped in, propelling his bulk into the middle section of the boat. It didn't sink to the bottom with him, which he considered a good sign.

There was a broken piece of oar and a couple of old cans and milk jugs, which had probably been used to bail the old leaky tub with. He picked up the oar and shoved off from the bank. The water was probably quite shallow along here, he thought, with the bank only ten or twelve feet high and maybe—tops—six or seven feet of water beneath the boat.

Silently, with the powerful arms and wrists and back that possessed superhuman strength, the behemoth dipped the piece of wood into the water and sent the rowboat gliding upstream, aiming quietly in the direction of the enemy's heartbeat.

BUCKHEAD STATION

Lee clip-clopped down the steps into the squad room to find Eichord with his chair tilted back, one foot hooked onto a desk drawer, the room otherwise empty.

"I can't go off and leave you, can I?" Lee said, shaking his head. "I come back—it'sa same damn thing everytime, hats, horns, drunken behavior, screaming, and wild parties. You're an irrepressible knucklehead, ya know that? What am I gonna do with you?"

Eichord calmly looked up from his book. "Well, look who's here, it's the Chinese Willie Sutton."

"Oh, cute. Real funny. Like they'd never think to put a you-know-what in here. Right?"

"I don't know. What's a you-know-what?"

"A mike. A fucking *MICROPHONE*," he screamed.

"Jeez, pal. Take a couple dozen Valium and get a hold of it."

"YOU get a hold of it," Lee said, dropping a newspaper on top of Eichord's book, *The Gentleman's Clubs of London*.

Eichord saw the headline "FBI LINKS ROBBERY GUN TO KILLING," reading "A handgun taken from fugitive Wendell De Witt, 31, has been identified as the weapon used in the shooting death of a Buckhead bank guard on July 3, according to testimony given by a Federal Bureau of Investigation forensics analyst.

"The unnamed FBI analyst verified that tests conducted on a .38-caliber pistol taken from De Witt at the time of his capture showed conclusively that it was the

196

weapon used in the killing of Floyd Coleman, 52, during the robbery of Buckhead Mercantile Bank and Trust.

"The gun is reportedly one of several weapons stolen from a Buckhead store on June 26. De Witt's accomplice in the bank robbery and shooting, John Monroe, 24, was granted immunity by the Federal Bureau of Investigation working with Buckhead County prosecuting attorney Arthur Wiegrath, in return for Monroe agreeing to testify against his accomplice in the July 3 robbery and homicide."

Eichord glanced at Lee and gave him a shake of the head and one of those thin-lipped you-stupid-asshole looks of exasperation as he finished the last paragraph:

"Wiegrath said that information given by Monroe had resulted in De Witt's capture. Both De Witt and Monroe have claimed that only $16,000 of the $28,421 taken in the robbery was removed from the bank."

"What I want to know is this," Eichord said. "Just tell me how anybody with your brains, can—" They finished in unison, "—be so fucking STUPID."

He'd always wanted to know how Chink and Chunk did that—but not THIS bad.

He picked up his book and tried to get back into the world of gentleman's clubs but he kept reading the same line. The last sentence of the story in the paper.

NEW CAIRO DRAIN

Locally it had once been known as the Iron Bridge, but like all the iron around here the exposure to the elements had eventually taken its toll, and as we all know rust never naps much less sleeps. When the Iron Bridge had rusted through to the point where it was long past being deemed unsafe, somebody from the county road agency came and made an assessment and work began. When the workmen were done after a summer's toil the rusting iron girders that remained were resting on huge, treated utility poles, X-braced, and it had become the Wooden Bridge. Then the flash floods came to eat at the banks.

But the county people had run out of money somewhere along the way toward completion, and they'd never gotten around to fixing the bridge right in the middle, nor had they rebuilt the sides. It was a nice potential Chappaquiddick as it stood there, some sixty feet above the ditch at highest watermark, no rails and no center, but safe enough in outward appearance to an approaching stranger.

They feared that vandals would take down the BRIDGE OUT signs, cut the chains and steel cables, and stand around with fingers crossed waiting for some hapless civilian from the city. So the county came back and blew the whole center section of the bridge out. Only the drunkest party animal would fail to see the bridge was gone.

To Daniel, looking up and seeing the blown bridge's sides arching out from either bank, miniature sandbars,

the tallest Johnson grass you've ever seen, gigantic trees
and weeds hanging over the brown water, it was a green-
choked world of paddies and tree lines and blown bridge
and quasi-jungle, and it looked more like Vietnam than
anything this side of the Phillippines. And his sensors
began blinking as he saw this blown artifact from his
past. And he smelled Cong.

Up on the high bank two pickups were parked side by
side. Three men were talking.

"Kenny caught a twelve-pound channel cat down there
around the eddy?"

"Yeah? By the ferry?"

"Yeah. Worked all up an' down there clean up to just
south of Kerr's Store."

"D'jew do anythin'?"

"Hell!" The other man shook his head in exasperation.

"Three"—he laughed mirthlessly—"'n a couple of damn
drum."

"Where was ya?"

"Number Thirty-six."

"They in close," he said.

"I was draggin' 'em off the bank."

"Get in there, boy," the third man said with a knowing
nod.

"Yeah."

"I put in off Whitetail and worked all the way back
down that bank where the drain north of Clearmont
Church is?" The other man nodded. "'N I shagged seven
and some bluegill." His head shook once in disgust.

"D'jew go crappie fishin'?"

"Naw. Me 'n Cecil's goin' tomorrow," he said, and
they talked about the fact it hadn't rained hardly at all
for two weeks, and about the big tater patch, and some
new pre-emerge one of them had heard about, and they
had got around to bait again about the time Chaingang
came out of the water and heard the three Cong chatter-
ing away in their singsong Vietnamese monkey gibberish,
and a huge hand holding a gleaming fighting bowie comes
up out of the muddy waters like the fin of a silver shark,
the back of the hand matted with hair as thick as an
animal's pelt. A huge head followed silently out of the
water, tiny, hard black eyes gleaming in the doughy,

scarred face, sun-brown, hard, steel-muscled, fast now, quick and sure with every move, one of the most experienced assassins ever, easing his massive body out of the water. The boat pushed up against the shore a hundred meters back, Chain had gone into the water when the voices first carried down into the ditch, the Woodsman in one hand, the chain in the other, the big fighting bowie clamped in those shark teeth, frightening, misshapen teeth that had never known a cavity, clenched down on that lightly oiled razor-edged blade, holding the heavy knife in his teeth like a pirate—what did they call them?—like a cutthroat. He was a cutthroat easing along the bank in among the deep weeds, looking for a way to get up there where he wouldn't be seen.

He'd come about a hundred meters in the water and he saw the near-invisible path made by fishermen. You could see where they'd come down the bank when it was muddy. He instantly read the sign for three or four men, putting a small boat in, putting in here where they could walk out on a little mud bank in their boots, dragging the boat down through the vines and mashing down the grass and weeds with the weight of the boat, their bootprints here and there amid the boat tracks in the mud.

". . . them fuckin' Cardinals."

"Yeah, but shit you shouldna bet that's where you made your mistake. He does zat for a living. You work in the pot room for a living. You don't see him comin' down 'nair and tellin' you how to pour iron, do ya?" The three men laughed.

"Hey, Cec," the one said to the third man, who was getting out of the pickup.

"Huh?"

"Ja ever see so many tators as over'n that Dalton ground?"

"They go right ta Amalgamated."

"Zat right?"

"Every damn tator. That's a syndicate operation. They got about six thousand acres they buy. Dalton's got—what?—maybe 650 to 750 right there. Another five hundred up yonder." He gestured. " 'Course they only buy irrigated fields. Ya got to have all them pipes laid and that—it's all by the numbers."

"Yeah, I figured that was a big-chip operation when
. . ." He trailed off. The first man thought he'd heard
something, but when he turned to look in the direction of
the sound the darkening sky rumbled and they all looked
up at the sight of the blessed rain they needed.

"All damn right!"

"Finally!"

"Speakin' of irrigation . . ." They laughed. "We finally
goin' to get some of that there wet stuff."

"Boy, I'll tell ya," the second man said, "I've never
seen anything like this last year f'r lack of moisture. I was
watching that—"

They never would know what he'd been watching because the last two or three chain links smashed into his
left temple and he made a noise and fell to the ground as
the other man, the first man, who was by himself, instinctively moved back and the blade of the fighting
bowie stabbed into him and he screamed and the third
man was very fast and he was out of the truck and
running hell for leather toward the road and Chain rested
a huge iron bar of forearm up on the truck closest to him
and squeezed off a shot low and another not rushing
taking all the time in the world that sixth-sense thing
telling him there was no traffic coming and pulling the
next shot up a little and catching the man in the right leg
and then missing again but catching him with the next
two in the back.

The others he put away with the bowie in two fast
carotid-artery slashes, saving that last .22 round. Jogging
up and starting to put the round into the runner but
deciding not to.

"You look near death's door," he told him with a
grunt, whispering it to the man in a friendly, concerned
tone as he took hold of an ankle and drug him back to a
copse of trees until he could figure what was what. He
didn't even get to slit his throat. He looked at the man,
who was already dead then, and said, "I think you're
gonna bleed to death." And he went back and drug the
other two out of the path made by the two adjacent
pickup trucks, and his mind was going a mile a minute.

It had been a while since he'd indulged himself with
this kind of a kill. Three humans at one time. Usually he

did so inside a home or away from prying eyes. The
butcher boys he'd carved up back in Chicago. But you
don't take down this many out in the open. Too much
gravedigging. Too many trucks. Too much chance of a
passing motorist. He started moving, squeezing his soaked
body up into the nearest pickup and turning the key,
grinding it to life and roaring down off the bank onto the
nearby road, pulling it into the first turn-row he came to
and wiping the wheel, keys, all the surfaces he might
have touched, the door handles, leaving the keys in it
and jogging back up to the second truck. He pulled it
right behind the first one. Still no traffic coming along.
So far so good. He ran back, breathing a little hard now
but not feeling it the way he would have six or seven
months back. He had to admit it. He felt good.

He started working on the blood trails and then decided he'd leave that temporarily. The rain would help
him some. This was a monsoon rain. It would pull the
water up to the banks and beyond. He had to get out of
there. The big man would not allow himself the usual
luxury of digging a grave. This big a mass grave would
take time he did not have. He started dragging the three
bodies down the bank through the tangle of vines and
weeds, rolling, sliding, pulling, horsing the three corpses
down by the water, taking note of the mashed greenery
and blood trails as he did so.

Perhaps it was the fact his clothing was still soaked
from the water or the rain that was coming down on him
as he worked, but something gave him the idea of trying
the water. He went back in, splashing down next to the
deep bank then going over his head and breaststroking
powerfully toward the bridge underwater. Suddenly one
of his fingers struck something metal as he swam, and he
came up for air, nursing a sore hand. He'd almost run
into the girder headfirst. He assumed that's what he'd
hit—part of the old bridge.

He took a mighty chestful of air and dove again, this
time opening his eyes. The water was quite dark and
muddy but he could make out a shape and then he
realized what it was and came back up. It was a car or
truck of some kind, a junker somebody had probably
either pushed or driven off the bridge long ago. He dove

again and powerful muscles strained and he was able to wrench a door open underwater. It would be perfect for a temporary holding cell.

Chaingang went back to get the bodies. One at a time he took them into the water and down below the bridge, pulling them down underwater with him and stuffing the corpses into the vehicle. It was extremely difficult work and the bodies were a lot harder to manipulate than he'd anticipated, but he eventually managed it, moving with the supple sureness of a natural athlete, the effortless fluidity of a competent stage actor, and the awesome strength of a power lifter. The three bodies were soon tucked out of sight.

Later he'd come back with wire, goggles, and a torch, and he'd do the thing right. And it would be then he'd learn of a wonderful subaqueous surprise down there waiting for him in the watery graveyard of the metal elephants.

BUCKHEAD SPRINGS

"**W**hatcha doin'?"

"Umm, everybody I can," he promised her, "and you're next. Pull up some mattress and park that gorgeous bod."

"Okay. You've made me an offer I can't refuse. Here we come." And a hand dropped something small and fuzzy and gray beside Jack. "Herrrrrrrrre's Tuffkins!"

"Well, hello, pal."

Tuffy attacked one of the pieces of paper scattered across the bed.

"MasterCard," Donna said, "we're bored and we wants some hot action."

"Did you say something about hot action?" She nodded. "You don't mean like THIS, do you?" And he jumped on her and began what he called a frontal nuzzling attack.

"AAAK," she screamed "Truce!"

"Say what?"

"Uncle! Help! Stop. I give. I'm not bored anymore."

"Uhhhh. How about you, Tuffy? Are you bored?"

The cat wisely ignored him.

"Tell me the truth."

"Yeah?"

"Who's the sexiest woman you've ever seen—and don't say me."

"Don't say me? Okay. No problem. I won't say me."

"You know what I mean. But I want to know. First one who pops into your mind. Not counting present company. The real sex goddesses. Marilyn. Those kinda girls. Who was your favorite?"

"Who wants to know?"

"I wants to know. Me and my pal Tuffkins want to know."

"Marilyn."

"Who else?"

"Bardot?"

"Yeah. I can see that. Brigitte at fifteen was unbelievable."

"My favorite Bardot was at forty, if you're serious. One of the loveliest pictures of a woman I can remember seeing was that shot of her next to the baby seal, talking about the seal-killers. She was about forty as I remember, no longer the sex kitten, but doing something about animal cruelty. I recall she hugged this gorgeous seal and said whatever it was she said about the seal culls—the harvests or whatever those heartless assholes call them—and she said a line I still remember. She said they killed seals to make fur toys and coats for stupid women."

"God"—Donna sat up in the bed—"you know, I remember that too."

"She was one of the first big stars to say that. I don't know if it did any good. But it was such a strong indictment of those rich . . . I don't want to say the word to you—you know the kind of woman—those hot-shit jet-setter Fifth Avenue sluts. Anyway, she went on to say to this little seal, she hugged it and said, But we'll *get* 'em. Meaning the furriers or the stupid women or the guys who slaughtered the seals for a living. And I said right back to her, No baby, no you won't, but it's a lovely thought."

"There's a lot more fake fur sold now. She may have helped, honey."

"You don't fight city hall and win. You don't screw with human nature and prevail. You don't alter the course of evolution. We like to run everything out to the edge. Push it to the max. It's what will take us down. We'll find safe nuclear energy too irresistible. Or we'll keep building that first strike capability against the other guys and one day some nutcase will find a way to leave his or her mark on history with the push of a button. It's human nature."

Donna wished she hadn't gotten this one started. He had seemed so gloomy and downbeat the last few days. He'd leave for the office, as she called it, in a good mood and come home that night bummed-out and depressed. She reached out and ran a soft hand across the side of his face. "Ooooh. Barbed wire."

"Yeah?" He smiled.

"Not shaving today, are we?"

"Just hadn't got the energy. I got a bad case of the lazies today," he told her, scratching the kitten behind the ears.

"Do you know something?" she said, leaning very close. "I've never told you this, Officer, but I've never kissed a man with a beard before."

"That's a coincidence," he said. "Neither have I."

And she laughed into his mouth.

STOBAUGH COUNTY

Daniel Edward Flowers Bunkowski's world was that strange and unexplainable twilight swamp in which there were moments of apparent normalcy. He was a madman, of course. Totally insane. But yet much of the time he functioned on what appeared to be a normal plane of existence. When he returned to the sharecropper's house, to get supplies from the hootch, he was still firmly planted in Southeast Asia and in the middle of a running mission. It was the high and tiny voice of his woman, the soft tones of Sissy Selkirk, now hugely pregnant, that pulled him back into the middle range between raving lunacy and what passed for humanity.

"What happened to *you*?" The voice somehow pierced the fog of murderous thoughts, pulling at his consciousness like a tugboat trying to move a battleship. She tried again, "You're hurt. Howdja get cut?"

"Eh?" He rumbled a monosyllabic grunt at her, then realized the battle dressing had come off and the wound was bleeding again. In just that second his twisted mind embraced three thoughts.

First, he realized how stupid he had been to inflict a wound on himself over here, even jokingly, because the severity of the bacteria problem was an ever-present danger in this environment and . . . Second, he knew even as he thought the idea that "over here" was wrong, that he was flashing back again, that this was another time and place. And third, he must have her buy a car. Put it in his name, trade the Caprice immediately. Thinking this because he knew in just that moment she'd have to go before long, even as he answered her, his mind calculating what sort of a response this human expected, forming his lips around the B-sound of barbed wire, saying, "Barbed-wire cut. Just a scratch," moving away from her before the red tide could wash over him and he'd kill her for the hell of it, drag her back to that place under the bridge, put her in the car and be done with it. He knew now that he would have to kill her soon.

"You want me to get some whatdya call it and put onnit?" the little voice said.

"Yeah," he forced himself to say. He must not allow himself the great pleasure of exploding in a scarlet tide and stomping this cow and her unborn child out in one stomp of fifteen-quintuple-E bootprint. He had gone to all this trouble so he would be able to kill freely, and later so that he could safely approach the hated cop EICHORD and introduce him to the tearing and pulverizing delights of Chaingang's special world. He must not blow his cover now. At least wait until the idiot dropped her frog. Find the cop with a woman and baby as his shield.

"Okay," she said, surprised and delighted that he would allow her such a privileged intimacy. She ran in to find something to put on his wound, which he noticed was beginning to coagulate again. She came running back out and he was gone. He had taken off back toward the big ditch and his nighttime business.

When he finally got back under the bridge that night, shining the underwater light on his grisly work, he was delighted to find that there was a mini-junkyard of rusting vehicles submerged under the bridge. At one time some back-yard tinkerer, or perhaps some thief in the spot-and-steal game, had used the bridge as a convenient dumping grounds for the stripped junkers that were not worth hauling off for their weight in iron. As he wired his three new friends in place as a precaution, then wiring the doors of the rusting enclosure itself, he decided that he'd come back and create a very special graveyard right here in what he'd think of as the final rusting place of the metal elephants.

For weeks he worked by day and killed by night. Each day quitting earlier and driving farther, ranging out more and more, but almost always bringing his victims back to be placed under his beloved wooden bridge. He was killing with a serious vengeance now, goaded by the annoying yet tolerable ambiguity of the girl's constant presence, an irritant he had himself caused to exist and that—for the time being—he could do nothing about.

He would see her only briefly. Occasionally at a meal-time, or when his biological needs would force him to notice her proximate presence and he'd summon her to her knees for a quick head job. Then he'd be out the door, slamming the thing in a rage, driving wherever his killer vibes took him. He'd come back after his night business, sometimes wet as if he'd sweated through his clothing, but back to her to sleep beside her in that placid, soothed state that always settled over him after he had slaked his angry hunger with a living human's heart.

Sissy thought he probably went out and "went into bars and got into fights," as previous men in her life had done. She was beginning to find the last weeks of preg-nancy unpleasant. It was hot in the sharecropper shack, and hotter still outside. Even in the shade she suffered. She had some swelling of her fingers and her ankles. The hotter it got, the more her ankles swelled. It was if she had literally traded with her man: the more weight he lost, the bigger her stomach got. The stronger his ankle, the weaker hers became.

One day she came waddling up to him while he was cutting weeds and said, "Sorry to bother ya." He looked up at her. "But can you take me to see a doctor."

"You having it?"

"Huh uh. I don't feel so good. I feel like I'm gonna puke and my feet are killing me and I'm hurting here an' . . ." She started to go on with a whole catalog of prob-lems. He sighed disgustedly and dropped the weed slinger, motioning for her to follow him as he headed for the car.

In town the doctor said to them, "This here," he was talking about her sickness, "is prob'ly just, uh"—he started to say psychosomatic but caught himself in time—"nothin' to worry over. Step on the scales here."

"Okay." She obliged.

"Yeah." He marked something on a chart. "Step down." She did so with an effort—each movement was a massive expenditure of energy. "You've gained about six and a half pounds, maybe seven. Perfectly normal. Your blood pressure is only slightly elevated. The diastolic, uh, lower reading is ninety. I wouldn't worry, really. You're doin' fine."

"I'm so hot alla time I feel like I'm gonna faint."

"Just git a lot of rest," he told her with a chuckle. "Remember, you wanna keep eatin' good. You're eating for two." He'd only said that two thousand times.

"Come on," Daniel told the girl as she waddled back out to the car, "we'll go get you some pizza and have a picnic." He beamed in a vocal tone so solicitous and warm that she looked over at him.

"Yeah," she said, beginning to cheer up with his tender, loving offer, "that sounds good." And she settled back beside him, Chaingang's baby inside her like a seven-pound basketball.

Without exception, each week of his prolonged agony and self-imposed starvation on the fat farm, Daniel had allowed himself one meal as a reward. He would often take Sissy with him and they'd drive in and feast on cheeseburgers, nachos, fish platters, whatever fast-food place caught his eye first would find him as a customer. They gravitated toward places with drive-in windows, as the size and appearance of "that there new man works for Hora" was already a topic of discussion within the tiny agricommunity.

It was close to his weekly treat time and he pulled up at the busy drive-in window of a Pizza Palace. He'd phoned ahead while Sissy was at the doctor's.

"Yes, sir. Welcome to Pizza Palace. May we take your order?" the squawking intercom asked him.

"We called in an order. Name's Selkirk," he told the box.

"Yes, sir. It's ready. That'll be $18.90, please drive to the window." He drove the Caprice up and pulled out a fistful of disreputable-looking crumpled bills, counting off nineteen in fives and ones. His massive sunburned arm shoved the money up into the window. Sissy loved to touch him on the arms and back and he sometimes let her. His muscles were rock-hard. His arms, legs, back, neck—all looked as if they'd been carved from solid hardwood. There was not an ounce of fat anywhere except on his belly, chest, and haunches.

They drove away and stopped on the way back to Hora's at a favorite spot for their "picnic feasts," a spot where Chaingang had once buried a kill. It amused him to bring the pregnant woman there.

"Ummm," she said, a mouthful of cheese and pepperoni not yet swallowed as she spoke, "this is good." She ate two pieces from the two giant-size pizzas as usual. She was always amazed at the amount of food he would eat, but she said nothing. "Ain't you hungry?" she asked him now. He said nothing. He had eaten only eight slices of pizza and, to his great amazement, he was full. It actually worried him momentarily, until he realized that he had shrunk to that extent.

"Watch," he told her, and in something so alien and uncharacteristic for him Daniel stood up and, sucking in his gut slightly, pulled the belt in, cinching it in as hard as he could. The pants he'd just bought two months before to replace the ones that had been falling off were already too big, and he pulled the cow-long belt in nearly a foot. He'd already cut a good foot of leather off the belt.

"God! You're gettin' skinny." She smiled. This was her idea of clever wit.

He beamed back and nodded. But the only thought going through his mind as he rebuckled the belt was, he would like to say to her, Do you know where you're sitting? And when she said, No, she didn't, he'd tell her she was having a picnic on a grave. And then he'd ask her if she would like to see what was in it. He thought what great pleasure it would bring him when he removed both her and her mound of a gut from his presence. He allowed himself the barking cough of a laugh.

"That's me," he told her, "skinny." This was the longest conversation they'd had in months and she wished she could put her arms around him and hug him, but she was afraid if she tried to move she'd puke the pizza up.

"Could we buy a fan?" she asked him.

"I don't see why not," he told her, again surprising both of them. "After all, we want you to have a healthy kid, eh?" He wondered, idly, what the kid would look like if he took his bowie and sliced her watermelon open, and took it out of the oven a little early.

"Right here," he rumbled to her and patted her stomach, where his child was being carried. That's where I'll make the cut, he thought. He traced a line across her swollen belly with a steel finger like a knife point. "This is where a baby is."

'That's right," she said. "Feel your son in there."

And he did.

BUCKHEAD

"**Y**a jes' fuckin' with me. Bloated GAWDAMN *SHOAT*," he shouted at the agent who yanked him backward and he fell over on the hard floor. "Iffn' I wasn't tied to this weuns d' have us a different story then, tubby." The standing man kicked him hard and the man tied to the chair spit, started to say something, changed his mind and stared straight up at the ceiling. Fuckin' faggots.

"You're a real piece of work, aren't ya, Mr. De Witt, or Mr. De Half-Witt—which is it?"

"Yo're a big fuckin' man now."

"You're an ignorant, redneck, no-account piece of SHIT, boy. You know that."

"Fuckin' fa—" He grunted in pain as the man kicked the top of his head.

"I hated to do that, Mr. Witless, youuns git gooey kid stuff on my shoe. And what kinda language is that anyway, peckerwood? Cain't *YOUUNS* talk too good?" He mimicked the man tied to the chair. "Are you a fuckin' hillwilliam, dummy? Is that *YOUUNS* problem."

The man named Wendell De Witt stared up at the ceiling without blinking an eye. He'd put up with horse-shit like this all his life. It didn't faze him. He looked over at the agent looming over him. "Iffn youuns talk real sweet to me I'll let ya' suck ma pole later on." He almost blacked out for a second when the man kicked him again in the top of the head. He kicked with the flat of the foot to leave as little evidence as possible, not that

213

he was particularly worried about it. The tough country bumpkin appeared to have passed out, so he passed smelling salts under the man's nose and he came back with a cough and cursing.

The agent opened the door and said to someone in the hall, "Gimme a hand with this, will ya?" The other agent entered the interrogation room and they lifted the subject up so the chair was upright again.

"Listen up, Mr. De Shitt. I'll be back in a few minutes with a couple friends of that cop you assholes shot. And the four of us will play bridge, okay? And YOU'LL be the fuckin' bridge, tough guy." He slammed out of the room.

"You okay?" the second agent asked with genuine concern in his voice.

"Yeah. I'm jes' fine."

"He loses his temper. I'm sorry about that, man."

"That's no problem."

"You know, Mr. De Witt, if you'd cooperate with us it could make a big difference for you." He sounded so warm and friendly. "This is the time to work something out, you know?"

"Commere." De Witt gestured with his head. "Lean over here an' I'll tell ya somethin'." As the agent leaned over slightly De Witt hawked up a big goober of bloody phlegm and spat it into the man's face.

"OH FOR CHRIST'S—" The man watching all of this through the one-way got up, his wooden chair scraping on the floor, and walked into an adjoining office, where he picked up a phone, dialing.

"Howard Krug," the SAC said, picking up his private line.

"No goodski. Sorry."

"You didn't really believe *that* animal was going to fall apart behind some bad cop/good cop, did you?"

"Nope. So what now? What, uh, you want me to put Joe back in there for a while?"

"Huh uh. Just put 'm back in lockup and pull James Lee in and see what you can do."

"How long I get with Lee before Buckhead and IAD are in on it?"

"What do you need?"

"Can we keep him overnight?"

"Negative."

"Well?"

"Pull him in and act like you got him nailed. The usual. Keep him till close of business. You know, five-thirty, six o'clock tops. Cut him loose and let him go home for supper to think about it."

"You got it."

"Remember—he won't know they got to John Monroe somehow, so make sure you don't tip it."

"He's gonna know when he goes home tonight."

"Maybe so. But just play it like he doesn't know. Maybe we'll get lucky. Depends what kind of poker player he is."

"Okay. We'll see what happens."

"Call me later at home."

"Will do. I'll let you know."

"Just a couple things. First make sure first thing you do is the bit about the special, hidden cam we got him on in the entranceway. Run that right at the beginning. Don't wait for him to crumple. He'll stonewall. You just gloss over it like you don't care if he denies. Then—"

"Right, he's gonna go, Hey, that's bullshit, or whatever, and I can just say. Like, I shrug and say, Hey, you and your attorney will have a copy to study. I mean it's all there where he picks up the money, I mean where YOU pick up the money, and if he goes, BULLSHIT you couldn't have it because I didn't do it, I just shrug as if I expected him to say that and plow right into the next thing."

"Remember, though, somewhere before you cut him loose you're gonna have to say something like, Hell, man I was just kidding. You want to leave it as light as you can. I was just puttin' you on, Jimmie old boy. I mean, you never know how bent outta shape these guys are gonna get and—just remember you might have to get on the stand behind this."

"Okay," the agent said, thinking to himself, What a schmuck.

"Now, let's say he's a good actor. He stonewalls. He didn't do it. No way. Not only do we have this famous surveillance cam in the entranceway, all that shit, but then that's when you hit him with the business about the computer-enhanced crap. Simulation-of-sequence time study. All that crap. I mean, we got him there. He's righteous for it."

"Right."

"We've looked at the pictures and we've got you picking up on camera. And in the study you can see that mathematically you were the only one coulda got the money—"

"What about John Monroe, do we—"

"Oh, yeah! That's the other thing. Imperative you don't let Lee know that John Monroe's been killed."

"Sure. Gotcha. I meant, we make sure he thinks, you know, there's no way the perps could have got the money out of the bank. The polys, all that."

"Right. Just stonewall it," he told him, breaking off the connection. What a schmuck, the agent thought. General Stonewall, he thought contemptuously, which is the nickname by which SAC Krug was known within the Bureau.

STOBAUGH

Chaingang was wailing away at the vetch, what there was left of it, and sensed eyes on him. Slowly he let the swings of the weed slinger turn him around and squinted through darkened lenses at the image of Michael Hora walking up to him. He stopped what he was doing and wiped sweat from his neck and forehead.

"Yo."

"Hey."

"We gotta talk."

"Mmm?"

"See where they still haven't found them three dudes disappeared up around the New Cairo Drain. Man, that's really sompin'—people vanishing like that."

"Yeah." Chaingang just looked at him.

"Hey, my man." Chaingang not moving. "Awful lot of people goin' up in smoke lately, ya know?"

"Yeah?" He noticed Hora had a hand back in his hip pocket. Probably a piece in there. He was well out of reach of a thrown chain or a whipsickle.

"Yeah," he said.

"So." Chaingang moved slightly and Hora tensed.

"Too many folks turnin' up missing. Gonna have to call it a day, ya know."

"Whatdya mean."

"I think you all better be moving on. No offense, my man, but I don't want any problems. I've already had heat around asking questions and shit."

"I'm paid up for this month."

"That was then. This is now. This is different. You got to git."

Neither of them blinked. After a couple of heartbeats Chaingang said, "How much time you give me to get out?"

"Now. Pack up, my man. Got to do it. Sorry." The hand still in the hip pocket. The eyes hard and cold.

"How much more to finish out the month?"

"Can't do it."

"Five thousand cash?"

"Wheeeew," he whistled. "I might could handle that. Up front with the money, of course."

"Yeah."

"When?"

"I go get it now if you want it."

"Yeah. All right. But that's it, then. To the end of the month, but I make no guarantees if the cops come around again."

"Okay." This was the longest conversation they'd ever had. Hora backed away carefully and when he was out of range turned and walked quickly in the direction he had come from.

Chaingang walked back to the sharecropper's shack and surprised Sissy, who was washing out some clothing in a tub, washing by hand, slowly, with an old-fashioned washboard, her belly swollen like she was carrying triplets.

"Hi," she said.

He grunted and went inside to get his money. He had about nine hundred dollars left. He tore up some paper and carefully cut it to look like bills, put the real money on the outside, and rolled it into a tight roll. It didn't look good enough. He smoothed out the bills and the cut paper and made a stack, put a rubber band tightly around it, and put that into an envelope. Then he quickly wrote something on a sheet of his ledger paper. Printing in heavy, firm lines that left clear marks on the next page.

The thing looked okay when he read it back, and the envelope felt right. Daniel took a small leather case not much larger than a shaving kit out of his duffel. There was a covered compartment that he kept the Colt Woodsman in, covered by a flap of yellowish vinyl that held it out of view. He laid the sheet of paper he'd written on and the envelope with the money and stuffing on top of the gun and it looked good.

He pulled a small red box out and his huge fingers as big as thick, steel cigars delicately removed a half-dozen of the .22 rounds. He took the clip out of the pistol and pressed the round down into it. They had the word "SUPER" stamped on their bases. He pushed the clip up into place and racked a round into the chamber, thumbed the safety on and off again, then slid the Woodsman back into the case, covering it with the money and the paper.

Hora was very good. He was experienced and he knew how good Chaingang was. It was one of those things where he'd just have to see what was what. If the time was right, then fine. Otherwise he'd use the contract to stall with and take the five-thousand-dollar mock-up package back under some pretext. No way would Hora sign anything.

He went up on the porch of Hora's house where the slow wife was sitting.

"Howdy doo."

"Uh," she grunted.

"Michael here?"

"Yo," a voice said from the yard. Hora watching him, the hand in the pocket as before. Nothing personal. Just letting him know.

"Hey." Chaingang's face lit up in his least dangerous smile. Nice and natural. "Got it here."

"Bring it down if you don't mind."

Chaingang nodded pleasantly and tromped down the rickety wooden steps. He was pleased the boards didn't groan under his weight as badly as before. He held the case in two fingers the way you would if it was very light.

"Like to get you to sign something, you know, just to protect both of us." Hora didn't say anything or move. Daniel reached in slowly and pulled out the envelope, which he held with the case between thumb and first finger and then went back in with his right hand where Hora could see and removed the sheet of paper.

It was very deft, the kind of move that a skilled killer practices the way other people work on a card trick. Doing it over and over in front of a mirror to get it slick, organic, so natural that it would put a move on anybody.

Like a real head fake that leaves the other guy coming out of his shoes as he tries to check himself in time. Hora tensed, waiting for whatever it was, his reflexes honed to a level of lightning-quick speed. Daniel going in as the muscles clenched up, tightened, coming out with something, something harmless-looking, jerking it back just as Hora reaches, then smiling, saying, "Guess you'd like the money first." And the envelope coming out and pulling *that* back as he goes back and gets the envelope *and* the piece of paper that begins, "Upon recpt of $5,000 I do hereby agree . . ." and making the two fakes, the offered item, pulling it back, the other offered item, going back again, now coming forward a *third* time with paper and packet of money, it sets up a reaction of tense apprehensive movement.

The third time the hand comes out you've bought it and the sudden thrust of the hand looks more natural and it is just in the first half-second of vulnerability that the trigger gets pulled. You have to know what you're doing. It's all in the timing. The fake-out depends on many things: position of the head, rapid eye movement, the mouth, the set of the chin, the upper torso, how you're holding your arms, the body language as you tell the other person without words just how nervous YOU are.

"Here's the . . . Oh, sorry, I mean HERE it is. Well, shit I'm sorry." I know you want the MONEY but look at THIS too, and the five thousand is coming out at you, and a piece of paper which is now the substitute threat and the interlocking moves and smiles and vocal tone is all very complex and manipulative and you can be very good but you can only look at the broad, blurred field of semicircular vision as the pass and the force are accomplished and you never look at the left hand—you just don't, it's not where the action is—and the trigger is squeezed and a .22 SUPER smacks into your chest and you go right to your knees trying to pull the Llama out and just never get that extra half-second because fire is jumping out of gunmetal blue, and putting out your running lights and that's the name of that tune. *Adiós, muchachos.*

And this is Michael Hora and so Chaingang goes right up close and puts one up in his ear and kicks the Llama away and is going up those rotten stairs but the slow lady she moves pretty good she's damn fast for being slow and she's already inside fumbling with a 410 when he plunks her in her pig back and she turns as if to say, Hey, watch it, and he plugs her right in her forehead and she goes down with one of the little chunks of dirty lead in her brain and he's grabbed the 410 and at a window, making sure Hora hasn't moved, and Sissy hasn't come outside but she could be looking out a window and he's got Hora by a boot and dragging him into the delapidated tool shed in thirty seconds. It went all right.

He goes next door.

"Hear that shootin'?"

"Yeah," she says, still washing a huge shirt by hand out in back. Stray hair down in her eyes. Sweat pouring from her. She looks whiter than he's ever seen her. Shooting, shmooting, her body said. "I feel like shit."

"Go to town. I want you to see the doctor. Ask him to give you something so you'll feel better."

"I'm okay. I'm just hot."

"Do as I say. Tell him you feel like you're gonna pass out."

"I do feel a little faint." What an idiot.

"Right. Here's the keys. Drive carefully."

"Okay." She goes out and heaves herself into the vehicle. She can barely get behind the wheel even with the seat pushed all the way back. She starts the car and drives off at about fifteen miles an hour. At that speed she'll be an hour just getting to town and back. Fine, he thinks, getting the keys to Hora's pickup and starting to clean up the messes. Get the slow sow and Hora loaded and covered. Start for the bridge. He puts them down in the graveyard and drives back. Takes a marking pen and makes a sign for the door of the house and starts packing. He has everything ready to load into the Caprice by the time she comes back from town to find they're leaving.

"He said I was okay."

"I don't trust small-town doctors. Now that you're getting this close I want us near a city doctor who really knows his stuff."

"Okay." He seemed so considerate lately.

"I want somebody good nearby, in case there's any

trouble with the, uh, delivery. First, though, I want to give you some more acting practice." It was a word he hadn't used in nearly eight months, the whole time she'd been with him, and her face lit up with the luminosity of the eternally hopeful.

"Sure."

"Need some new wheels." Also need some new money. He'd turned up nearly six hundred dollars squirreled away inside Hora's place, but that wasn't nearly enough now. He wanted a nice cushion. But he could go out and get what he needed that night . . . Or the next day . . . He'd get it.

Daniel Bunkowski almost never killed to rob. He had little intrinsic interest in material goods, and certainly none whatsoever in the accumulation of monetary wealth. But he enjoyed the sport, the challenge, and the RIGHT-NESS of thievery. It was important to him to rob now and then. Those scum out there OWED it to him.

His precognitive computer of a mind stored his next steps for later retrieval. The distancing of themselves from Stobaugh County. The best way to get the next legal wheels and how he would coach Sissy to buy the car. How the second legally bought ride would insulate him. Next the new identities. Clothing. The physical make-overs. His, anyway, almost no point in wasting anything on this one. Let her drop the frog first.

Daniel understood the process of ovulation by which the female egg is fertilized by male spermatozoa. How it develops into an embryo and fetus and after the three requisite trimesters, what the doctor kept calling "the thirty-seven to forty-week gestation," an infant is miraculously produced. It meant no more to Bunkowski than the lunar cycle. It was just something that was. He had never had any reason to come to terms with the fact that *HE*, this beast on two legs, was capable of producing a normal, human, viviparous response. When the time came, he would learn the meaning of the phrase "a sense of wonder."

BUCKHEAD SPRINGS

"**J**uggy," he said to the PR guy, "f'r Chrissakes."

"Hey, Jack, what can I say, booby?" He spread out his hands expansively in a totally insincere gesture.

"Hey, this is home, ya know?"

"I hear ya, *paisan*, but this was the deal," he whispered conspiratorially, smiling some orthodontist's Bermuda vacation.

"Donna too? Jesus." Eichord was just a hair away from boiling over and he knew he didn't want that to happen. But the PR dude should have handled it so it wouldn't have ended up on his fucking doorstep.

"It's a PHOTO *OPPORTUNITY*, poops," Juggy Jay told him. Juggy and Eichord got along well because they both had a sense of humor, and Juggy had earned his nickname out in the wet trenches, something Jack knew all about. All too well.

"Uh huh," he said, feeling like a fatuous fool in his old Mets cap.

"What can I tell ya?"

"Right." Where was a houndstooth cape or a meerschaum when you needed one.

"You guys are news. People wanna see. Superflyyyy." He grinned.

"Cut me a huss," Eichord said, without moving his lips.

"It's good for the shop."

"Real smart. And down the line I'm on a homicide and

some crazy hump sees this and he knows what my lady looks like."

"They got fifty GRILLION shots of her in Dallas, bunky, and one more ain't gonna hoit. Also, that's why the wig." Booby. Poops. Bunky. Poopsy. Juggy. Christ, it sounded like the fucking East Side Kids. Eichord sulked.

"It's all right, hon," Donna whispered to him, having already quite obviously accepted the fact that a photographer was waiting to take a picture of the Eichords.

"No. It's not, actually," he said to her quietly in his most brittle whisper, and he smiled to soften it. "But what the hell."

"Come on." She held his hand. "If we don't give it to them with our blessing they'll just get it anyway under worse conditions—that's what you've always told me." She'd acclimated herself to Jack's unwanted celebrity, as well as her own. She'd had her fill of the spotlight too, such as it was, but ever since Dallas there'd been enough vestiges of it from time to time that it no longer jarred. It was certainly part of her husband's life, and for good or bad she figured she might as well do the best she could to accept it gracefully. Jack was hot and cold on it. One time he'd grin and go with the flow. Next time he'd stomp his feet a little.

In Dallas, where Donna had been abducted and raped by the brother of a psychotic killer, she'd had her fifteen minutes of stardom and then some. She'd been hounded by print and electronic media, the American version of the paparazzi, and had not handled it well. They'd talked about it. Jack talked about it. "You have to understand the public's curiosity. The concept of serial killings holds a perverse fascination for these people." He was talking about a woman buying supermarket tabloids, but he meant everybody. "The horror of it is kinda like terrorism itself, you know? We can't quite put it in any of the accepted pigeonholes.

"We try to comprehend the mass horror of the Reverend Jones, the clown who tortures and kills boys—whose names begins with the ironic John Wayne, the mystical, demented monsters like"—he started to say Joseph Hackabee, but swallowed the words and said—"the so-called Lonely Hearts killer. And more than anything else we want somebody to have answers.

"They want to believe some cop has genuine insight into the mentality and psyche of the serial murderer. It's the supersleuth syndrome, that desire to have a hero we can put our faith in. Sherlock's on the job, gang. We can sleep safely tonight. But where was I in Atlanta, for example, when that nut was killing the kids? I've struck out more times than I've hit homers, but the press don't talk about those.

"Part of it is the guys I work for. The brass with the hash-marks and big bellies and Swiss bank accounts. I'm a media tool, they say," he pronounced the words with a vengeance, "and they're going to use whoever or whatever they can because to them the balance of the scales rests on manipulation of the public perception. It's not so much catch the bad guys as make sure we LOOK like we caught the bad guys." He shook his head in frustration. "Finally you just shrug and say, What the hell." And that's what Jack was doing now.

This would get a lot of coverage. The big regional daily was doing a piece on law enforcement. It was pro-cop, with a pictorial section on the Major Crimes Task Force and—central to that—Jack. These were the kinds of public-relations pieces in which the top cops, Eichord's rabbis within the system, could use print to spoon-feed whatever the latest official thinking was. This week's install-ment in the continuing efforts of the establishment to keep the old upscale image in motion. Jack and Donna Eichord at home. It went against his grain but he was smart enough to know he wasn't being asked, he was being told. It went with the territory. So you give in here, whether you think it's right or wrong, and later—when something is too tough to swallow—you stomp and scream and kick holes in the wall and maybe then it's your turn and you get your way.

"Okay, gang," the woman from the paper said to them, "let's do it."

The young man with the camera got down on his knees as if to pray, and he motioned for the Eichords to move to the right. "Could you come over this way, please?"

"Sure," Juggy Jay said, as if he'd been asked.

The cop and the cop's wife moved over as directed. The sun hit Eichord right in the eyes like a couple of steel knitting needles. He made a kind of humming noise in agony and the photographer said, "Good. Hold THAT!" And something clicked and a car squealed up and Eichord saw fat Dana lurch from one side, Chink from the other, and Jimmie motioned him over.

Donna saw them say something to him that made him change the set of his big shoulders—bad or good she couldn't tell but something—and turned back and shouted, "That's it. Sorry! Gotta go. Donna," and he sort of pointed with his head, which she knew by now meant, Better go on back in the house. She'd been through enough with him that she knew he didn't futz around. When he looked like that, it was time to move. She just said her thanks, made a couple of quick apologies, said good-byes, and went inside, wondering if it were something bad.

"Thanks," Eichord said from the back seat of the car as they pulled away, "gave me an excuse to put an end to that shit."

"Our pleasure."

"Okay. What happened?" The unmarked car's radio was blasting. Lee leaned back over the seat with his hand over his face, as if he didn't want anybody reading his lips.

"I got pulled in on the thing yesterday. The feds." Eichord's heart started to sink. "No. Really. No sweat. They don't know jack. They don't know babyshit. Gave me this hilarious thing about a secret surveillance camera or something, said they had me dead-bang. I said, Fine, assholes—arrest me then, right? I'll sue you from one end of the fucking city to the other." Eichord didn't appear relieved. "They later cop that it's bullshit. They run some crap by me about computer-enhanced doo-dahs, and the electronic reebus-feebus. All this good craparoony. And the bottom line is—they cut me loose. Nothing. I go home—right. The blimp here's on the landline. Meet me outside. He wheels by in the blimpmobile and lays it on me." He looks at Dana Tuny.

"They had this moke John Monroe in Segregation and, funny thing, somebody didn't like the way he ratted out his partner and what not. They convinced him he didn't have anything to live for, and the booger just goes over, takes a towel, and hangs himself." Chink tilted his head over like he was dead. Dana's hung-man neck schtick.

"So now what?" Eichord felt like he was being booked on the *Titanic*.

"Who the fuck knows?" Lee said. He looked over at his pudgy partner and shrugged.

"What a handjob."

"They'll watch you the rest of your fucking *life*, man." Eichord told him. All for twelve fucking thousand. "This just keeps getting worse and worse." And he didn't know anything. He hadn't even seen the tip of the shitberg. "Jeezus, Chink—I mean, seriously, you're a logical person. You knew there was no fuckin' way you could get clear with the money in that sort of a controlled circumstance. You knew it would mess up your job. They'd be suspicious of you forever. It might even get you thrown off the force not to mention *into* prison. Why in the flaming *FUCK* did you do it?"

"Everybody else gets THEIR slice of the American Pie, papa-san. I looked down there and saw that fucking money, and that was *MY* slice. Hey, I'll tell you the truth I only wish it had been *MORE*. I wish it wasn't twelve I wish it was a hundred twelve. And as far as them watching me the rest of my life, fuck 'em. And I'll tell you something else, Jack. You know something: if I had it to do over, I'd do it *AGAIN*!"

"Dana," Eichord said, looking into the bloodshot eyes in the rearview mirror, "what the hell are we gonna DO with this maniac?"

"Fucked if I know. What do I look like f'r Chrissakes, a"—he couldn't think of the name "halfway house" and he trailed off sleepily—"a goddamn whaddyacallit?"

"Yeah," his partner said to him reflexively, "for once you got it right, hippo hips. You look like a goddamn whadyacallit."

They rode in silence and finally Eichord muttered, "Well, at least there's one thing to be thankful for: it's still a secret. Only seventeen people know about it."

"That's a lotta yak shit. Nobody's knows but you, me, the human blimp, and"—he narrowed his eyes and in-

toned in his best Sessue Hayakawa—"Admiral Yama-
moto. Nobody else knows that on the dawn of December
twenty-first, my men and I will attack Pearl Bailey."

But Eichord wasn't going for it. He said in a serious,
soft voice, "Jeezus, man. I just can't come to grips with
it. You FUCKING GOT TO COUGH IT UP, BUD.
Get it? You gotta give it back. Either Dana can get it
back to 'em, I can get it back to 'em someway, or
whatever, but get rid of that damn stolen money."

"Don't talk nonsense, Amellican G.I."

"One, it's the right thing to do. Two, it'll show you
are a honest person who just fucked up for a second,
came to your senses, and decided to play it straight.
VERY important, *mano*, when they descend upon your
silly butt with the warrants and the hoo-hah. Gon' be too
late then. Get the money back *now* while you still got a
shot."

"You spleek suplisingly good Engrish for a total roon-a-
tic. But your thinking is unsound." Still with the put-on
voice.

"Yeah." Wonderful. His best friend was going to prison.
He couldn't get it up half the time for worrying. And
down at the office he had twenty-nine fucking dossiers
from the task force. Missing persons all having vanished
in the same sixty-mile radius during the past six or eight
months. Sometimes life was just a bowl of cherry pits.

MOUNT VERNON

Howard Kresse, Kresse and Co., Inc., Kresse Enterprises, Inc., Kresse Entertainment, Inc., Kokress/Amalgamated Industries, Inc., Midwest Investment Partners, Ltd., Kresse Art Museum, and a young man purporting to be his son despite the name "Richard Cross" on his credit cards had to drive in all the way from Kresse's exclusive country club on the other side of Mount Vernon, just so—as he elequently put it—his hotshot kid could put a night deposit in some shiksa's sperm depository. "Turbulent" was the most genteel word that could accurately be applied to their father-and-son nonrelationship.

Richard had gone through a period where he had even started calling his father "Howard," but his mother had been so hurt he'd returned to "Dad." It was a small hypocrisy to pay for a loving mother. In fact, this inquisition of the day was all for his mom's benefit, and for his fiancée's, to see if he could lay a foundation on which to build a new relationship. Sharon was a traditionalist who insisted they have all the family ties and niceties of holiday gatherings and all the rest of it. So far it had been a mitigated disaster.

Richard could never understand what made his father tick. He seemed enamored of money, but when his son took over the famous Marsh-Endicott Agency in Chicago, and he became the official guru of record to one of the biggest accounts in local print advertising, he'd thought that would have turned the tide. But no. It only managed to widen the gap between them. Richard could NEVER please his father in a thousand years. Finally, he'd learned to accept it. The unfairness of it rankled, but he'd please his favorite ladies and bite his tongue until he could shake loose of his carping father.

"You really turn onto this shit or you just doin' this to bug me," the father asked his kid rhetorically.

"I don't TURN ONto it, Dad, gimme a break here, will ya?" The kid was twenty-eight years old and making a hundred and fifty thousand a year running one of the biggest agencies in regional advertising.

"You still play the rock-'n'-roll on the radio, look at this hair down to your ass, live like a MENSCH for a change. Be a man, what d'ya—seventeen years old with pimples? Act like a grown-up person."

"Lighten up. Riding with me was your idea."

"Mother said make an effort. She blackmails me. Make an effort with the boy. So I make an effort, I cram myself in this kiddybopper car the hotshot drives to go put a few hard earned dollars into the bank, we can't go down in the daytime like normal people, we got to drive down and in the darkness yet. And I'm crammed in the front with my son the hotshot here, I can't feel my legs they're numb already, I'm getting such a migraine from this music noise here you gotta play."

"So what did you want to talk about? Come on." He reached over and killed the tape deck. "I know you're pissed about somethin'."

"No. Why would I be pissed? My wife is going to Europe by herself. I'm stuck here working my ass off. I gotta kid don't care enough about his old man to bring the girl he's goin' to marry over even if she is a shi—uh, even if we don't know her from nothing. Why would this be a possible irritation?"

Howard Kresse was a business genius. He was responsible for developing some of the biggest shopping malls in the Midwest back in the early 1950s, a pioneer from the dawn of urban renewal. He'd been in on the first teams to steamroller the old ma-and-pa stores for the vast parking lots and huge shopping centers of the new American merchant's dreamworld. Howard Kresse was a dream salesman. He dreamt of big bosomy blond women, shiny limos with wet bars and telephones, leveraged buy-outs, and sprawling shopping centers. And not in that order.

"You know why I haven't brought her with me. Why would you want me to subject my fiancée to this sort of abuse? I know how you'd behave." The kid was Dick Cross, he couldn't even be Dick Kresse, like a man, he had to have a "professional name" like this was Dachau in the 1940s, he couldn't be a Jew in public. What a disappointment this kid had turned out to be. He and his father had not loved each other for many years. They were a kind of family accident that kept looking for a place to happen.

By the late 50s Howard Kresse had filed Chapter 11 twice and made his first seven figures and lost it twice and was on his way to a third when he got into such a swindle he couldn't even believe it was happening. It was called West Hills and a giant conglom wanted him to put it all together for them and it was to be on land HE owned through a dummy corporation and such a license to steal he couldn't believe his luck. BIG bucks, we're talking. And the dough went into smart stocks like Dr. Land's clever camera thing, and he became very rich.

So when Dick that little shit decided to go to some no-prick, goyem school nobody'd ever heard of, and come back with a half-assed major in COMPARATIVE FUCKING LIT that you couldn't get a decent fucking teacher's job with much less anything in business—it was enough to make a father sick. Then, this disappointment goes to work for Lawrence Cain's agency, another little hotshot can't own to being a Jew, and he teaches the kid to dress like some faggot preppie and talk like a hippie, and before you know it, his son is gone and somebody named Richard Cross is making a living in advertising, which, he had to admit, the kid had made a few dollars at. But what a disappointment to Howard that the boy didn't come in with him.

Then the kid winds up running Marsh-Endicott and rubbing the old man's nose in it that he's a big success, you call this a big success running around in a little car with legroom like a fucking Nazi wagon, hair down to your ass, you call this wonderful? And now he's marrying some shiksa named Sharon Souther he never heard of,

God only knows from their family what does the father do—a fucking poet, for all he knows—and never mind where the Kresse and Company, Inc., money is all going to end up someday. It's a heartache. But Mother makes him promise so they're spending the day together and they play golf and dinner at the club so he can't even get to the bank, and now this aggravation.

And some big guard is coming up to the window and the kid rolls it down and the guy is saying something about the night deposit being temporarily closed and all the old man can see is a cap and a badge of some kind and there's the loud bang and Dick is slumping over my God something shot him OH GOD DON'T NOOOOOOOO THE EXPLOSION AND BLINDING FIRE AND THE SMACK OF THE TINY LEAD NEEDLE THE BULLET EMBEDDING ITSELF IN HIS NECK AND OH MY GOD WHY ARE YOU KILLING US LIKE THIS? And the guard leans in and shoots the man on the passenger side again but still it doesn't kill him. As he shoots the car starts moving as Dick Kresse/Richard Cross slides down and to his right and into the man beside him and his foot is off the brake and the car's idling engine is tuned up so high that it surges forward slightly as the huge man tries to wrench the door open but it is locked and the car keeps going until it hits a concrete abutment and it stops and the man has charged after it on strong, tree-trunk legs and he smashes the window and pulls the driver out of the way, taking the checks and cash in the zippered envelope between them, pocketing the checks, which he'll destroy later. He will not try to dispose of these bodies, and he senses the older man is still alive and he puts the long-barreled .22 to the ear of the one on the passenger side and fires another round killing him.

Chaingang takes the two wallets containing, respectively, $68 and $170, and then he finds two hundreds tucked inside a "hidden" compartment in the wallet with the $68 in it, and he doesn't stop to count it all but in less than three minutes he's made about $6,300 and change. More than satisfactory, he thinks, quickly obliterating the prints on the envelope and door handle, and moving toward the car parked nearby, wiping off the empty billfolds and pitching them in the street as he walks. He will not endanger himself further here but soon he must satisfy his hunger for bloody essence of human. He craves a fresh heart.

Even the girl's would do, he thinks, letting himself toy with the idea in his twisted mind as he drives back to her, although he knows he needs her if only for the time being. Soon, however, he will slice open this albatross.

BUCKHEAD SPRINGS

Eichord, who has not had one of THOSE nightmares
for over a year, comes floating up to the surface of a
screaming hell, dreaming the word "INTEGUMENT,"
something that covers or encloses, an enveloping layer of
skin, a membrane or husk. He is unable to break through
to the air, but finally comes up fighting, lungs bursting,
and it is one of the worst of the screaming dreams. It's a
nightmare of tortured, mad, blue-eyed twins from the
Mengele clinic, a fearsome thing borne of his most re-
doubtable adversaries. Searching for parallels in the de-
monology of classical antiquity, he finds a face that
resembles a dead assassin in his dream of the necropolis,
and he comes awake screaming in fear. No! HEARING
a shrill, frightened scream, the agony of his amanuensis,
and he comes out of the dream fighting for the surface
hearing Donna Scannapieco fighting her assailant.

He breaks through the integument woven across his
old boozer's face to find himself facedown on his own
bed and safe, but Donna *is* screaming. He is wide awake,
dazed, on his feet with his revolver in his hand. Stubbing
his toe against something as he runs through the house
toward the back door.

"JACK! JACK!" Donna's screams fill his head as he
crashes through the door nearly taking it from its hinges.
Donna has the kitten now and he sees that she is safe and
the cat is hurt my God it was just the kitten not Donna
oh Jesus not Donna oh God his heart is thumping pounding threatening to burst through his chest and then he sees

234

the black cat the mean fucking little yellow-eyed tough-
guy tomcat and he draws down on it drawing down on all
the Cabreys and Mansons and Zodiacs and Williamses
and Houtchesons and Gaceys and fucking Spanhowers
and sniping, torturing backshooting crazies and squeezes
through sleep-encrusted eyes.

BAAAAAAAAAAAAAAAAAAAAAAAAMMMMM-
MMMMMMMMMMMMMMMMMM! The fucking thing
sounds like an H-bomb going off in his back yard and of
course Christ he's asleep and the little cat is fifty feet
away and moving and Eichord can't hit shit with a handgun
and never could and all the missed shots that have cost
him, perhaps even the ones he doesn't know about yet,
all those fantasies from a thousand Johnny Mack Brown
and Durango and Wild Bill Elliott westerns in the Up-
town and all those movies and TV show cowboys and
cops and perfect, perfectly wonderful sharpshooting moth-
ers come back to kick his ass as he misses. Nothing but a
fucking yellow-eyed bully of a tomcat. Still, the noise
scares the poor kitten and it scratches Donna, who screams
again and runs into the house with the little cat. Tuffkins
has a mangled ear, and Eichord is filled with a blue-eyed,
dadgummed Mengele clinic rage the likes of which has
not possessed him since the old hard-drinking days of
alcoholic, mindless frustration and self-flagellation. He
stomps in through the house and out into the garage,
where he pops the cartridges and the spent shell casing
out of his service revolver. For whatever combination of
reasons—out of control, fucked over and fucked up by
the thousand and one inequities and irritations and shit
he's had to swallow—he cranks that vise handle down
tight, cranking down on case-hardened steel, twisting
down on good ole Mr. Smith and Mr. Wesson, tightening
down on his weapon. Shit—he can't believe he's doing it
even as he twists the vise—he's just so fucking mad! If he
could only laugh, stop for a second, count to ten. But
he's out of goddamn maniacal, shit, fucking CONTROL.
He just can't take any more and there are limits. But
maybe part of his brain is still asleep still fighting his way
through the husk or whatever it was, as he puts it all into
the first shot, with the four-pound mini-sledgehammer.
Jack puts all his weight, his shoulders, his upper-body

strength his biceps, his triceps, forceps, foreplay, foreskin—
FUCK FUCK FUCKKKKKKKKKKKKKKKKKKKK!

He's pounding that barrel, that sight, that trigger guard,
that hammer, slamming down on all the bullshit and the
bad guys and the B-movies and the bad jokes and the
bad shots and the people who would hurt sweet ladies
and innocent kittens and oh fuck do you want a list of
them—DONT YOU FUCKING KNOW WHO THOSE
SONS OF BITCHES ARE? ARE YOU A FUCKING
IDIOT—? CAN'T YOU *DO* SOMETHING ABOUT
THEM? CAN'T YOU STOP THEM SOMEHOW YOU'RE
SUPPOSED TO BE SOME HOT FUCKING SHIT GE-
NIUS THEN PROVE IT STOP THEM FUCKKKKKK-
KKKKKKKKKKKKKK SHIT PISS DAMN IT TO HELL
pounding as hard and as fast as he can and then falling
apart laughing just roaring to think he was so nuts
for a minute that he has taken a four-pound hammer,
this is Mr. Control—now—Jack Eichord for Chrissakes
we're talking about here, and he's turned his service
revolver, a PERFECTLY good weapon that he actually
liked and trusted, and he just can't believe it he's ren-
dered it into a full month's take-home worth of metal
garbage. Just brilliant. And he gets up, lays the hammer
down, leaves the semi-unrecognizable Magnum in the
vise, and goes in to see how his wife and their cat are
doing. Thinking as he does so that they will almost surely
never film the Jack Eichord Story now. Mr. Eastwood
would probably balk at starring in anything titled *Magnum Farce*, particularly when he would have to play a
character called Stupid Harry. It just doesn't have that
same ring to it. Oh, well. He walks in and Donna is
standing there. Looking at him as if to say, Okay, what
OTHER weird tricks can you do?

He makes that total body gesture that begins with the
wrinkles in the forehead and goes down through the
hands that says, "I know. I'm sorry. What can I say?"

And turns and goes back to the bedroom and goes
back and gets his oldest 12-gauge down and carries it
back through the house, saying to Donna on the way out
into the garage, "Don't worry. I'm not going to do anything else weird," but he goes out into the garage and does
something very weird indeed. He pounds his workbench

vise open, drops the remains of his revolver in a box to be buried with full honors later, and wrapping an old oily towel around the gun, he puts IT in the vise, takes a hacksaw, and begins sawing the barrel off. Gunsmithing for the terminally insane.

NASHVILLE

"Uh, Daniel," the girl said in her little soft voice, and he glanced over at her quickly, then back at the busy traffic on Interstate 24, "I'm sick. Could we stop pretty soon?"

He just grunted and nodded and said, in his basso profundo rumble, "Yeah." Within ten minutes he was registering them into a decent motel. She lay flat on her back, breathing like a beached whale, while he carried in such luggage as they possessed by now, which included a duffel bag most people couldn't even lift off the floor much less carry.

"I hurt," she told him when he'd come in and closed the door. Her incessant stream of birdlike chatter had slowed to a trickle and then dried up completely during his most recent southeastern journey.

"Spread your legs," he said.

"I don't feel like doing it," she said, misunderstanding his intentions.

"SPREAD 'EM." She spread her legs and he examined her. Dr. Bunkowski noticed a small "blob of blood" which was the result of the displacement of a mucus plug from the uterine cervix. He told her, "You're all right." She smiled and rolled over on her side as best she could, propped on a mound of motel pillows, and immediately fell asleep.

He set his mental clock for six hours' sleep and was snoring peacefully within sixty seconds.

"Wake up," he told her. He had slept for five hours

and fifty-four minutes. He went into the bathroom and when he came out she was still lying there unmoving.

"What's the matter?" he asked.

"I think it's getting to that time."

"You hurting?"

"Not exactly." She was feeling contractions of her uterus. Daniel had her walk around a little. It didn't make any difference. He carried the desk chair into the bathroom, ran hot water into the bathtub, and had Sissy sit in the chair with her feet in the hot water.

"You feeling good enough to travel?" he asked after a few minutes.

"Sure" she said, rather unconvincingly. "I guess so."

They got back in the car, heading in the direction of Chattanooga, the next stop on the route that made a slow, curving arrow pointed at the heart of one Jack Eichord.

HUBBARD CITY

"**Y**es, sir," the cop was saying to him, "that's really all we can give you at this point." At least he hadn't been one of those people who would genuflect, then take it out on Eichord that he'd been made into a star; or an autograph hound; or somebody who wanted to know what Dr. Demented was really like. This was a dude trying to do his job, and for that Jack was grateful.

"Okay. Appreciate your help. I'm gonna get going."

"Okay. Good luck with it."

"Thanks." He shook hands with the local guys and went outside where the chopper was waiting for him. That was the thing about the task force, there was no scrimping. They went first-class. They got you in "yesterday" and sliced down through all the layers of red tape like a hot knife into the lard of bureaucratic paperwork. They got things done.

Eichord had been sitting at his desk in Buckhead Station one minute and was literally in a vehicle heading for the airport the next, summoned with an emergency forthwith by the Major Crimes Task Force. MacTuff, as the acronym was pronounced, wanted him in Stobaugh County, Illinois, and yesterday. And when they reached out for you like that, you just relaxed and went with it.

It seemed to take longer to get to the crime scene than it had to fly in from Buckhead. He choppered from Hubbard City, which was in southern Stobaugh County, down to an impromptu landing zone at a place called Bayou Landing, where he was met by a pair of feds, one of whom he already knew.

"Hi, Tom," he said as they shook hands quickly, shielding their faces as the helicopter lifted in the invariably threatening windstorm.

"Jack. Come on," Tom said loudly over the noise, and they ran for the waiting car.

"Jack, this is Walter Belcher," he said. "Jack Eichord." Tom D'Amico and Jack had worked together on a couple of things in the past, if only nominally. D'Amico was a competent, career-type federal agent. Eichord didn't know him well, nor did he feel like there was a lot to know. Just somebody he'd seen around on task-force assignments.

"Where do you want to start?" he asked Eichord as soon as the vehicle was moving.

"I'd like to see the bridge, then go look at the bodies. You still getting corpses out of there?"

"Negative. I think we may have 'em all. Fourteen bodies. That includes the trucker."

"How'd the other pictures turn out?"

"Okay, considering." The first batch of stuff they'd taken underwater had been ruined in developing. "Here's some of the new ones." He reached back across the front seat and handed Eichord a thick manila envelope. There was a smaller white envelope inside that, and Jack looked at the shots.

"Christ," he said softly. You really couldn't see much in the shots. A couple of the underwater shots showed the cars pretty clearly, and one in particular with a corpse's face in a window would make for some interesting new nightmares for everybody who looked at it.

The shots of the cars pulled out of the water were so bizarre and terrifying that they almost had a fake look about them, as if a Hollywood shlock producer had decided to film *Demolition Derby of the Undead* and this was the big chase scene, featuring rust buckets full of cadavers in various states of bloated decomposition. He'd seen enough for the time being and handed the envelope back to D'Amico.

"We'll have big blowups by tomorrow. Better resolution and whatnot. The diagrams are here"—he handed Eichord a thick dossier—"with everything we've got so far. Which isn't much."

"Jack," the other agent said, "five of them were locals, did you notice?"

"Any theories on that, Walter?" he asked the man sitting beside him.

"Nah." He shook his head. "We may have an ID on this one." Belcher leaned over and pointed at one of the Jane Doe descriptions. "We're waiting to get the word on this one right now, but barring a surprise, I think this will be Rosa Lotti. Housewife married to a sheet-metal worker in Varney. Been missing a couple weeks. We know this is a farmer, name of Perce F. Shaunessy. Farms some ground not too far from where these two lived. Hora and his common-law wife. They haven't been in the water too long from the looks of 'em."

"The one named Lee Moore is a friend of Shaunessy's," Tom D'Amico said. "There's no connection between the Horas and Moore and Shaunessy other than geography, so far as we know. Shaunessy is believed to have known who Hora was. He's the one that wholesaled to nurseries, landscapers, gardeners, and so forth. Moore worked in some blue-collar job. It's there. I forget."

"A karate instructor?" Eichord read. "Sophomore in high school? Jeezus, these people look like they gotta be random kills."

"It really looks that way," Belcher said.

"Couldn't be some kinda drug thing?" No comment. "You know—a mob thing maybe. They want to do a copycat number. Make it look like the Chicago killings."

"I don't much think so. Shit, the dopers around here all grow their own out in the back yard. There hasn't been much. They busted a pretty good-sized operation up in Centerburg a few months ago. But God, nothing like, you know, these mutilations and so on."

"Cubans, maybe? One of the new Latin gangs? Vengeance killings?" The shrugs were almost audible.

"Well, surely do have a bunch of John Does here. Could be anything. Any damn thing at all."

One phrase kept leaping out at him off the page, and it made him feel sick and he stopped reading and leaned back in the seat and said. "Tom. If you don't mind. Run it down for me again, wouldja? Right from the point the sheriff gets into it?"

"Last night," D'Amico said, turning in the front seat beside the uniformed driver, "Sheriff Bob Anderson gets a call about this tractor trailer going off the Iron Bridge—that's what they used to call the bridge, it's in the folder as the Wooden Bridge, same difference. Anyway, driver was looped and thought he was taking a shortcut and goes right off this old bridge. I mean, you'd have to be totally out of it not to see there wasn't anything there, but if you were tired, and drunk, and it was the darkest night of the year . . . Anyway he didn't see the barricades and just blasted through the steel cable and chains and whatnot and—wham!—sixty feet straight down into the muddy water. Couple people came along, God knows what they were doing out here at three A.M.—making out I suppose. They see the truck in the water down there, the mess all over where it crashed through, they call for an ambulance, the ambulance guys call the sheriff."

"Eula Minery and Dub Ziegenheimer?" Eichord asked. "These the two that noticed the truck."

"Right."

"No satisfactory explanation as to what they were doing on a dark road at three in the morning. Looking down into a swampy old creek sixty feet below. They got priors or anything?"

"Nah."

"Something's funny about that. I don't know. Anyway, so the sheriff gets a call."

"Right. He gets outta bed and comes out. Gets the state rods and whatnot. They call us. The guys who did the diving with lights to try to see if there might have been another body thrown out in the impact, they see a car with three corpses in it and assumed that this was like—you know, an ACCIDENT—and then they go back down and find another car. And another. All old junkers. It was totally weird."

"I imagine." A note on another page caught his eye and he said, "This one corpse marked as John Doe #2. Badly decomposed. Mutilated body. Heart missing. Estimated to be in the water six to eight weeks. What the hell is going on here?"

"Nothing good."

"That's for sure."

"Jeezus." He read the composite sheet of recent missing persons in southern Stobaugh County.

Heather Annenberg. Daughter of a podiatrist. Probable runaway.

Mary Anne Brimer. A married dietician.

John Davis. Another truck driver.

Ernest Jones. A cook. Another Jones. A Johnson.

Bill Judd. A computer programmer.

Jesse Keys. A carpenter and jack-of-all-trades.

Rosa Lotti. Housewife. A kid named Lingle. Thirteen.

Royce Maxwell. Unemployed.

Melba Murphy. College freshman.

Nuyen. Obergoenner, Odum, Olivera, Pyland, Reeves, Robinson, Rothstein, Rudert, Schmitz, Shanda, two Smiths, Sneathern, Stewart, Tewls, Timmons, Wade, Weiss. Which one of you is the face in the window?

Is it you, Royce Odum, twenty-seven, on your way home from representing the Monroe Implement Bowling League in a regional tournament, driving home to tiny Texas Corners after a great 259 game, never reaching your destination, your car found locked and empty in a field? Is it your face plastered there in the window of the rusting, wheeless car—a bloated freaked-out concentration camp photo to frighten your survivors, that look of horror caught on what was once your face in midscream? Is this your skull face, Royce? Talk, ole buddy, and tell me. Whodunit?

But Royce Odum is not talking now. Perhaps later. Later tonight when Eichord has spent a tiring and brutalizing day with the hideous cadavers and the frightening death-camp scenes, and he's back in his bed in the Hubbard City Motel; perhaps he'll be ready for a chat. Maybe while dreaming of Sugar Lake, Jack will spit into a visor and pull his mask on and dive down for a look-see, Royce. Down in the cold, muddy waters of dark Sugar Lake.

Perhaps tonight Jack will swim along through his own bubbles as he circles through the frigid underwater shadows of his childhood friends Whortley Williams and Cabrey Brown, his unforgettable pals of long ago, the bully boys who terrorized him so. And maybe he'll find them, each wearing a twisted chain around their elongated necks, each bloated, rotten body chained to the other and then wired to the roots of a mysterious dream tree, a leftover from the Houtcheson case. And then he'll swim by Royce's car and he'll be ready to say hello—speak to him then from that screaming skullhead and tell him all about it.

And seeing the imaginary and the real murder victims will somehow jar loose the old memory of a phrase— "salt walter taffy"—a combination of a cop's first name, the label of a waxy paper-covered piece of candy he once saw that he misread for salt water cadavers, a particularly gruesome pictorial chapter of a police forensics book, and God knows what childhood nightmare.

Will you speak to him then, Royce Odum? Telling Jack of the final minutes and seconds of your life, and of the monster of a man who took you down with muscles of steel and a neck, chest, leg, forearm, hip, gluteus max, pectorals triceps belly hardened by the cruelest regimen of bench presses, deep knee-bends, power squats, sit-ups, arms curls with stacks of landscape timbers, a thousand then ten thousand reps with the weighted whipsickle through impenetrable vetch, his cumbrous bulk and weight sweating, hardening, melting away, the fat dripping off, the steel tendons and muscles preparing to take you to the edge as you ascend the mountaintop funicular and your car breaks loose from the cables and you plummet down out of the sky toward an unyielding death that waits to flatten you—a final, bloody scream trapped in your throat.

And the dream will be very real and in the morning Jack Eichord will not awaken with a hangover as he has done on so many hundreds of shaking, booze-battered mornings in memory. He will awaken with the taste of taffy and the lingering, distinctive smell of a neoprene wet suit, and the thought of Royce's face in the window to chill him to the core. In his heart he will be afraid yet as he comes awake he will not know why.

"I think we may have 'em all," the guy told him. "Fourteen bodies," and the number 14 stayed in his mind but he couldn't remember why or where or what. He remembered what it was when he got dressed the next morning, picking up the small fourteen-inch cardboard box that he carried everywhere now, the box that was only fourteen inches long, EXACTLY fourteen inches, but it felt like it weighed fourteen pounds. The box he carried the thing he'd made in—that day of his other recent nightmare, when he'd woken up after the blue-eyed Mengele clinic twins and the screaming voice that proved not to be a dream at all—the thing he'd made with his own wittle hacksaw.

One could no longer see the part that said it was "Made in New Haven, Conn., USA." It no longer carried the maker's marks or the proud "Winchester Proof Steel." All that was left said "L1653799," and the thing was good for only one purpose. Up close, he could point this at four guys all at the same time, and this baby would quell a fucking mutiny. Because anybody could see that this thing Eichord carried in the box was ready to kick some serious ass. Eichord had grown weary of missing what he shot at. He didn't know *how* weary.

Jack Eichord had that feeling you get when the long double lane of cars is rolling through the tunnel under the river, the traffic bumper to bumper, everybody tailgating, everybody in a hurry, and suddenly somebody way up ahead slams on the brakes for whatever reason and all these vehicles screech to a stop. And you wait. And you know the cars will all start moving pretty soon the way they always do. And a few assholes start honking. Then you turn off the engine and kill your lights and just sit there. Waiting. Wondering what's happened up ahead in the darkness. Realizing for the first time there's a RIVER over your head on the other side of all the concrete and steel. Knowing that there's trouble up ahead. And with each minute that passes, the odds grow greater that the trouble is serious. And you can't help but say to yourself, If trouble had to come, why the hell couldn't it wait until I made it through to the light at the other end?

CHATTANOOGA

Chaingang is in his new used car. Legit wheels. Insulated now by the paper trappings of the real straight world that will protect him from the law's curious gaze. The endless need to steal another ride and more disposal problems that often attend such an acquisition have ceased to exist. He is a citizen. He has rights. Papers. A hugely pregnant wife beside him.

"God," she says, letting out a quiet moan. She has turned into a little whining noise that he keeps tuned out for the most part. It is getting close to the time. The blood had appeared yesterday. Then a watery, colorless gush that finally thinned to a dribble, and not long after that the serious pains began.

"Just take it easy," he tells her solicitously, but she seems to have tuned out on him the way he has on her. She only lets out a noise, "Mmmm-mmmmm," a half-hearted whine that has become her shorthand for okay. She is hurting now at regular intervals for the first time. The pains hit every couple of minutes now. He finds a motel and all but carries her into the room.

"This better?" he asks.

"Jesus," she says as another pain hits. They last half a minute, or so he thinks, watching her. He removes her clothing and pulls a sheet over her and as an afterthought takes one of the big plastic sheets he keeps in the trunk for emergency body bags. He spreads it down and has her lie back down on top of a blanket over the plastic. This figures to be a mess.

"The pain is"—she winces, biting her lower lip, looking like a disco queen in some dance reverie, then she closes her eyes for a minute—"getting kinda bad."

"No problem," he says. Solicitous. Paternal. Dr. Daniel Edward Flowers Bunkowski, Doctor of Death in residence here at Motel Pediatric. All the amenities. Hot and Cold Running Water. Unsterilized equipment with all the latest germs. Color TV and the Movie Channel.

His life has changed. His baby is in this cow's gut. He owns a three-piece suit now that he will put on tomorrow for his urban camouflage. He has lost as much as some men weigh. He owns a maroon used car. He is delivering a baby.

"Ooooooooooooh, shit," she says. He goes over and turns up the volume on the TV. There are no cars beside theirs. The motel is doing a flourishing business. Chaingang has read about delivering babies once while in jail and it is still up there in his data bank. The average length of labor from the first contraction to delivery with a first pregnancy is about twelve hours; this being Sissy's second frog it should pop out of the oven after about eight hours from the first contraction time. The frog is overdue.

Dr. Frankenkong feels the cervix through the vagina. He finds the cervix to be thinned out and dilated to a diameter of about four centimeters. The doctor knows there are 2.54 centimeters to an inch. They have been in the motel for almost four hours and the cervix is now completely dilated. About ten centimeters. Sissy is biting on a washcloth to keep from screaming. Daniel says it is now necessary to tape her mouth shut so "they don't get kicked out." She nods okay.

He also ties her wrists and swollen ankles to the bed. Sissy is spread-eagled, nude under a sheet, eyes closed, moaning in great pain. Mouth duct-taped shut. Now the eyes open wide in terror.

"That's okay," Daniel rumbles gently. He's enjoying himself immensely now. He reaches down and feels a membrane over the fetal head bulging with fluid and he ruptures it by poking it with a finger the size of a steel Monte Cristo #1. Fluid gushes from the vagina running onto the blanket. He has left her plenty of slack and Sissy's knees are in the air.

"Yes," he says, watching her push again, and he sees the light-colored pubic hair part slightly and the dark hair of the fetus can be seen within the stretched introitus. He senses blood and then he spots a trickle where there is a slight tearing of the vagina. That is his CHILD in there wanting out, and the bitch's hole is not big enough.

The storage banks tell him what to do next. He sees a word that means cut and he can cut—no problem. He even carries surgical scalpels. Sterilized, more or less, he thinks. He has a scalpel that Sissy cannot see—you know, just in case. So many things can go wrong. What if the palcenta accidentally implanted low on the uterine wall, just as an example? What then? What if there is a breech and Danny Junior comes out ass-first? What if the umbilical is wrapped around the head? What if a hundred things? What if the motel air-conditioning freezes the kid, or what if it comes out with its ears on backward? What then?

So if the bitch's HOLE is the problem you just make a slightly larger cut but God it's just too tempting isn't it, taking that scalpel and the stupid cunt is spread out here right in front of you on PLASTIC and the TV is LOUD and your KID is in there wanting air and she's an IDIOT you'd be doing her a favor and enough is enough and this is Dr. Bunkowski making his small incision only whoops it just keeps cutting doesn't it that nice easy pressure very delicate there at the vaginal opening the baby's head is there but then the blade is so sharp and it's her fault the bitch strains and arches up as you cut so how can you help it as the blade just keeps going, MAKING THAT BEAU-TIFUL RED, PERFECTLY STRAIGHT OH GOD DON'T YOU LOVE THE WAY IT LOOKS LONG AND STRAIGHT AND OPENING HER RIGHT UP WITH THAT FIRM AND PERFECTLY HELD SCALPEL CUTTING STRAIGHT UP CUTTING DEEPLY NOW THROUGH THE FATTY TISSUE OF THE ABDOMEN JUDGING IT JUST SO MUSTN'T CUT BABY AND CUTTING HER RIGHT IN HALF JESUS CUTTING STRAIGHT ON UP THE CHEST SLICING RIGHT UP THERE AND THEN ONE LEFT TO RIGHT FOR LUCK AND PEEL THAT SHIT OPEN AND TAKE THE BABY JUST REACH ON IN THERE AND LIFT IT OUT OF THAT STEAMING STINKING SCARLET SHIT PILE

OF GUTS AND BILE AND BLOODY THINGS AND BEATING HEART AND SCREAMING AWFUL SUDDEN DEATH AND AGONY AND TERROR BEYOND ANY MORTAL EXPERIENCE, THAT LONG, STRAIGHT, DEEP, PERFECT SLICE UP THE CENTER OF WHAT WAS SISSY FUCKING SELKIRK. CARVING HER OPEN FROM POOP CHUTE TO MORGAN FAIRCHILD CHEST, AND THOSE STEEL-MUSCLED HANDS REACH OUT IN THE SUDDEN, VIOLENT EBULLITION OF THIS BRIGHT-RED MOMENT AND PEEL HER BACK! GOD HOW WONDERFUL IT IS AND CHAINGANG TENDERLY CLEARS THE NEWBORN'S MOUTH AND THROAT AS HE TIES THE UMBILICAL CLOSE TO THE BELLY LIFTING IT OUT OF THE DARK, BEEFY PLACENTA AND THE AMNIOTIC MEMBRANE, AND OH SO GENTLY TAPS THE LITTLE DEAD MONKEY ON THE BOTTOM OF ITS TINY FEET AND IT GOES "wwwwwaaaaaaaaaaaaaaaah," and Chaingang's son is alive. Ten fingers, ten toes, a pair of testicles, and a penis, all orifices clear and with a functioning brain. Dr. Bunkowski, he of the first hundred known heart transplants that didn't take—well, not exactly transplants, open heart surgery we can call it, the good doctor has delivered his own child. The wife, ahhhh, that's another story. She doesn't look like she's going to make it.

That's all she wrote for Sissy, it looks like. It was a weird relationship while it lasted. Poor Sissy-girl walking a kind of razor's edge, never knowing when she'd go too far and her violent madman would have to lash out at her and she'd fall across the blade. When you slide down the banister of life you gotta make sure nobody's hidden anything real sharp in there.

STOBAUGH COUNTY

"**M**r. Schott?" Both Eichord and the agent flashed shields and IDs. "Special agents. Can we talk to you about the—"

"Oh, shit, betcha wanna talk about them bodies. I knew it. Christ's sake I told Larry, the boy I work with, it's that spooky big sumbitch out there at Hora's. You know that Hora was a weird duck hisself 'course I don't hold with talking about the dead. I mean rest in peace and whatnot. But he never did associate with nobody 'round here. Had this woman he lived with out there on that there farm who was playin' without all fifty-two cards in her deck if you get my drift."

"Wonder if we could talk inside?" Jack said, and the man stepped back as he kept up his running commentary. "He come here I dunno—it's been several years back, I think he was in Veetnam and maybe got shot in the head or whatdyacallit shell shock? Anyway, he took up with this ole gal—she didn't have a front porch onner house if you get me—and man he just never—"

"You said spooky, big man. Who did you mean—the one who worked at Michael Hora's?"

"Yeah. BIG mother. Like to go four hundred pound. Stood about seven feet tall. Fill up a damn doorway. Ask Buddy Retter about him, he seen 'm load about three or four ton o' them damn railroad crossties onto a flatbed truck in a couple hours. You couldn't do it with a goddamn FORKLIFT. Strong as a damn OX. Went out there and cleaned out every weed in Hora's pasture with a little

251

old sickle like yea"—he gestured with his hands—"I know where he bought the damn thing 'n you go over to Western Auto if you wanna hear some stories about that big ole boy. He only come up here about a year ago, I remember saying to Larry, this boy works with me? When he come to town I seen 'm one day I said to Larry I said—"

"Uh, Mr. Schott, we have a couple of composite drawings of this Mr. Selkirk, the assistant to Mr. Hora that's missing? I wonder if you'd take a look at these and tell us if they resemble the man."

D'Amico was pulling out the drawings.

"Lemme see 'em," the voluble man said, pulling a set of spectacles from a case in his pocket. "I don't really need these I only wear 'em when I wanna SEE somethin."

"Right," Jack said softly. Schott shook his head.

"Naw. That don't look nothing like . . . Ahhhhh, yeah, that's more like it only this here is wrong. It's more of a triangle, and the face was holes not scars. This looks like scars. He didn't look like that. Djew ever see Killer Karl Kemp rassle?"

"Pardon?"

"He looked just like Killer Karl Kemp's back. In the face, I mean. Killer Karl use to work over by Hubbard, an' we went up there to see him rassle in the amp'theater a coupla times. He had two bullet holes in his back real close together an' it sorta looked thataway, all puckered up. Coulda been anything made 'em. I ain't saying they was bullet holes but they LOOKED like the ones in Killer Karl Kemp's back and I know they WAS bullet holes 'cause I recall when Eddie Rogers shot him. It was over the woman Eddie was livin' with and they got into a altercation over it and had 'em a gunfight up in—"

Eichord was finally able to shut the man up, and they got him to agree to meet with the artist in the sheriff's office later and work up a new Identikit drawing.

They talked to two more persons and learned very little of substance and finally they were in the car and heading back to the temporary command post, Tom D'Amico, Walter Belcher, with one of Bob Anderson's uniformed guys, Gary Ammons, driving them. The radio crackled, and the driver rogered it.

"Task force call for special unit on frequency two."

"Roger, switching to two" He flipped a switch. "Kay zero niner on two, over."

"Is special unit in the vehicle?"

"Affirmative."

"Jack, this is Bob Anderson. Patching a call through from Buckhead, stand by one."

Gary Ammons handed the mike to Eichord, who leaned forward and keyed the press-to-talk switch.

"Eichord standing by, over." He waited.

"Jack, can you hear me?" It was James Lee.

"That's a rog. Loud and clear, Jimmie."

"Need to talk to you on a land line *immediately*." His voice was very cold and businesslike. Jack's first thought was that Chink had just caught the shit from IAD.

"Let me call you in . . . oh, five or ten minutes. Where are you?"

"Squad room."

Eichord almost said, What are you doing there? He figured he'd be at a pay phone.

"You want me to call you back at the squad room?" Eichord repeated, knowing Chink would get the point of the question.

"Yeah. Immediately. Soon as you can."

"Ten-four. Out." The ride took a long six or seven minutes and Jack was outside in a pay telephone calling Buckhead Station and asking for James Lee in homicide.

"Jack, listen. Maybe it's nothing. Maybe something. Listen. Just heard about a mutilation homicide matches your MO there. Did anybody say anything to you about—"

CLIK. BBBBZZZZZZZZZZZZZ.

"Hello? Jesus, oh man, HELLO. SHIT." Click, Tick . . . tick . . . tick . . . tick . . . Is he going to call me or is he waiting to get MY call but if I call HIM and my line is busy when he calls ME then he can't get in and . . .

RIIIIIIIIIIIIINNNNNNG.

"YEAH!"

"—Were cut off. Listen, did you get that about a mutilation homicide?"

"No, what?"

"Can you hear me?"

"YES I CAN FUCKING HEAR. What about a mutilation homicide, Jimmie?"

"This side of Chattanooga, man. I-Seventy-five. A motel. Scene straight out of hell. The maid goes in to clean and runs out into the street screaming. Young girl in there ripped in half. Bed is covered in blood. Sliced open and gutted. Heart removed. Sealed up." There was a noise like he was coughing. "Heart sealed up inside a little plastic bag and put back in the chest cavity. You still there?"

"Yeah. I'm here."

"Medical examiner thinks a baby was removed from the womb of the girl."

"ID?"

"Not yet."

"Let's have the rest of it."

"Yeah. You sittin' down?"

"Yeah."

"Okay. The plastic bag in the chest cavity with the heart cut loose and—you know—sealed up in it. The killer printed your name on it. There was a long pause. Same MO as Bunkowski in Chicago."

"That doesn't mean shit. He could be a copycat, you know that. Let's not get crazy here."

"I thought you oughta know. I mean, the description of the dude matches the guy there. Big, massive Cauc. 'Course that don't mean anything. All you white guys look alike anyway," he said, trying feebly.

"Right."

"Hang tough. I'll have the results datafaxed right to you soon as we get. And call. Perp left prints ALL over the scene. We'll have something from docs on the plastic-bag printing. Get it right to you."

"Yeah." Eichord took a deep breath and let it out slowly as if he had a lungful of smoke. "Other than THAT, how's everything."

"Samey same, papa-san."

"Wonderful."

"I just thought," Lee paused. He was acting like he didn't want to hang up yet. "Uh, you know, if it IS anything, the fucker was in Chatanooga this morning. Sort of on the way here, you know?"

"Yeah. I know. Lemme hear what you get." The connection was broken.

And as he broke the connection he could only think of one thing: a phone call to a Virginia pay phone compliments of his old colleague Sonny Shoenburgen, a career colonel in the intelligence racket who had managed to survive the purges and climb into the senior strata of clandestine spookery. The call had been to an anonymous spook chief who had told him next to nothing about the man he'd been hunting in a notorious serial-murder case. A conversation pried loose through the sticky need-to-know tape that seals the doings of the folks who come out of various compounds and complexes and camps and forts with that special and unique attitude that is part mean and part tradecraft.

"This bridge is burnt. No matter what," he'd said. It was after he'd told him about their "experiment with mercenaries in Southeast Asia," and about this self-taught genius of assassination who had developed a taste for raw, fresh, human heart.

"What makes him kill?" Jack had asked. He'd never forget the sound of those three words down the long, hollow umbilical to spookland.

"He likes it," the man had said.

Even though Eichord was not prepared to believe it was happening, he was galvanized into an orgy of action. Each phone call, each successive interview, every new fact that emerged, each word down the task-force line brought the distant image into sharper focus. Try as he might to build air castles of theory about copycat killers and this and that and the other, he was beginning to see the shape of the shadow that was blocking the other end of the tunnel. And it made him shudder with the icy reality of this terrible thing that could not now be denied.

I-75 EAST OF WINDER

"White-Merrimen," the operator said crisply.

"Good morning," the deep voice rumbled resonantly into the phone, eighteen-wheelers whizzing by not far away. "I need some information related to newborn infants for a piece we're doing for the *Buckhead Advertising Guide*, a new newspaper. Could I ask you just a couple of brief questions?"

"One moment please." A busy receptionist passing the buck to somebody. A pause and then, "Yes? May I help you?"

"Yes, ma'am, we're doing a piece for a new newspaper here, and I just wanted to get a couple of answers about newborn infant care. Okay? I'll be real fast—know you're busy."

"Sure. Okay. Who's this now?"

"It's called the *Buckhead Ad Guide*. It won't be out for a couple of weeks but it will have a lot of information for newly marrieds, people moving to the community, that sort of thing. We won't quote you unless you want us to, okay?"

"What did you want to know?"

"What do you recommend for the feeding of a newborn child? Let's assume the mother doesn't breast-feed for whatever reason, and . . ." Chaingang in his three-piece suit, looking extremely large but quite proper, talking into a pay telephone within .22 range of the southeast lane of I-75, talking his line of con into a phone, looking into the window of a used maroon Sedan DeVille, amaz-

256

ingly legal, at the tiny, wrinkled monkey packed into a soft nest of covers.

"Yes," he said, "uh-huh," as he milked the woman for all the information necessary for the proper care and feeding of the newborn monkey.

"Thanks," he told her. He hung up the phone and got back into the car. "Now, little monkey," he said in soft tones, "we'll get you some goodies." The child was fast asleep, and he slept through the closing of the car door and the starting of the engine.

Bunkowski drove to a nearby shopping area and was soon back in the car with formula, appropriate containers, bottles, boxes of diapers, and piles of things that he stacked methodically across the back seat. He pulled the car over into a shady area behind a building and told his son, "You're such a fine monkey. Monkey doesn't hardly cry at all," and beaming with pleasure and amazement he gently lowered a nippled bottle of formula toward the wrinkled monkey, who gratefully began to feed. Daniel remembered something about how you were supposed to test the formula first by shaking some out onto your wrist to see if it was too hot. It made his smile even wider—the thought of putting formula on that huge, steel-hard wrist. Life was actually rather amazing.

"Good monkey, atta boy," he said paternally. The monkey fed. Slept again. Daniel knew he must find a safe place for the baby. A nice, quiet motel where he could care for the baby while he marshaled his forces. There was a way he might even pay someone to rent him a small, secluded home or apartment for temporary quarters. He drove around the corner and paid for a newspaper. He would see what his options were.

He was scanning the paper as he always did, speed-reading blocks of words, his eidetic memory sorting chaff and wheat and saving only the survivalist data of possible importance to him. He saw the headline buried on page six: BRIDGE (contin.— Page 2)" and the words "southern Stobaugh County," and he thumbed back to the second page and saw the big headline and the picture of the semi being hauled out of the water. There was a photo of the buried vehicle graveyard in a long shot from the road, a crowd of people milling around. The headline being

14 BODIES FOUND AFTER TRUCK DRIVES INTO CREEK, and he read:

Stobaugh County sheriff's deputies, aided by emergency workers and agents of the Major Crimes Task Force, pulled four vehicles containing bodies from the shallow waters of the New Cairo Creek, following an accident Wednesday morning in which a tractor-trailer rig was driven off a closed, abandoned bridge.

The tractor-trailer rig's driver, whose name is being withheld pending notification of next of kin, plunged from the long-abandoned bridge into the creek sixty feet below, instantly killing him. Passers-by noticed the truck in the water and notified authorites, who found the vehicles containing the other bodies while searching for additional passengers who might have been thrown clear of the truck.

"Some of the bodies have been identified but their identities are being withheld," Stobaugh County Sheriff Bob Anderson said. Anderson would not speculate as to the cause of death of the thirteen other individuals whose bodies were found in abandoned cars and trucks that had apparently been placed in the creek over a period of many months.

"It is a scene out of hell," one unnamed worker told reporters, "and I hope I never see anything like this again as long as I live." Divers and emergency personnel were still looking for bodies as late as nine hours following the removal of the tractor-trailer rig from the creek. "In the first place, it was extremely dangerous to leave a bridge like that. Even with it closed on each side, there was always the chance somebody might have an accident here at night," the worker said. "Nobody knows where these others came from."

The bridge is situated southeast of Mount Vernon, about twelve miles south of Hubbard City, Illinois. The Stobaugh County Army Corps of Engineers issued a brief statement blaming "insufficient funds" for the fact that the bridge over the New Cairo Creek had never been rebuilt.

The designer of the original bridge, which was built over forty years ago, said that flash flooding had originally been the cause of the erosion of the bridge supports which led to the bridge's collapse nine years ago. "I've built over six hundred bridges in my time," B. L. Drake told one reporter, "and I never had any problems with any of the others." Drake was head of the United Engineering Design Corporation of Chicago, the firm that built the iron bridge in the late 1940s. "It was extremely irresponsible not to rebuild the bridge," he said.

Federal authorities on the scene would not speculate as to the nature of the—" Chaingang glanced over at the photo again, captioned with the bold title, "BIZARRE UNDERWATER GRAVEYARD HOLDS 13 MORE BODIES," and crumpled the paper savagely.

"This changes lots of things, little monkey," he told the newborn infant. "We'll adapt accordingly," he said, starting up the car and driving toward Buckhead. "We'll pay a little courtesy call on our good friend Mr. Eichord and then we'll find us a nice, temporary shelter. How does that sound, little monkey?"

As if in reply, the newborn baby did its best to smile and made a kind of contented gurgling noise.

"Monkey is a GOOD baby," the huge man rumbled, thinking how much pleasure it would give him deep inside to rip the arrogant cop into shreds of bloody payback, how good the anticipation felt, how wonderfully his new life had come together, how bright the prospects were, how enjoyable it was to be alive and invulnerable.

BUCKHEAD SPRINGS

"**O**h!" Donna Eichord was surprised by the little kitten, who had stood up on his hind legs sinking his tiny front claws into her leg. "Ouch! Don't!" she said, disengaging the cat from her flesh. "That hurts, you little stinkpot. You're so quiet. You nearly scared me to death, sneaking up on me." She was cleaning a chicken and she put the naked fowl down, washed her hands, then picked the kitten up and carried him into the living room, sitting him down on the floor and dropping down beside him.

"Wanna play?" she said, and the cat meowed loudly. "Okay, come on." And she tossed one of his toys. "Come on. You wanna play, let's play then. Chase it, Tuffkins." She threw the fake mouse across the room. The cat cocked his head at her and let out a meow of disinterest. "Not into that, eh?" He yawned. "You sleepy? You couldn't be sleepy, little guy, you've been asleep half the day. You want your dinner?" The car cried and she got up with a sigh and looked at the clock. "Okay. Dinner coming up."

She took the can opener and opened some cat food. Tuffy sniffed it a couple of times, then walked to the back door.

"Okay. I give up. I'm going to let you out but only on one condition: you have to promise you'll come in when I call you. No making me come chase you down like last time, okay?"

The cat blinked, or so she imagined, meaning, yes, I promise, and she said, "All right. Just remember,

260

pal, a deal is a deal." She opened the door with a flourish. "And it's little Tuff coming out of chute number one. Wheeee!" The small ball of gray flew past her into the freedom and excitement of the yard and the big, wild, outdoor world.

BUCKHEAD STATION

"**S**till no answer in Room 117?" James Lee asked the switchboard operator.

"No, sir. I'm sorry. I let it ring twenty-five times like you said."

"And the messages I left with the desk. No chance he could have come in and picked them up?"

"No way. Everybody knows it concerns official police business, and he hasn't come back here today as far as we know. I had a maid go down and unlock the door just to make sure he hadn't come back without any of us knowing it, and he's not in the room."

"Yeah. Okay."

"Sorry, sir. We'll notify him as soon as he comes in this evening."

"Yeah. Yeah. Good. Right. Thanks a lot." Lee hung up and called the sheriff's number.

A man answered. "Yes. Is this the same gentleman I spoke with about half an hour ago? This is Lee out of Buckhead Station."

"No, sir. You're the one trying to reach Special Agent Eichord?"

"Correct."

"We have been unable to reach them since your call earlier. However, Tom D'Amico was with him just a little while ago. Would you like to speak with him?"

"Please."

A pause.

"Sgt. Lee? Tom D'Amico."

"Hi. Listen, you have any idea where the hell Eichord went to today?"

"We were together some of the day. I haven't seen him for the last couple of hours. They said he isn't responding to the radio, so wherever he went with the driver they've left the car. I imagine he'll be calling in anytime now."

"It's imperative I get in touch with Jack right away. Life and death, my man. Can you help?"

"Best I could do is take your message. Either give it to Jack when they call back in or have him call you right away. I guess you tried the motel, right?"

"I've called the Hubbard City Motel five or six times," Lee said. Six times, D'Amico thought silently, according to our count. But he said, "Well, don't worry, he'll be in touch soon. Do you want me to give him any message or have him call you or what?"

"Okay, first give him this, then get him to call me right away. If I'm not here I'll leave word with the dispatcher on the phones. Okay. Tell him I want to make sure he's got everything on the Chattanooga killing. Prints has positives on the perpetrator. Daniel Bunkowski is still alive. Tell him that as soon as he calls in or radios in and make sure he phones me right away, okay?"

"Gotcha. Will do."

"Thanks a lot."

"Okay. No problem. Talk to you soon, then."

"Sure." Lee hung up. "Shit! Goddammit." Lee was worried. Mad that he couldn't find Eichord. Where the fuck WAS he? Why didn't the coppers up there know anything? Why didn't Eichord ever have his fucking call-beeper on him? He had to get the word to him. Somebody had to get Donna out of the house, put round-the-clock surveillance on Eichord's place, the station house itself. He tried to remember everything Jack had told him about the Lonely Hearts maniac.

He had made up his mind about the money that morning and it irritated him further that he couldn't say to Jack, "Hey, pal. You're right. I gotta do the right thing." He'd figured a way to get it back to the bank without copping to it himself. He'd explain the whole thing to Jack. He knew he could count on Eichord to help him.

Reluctantly, he'd already taken the first step. It was one he couldn't take back and already the weight of the guilt had lifted from him like a cross being lifted from his shoulders. He smiled at the thought of the Christian imagery, amused, as he sometimes was, to find that he no longer thought in Chinese.

"I'm a helluva guy, you know that," he said to his fat partner sitting at a nearby desk, who blew an enormous raspberry-flavored fart at him without looking. "C'mon, super-pooper, we gotta go take Donna somewhere safe."

"I'll handle that. I'll take her to a motel."

"Good idea," he said. "She *would* be safe with you in a motel, dinky-dick." He took the stairs two at a time. "Hey, babe," Lee said to the girl at the switchboard, who lifted her frizzy head and smiled at him, "do me one. Call Peggy and tell her I need her to wait around the house. I'm gonna be bringing Mrs. Eichord over there. Nothing's wrong, I'll explain to her when we get there. Just tell her—ah, just say that, okay?"

"Sure." The girl started dialing his number.

"Peg'll worry now, schmuck," fat Dana said to him as they went to the car, "all the time till you get there. She'll wonder if Jack and her had a fight or something. What a dummy."

"Hey. That's show biz," Lee said, starting the car and roaring out toward Buckhead Springs in the fast lane.

Twelve minutes later they were pulling into the street leading to the Eichord's subdivision. Daniel Edward Flowers Bunkowski and his newborn son were a half-mile away, driving at the speed limit, and looking for the street in the newspaper piece on which the Eichords lived. Bunkowski had the newspaper that he'd had photocopied by the Buckhead Library spread open in the seat between his massive body and the baby's nest. The microfiche had made grainy but usable copies. He had found the street and now had the chore of spotting the house that matched the one visible behind the smiling couple in the photo.

He looked at the monkey with the little tiny hands and feet all bundled up in the pile of blankets and thought he could make a perfect and safe bassinet out of his camouflage tarp and the enormous piece of mosquito netting he sometimes used in his night ambushes. He looked back at the houses, driving slowly, and missing nothing, every house automatically checked against the image retained in his mental computer, he concentrated fiercely with the total dedication that marked all his moves in combat situations.

Bunkowski spotted the house, the name "EICHORD" across the side of the mailbox at street level, and mashed the accelerator a little, heading for the shopping mall he'd seen. All the time the mental computer gears whirred, sorting possibilities, permutations, ways and means, options and escape routes, logistics and countermeasures. Was parking the baby on a darkened side street, hidden on the floor of the DeVille, the best way? The only way? Ample oxygen? Peril assessment? It was the last calculated gamble he'd make with his little monkey. He'd park two blocks from Eichord's. Make the car switch within seconds of the "calling card."

While Chaingang was taking care of business Chink and Chunk were parking out in front of Jack's and Donna's house, feeling oddly out of place to be here on cop business instead of socializing, and they headed up to the door and rang.

"Wait here, I'll go around back." Dana stood on the front stoop and Jimmie ran around in the back yard. No Donna Eichord in sight. He banged on the back door. Nothing. He went back around. Tuny shook his head.

"I'm gonna see if I can slip the lock."

"Eichord have yer yellow eggs for an omelet if you go walkin' in on her in the can," Dana said, followed by something else Lee didn't catch as he was halfway around to the back again, slipping the back door lock only to find the door was open. He went in, thinking about his Magnum almost as an afterthought, the way one does when one goes through a door and nobody's there.

"Donna?" He called out louder as he walked through the home, "DONNA, IT'S JAMES LEE. *DONNA?*" Nobody. He opened the door for Tuny.

"She ain't here," Dana told him as he came in, unnecessarily.

"Yeah, I can see that, Jumbo. Listen. Uh, whyncha go hit the neighbors' houses. Maybe she went next door for a cuppa coffee, whatever. I'll wait in case she comes back."

"Yeah. Awright," his fat partner said, and went out the door and down the stairs, taking off at a brisk waddle.

Lee went over and sat in the front window, where he could see Dana going up to the door to the Eichords' east and ringing the bell. Waiting, then moving off and trying the next house. Lee turned back to the window and put his feet up on the ottoman and waited impatiently. He picked up a magazine and thumbed through it. Put it down. Listened to the clock tick. Picked up Jack's old Mets cap. Fooled around with it, trying to spin the bill on his finger. Stuck it absentmindedly on his head, whistling softly, waiting.

Chain parked in the center of the street, the motor running, in park, door open, came out hard and fast and tough and mean. An amalgam of pent-up, murderous emotions housed in the body of a twisted giant, controlled by the tortured mind of a genius, a physical precognate, running up the bank on those steel tree trunks, not an ounce of fat on the enormous body, lightning-fast now, so far from the Chaingang of old as to be unrecognizable in motion, none of the inertia problems of the massively ponderous, no pachyderm ludicrousness, all fast well-oiled blur, the hands, fingers, muscles in the arms and shoulders rippling, the muscles capable of squeezing a flashlight battery, those HANDS, the steel-fingered hands that could rip a human's rib cage apart, that could rip a girl open in a steaming stinking ghoulish goulash of horror, three-hundred-plus pounds of rock-hard killer hurls the satchel charge through the front window at the image of the man in the Mets cap, grainy microfiche trigger of data retrieval feeding the on-line terminal, the body flattening on the bank as it blows upward and outward.

"BLLLLLLLLLLLLLLLLLLLLLLLLLLLLLLLLLLLLLLLL LLLLLLLLLLLLLLLLLLLLLLLLAAAAAAAAAAAAAAAA AAAAAAAAAAAAAAAAAMMMMMMMMMMMM!" Wood asbestos insulation glass flesh offal intestine steel rock earth kidney face iron shingle shutter door finger-nails doorknob window lungs skin nails screws balls sparking sizzling shooting red yellow white blue hot slag sparking flying metal melting wood splintering shrapnel whistling people screaming sonic booms crashing autos diving planes bomb blasts ripping the quiet suburban air in a molten metal blast furnace of death and destruction putting an end once and for all to the earthly woes of one Detective Sergeant James Lee in a million microscopic shrapnel bullets designed to cut, rip, tear, mutilate, shred, cut off, cut out, cut down, and permanently excise.

And Chaingang Bunkowski is in the car and gone, his maddening hunger for vengeance slaked, as the terrorizing blast still echoes in the litter-strewn street.

LAKE BUCKHEAD

Chaingang at five hundred pounds, six feet seven inches of killer gorilla, had first faced the seemingly impossible challenge of obtaining a low profile. Where could he possibly hide?

He had emulated his former enemies, the NVA hard core, who hid by day, emerging at night to kill, resupply, move, then vanish again without a trace. They went down into the vast tunnel complexes that spanned the whole of Vietnam . . . to hide, to sleep, nursing their wounded, planning strategies, shaping tactics. And so this is what Bunkowski did.

Knowing how his enemies live by their utilities, he goes to their source: the water supply, sewage disposal systems, electrical hookups, telephone cables, pipelines, subways, underground linkages. The subterranean world that charges and flushes and rumbles beneath the surface of urban America.

Now he is down to 320 pounds, but he knows he will be very hot. His face or a reasonable facsimile—scars, dimples, warts, and all—will be plastered all over Buckhead. And there is the little newborn thing that must be cared for. He cannot go back into the sewers.

It is pitch-black night and Chaingang is behind the wheel of the maroon Sedan DeVille cruising through a rich residential section of suburban Buckhead. He is looking for a certain type of midrange home. Medium wealth. Somebody on vacation, maybe. No house-sitter.. A certain look that will make his sensors purr. The look that says, NOBODY HOME.

He spots a couple of houses that both feel very good to him. He drives on past, cruising the neighborhood. He doesn't want the kind of Beverly Hills-Bellaire thing where you have a private security force running the streets constantly, yet the homes should be monied. The kind of families that can take long, unhurried vacations.

He stops at an all-night convenience store, buys a paper, a quart of Wild Turkey, and some junk food. Why deprive himself? He deserves some R & R now. He worked for it. He buys some fruit juice. He will wean the newborn monkey onto some juice soon. He will get out of this suit. Put his feet up. Enjoy the pleasure of having paid back that arrogant cop.

Chaingang drives back to the darkened area that still beckons him with its aura of vulnerability and access. One of the houses feels especially good and he has long ago learned to trust these vibes. He pulls up to the rear of the house in a shelter of trees and shrubs. It is a perfect place. Isolated. Total privacy. He checks for the signs of "bells" which can be anything from special wiring to the light beam type detectors. The good feeling is still there. He silently opens the back door with one of his special tools.

Had he not opted to be a killer he would have made a wonderful thief. His burglary skills are superb. Soon the baby infant is inside and safe, and Chaingang, working with a penlight, is securing the windows of a back room so that he can turn the lights on. He does so and completes his initial inspection of the house. His estimate is that a family of 5 lives here. The father owns an insurance agency. They have been gone for 8 days. That means he has anywhere from 2 days to 5 days time here if his assessment proves correct.

After he changes the little guy's diaper and washes his hands, he and baby take their bottles. Monkey gets formula—Chaingang Wild Turkey on ice—just the way he likes it. He hangs the suit up carefully and sits on the bed in his skivvies, watching his son contentedly suck down formula as he sucks down whiskey, still the killer, still the madman, but changed.

Gone is the old necrophagiacal heart-eater. Sissy will prove to be his last mutilation. There will be no more hearts. He has partaken of his last ritualistic devouring of the enemy.

He turns to the story he senses he'll find in the paper and reads with more than a bit of amazement that he has blown up the wrong cop.

> BUCKHEAD DETECTIVE KILLED IN BOMB BLAST (BP)—A bomb thrown into the home of a well-known detective, serial murder expert Jack Eichord of Buckhead Springs, killed detective James Lee, 46, police said. Lee had been conducting an inquiry that led him to the home of the special investigator who was out of town on another case at the time of the explosion. "We cannot comment on this at the present time," Buckhead detectives said, when asked about who they thought had thrown the bomb.
>
> The Buckhead Bombing and Arson Unit said the bomb appeared to have been "a high explosive such as C-4 or plastic explosive, something with a detonation velocity of 25,000 feet per second, like a military explosive, and that the bomb had been built with fragmentation shrapnel such as the satchel charges used in the Vietnam War."
>
> The blast lifted the roof from the home at 2771 Spring Hill Drive, blowing large holes in the walls and floor. "It even blew the window frames out," one observer said, "and you could see right down where it blew holes all the way through the floor joists."

The baby began crying and Chaingang tossed the paper onto the floor and looked over at the infant beside him on the bed. In just that heartbeat there was a flash of insight that somehow penetrated through to Chaingang's core, and for just that flicker of light Bunkowski realized how insane he must be. Just a flickering hint of the monstrousness of what he'd done, the tableau of depravity and murder revealed itself to him. The revelation was so surprisingly disgusting to him that he felt himself shudder at the awful, bloodsoaked picture that was the sum of his repugnant past.

The huge man gently reached out a steel cigar finger and tried to put it in the baby's tiny fist, and he knew why he had shuddered in that flash of insight. For the first time in his horror of a life Daniel Bunkowski had something to live for.

SOUTH BUCKHEAD

"I'm sorry." It was all he could say. Peggy was on his shoulder, collapsed, and he held her and rocked her like a baby for a moment as she sobbed. Donna had to physically pull her off and lead her into a bedroom. Bev Tuny had readied their guest room and the doctor was going to sedate Peggy. Donna was going to stay with her the rest of the afternoon. Tonight they were moving everybody to another location. Federal marshals were already working on a transportation plan that was as elaborate as could be devised and quite impenetrable. It would have to be, considering their adversary.

"He tried every way in the world to warn you. He couldn't find you," Dana was saying.

Eichord answered in a cracked voice, emotionless and flat, saying the words not for the first time, "He datafaxed the latents to me about the time I got the rundown from docs on the note. It tested as Bunkowski's printing. Hair and fibers cross-matched the two locations, and so forth. And so on. It was him. Hadda be. I knew I had to get out of there. He was obviously on the way. But he's capable of anything. I had 'em put a lid on it up there. I thought it might give us an edge. Shit, all it did was get Jimmie killed."

He broke down and Dana hugged him and said, "Don't say that, man. You didn't get him killed. No fuckin' way. It was just—shit—his time." They both sobbed. "If we'd found Donna there. Jesus, Jack, we would have left with a warning to her, or just put surveillance on the house and that insane piece of shit would probably have taken me and Jimmie out and gone in and got Donna, too. Just look at it like this—Jimmie saved her life."

"If she hadn't been outta the house because of the cat . . ." He trailed off. Donna had called Tuffy and the kitten hadn't come and she'd gone outside looking for him. The black tomcat had him cornered and she'd seen the cat attack the kitten again just as she went running toward them. The tom had Tuffy about half-killed by the time she chased it off. She had gathered up the injured cat and a neighbor lady had been kind enough to run them over to a nearby vet, where Donna had waited while they sewed up Tuffy's injuries, and they told her they'd keep the kitten there overnight. She took a taxi back to find her home, or what was left of it, in ruins, police cars, ambulance, God knows what all from the fire department to the bomb squad parked in the litter-filled street.

Eichord had been on the scene within an hour and a half. It was then that he learned Jimmie had been killed in the explosion. Donna and Dana Tuny and Bev had gone to tell Peggy and they were with her when Eichord arrived.

Dana and Jack went outside and sat on the front steps.

"It don't seem possible." Dana shook his head.

"Yeah. I know." Jack took a pen and pocket notebook out and began making notes. He would have sketches made of Bunkowski in every possible wig, facial hair combination, glasses, anything he could think of. He'd use his position with the media. He had an idea: a way he could make it very hot for the killer, whom he knew was still close. If not now, as soon as he found out Eichord was alive, he would be back to try again. Eichord could use himself as bait if he could devise the right sort of a trap. He tried to make some preliminary notes but all he could think of was Jimmie.

"Jack? Dana?" Donna was at the door. "Peggy wants to see you both."

The two of them got up. Eichord started through the doorway, but then stopped and held his arm out for his friend to join him. Chink and Chunk had a thousand little routines they'd always do. Like when they went through a doorway they'd try to go through at the same time so they could pretend they'd gotten stuck. Fat Dana's wedged-in-the-doorway shtick.

Dana realized what Jack wanted and he stepped up into the doorway and they squeezed through together, both of them laughing and then sobbing at the same time.

Jack looked at his fat friend. "I've never loved you any more than I love you right now, Dana." And Dana hugged him and Jack sobbed. "Of course, I've never loved you any less either," and broke up completely. He finally got control of himself and they went back to see Peggy, blowing their noses and wiping their eyes.

"Come in, guys," Peggy said, and they went into the bedroom. "He would have said, Hey, you two look like you-know-what." And they both smiled and nodded.

"That's right," Jack said.

"Listen. I know you two are willing to do everything, but I'm okay. I've always been waiting for something like this. You're not ready for it, naturally, but I know what I have to do. I'm going to take care of the details. I've called Jeff and told everybody. I'm about to notify his family in China when the call finally goes through. I've been making some notes. I'll arrange the funeral details and all. I'll be okay.

"I know there was something going on and whatever it was it's all over now. I don't care what it was, but I know that at last he'd decided to do something different and, I dunno, change whatever it was so that it would be right. He was going to make things right. He said to me—one of the last things was, 'Dana and Jack'll be relieved.' So whatever it was he'd got it out of his system and I thought you both should know he'd said that to me."

Neither of them said anything.

"He loved you both very much, you know," she told them, and the tears came in a screaming, uncontrollable flood, and both men went to her and the three of them held one another and cried.

It would be early the next morning before Peg told Jimmie's family about her husband's tragic murder. Nighttime, a day later, as a family friend would listen, carefully taking notes on the other end of a conversation that spanned an ocean and the international dateline. The friend would convey the news of the sad and tragic, faraway death of James Lee to a man who had no voice with which to cry and whose steel hard eyes had long since lost the capacity to shed human tears.

LAKE BUCKHEAD

For two days Chaingang had busied himself with plans, strategies, options, looking at the realistic future and the course of possible actions open to him. The rest of the time he relaxed with baby monkey, playing with it incessantly, loving it the way you would a small puppy, amazed by its microscopic features and the parallels of its biological clock.

Like him, it was little more than a machine. All but without a soul or personality or character. Only the raw mind there for whatever input the river of experience and data would leave in its wake as it washed across the brain wrinkles. A human being in microcosm, designed to ingest formula, convert the matter into energy and bodily waste, sleeping, building, growing, repeating the process. It amazed him. He suddenly realized that a newborn human was the exact mirror opposite of an old person, who slowly degenerates with the intake and expulsion of matter. He saw humanity as a miraculous eating machine.

Chaingang could look at the tiny features—the wrinkled face, the mouth, the miniature hands and feet—for hours and hours. This was his human son. It was a miniature Daniel Bunkowski. He had performed a miracle. He had duplicated himself.

Bunkowski retained only survival information, but that ran the gamut from the basics of high technology to the most incredible trivia. He understood that criminology had made advances far beyond what the public knew about. Just within his own personal history of capture(s) and imprisonment(s) he had experienced many didactic and mind-expanding events that gave the lie to the stereotypical dumb-copper image. What little the public, cons included, knew about the latest advancements in ultrasophisticated weaponry or ultrasound detection was a mere trickle of disinformation filtering down through the media.

A man as large as himself, a man alone with an infant, it would only be a matter of time before they zeroed in on him. He had killed another policeman. Never mind that it had been the wrong one. They would hunt him down as relentlessly as if the victim had been Eichord.

In this new introspection the bestial killer was permitted sufficient insight to realize that his quest of vengeance was meaningless. It was the sort of thing he did when he was out of control. Eichord would now be surrounded by such a steel circle of protection that to attempt to penetrate it again would be virtually suicidal. Yet, to this physical precognate the copper Jack Eichord remained the key to Daniel Bunkowski's future. He represented the police to Chaingang. He WAS the long blue arm.

As always, the huge man was not bereft of plans. He knew that to escape that claw full of sharp, legal talons he would have to vanish again, as he had in Chicago. What was the best way to disappear? To remain in view. The last place they'd look would be right under their noses. He could hide here with his son, and take on the colorings of the locale and its people with his consummate actor's skill. Change. Blend in. Disappear. But to do this there was one major prerequisite. He must have money.

It was this need that had him putting the baby to sleep in its mosquito-netted bassinet and surveilling the traffic at a remote construction site there on the outskirts of monied Lake Buckhead.

Chaingang saw the man get into the van and pull out from the construction site. The van said Catton Construction Co., Inc., on the side of the door and he pulled out a half a block behind it. They went through a newly planted line of scraggly tulip poplars and small, spreading yews, and passed under a huge sign saying WELCOME TO

SOMETHING VISTA A NEW SOMETHING VILLAGE. The two something-words had portions of banner stuck to them and Chaingang couldn't make the words out. At the bottom of the sign that spanned the entranceway and exit to the new project it boasted that this was *New from Concept Environments*, whatever that was.

They went by a vast work site of cats and backhoes and diggers and scoopers and haulers and movers and shakers of every description. Water sluiced down into the muddy earthen pit from a half a hundred pipes and hoses and lines. The lake was about twelve feet deep at the finished depth, and appeared to be five or six acres in overall size. Catton's job would be limited to the construction of the lake, which would ultimately be stocked to keep the standing water from becoming stagnant, at least until they got the place filled and paying for itself.

Concept Environments, Inc., was a work name for the Bernard Grossman Co., who had designed, sold, and erected these "villages" all over the South and Midwest. The man driving the Catton van was on his way to discuss a problem with Mr. Grossman, and the problem was occupying his thoughts when a loud, metallic crunch and a slamming jolt whipped him back and forth in the seat as a vehicle had come from out of nowhere and rammed the van from behind.

"You STUPID son of a bitch," was all he could think as he heard that awful and unmistakable crunch that most motorists end up hearing at some point in their lifetimes, and Bob Byrd came out of the van hopping mad and ready to kick some ass.

For most of us tame citizens, jumping out of our company van with our schedule our precious *time schedule* tampered with in this unexpected way, our mindset rudely altered, our busy life now more cluttered by some inept motorist's stupidity, a pile of forms and phone calls and ennui, added to an already hectic life and workload, there is the moment of anger, understandably, but when we see the man coming out of the other car is a fierce, gigantic six foot seven inch 320-pound scarred, sunburned, tough-looking hard case who looks like he might be able to tear us in half, the moment of anger has this way of suddenly vanishing. Not Bob Byrd. Not this hothead.

"Whycha look where the FUCK you're goin'?"

"Ahhh, hey, man" Bunkowski is saying, the face crinkled with sincere remorse, "I feel like a fucking IDIOT," he says even as Byrd is going, "Why didn'cha hit cher BRAKES when—"

"STUPIDEST damn thing I've ever done." The head about to come off he's shaking it so hard, so abject in his apology, looking all around like he just can't believe it, the big head bobbing around as he admits his stupidity,

"Jeeeezus," Byrd says as he looks at the damage to the van.

"I just can't tell you how sorry I am," Bunkowski is saying, that face in constant motion, that head going all over the place, what he does—he looks around as he talks, looking for a curious passing motorist, looking for the cop car, the rod out of nowhere, the interested construction worker leaning on his shovel a block away drawn by the impact of the vehicles, and moving back up to the van to get a clear view of the front seat, moving the body, the arms, the hands, the face, that huge shadow of bulk in sudden, constant motion. "I just hope I can make this up to you, buddy," he's saying to Bob Byrd, who is still irritated but how the hell can you keep cussing out a guy who admits he's wrong, says he's stupid, and it's all his fault, he's going to make it up to you.

"This is going to cost me—"

"Not to mention fuckin' up your busy schedule," he's telling the guy what he was about to say, he knows just how this man feels, he is genuinely SYMPATHETIC—well, hell, accidents happen—and Byrd is still mad but he's beginning to see there is nothing to be gained by flying off the handle.

"Man, I just wish my foot hadn't slid off that damn brake." And all the time with the body language and the hands, now, HANDLING him so very gently, he couldn't really tell you how it was happening, this big guy TOUCHED him somehow, just a light rap really a pat on the shoulder but the unwanted intrusive familiarity makes you back up and that is how he HANDLES you, MOVES you, MANIPULATES you like a human chess piece.

"I'm always having to drive defensively because of

some IDIOT," he's saying, "and now to go and be one of the idiots—well, I tell you." He keeps up the flood of words, always words coming out at you as that huge head bobs around, the expression constantly changing, so much to look at, to hear, to contend with, to assimilate, the flow of information coming at you so rationally, the words coming in the exact cadence of your own speech pattern, because this is CHAINGANG, who practiced the art of vocal camouflage as a SURVIVAL SKILL.

And 99 percent of the time all the bullshit and the sudden waves of input overload your ordinary thought processes and it's just too much for you, but Bob Byrd is a hothead, you see, and something about the guy, the bigness, the familiarity, the unwanted intrusion on his life just hacks him off and he bristles and PULLS AWAY from the immense man, almost as if he was going to RUN, and the plan, which was to get hold of him with those hands, snap his neck, toss the rubbish back in the van, and get what there was to take and be gone, the plan is changed and Chaingang pulls out the Colt Woodsman and drills the hothead right in the pelvis with the first one, but it's only a .22 long rifle Super and the hands come up as Chain triggers another one, making a nice perforation in the left palm, but by then, as Bob Byrd slips and goes down, Death is right on top of him and he lets him hold one up close and personal the ABC way and pockets the weapon and with one hand the sack of shit is being hauled up off the blacktop and packed back into his van with one of the nasty little chunks of lead in his gray matter, Daniel Edward Flowers Bunkowski having just permanently revoked and canceled Bob Byrd's birth certificate.

The long, strange-looking leather wallet thing is attached to a small chain that is locked to a thick leather belt and for most of us it would take wire cutters to snip through it but Daniel just puts a little crimp in the chain and wraps the slack around a couple of steel cigars on either hand and WHAP the sucker is in two pieces and he is back in the car and moving away from the scene. And a dirty van with Catton Construction Co., Inc., on the door is sort of in the way of the traffic but you can get around it so it will be a few minutes before a semi tries to pull around it, going down on the shoulder a little, the driver sitting high up looking into the van seeing the man who obviously had a heart attack or something slumped down on the floorboards and taking time to signal to a passing scout car.

Even as Daniel drives away the on-line terminals are filing the information away and his bizarre but impressive mind tells him "two men in front of bank" and all the other ones he's shot, from the Horas on going back to the kid in the shallow grave down by the river. Even though he is linked to these deaths in other ways he knows the unpredictability of the law and as a precaution he brakes and fires the rest of the .22 rounds in the magazine, and holding the gun in his open door ejects the spent brass into deep weeds beside the road, and the first small creek he drives over Daniel tosses the Colt over the railing. Just a feeling he has.

How does he know to take just that one car in his guard hat and shield in front of the bank's night depository? How does he know a meat market will have $15,000 in cash on hand? How does he know to hit this dirty construction-company van with money for a payroll deposit in a long, beat-up leather pouch? He's "lucky." He goes with his vibes. Whatever.

Daniel has a plan, an involved plan involving a computer hacker he's read about. He can kidnap the boy. Terrorize him. Make him do a certain thing. Bunkowski can walk away with $50,000 *MINIMUM*. It will be enough to give him a fresh start somewhere. First things first. He has to get the police off his back.

But he still has a day or two before the family returns home to find a very deadly houseguest filling up their clothes hamper and garbage pail with befouled diapers, a newborn boy nestled in a hammocklike bassinet made of voluminous sheets of camouflaged tarp and mosquito netting.

He will go "home." Drink a little Wild Turkey. Work on his next move. Play with the little monkey boy. Count his score.

Daniel will squint those hard black pig eyes and take a close look at the next penetration problem. It will be a simple exercise in rudimentary character analysis. The ring of steel that surrounds this cop Eichord—is it organic? Is it made from a single block of impenetrable metals, vulnerable only to a burning bar or a recoilless rifle? Or is it a ring with a welded join, a point of weakness, and if so, where is that point on the ring?

A man or woman who is all policeman or policewoman inside, they have a common trait. It can be perceived as a strength or a flaw, depending on your viewpoint, and what it is, is the peculiar vein that each of them has at their center. That rich core of pure copper in there. Jack Eichord is one of those curiosities. And copper is not an impenetrable metal.

So Daniel Bunkowski takes equal parts of copper, and ego, and that thing he knows so well—the desire for retribution—and a dash of anger, and a pinch of confidence, and a tablespoon of Duty, and a few shakes of impatience with bureaucratic rules, and he stirs all of this in his mind and he sees how utterly simple it will be to reach out for this arrogant irritation. How pleasurable it will be to finally pluck the thorn once and for all.

And now he knows precisely when and where he will take him down, and a barking cough of amusement escapes his throat at the sheer appropriateness of it.

VIP LOUNGE—BUCKHEAD AIRPORT

"I'm gonna get awfully lonesome for you guys." You guys included the little kitten. Tuffy lay peacefully at Donna's high-heeled feet, asleep inside a white fiberglass carrying cage.

"We're gonna miss you," she said, with her softest voice, and whispered, "Wish we could stay here with you."

"Me too, see." The cat stirred. "How's our little pal there?"

"He's okay." She looked down and in her cat voice purred, "I'm not gonna be real purrrrty for a while, but when I get my stitches taken out I'll look just as good as new."

"Yeah. Absolutely."

'They said there's no idea how long—"

"No"—he knew what she was going to say—"it's totally unpredictable. Can't take any chances though," he said with a smile he didn't feel.

"I know."

"We can't call either. Won't talk to you until this is all over with, so it might be a few days."

"They told me. I'll be fine, honey. Don't worry about anything. Just, you know, take care. Okay?"

"Yeah. Sure." They sat there in silence for a bit. There were marshals at both of the locked doors. Only the Eichords, Peg Lee, and the Tuny family were in the lounge. A company Lear was taxied and parked nearby, filling its tanks for the journey. There were more marshals in unmarked vans parked right by the gate, flanking the black stretch limo that would take them to their protected destination.

"Come're," he said, and she snuggled over as close to him as she could get and he kissed her so hard it pulled her out of her chair.

"My stars," remembering old expressions he whispered to her, "can you remember when they used to say, my stars?"

"Sure," she said, snuggling.

"Land's sakes."

"Land sakes alive."

"Land a' goshen." They laughed.

"Lawd have mercy."

"Lawdy, Miss Claudy."

"Tooty fruity all-rooty?"

"That doesn't count."

"I see. YOURS are okay but mine don't count. I think I have the rules clearly in mind now."

"No song titles. My stars. My lands. That's the kind of thing. Old expressions."

"Well, in all my born days."

"Okay, that's more like it. Gosh all hemlock."

"Croop."

"Excuse me?"

"Croop. Whooping cough. Dropsy. Scarlatina. Mustard plasters."

"I'll accept those, but they're borderline."

"Borderline or not, it's your turn."

"Hully gully, guess how many."

"Bless my soul."

"Hubba-hubba."

"Mrs. Eichord?" a federal marshal said. She stood up. They had agreed beforehand not to say good-bye. They kissed again. And Donna walked away with the kitten in the carrying case. At the door he could overhear Peggy saying something to a marshal about what to tell the family when they arrived from China. The police were going to try to head them off before they changed planes for Buckhead.

Peggy looked over at Jack as she went out the door, Bev and Dana behind her. There was the rigmarole with the boarding tube, the portable thing that was connected to the limo, and then they were all safely behind the bulletproof privacy glass and the shiny car was moving to the small jet.

He watched through the window as they boarded. He could see Donna, voluptuous even at that distance, carrying Tuffy aboard, followed by Peggy, and Bev, and then Chunk's distinctive waddle as he climbed the steps and a marshal pulled the door of the plane closed. They were in the air and gone within a couple of minutes. And the guard vans returned to Buckhead.

Donna, Tuffy, Peg, Bev, Dana, were all in the back of one of the vans, and some very competent matrons and an overweight federal marshal on their way to a paid vacation somewhere. Nobody was taking any chances with this.

The real problem was that Jack Eichord didn't believe it. Not really. Not deep down inside. He knew he'd killed Daniel Bunkowski under the streets of Chicago. He knew that Jimmie Lee was not dead. He knew that their home had not been blown up by a satchel charge. He knew that he would wake up in the morning and the awful dream would be over, this madness of dead killers coming to life, this insanity of his friend's murder, this endless nightmare.

And then, of course, he knew THAT was bullshit.

KOWLOON

The airport was about five miles northeast of downtown. He drove slowly, his mind like a frozen stream, icy white and untroubled.

At Kai Tak, he locked the car and walked to the departures counter. Being a careful man, he checked his notes again before handing the message across the counter to the man, who read it and asked, "Round trip, first class?" To which he nodded yes. The man behind the counter said okay, tabulated quickly, and told him "That will be 32,169 Hong Kong dollars, sir." He handed the exact amount in currency across to the ticket agent. The brotherhood had helped him with the air fare. He would repay the money later.

He would not board for another two hours or so, he was told. He nodded again, took the tickets, and walked through the airport to find a seat in the vicinity of the departure gate. He'd cross the dateline on the long flight over but actually arrive on the same day due to the idiosyncratic nature of the international calendar. He'd leave the following Sunday morning at eight-ten A.M., deplaning back on Kowloon at six P.M. the following day.

He reread his notes once again, reading carefully, his eyes hard as tempered steel and black as a midnight grave.

BUCKHEAD STATION

Only two detectives were in the squad room, Eichord and Brown, each slumped over a desk, each with a phone growing out of their ear, on separate missions, each muttering into a hunk of plastic whose microphone apertures retained the traces of ten thousand breath mints, a quarter-century of cancerous tobacco smoke, a couple of tons of burgers with onions, a small lake of back-to-work tighteners, eight million heartaches in the big, naked city, nine million hours on hold, or, as Chink and Chunk might have said, ten million Wong numbers in Chinatown alone.

"Hello?" Nothing. Nothing but a clicking noise in Eichord's ear. He was calling a TV station to try to keep the lid on the exploding resurrection of the Lonely Hearts case. No please hold, no please stand by, no please please please, just click. Not even a simple "We're too busy to talk right now but if you'll shove the phone receiver up your ass a proctologist will be with you in a couple of weeks." Finally a few more clicks and a lilting voice told him he'd made contact with the mother ship.

"Ginny Snow please," he told the voice, and he sat there waiting while it went one ringy-dingy and two ringy-dingies, and finally another voice and another click and Whom shall I say would like an audience with her highness? Eichord was singing tunelessly to himself as he sorted through the voluminous crime-scene reports that now threatened to shove his desk down through the floor, the voice in his ear stabbing him back to life and he began a soft-shoe tap dance with a local television anchorwoman, conning her for all he was worth, doing his best to keep the lid on this thing.

Finally, his task accomplished, he thanked her, made the obligatory promises about dispensing information, all the usual media bullshit, and hung up. Sighed. Checked his directory and then remembered he had a call card on her and dialed Letty Budge over at the *Buckhead News-Gazette*, slipped his feet back into his patent-leather dancing shoes, and started tapping again.

Letty was a total pro who bought nary a word of it, so he gave up his scam and leveled with her. They were friends. She was a responsible journalist. Blah blah. He needed some slack, and he needed it now. Finally, one more odious task was completed, with promises of exclusivity, a bit of a ribbing about "trying to pull her chain," and he'd managed to buy a few more precious hours.

Eichord knew what it was like when a city was swept up in the awful tide of a pattern of serial crimes. One of his primary functions beyond apprehending serial killers was to placate the media, pure and simple. He was by now such a high-profile cop that anything from him was newsworthy and he didn't blink an eye at using the press the way they so often used him. He didn't like it. He wasn't crazy about it. But it was a vitally important part of his job to keep the flow of ink as managed as he possibly could under the circumstances.

More phone calls. The mock-ups of Bunkowski were almost ready. He told somebody he'd be over in an hour and a half and wanted three copies of everything, plus the master for the new expanded circulars he figured they'd be saturating the town with soon enough. More details. More paper logjam to cut through.

And then, for just a few moments, Jack sat there at the desk in a kind of stupor, listening to Brown murmur in the background, and he thought about his nemesis, Chaingang.

Where are you? What are you doing with that little baby you ripped from the girl in Chattanooga? Why did you take it? Here was a beast who had come back from the dead. Something that ate human hearts. Mutilated. Tortured. Fed. Cannibalized. Gorged to capacity until its vast, demonic hunger was satiated. WHAT IN THE

NAME OF CHRIST WOULD IT DO WITH A TINY BABY? He could hardly stand to think of the possibilities.

While his mind was temporarily in the floating state of hold he seized the opportunity to begin what he called his mnemonic doodle. Years ago he'd taken some courses in speed-reading, improved retention, various self-improvement studies designed to aid him in his work. He'd found mnemonic devices well suited to his work style. Mnemonics gave him a way of retaining large amounts of seemingly unrelated data in a manner that was particularly useful when his ever-present pocket recorder wasn't filing it all away on cassette for him.

In an interrogation or during an impromptu interview or at a busy crime scene he could file away reactions, responses, facts, figures, anything imaginable with his mnemonic system. He'd committed over sixty graphic, numerical images to memory, and these are what he drew now as he began doodling:

1. A picture of a gun beside the number.
2. Glue. A bottle of glue tipped over. Spilled. A lake of sticky glue.
3. A crudely drawn tree.
4. Open door.
5. A hive swarming with bees.
6. A pile of sticks.
7. A billowy cloud with the word "HEAVEN."
8.

Eichord stopped his mnemonic doodle in midstream and thought about the realities of what faced him. He knew what his chances were against this seemingly unstoppable monster.

8. ATE. The things it ate. He doodled an enormous heart with his felt-tip pen and began shading in perspective. Drawing to kill time like some little kid in study hall waiting for the bell and the summertime playground ball game, he doodled the phrase "TO KILL TIME," and he drew a clock with a dagger in it.

The thing had been honing its skills. Dieting. Starving, no doubt. Healing from Jack's pathetic attempts to destroy it, planning its revenge with the acute foresight of a presentient being, killing for pleasure as always. Killing for the basic love of taking human life, guided by the

unerring premonitions and previsions that were the gifts
to be enjoyed by this rare subspecies of humanity.

He looked at the drawing of the gun beside the number one and his mind slipped back into gear. He got up
from the desk and started up the stairs. His chances were
marginal. He smiled to think of it. At the moment he
didn't care. Later he could think about it to his heart's
content and pee his pants in mortal terror.

He went out of the building and drove to a pawn shop
nearby run by the cop's unofficial gunsmith, Shorty
Wallhausen.

"Hey."

"Yo."

"Can't change y'r mind?"

"Nope."

"Okay. I still say if it was me I'd take and get me
something like this." He was holding a .45 Colt in his big
fist. It was pointing at the ceiling and it had jumped into
his hand from out of nowhere.

"If I could handle one the way you can, I would. But
I'm dirt worthless with one of those."

"You don't have to be Wild Bill fucking Hickock,
baby. Just blow about seven dollars' worth of Teflon-
coated KTW power load in his general direction. WAX
that mother-flogger."

"I trust this," Jack said, lifting his heavy fourteen-inch
cardboard box of steel and grip. Shorty held out his hand
and Eichord relinquished it. He always enjoyed watching
somebody like Wallhausen when he examined a weapon.
Any kind of weapon. It was watching a master craftsman
with a fine, precision tool. He showed so much respect
for the ability of the thing, such a great affinity for it. It
was just a kind of awe for the purity of the professional-
ism. Now he felt nothing.

"Well," Shorty said, taking one of the thick red shells
by its brass base and holding it up in the light, "you got
your basic death hurricane here." He wiped off the brass
as he checked the sides of the waxy container, shoving
the two shells into place, wiping the exterior of the am-
putated shotgun as he returned it to its innocuous resting
place in the box. "The master blaster."

"Let's hope," Eichord said quietly.

"Remember our deal. You have to use this on our boy, you doctored the loads yourself."

"That's right, I did."

"Now let's see how you did it," he said, as he handed Jack a hunting knife. "Open the crimp."

"Like this."

"No." Shorty showed him, making it look easy.

"Okay."

"Shake everything out."

He did so, and the little lethal pellets rattled into the metal pan.

"Now watch how I load the crystals." Shorty stuffed the crystalline poison in, repacking the pellets at the same time. "I'm not doing it right, but just so you know how to, if you have to prove you done it. Okay? Now you take an' give this a shot, and a little epoxy"—add a teaspoon of nitro, a pinch of oregano—"and crimp 'er back 'n wipe all the excess. That's an easy way to do it," he told him, making it look easy again.

"Gotcha. I 'preciate it a lot, Shorty."

"Nothin' to it. Jus' do it."

"Long as it gets the job done."

"Put 'er this way, pohdna'. You hit a rhinoceros in the big TOE with this load an' that sucker's dead 'fore he can FALL."

"That MIGHT do it," Eichord said, meaning it. "Thanks." He had little faith in guns, and for damn good reason as he looked at his own sorry track record. He had little faith in his own judgment, seeing as how it had caused his pal Jimmie Lee to die a horrendous and sudden death. He had, when you get right down to it, very little faith in anything right at this moment. He went out and started his car and to his relief it didn't explode.

Jack missed the hell out of his wife. He thought of her more than he'd planned since the bit of hopeful misdirection at the airport. He wished he could talk to her right now. Just hear that sweet voice over the phone. To be able to whisper love talk. To tell her the honeymoon WASN'T over, that there'd be better days. To tell her that nobody said "commence" anymore.

He thought of a bad joke one of the guys had told him about hazard pay, danger pay, something like that. He suddenly felt very cold at the thought of flying solo on this one, but he knew the MO of Daniel Bunkowski. To insulate himself and hide behind a shield of cops would achieve nothing. It would only delay the inevitable confrontation. It would mean more uncertainty for everyone, more innocent victims would surely die. It was better to let this thing come to a head. Easy to say, but when the bull's-eye is painted on your back it's another matter.

He ached so bad with the loss of Jimmie he could put himself at risk again in the hopes of drawing the killer out in the open. This time Eichord wasn't going to miss. No matter what. The man they called Chaingang would die.

For all the pissing and moaning about his status as a media darling there was an up side to it. He could manipulate the ink. His tendency to be nonconfrontational with the brass, somewhere between iconoclast and ass-kisser, had a curious side effect. The powers had now begun to believe the press THEY had created as a buffer between the police and the public. To them Jack had in fact become a supersleuth. It was the way they looked at things. You said something enough times with a perfectly straight face and it came to pass. A nutty sort of egoistic self-confidence bred of supreme power of authority.

But their attitude resulted in Eichord having autonomy now when it came to this sort of situation. And since he was the one who would pay in spades for having allowed Bunkowski to come back, as it were, from the grave—he was going to go for broke. Make himself as vulnerable and unprotected as he could and let the monster come for him. He wanted it one-to-one now. But most of all he just wanted it to be done with.

For a second he could visualize Lee watching him and he said softly, "We'll get him, Chink." And for a second he was the Eichord of old and he looked in the rearview mirror and intoned, "Or my name isn't Michael Lanyard."

BUCKHEAD HIGHWAY MALL

On Tuesday evening, Daniel Bunkowski, in his neatly pressed suit, with infant safely nested beside him, was driving out of the crowded Buckhead Highway Mall and turning at the third light, a now-familiar interchange to him as he drives a route leading to money. He will check a rental property tomorrow morning, and if it seems adequate inside, having already cased the lay of the land and assessed its isolation factor, he will rent the base for his next operation.

The immense killer is not the same anthropophagous wild man who devoured the heart of a fresh kill only a few weeks ago. In fact, he can still feel himself changing. That *thing* that would come over him is growing weak inside him and he can feel its hold on him lessening. The thing that would force him to kill to appease the boiling pressure cooker, to make the awful heat subside, to do violence—the only kind of act that would slake the burning red thirst—no longer had its sharp fangs suck into his innards. He was changing.

All because of the little baby son. It was, indeed, a miracle. Bunkowski for the first time was acting out of regard for someone or something beyond his own survival. Above all else it was now crucial to him that the newborn be protected. His long-range plan, the creation of a self-sustaining safe environment for his pet monkey—involved the acquisition of money. To even make the move involving the computer hacker he needed lots of working cash. One more score on top of the recent windfall. Just a thousand, twelve hundred, would do it. Walking-around money.

"That be all tonight, hon?" the bored lady at the cash register said as he slid a quart of Wild Turkey along the counter together with a crisp new double sawbuck.

"That's got it," he rumbled with a wide smile.

"How you been gettin' by?" she asked with her usual familiarity. Having seen him five or six times he was filed away as a regular.

"Just so-so. I guess I can't complain."

"Well, you can complain but it won't do you a goddamn bit of good."

They both roared with laughter at this brilliant conversational diamond.

"That's for goddamn sure," the big man agreed in his most jovial and pear-shaped approximation of ingenuousness.

"Ohhhhh, my God," she said, stretching like a cat, pushing her chest forward to emphasize what Bunkowski suspected were outrageously padded breasts, "I got a back that's just KILLING ME, ya know?"

"Really?" he said. The state of her health and well-being was clearly the most important thing in the huge man's life. Everything about the sincerity of his facial expression, tone of voice, and the steadiness of his gaze said that her back pain was FASCINATING to him.

"I got the goddamnedest crick in my back I ever had in my life. I tell you it is MURDER." She stretched again in the white sweater, moving her head from side to side as she did so. "I didn't sleep in my own bed las' night and shit I tell ya I can't hardly move today. I stay over at my boyfriend's once in a while, ya know?" Daniel nodded. "An' last night, God, I promise ya it wasn't cause we . . . you know. BELIEVE me, we DIDN'T." She shook her head knowingly, letting him know it wasn't because they'd done the deed hanging from a chandelier or anything. "But hell, you know how it is when you're not in your own bed."

"I sure do. I just don't sleep worth a damn when I'm not in my own bed," he said.

"I can't even sleep good when I'm, you know, on

VACATION or anything. I like my own bed." Her head shook at the very thought of her own bed.

"Boy I hear that loud and clear. You know, I guess this job gets kinda *scary* once inna while, you know—guys coming in and sticking up liquor stores and that." He said it innocently, shaking his head just the way she did as he slowly folded up the bills, letting her see the humongous wad of money he carried so she'd know he wasn't interested personally, just making conversation. A friendly non sequitur.

"The scardiest I've ever been was about four, five months ago this Mexican comes in here—well, I say Mexican, he LOOKED Mexican. Anyway he comes in somethin 'bout a flat and hasta call somebody, he's lost his wallet, hell, I don't remember what all, so he's got a pint of whiskey and he comes over and he says, Put this on my tab."

"Uh huh."

"And I go, You haven't got a tab here, mister. I can't do that."

"Wow."

"And he says, You BETTER do it. And, you know, he just stares. And I stare back at him. And I mean he is STARING at me, you know. I figure he's gonna shoot me or stab me with a knife or somethin' bad is gonna happen. And I move on across like this"—she moved down the length of the counter to show him—"and I said, Listen, mister, if you don't get outta here I'm gonna step on this buzzer back here, and as soon as my foot hits THAT, the shit hits the fan down at PO-LEECE headquarters. NOW GIT THE HELL OUTTA HERE!"

They both laughed at her amazing audacity in the face of peril.

"God! That's really something," Chaingang said, amazed by this woman's bravery and quick thinking, moving around to look where the buzzer was as he told her how great she was. "That was really something!"

"There AIN'T NO BUZZER," she screamed, and they both roared again with laughter.

"Wow! Goddamn, you sure were great. That's pretty fast thinking." He obviously admired her for her cleverness.

"Well, you know, I had to do somethin'. It was all I could think of."

"I don't think MY mind would have worked that fast."

"Wally don't have nothing in here. We don't even keep a gun."

"Hell. Looks like they'd have an alarm to that—whatdya callit—that security company deal."

"Naw. We ain't got shit in here."

"Well, don't that beat all. Hell, I bet if some stickup guy hit you now he'd get a thousand dollars cash!"

"Shit. He'd be lucky to get a hunnert and a half." She leaned on the counter. "Weekends when the money stacks up good."

"Bet you could hit a liquor store like this on a Friday, eight, nine o'clock, come away with plenty."

"No." She shook her head. She knew what she was talking about. "I'd make it Saturday night about ten or ten-thirty," nodding firmly, "yep, that's when the most cash would be on hand."

"Hell, a guy'd probably get two, three thousand on a Saturday night," he agreed.

"Ummm." She shrugged, obviously disagreeing. "He might get fifteen hundred, MAYBE two thousand on a real good Saturday."

They bid their friendly good-nights after a bit and Chaingang got into his car and drove off. It never failed to astonish him . . . the remarkable degree of openness with which people revealed their innermost secrets to casual strangers. He in particular had this ability with people. He could just look at someone and they'd be telling him their life story inside of five minutes. Something about the look of him. A trust thing. Something across the bridge of the nose, in those doughy wrinkles and crinkles, all he lacked was a white beard and a ho-ho-ho. And now—a pillow for padding.

He had a reason for every move he made, if only subconsciously. He'd picked this liquor store to patronize for a specific reason. He was going to hit it, and this imbecile had just told him when the best time was and how safe it would be for him. She'd even given him a guided tour of her behind-the-counter surprises and a peek at her hole card.

It was what he did, this matter of sizing up situations and making instant assessments of the vulnerability and access quotients. He'd gone into the mall nearby and

turned at the third light instead of the second light, by
mistake, and seen this little cluster of stores and services.

A fast-food chicken shack, a car-care center, a disreput-
able-looking motel, a busy gas station, the package store,
a small ma-and-pa operation, and the assessment print-
out was there in that first heartbeat.

When one looked at the chicken shack one saw food;
Daniel saw a bustling interior full of witnesses and a
drive-in window with one of those shatterproof, revolving
Lok-Tite jobs, and looked away. The car-care center
smelled like easy money but there were eight, nine bozos
milling around. Again, too many people. The run-down
motel was okay as far as the access, isolation factor and
vulnerability quotient went, but it was TOO run-down.
Paint chipped from the doors. No guests. Nickles and
dimes. The busy gas station. Impossible for his current
needs. He wanted no witnesses and no MO. He'd probably cold-cock the clerk as soon as he had the money, pop
them into the open trunk, and be gone before the next
car pulled in. He'd hit the store right after dark Saturday.
Daniel figured it to be his last small job.

The next step was the cop. He needed to summon all
his powers of persuasion. He'd charted it out on paper
and it could work. The policeman Eichord was a known
quantity within certain boundaries. If he didn't overreact
to the killing of his friend, and to Bunkowski's track
record, it boiled down to a simple trade-off. Would the
cop be willing to guarantee him unofficial amnesty of
sorts in return for Bunkowski's guarantee that the killings
were over for good? It was a shot.

What did the detective have to lose? He didn't know,
of course, that Daniel had lost his taste for murder and
mutilation. That at last the normalcy of building a regular
life and raising a child had pulled Chaingang's head out
of the sewers. Such was the uniqueness of Chain's madness that he could have this dream, and it was so real to
him he now believed it. And for this strange, bizarre
killer of hundreds, to believe was to be.

He would first try to convince the cop that the killings
had come to an end. He knew this arrogant man would
let him get close. The lure of a confrontation would be

irresistible to him. And he would pay for his temerity with his dying screams and the thought of this filled Chaingang's head with a hot crimson wave of overwhelming need. A final kill.

BUCKHEAD STATION

Back inside the cop shop, Eichord stared at his messages. The first pink call-back note was from the task force, and he tried to place it but all the lines were busy. It would only be more corroboration of the obvious now. The next one was a call to the 312 area code. He dialed it and asked for the extension number specified.

"This is Jack Eichord in Buckhead, returning a long-distance call," he told the male voice that answered.

"Just a second, please."

He waited.

"Jack Eichord?"

"Speaking."

"Can you hear me okay?"

"Yeah. I can hear you fine. Who is this?"

"Having one helluva time hearing you." There was an earsplitting burst of static on the line.

"In Chicago. You remember me?"

"I'm sorry your voice cut out just then." Jeezus. The fucking telephones. It was like living in a goddamn war zone. "I didn't hear you just when you answered me. Who is this please?"

"Scheige in Chicago. Remember?" A little pause as Eichord tried to place the name. "We worked together when you were on loan to the Eighteenth on the Kasikoff case."

"Oh, hell yes. I'm sorry. Sure. How ya doin'?"

"Good. I'm outta the West Erie substation now. Listen I [STATIC] know if Lee told you about me calling him?"

"Sorry. The phones cut out again."

"Yeah. We have problems with the telephone system here. Anyway, I didn't know if James Lee got that message to you about me calling him. I just heard about it, man. Very sorry. Helluva thing."

"Thanks. No. I didn't get the message, I guess." He glanced through the stack of notes as he spoke.

"Well"—Jack could hear a sizzle down the line like bacon frying—"I think we had a tip on this Bunkowski. A fuckin' HYPE came in here trying to sell it to us—how he'd seen him right after you killed him and so on. We didn't give it any credence naturally, but now, I mean, I saw the new circular and the sheets on those killings and I put two and two together. It looks like it was on the square, you know?"

"Yeah. Hey, Scheige, I appreciate it. But I gotta get going on something here, so was that all you needed?"

"Sure. I just thought you might want to know." Eichord realized how rude he was being and how abrupt he must sound. No point in being a horse's butt and telling Scheige it was too late to be telling him what he already knew.

"Hey, I really appreciate your call. Might be a big help to us. That's good policework, Scheige—thanks."

"No sweat," he said, and they rang off.

Eichord took a very deep breath and stared at the cursed telephone hoping no more bad news would come across it, searching for his ear, working its way into his head. If only the madman wouldn't kill again as he had only the day before with that fucking .22, if only hell had ice water. If only elephants could fly.

The next phone conversation was in an elliptical sort of doublespeak between Jack and a federal marshal, confirming the brief rites that would be conducted for the immediate family early in the morning. Neither Donna nor Bev Tuny would be allowed to attend, for security purposes. Only Peg, her son, Dana Tuny, and Jack, with a couple of marshals riding shotgun. It'd be a very fast graveside service, what the funeral home guys privately call a "peekaboo," and then back into hiding for the family. The latest word he'd had from Peggy was that there'd been a problem in getting her husband's family in China flown here in time for the service. Jack had never fully understood—either the brother had tried to board without his passport, or somebody else had used the wrong passport, but there'd been some problem. The Chinese contingent might not be on hand. As if that mattered to Jimmie . . .

MEMORIAL FOREST

If you wish to see with the killer's eyes you must first think with the madman's brain. What you and I will see on our way to the remote, suburban cemetery are the broken boards of a deserted loading bay behind a J. C. Penney's with the legend RCVNG 8–12 & 1–2. We pass a mobile-home park and what appear to be three or four hundred mailboxes in an endless row of letter Quonsets. We see a small field of graves backed up against a pastoral, wooded setting. But what you and I see are not what he sees.

He sees beyond the superficial. When we see the ordinary and the obvious he looks beyond to the extraordinary and the remarkable, and his mental computer files them away for planning. Instead of a loading bay, mailboxes, a burial place, he sees victims, opportunities, hiding places. And his eyes lock on to the woods, a vantage point, and a method of evasion and escape.

It was almost as dark as night at 6:48A.M. Heavy black clouds threatened to open at any moment. It was the gloomiest, saddest possible time for this gloomy and sad event.

Peg's son helped his mother out of the blue Thunderbird with the privacy glass—what would have to do as their courtesy limo. Eichord patted the boy on the back, and Peg came and hugged Jack, who had breathed enough of his own alcoholic fumes so he could spot the scent easily. His mind left the images of Chink for a moment as he realized how hard this would be on Peg.

"I wish there were words. Something I could say."

"Me too, Jack." She tried a brave smile. "But nothing can hurt him now. He's at rest."

They exchanged a few more words, then Peg and the boy walked toward the closed casket. There had been heartbreakingly little to put in there for burial, and the cops dealt with it the way they always did.

"Ain't got nothin' in there but his fingernails and some pubic hair," Dana whispered irreverently to Eichord as they walked slowly up the sloping hillside toward the gravesite, a marshal in front and in back.

"I swear to CHRIST, Chunk, you got more shit in your head than a fucking busted toilet."

"Say what?"

"Say what. You oughta have a fucking handle mounted on your forehead so we could flush your brain once in a while."

"Not my fault they gotta bury a ninety-five-pound coffin with about six ounces of Chink innit. Shit!" He flecked imaginary filth from him. "He's STILL coming down."

"I can't take you anywhere," Eichord said as he brushed against the heavy cop's arm. "You know what—you're about as much fun as prostate trouble."

"You know something, Blackjack? You're about as much fun as a fucking root canal."

They put their arms around each other's shoulders as they walked. When the sky opened up with a crack of lightning and the beginnings of a heavy downpour, they both ran for umbrellas.

"Sheeeeeeit."

"Just great."

"I just had my hair styled, too," Dana puffed. "Ain't it the shits?"

"Can't you do anything right?" Eichord said as he looked up into the soggy sky.

He shivered from the cold of the chill rain, or something else. It was a sense of foreboding, the kind of thing that's often written off as a lucky guess or pure coincidence, but Eichord had long ago learned that hunches were as good as anything else. There was something right there in front of him, asking to be noticed, and yet he couldn't see it.

The harder he tried to focus on it, the blurrier it became, and he shrugged it off the way someone will an elusive phrase or word that's right on the tip of the tongue but refuses to hop out. He sensed that he was trying too hard and he relaxed.

Despite Dana's crudity there was a blackly laughable aspect to the formality of burying their dear friend's skimpy remains. The family had wanted a service of this type, which had surprised everybody, but Jimmie had made his fear of cremation well-known and they all understood the desire to pay tribute to a loved one, bizarre as the circumstances were.

The brief service began but Jack heard not a word of it. He was standing facing the woods trying to keep his mind in neutral, trying not to think of anything, and it came to him in that relaxed state: a dark shape sensed more than seen, a flash of light off something metallic perhaps, a discarded can, or just a trick of the weather. He'd spotted it as he and Dana had run for the umbrellas.

It came back to him the way a lost object can be found by retracing one's steps. He'd relaxed, taken his brain out of gear, and allowed the current of information and thought to pour over him. It was in the killer's frighteningly brilliant MO. He had studied it the way a kid studies his catechism—religiously, doggedly, committing it to memory, taking it to heart and soul. In that flash of light he saw the deeper reality. He KNEW that the man he wanted was out there in the woods somewhere watching and the knowledge of it fell across the back of his neck like that cold, itchy feeling he got when somebody was pointing a gun at him. He sensed the cross hairs, the foul breath, the pig eyes squinting through a high-power scope. It matched everything in Bunkowski's package: the precognate's unique vision, the killer's genius IQ, his coldly logical ability to analyze. It was absurd of them to think he would have fallen for a lame ruse like the airport theatrical. He would have found it child's play to stay a jump ahead of them as he always had.

Someone had mumbled to him.

He turned and said to Dana, "Huh?"

"What?"

"I asked you what you said."

Chunk looked at him as he turned and replied, "*I* didn't say anything." They were whispering back and forth as a man who hadn't known Jimmie spoke profound but profoundly meaningless words. Eichord realized that he was afraid, and he shivered again, chilled to the bone.

This would be the perfect place for Chaingang to nail the cop he hated, to scope him down with a rifle from those dense woods, beyond the protecting umbrellas and the federal marshals. The knowledge of this filled Eichord with a fiery hatred that suffused his face, leaving his cheeks flushed scarlet, and he could no longer contain the rage. A scream of defiant pain escaped. A howl of anger and sadness and loathing for the madman who had snuffed his treasured friend. A marshal started after him as he ran from the graveside into the nearby woods, dropping his umbrella, but Dana stopped the man, tears mixing with the rain on his face. "Let him be alone with his grief," he told the officer, thinking Jack had screamed from anguish at the loss of Jimmie, and the marshal allowed himself to be turned away and led back to the service.

Eichord plunged headlong through the woods, the crazy amputation of a shotgun clutched in a death grip as he tore his best suit on things that reached out to snag him, and sunk his best shoes into the mud, and as he reached the center of the dense woods, he stopped and held his face up to the rain and shook himself like a black Labrador who had just jumped out of a lake.

"What a maniac. Dumb piece of shit," he cursed himself aloud as he slogged on through the woods. That was really brilliant. Ruin the services for everybody else so he could play Hairbreadth Harry. Dumb fuck. He was freezing in this rain, but he didn't turn around. He had to satisfy his curiosity now that he'd made a total moron out of himself and he kept on going, drenched to the skin as the heavy downpour intensified.

Then he saw the car backed into the little opening between some trees on the other side of the wooded area and he started running for it, but he was too wary to get trapped and he stopped. Waited. Listened. The hairs on the back of his neck were standing up just the way they had earlier. He knew somebody had a weapon on him. He stood motionless. He couldn't hear anything for the fucking rain and there was no movement. Only the empty car.

"Hey," he said loudly, just to hear his own voice, and it sounded wet and hollow, the word swallowed by the rain and the trees.

"I know you're here," he said, feeling like a fool. Nothing. No answer. No gunshot. He took a deep, shuddering breath, letting it pour out of him like a chainsmoker, trembling not just from the cold damp day, and he took a few slow and cautious steps as he moved around the car.

"COME ON YOU FAT YELLOW SHIT," he shouted into the rain. Not caring how ridiculous he looked or who heard him. He felt a momentary pain in the vicinity of his heart. Gas. A little morning heartburn from all the anxiety and the aggravation. No response. He allowed himself to cast his eyes downward, looking for the huge, fifteen quintuple-E footprints of the monster's feet in the muddy earth. Nothing. No sign of anything but Eichord, and the empty car.

He moved closer to the side of the vehicle. The watersoaked cardboard box that held his sawed-off shotgun was collapsing in his hand. The outline of the gun felt hard and dangerous in his grip. There was no movement. No noise. No sunlight to flash on metal this time. And he just stood there by the car, wondering for a second or two if he'd given in to professional paranoia. This could be somebody who had car trouble and left their . . .

And in midthought the thing was on him, roaring, crashing out of the woods on its tree-trunk legs, huge and powerful and blindingly terrifying as it charged out at him with something in its hand. Eichord saw it just as he had leaned over toward the car and spotted the little newborn baby in the seat. The thing in his hand flashing again suddenly, as the lightning cracked down around them close by in the dark woods, and he saw metal, and the enormous thing was coming at him, but he jerked the car door open with one hand pulling the baby out roughly holding the sawed-off Master Disaster Blaster to the baby's infant head on instinct, screaming, "ONE MORE FOOT YOU UGLY SHIT!" Not even knowing why he did it. Why not just shoot the sonofabitch? Shoot the man charging toward you this beast that will not stay dead. But his brain was at some level analyzing that thought and telling him, Hey, no way. Too far. A shotgun, especially a hacksawed shorty, has no carrying power. This guy is like an elephant. You've got to let him get close and make sure this time.

"PUT IT DOWN," that bass voice growled.

"ONE MORE FOOT THIS BABY IS *DEAD*!"

"I'LL RIP YOUR HEART OUT," he bellowed back at Eichord, but the thing stopped in its tracks.

"JUST ANOTHER FOOT YOU SHIT! I'LL BLOW THE HEAD OFF THIS BABY!" What if he didn't care? Then he'd shoot the son of a bitch. He didn't see a gun. No telescoped hunting rifle after all. Just that THING he carried. He jammed the twin death hurricanes against the infant's head. "I MEAN IT."

"YOU CHICKENSHIT FILTH!"

"You want this baby splattered all over these woods? Listen to me goddammit I MEAN IT YOU COCKSUCKER STOP MOVING I *WILL* BLOW THE BABY TO BITS. YOU THINK I'M BLUFFING?" He screamed it with a cracking voice, scared out of his wits at this second, as much as anything because at that very instant he meant it. He would pull those triggers all right, but not with the gun aimed at the newborn. He'd blast Daniel Edward fucking Flowers Bunkowski out of his looney misery once and for all. Oh the sweet feel of those triggers and the power of the poisoned loads at his fingertips. He wanted to kill the son of a bitch. HE WANTED TO SHOOT HIM AND SEE THE MONSTROUS HEAD COME OFF AND ROLL INTO THE WOODS. HE WANTED . . .

"I'LL KILL A *THOUSAND* OF YOU WORTHLESS SHITS IF YOU TOUCH A HAIR ON THAT BABY'S—"

"FUCK YOU, YOU SON OF A BITCH, COME ON IF YOU THINK I'M BLUFFING I'LL KILL THIS BRAT," he said, spitting out the word, "and then I'll blow your crazy ass all over crea—"

"Listen to me, listen you arrogant garbage. Listen to what I'm—DON'T HURT THE—don't," forcing himself to speak normally. "Would you trade your desire for revenge against me, the desire to see me suffer retribution which you think I have coming, if it would spare the lives of many?" Moving slightly as he spoke, trying to get close enough to make a move.

"Come on you piece of shit. Keep coming. Get a little closer."

"I thought about killing you for a long time. Making you pay for what you did to me. I missed. I killed your friend. So we're even."

"Bullshit."

"The score is tied."

"There IS no score. This is no game, you're crazy as a fucking bedbug and you should be put to sleep." Only one chance. When that trigger was pulled he was a dead man if he missed. God, if only about two dozen feds would come tearing out of those woods like the cavalry in a John Ford western.

"In due time," the deep rumble said, "but not by you. Put the baby down you gutless wonder. Let's make it just you and I."

"A fair fight, eh?"

"If I'd wanted you dead at a distance I could have taken you out a couple of times already. At six-twelve you were parked at the red light at East Main and Buckhead Highway. I could see your head clearly through a reticular starlight scope. If I only wanted to see you dead I could have scoped you out with a gun. But I want a PIECE of you," he said, and just as Eichord was starting to answer him, saying, "I'm suppose to—" something or other, the flexible club of tractor-strength chain came snaking, whirling, whipping low, boloing out like a flying chainsaw, aimed at the legs, a daisy-cutter, sure to cripple and maim, flung hard but low enough to miss the child, and the beast charging forward as Eichord pulled the trigger just as the chain reached him, jerking the shot for fear the baby would be hit by the deadly chain— throwing the little boy back into his nest in the car seat knowing that those two hot loads of poisoned pellets were gone and nothing was between him and Death and the hands taking him and powering him down to the ground, Eichord immobilized in a grip more powerful than any he'd ever felt. It was like being caught in a pair of huge, steel vises. The idea of putting any kind of move on this mountain of muscle was out of the question.

"Now," the hard voice hacksawed into his ear, "you will feel my wrath, you insolent—"

"AAAAAAAAAAAAAH!" Eichord screaming in pain, screaming over the thunder as he felt the little finger on his left hand being bent back but for some reason not just being bent back, the beast not stopping, bending it all the way, keeping on with it, breaking it easily as he intoned the word "insolent," snapping it with almost gentle insouciance, Jack yelling into the rain and thunder as Bunkowski's steel cigar-thick fingers that had once furiously squeezed a FLASHLIGHT BATTERY began to twist and rip and Eichord passed out.

The pain was not of this world. It was like slamming one's finger in the car door again and again, and Eichord blacked out, collapsing, coming back, blacking out, coming back, the pain merciless but not quite enough to send him completely over the side into blackness. My God why would anyone want . . . Ohoooooooooohhhhhhhhhhh the pain washed over him in a wave of dizziness and that fearsome voice grunted in its distinctive bass register, "A little souvenir for you," Jack gagging as he felt the bloody thing being forced into one of his suitcoat pockets, the wet clothing wrapped around him like a shroud. "Your *FINGER*. From the hand that touched my picture that time on television." Eichord began retching. It was a voice that made no concessions to the social amenities. Rough-edged like a hacksaw. Tough and sharp. Crude. Like a jailhouse knife ground from a file. Not pretty but it got your attention with its surprising edge. A voice made to cut. It said, "And now, Mr. Policeman, do you know what I'm going to do?"

Eichord felt himself being manhandled over onto his back. He screamed again in pain as his hand struck something. The monster loomed over him. He could feel the thing's hot breath on him. There was a shift in the massive body weight.

"Now I am going to rip your rib cage apart. It will be quite painful, Special Investigator Eirhoorrrrrrrrrrrrrrrr aaaaaaaaaaaaaaaaaaaaaaaaAAAAAAAAAAAAAAAA!" The rain or something hot and wet splashing down on him and he tried to turn and nobody was holding him and the huge bulk was starting to spin around, holding its throat where the carotid artery had been completely severed through and just then Jack caught a glimpse of silver in the bright flash of lightning and the blade arced down, the sword propelled with such—not ease, that isn't the word—perfection? SIMPLICITY. The movement like a choreographed ballet. A simplicity of movement. Simplicity not as design or format. Not as tradition or technique. Simplicity not as style. Simplicity as CHALLENGE. Seventeen syllables of flawless haiku. The perfect twelve bar blues. Subtle. Studied. Symmetrical as a Chinese brushstroke.

And the silver blade of vengeance made hard contact again smacking down through hair and scarred flesh and tissue and muscle and bone and tortured memories and making that awful wet thwocking sound of a cleaver whacked into a rotten melon as the long, razor-sharp and carbon-hard sword of honor and terrible retaliation came slashing down in those powerful hands slicing Chaingang's skull. The great blade split the head of the evil one in a foul horror of bloody bone gristle gray matter and only then did the immense behemoth topple and Eichord felt his consciousness ebbing away completely as the stealthy silent specter that to him would always be the Man from Kowloon melted back into the cloak of rain and shadow.

He fought to hang in. Clothing soaked in Bunkowski's blood. Some of his own. He tried to stand and slipped and fell in the bad wetness and almost went down again from the pain and OHHHHHGODDDDD who would believe a little finger could hurt so much and Oh Dana Jimmie if you guys were only here to make jokes about it and help me and he tried to retch again and again but couldn't and spat some more, backing away from the fallen monstrosity and the blood and filth that was soaking the wet ground and he saw the shotgun thing.

1. Gun,
and the lid of the box, and
2. Glue. He walked through the glue. Each step a major effort. Slogging through the bloody gluepond.
3. Tree. He fought to keep from going under and something or someone was near the tree, moving toward him, and

4. Door. He was there beside the car door now, and

5. Hive. The killer bees swarmed in his ear, buzzing noisily as he continued unsteadily on his feet, someone helping him and trying to lead him away from the vehicle and he could hear the cry over the sound of an approaching siren and he managed to get "wait" out of his mouth and with the most massive effort of will he'd ever made he leaned down and focused on the interior of the nearby car.

"The baby," he could hear himself say, "get it." He could hear his own voice over the bees buzzing.

"Frawfer mansions through horse pistols," someone said. How irritating to hear that sort of gibberish in an emergency.

"Bring the baby," he managed to say, and the man who spoke nonsense was doing something and then and then and then his knees buckled and

6. Sticks. The sound of broken sticks.

Sticks and stones will break my bones, but I will still get to

7. Heaven, and the sweet arms of the blessed savior Jeeeeeeeeeeeeeeeezzzzzzzzzus going dooowwwwwwwwww wwnnnnnnnnn and he could feel himself losing it for good and being swallowed by the cold dark jaws of shock.

SAINT FRANCIS MEDICAL CENTER

"**H**ere," he heard a voice saying, "we're rejoining the living," which Jack thought to be an unusually appropriate choice of words.

"How long was I out?" was the question he framed in his head, but it came out as smiling silence because he'd forgotten to open his mouth as he spoke, so he only smiled. It was amazing how much coordination is required to verbalize a thought, and the realization of this tired him. He left himself sink deeper into a sea of feathers as the doctor told him about sewing his finger back on—how could this be?—telling him how Jack should check back in a few days and something mumble-mumble nighty-night.

"—look like you're ready to go anywhere," and a hearty laugh. And Eichord thought he must have just drifted off for a couple of seconds, and he wished people would shut up so he could doze off but these fellows had him propped up and he was on his feet or maybe he had always been on his feet and something mumble buzz, "Gets too strong call me and we'll fix you up with a shot." He nodded at the kindness and rightness of it all.

He heard a friendly voice speaking to him but for the life of him he couldn't focus and he was sitting down again or for the first time and moving and he tried to speak but once again only a halfhearted smile reached his mouth.

311

The next time he woke up he was in a bedroom somewhere and Donna Eichord was sitting across the room
from him and there was a lot of attention to his every need
and he kept telling her to find out about the baby and she
kept saying, What baby? and it confused him so badly
that he was able to snap out of the druggy fog completely
and he said, "Hey, darlin'."

Or so he thought he said, but it was more of Aaaaaaaay
sound without consonants and he tried to bear down and
concentrate and managed to say it aloud.

"Hey."

"Hey yourself."

"Hey. Hey darlin'."

"Yeah," she said softly to him. "How ya doin?"

"Hey." [SOMETHING MUMBLED.]

"What, honey?"

"The baby?"

"What about a baby?"

"Yeah. Howaza baby?"

"Oh. The baby that was in the car. Bill had the baby
checked over while we were at the hospital with you.
He's going to be fine. The little baby's okay, hon."

"Thass good."

"Yeah. You feelin' pretty rough?"

"No. Feel ffff—fiiiiiiine." He grinned and she smiled
with him and patted him gently.

"That's great."

"I lose my finger?"

"No, honey. The doctor will tell you all about the
procedure later. It's a new technique and they think you'll
regain use of it, at least partially. They said it went real
well." She smiled.

After a few minutes he could feel himself snapping out
of the deepest part of the drug fuzziness but he knew he
was only halfway out. He didn't want to lose that glow
now. It was a good buzz and he figured when he started
to lose it the pain would hammer him to his knees. He
looked at the thickly bandaged hand and felt nothing.

When he felt himself coming to his senses he talked
with Donna about the confrontation asking her about the
killer.

"I got him, didn't I?" he asked. "I got him this time?"

"Yes," she assured him. "You got him this time."

"No!" He started to tell her about the Man from Kowloon and he changed the subject. "Know what? That little baby is going to be in a big world of trouble. I wish we, you know, could take care of him or something."

"I know what you mean," she said, and then she wondered if she did. "You mean like adopt him?"

"I know he had a killer for a father but that wasn't his fault. He's still a little baby."

"Sure."

"So tiny. All alone. I mean, we'd do the same thing for a cat or dog."

"I know."

"Would you be against it?"

"Adopting the little boy?"

"Yeah."

"No. I, uh, I just haven't thought about it. But no, hon, I think it's a sweet idea. If you, you know, wanted to adopt a baby. I don't know if we could do it, if they'd let us, but—"

"What do you mean?"

"I don't know if it's that easy?"

"How do you adopt a baby like that? What happens to it?"

"I don't know. I suppose the baby gets placed in a foster home eventually. I don't know exactly what the procedure would be in a case like this, though."

"Why don't we look into it?"

"Okay. Just remember, darlin', this is a serious commitment. I mean, if it's something we both really want I'd say give it all we can to make it happen, but I'm just surprised you want THIS baby, you know. Considering everything that happened."

"It breaks my heart to think he wouldn't have a good home. He had such a bad start." Eichord thought about the little infant being taken from the slaughtered mother and he shivered as he had in the woods.

"You cold?"

"No, I feel GOOD," he said. She kissed him softly and whispered several secrets then, so grateful that he was alive. And as tired as Jack was, it felt good to feel her touch and her nearness, whispering to him these secrets of romantic love and Romeo and Juliet and the love songs of troubadours and sonnets and bonnets and white dresses on virginal flesh, and he heard her whisper as he drifted off, "You're my dream man. There's nothing I'd like more than to be the mother of your children. You'd make a wonderful daddy." And he tried to tell her about the baby and how he felt, but the effort of holding his heavy eyelids open was finally just too much and as he fell into a deep sleep he thought that he *was* every woman's dream: a monster's kid, a one-eared cat, a nine-fingered copper. He'd given her everything, that's for sure. But he went to sleep smiling anyway.

BUCKHEAD COUNTY
MORGUE

"**I** think it's stupid. What the hell you wanna put yourself through this for?"

"Just let's do it, okay?" Tuny had stayed with him like a Siamese twin. Watching over him. Bodyguarding him. It was absurd, but Jack didn't have the heart to make him go away.

"It's stupid. Y'r a dumb fuck ta come down here. Doc told you stay in bed another day anyway."

"They don't know everything. Come on." They walked through the door simultaneously, but Eichord was amused Dana didn't bump him. "What a turkey," he said.

"I'll catch ya next time."

Jack made a morgue attendant pull out the stitched, headless cadaver. He ran a set of prints for his own files, checked known scars—the whole bit. Finally he made them show him the decapitated head, the autopsy reports.

Dana said, "Hey, fuckface, enough awready. We gonna stay down here all fucking day or what?"

"I thought you might like to eat down here. We could order some lunch sent in?"

"Hey, asshole. What d'ya think I look like anyway—a fucking GHOUL?"

"Yeah," Eichord said, leaning over and giving his fat

315

friend a little gentle punch on the tit. "That's what you look like around the mammaries. A fucking girl." But it wasn't funny like when Jimmie did it, so Jack just looked at Dana and smiled. "I guess it's all in the timing." They went back out into the hot Buckhead sunlight of the more or less real world of the living.

When he got home that night there was quite a bit of mail, but his heart sank when he saw the package that was waiting for him. He couldn't find any markings or anything on it. Obviously Jimmie's printing, with a joke return address from "I.P. Freely, of Vlasic, MASS." But even without the printing he knew what it was—that soft, rectangular heft of dirty money, so innocent-looking in the IGA brown paper wrapper and transparent tape. Rubber-stamped "RE-ROUTED BY BUCKHEAD MAIL CENTER."

"How did this come, Donna?"

"It came today."

"HOW did it come? In the mail or UPS or what?"

"In the mail."

"It doesn't have any stamps. How was it delivered. Where's the address?"

"OH! Sorry babe. The thing came off and I put it in the trash." She bent over and plucked something out of a wastebasket. "Here you go." He looked at the stick-on label and the cluster of postage stamps.

"Thanks," he said. He wouldn't open it for a while. He'd deal with it later. He didn't want to think about it right now. He took the package back to the bedroom and tossed it into the back of a closet shelf to gather dust along with the crazy, homemade shotgun and a cowboy hat he had paid too much for and never wore.

Much later Jimmie Lee's last note would be found, in with the stolen money. For now that was temporarily forgotten. Eichord's big concern at the moment was the baby boy. He'd been jacked around half the day by the bureaucratic jumble of the adoption process. He told Donna about it over dinner promising her, "I'm gonna hang in there. I'll find out tomorrow if the Major Crimes Task Force has any serious clout with the Department of Family Services." He laughed with her about fat Dana, who had said to him with his usual tact and diplomacy, "What makes you think they'd let YOU adopt a kid?" And he had to smile every time he contemplated the idea that he might find himself becoming the father of a baby son.

Later that night, Donna did the dishes and Jack went outside for some fresh air. He stood looking up at the dark sky, and he said to himself silently, "What the fuck am I going to do with a baby?"

All Pan books are available at your local bookshop or newsagent, or can be ordered direct from the publisher. Indicate the number of copies required and fill in the form below.

Send to: **CS Department, Pan Books Ltd., P.O. Box 40,
             Basingstoke, Hants.   RG21 2YT.**

or phone: 0256 469551 (Ansaphone), quoting title, author
             and Credit Card number.

Please enclose a remittance* to the value of the cover price plus: 60p for the first book plus 30p per copy for each additional book ordered to a maximum charge of £2.40 to cover postage and packing.

*Payment may be made in sterling by UK personal cheque, postal order, sterling draft or international money order, made payable to Pan Books Ltd.

Alternatively by Barclaycard/Access:

Card No.

Signature:

Applicable only in the UK and Republic of Ireland.

While every effort is made to keep prices low, it is sometimes necessary to increase prices at short notice. Pan Books reserve the right to show on covers and charge new retail prices which may differ from those advertised in the text or elsewhere.

NAME AND ADDRESS IN BLOCK LETTERS PLEASE:

....

Name ————————————————————————————————

Address ————————————————————————————————

————————————————————————————————————

————————————————————————————————————

————————————————————————————————————

3/87